THE
LAST FREE MEN
MEN

BY
JACK EVERETT
& DAVID COLES

A VIRTUAL TALES BOOK

This is a work of fiction. Names, characters, places and events described herein are products of the author's imagination or are used fictitiously. Any resemblance to actual events, locations, organizations, or persons, living or dead, is entirely coincidental.

The Last Free Men

Cover art by Craig Jennion (www.craigjennion.com)

Edited by Jake George (www.sageservices.com)

Virtual Tales
PO Box 822674
Vancouver, WA 98682
USA

www.VirtualTales.com

ISBN: 1-935460-18-8

First Edition: November 2009

Printed in the United States of America

9 7 8 1 9 3 5 4 6 0 1 8 3

THE AUTHORS DEDICATE THE LAST FREE MEN
TO THE MEMORY OF JACK EVERETT'S SON, GAVIN,
WHO DIED IN A MOTORCYCLE ACCIDENT DURING
THE WRITING OF THE NOVEL.

WE WOULD ALSO LIKE TO REMEMBER THE
INNUMERABLE GROUPS OF PEOPLE FROM ALL OVER
THE WORLD AND THROUGHOUT TIME WHO HAVE
HAD THEIR HOMELANDS ANNEXED TO SERVE THE
PURPOSES OF STRONGER, AVARICIOUS NATIONS.

ACKNOWLEDGMENTS

THE AUTHORS WOULD LIKE TO THANK THEIR
FAMILIES FOR THEIR FORBEARANCE WHILE THIS
NOVEL WAS BEING WRITTEN AND ALSO JAKE GEORGE
FOR EDITING THE MANUSCRIPT, CRAIG JENNION
FOR HIS COVER DESIGN, AND THE REST OF THE
STAFF AT VIRTUAL TALES.

ALSO AVAILABLE FROM JACK EVERETT & DAVID COLES

DEATH AND TAXES
JIHAD
MERLIN'S KIN
THE FACES OF IMMORTALITY:
A TRIBUTE TO THE WORK OF THE WRITER, JACK VANCE
AND ITS SEQUEL
TO RULE THE UNIVERSE

COMING SOON FROM JACK EVERETT & DAVID COLES

THE LAST MISSION
BRIGHT SHADOWS
THE TOURIST

WWW.DAVIDBCOLES.CO.UK
WWW.JACKLEVERETT.ME.UK

"We, the last men on earth, the last of the free,
have been shielded till today by the very remoteness
and the seclusion for which we are famed...

But today the boundary of Britain is exposed;
beyond us lies no nation, nothing but waves and rocks
and the Romans."

from Calgacus' address to his army
at the battle of Mons Graupius.
...Tacitus

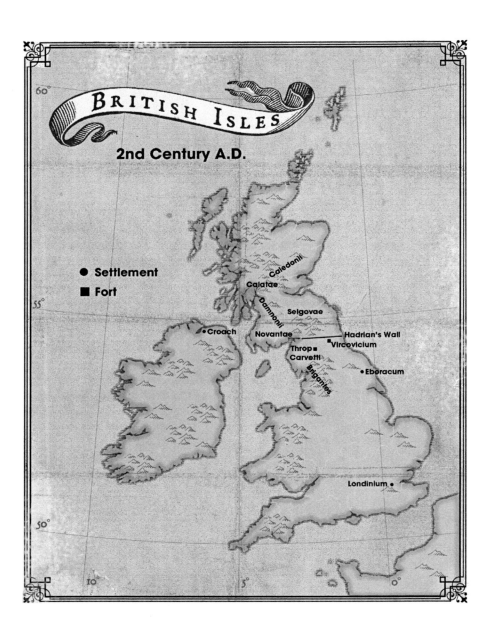

BRITISH ISLES

2nd Century A.D.

● Settlement
■ Fort

Caledonii

Calatae

Damnonii

Selgovae

● Croach

Novantae

Hadrian's Wall

■ Vircovicium

Throp ■
Carvetti

Brigantes

● Eboracum

Londinium ●

CHAPTER ONE

SELGOVANTIA—ANNO DOMINI 128

HE WAS DEEP INTO SELGOVANTIA, DUMFRIESHIRE, AND THERE were ten or more men ahead of him. They spoke infrequently and in low voices, yet their manner was not one of secrecy. They were subdued—fearful almost—and one seemed blind, having to be led.

Having come upon the group by accident, Marcus followed them, stepping silently fifty paces or so behind. Their way led through overgrown woodland with only the odd splash of moonlight to relieve the darkness and to reassure him that he still followed the narrow game trail.

At length, the group stopped, and Marcus left the pathway to approach from the side, well hidden by the undergrowth. The odd word came to him, but most of the desultory conversation was indecipherable. With the utmost caution, he crept closer and hid behind the partially cleft trunk of a great sycamore at the very edge of the glade. A bush grew close to the larger tree and added some concealment.

Dark clouds drifted leisurely across the nighttime sky to cast slow shadows over the small clearing. Brief glimpses of the quarter moon limned the ragged edges of the cloud rack with silver; the light gleamed palely from metal jeweler and weapons.

Apart from the stately progression of the clouds, the barest movement of leaves, the night had become still.

Twelve men stood in a close ring about a thirteenth, as near naked as the others although his head was covered with the skin of an animal and tied about the throat. All of them were rigid in their stillness—the twelve encircling, watchful sentinels and the apprehensive one within, whose occasional twitch of a muscle or a shiver belied his apparent composure.

Marcus could see little and he looked up at the tree above him. The trunk supported a growth of ivy, strong enough to bear his weight if he moved carefully. He began to climb slowly, hauling himself gently until he reached the first of the sycamore's lower limbs. Still cautious, Marcus settled himself against the trunk and stared downward.

A night bird called from a nearby tree and Marcus' heart froze, the others all jumped slightly at the sound. "Will he still come?" asked one of the twelve and his neighbor, a man built like an oak of seven generations, a giant, replied.

"He will, Manon, he will. He told me this: 'the sixth day of the moon.' This is the day he said. 'Twice three.'"

A larger gap in the clouds allowed the moon to drench the glade with sudden silver, and the waiting men shifted uncomfortably in the brighter light. Their bodies were covered from head to toe in intricate tattoos of blue dye Braided torques of hair worked with silver wire hung around their necks and waists. Each of the twelve held a long sword, and the fingers of the thirteenth were still curled from long habit, about the handle of a heavy though imaginary weapon.

Glances criss-crossed the circle watching faces that each knew as intimately as brother or father or son for all were close kin, even he in the center. All were tied by blood, born from the union of cousins and second cousins, uncles and nieces. The family resemblance was strong; it marked them all with heavy brows and strong jaws; pale eyes and fair hair; tall, big boned bodies.

A sound other than that of night birds and small creeping things brought them to full alert. The sound of feet running, no attempt to muffle the noise or to tread carefully, they relaxed and the runner broke from the nearby trees on the eastern side. "He comes, brothers, he comes." He fell to his knees just off the path and waited. Marcus, perched almost above the pathway, nearly lost his balance as he tried to see who was coming.

There was the sound of a second pair of feet; slower, the pace more measured, and those in the circle turned to face the newcomer.

"Keep the circle." The voice was deep, powerful, one accustomed to command and without the need to confirm that the wish was implemented.

A small whimper came from the hooded man at the center, and just as a cornered boar will do, he ran suddenly at the circle wall. But he had no tusks with which to gore, no weapons. He was pushed back again and again with no sign of family feeling. He stood quietly at last, shivering and sweating in the chill night air as though *he* had been the one to run ahead of the *Vate*, the Seer, and not the one who was just now rising from his knees. The captive's head hung in dejection—there would be no release but the one ordained by his deeds.

The old Seer came, his staff clicking on the rocky ground, punctuating soft footfalls. "What has he done?" The question was aimed at no one man—the tone one of total disinterest; a duty to be performed.

The big man who had answered Manon spoke again and the *Vate* seemed to gaze at the fellow's tattooed chest, an ascending moon atop a setting sun. "He lay with a young girl of the Cruagh and killed her afterwards. He hid her body under leaves in the deep forest in hope that a wolf might take his work." He was silent for a moment and then added, "He asked not her father's permission or that of our chief."

The old man, the *Vate*, nodded and threw back the hood of his cloak whereupon there was a great gasp at the sight of his dead white eye, which glared past the great hooked nose at each of them in turn. "Is there a Cruagh present?"

Dag Liogh, eldest son of the Clan Liogh shook his head. "No." The *Vate* had been too many times in his father's house for Dag Liogh to have been as overawed by the dreadful evil eye as his kin.

"But this is truth; the gods who have taken our sacrifices know that no Liogh lies in this, they are content for us to make our own justice."

Liogh. From his vantage, Marcus Gellorix heard the name clearly, knew the tribe. A small one, relative newcomers—no more than four, perhaps five generations. He shivered; a chill breeze blew at this height.

The Seer nodded. The questioning was pure formality, of little importance, and he took a long bright blade from within his cloak. Moonlight glittered from the interlocking patterns inscribed along its length until abruptly; he sheathed the knife in the condemned man's abdomen. The act was precise, the wound exact, inflicted with careless mastery.

The victim dropped to the floor as blood, black in the moonlight, flowed thickly. The *Vate* watched. Through his good eye, the one with mortal sight, he watched the convulsions attentively; through the dead eye, he saw the way the blood ran, the writhing of the spirit as it struggled free of the body.

Manon shivered, not because of his newly dead kinsman, but at sight of that dead eye, familiar but somehow more terrible at night. Behind his back, Manon crossed his fingers.

As the convulsions ceased and the body became at last, a corpse, the Seer looked up at the others. He smiled, a black grin punctuated by three ill-spaced teeth.

"I know of great deeds done and still to come. I know of warriors gone to drink with the Gods, and of others who will drink the blood of the invaders from the east. I know of a stone wall that stretches to the dawn, and a wall of turves stretching to the setting sun.

"I know what will come. What would you hear from me?"

"Tell us what is to come," cried all with a single voice.

The *Vate* seemed to grow in stature so that he towered above the others who surrounded him. He turned slowly from the west where he had been pointing, to the south, to east, to north, to west and round again and again. The sound of his voice mesmeric, compelling.

"In three days will come a wet mist from the sunset. I know that you will attack the wall by the river, and you will attack from the south, from the side of the Britons. And you, my sons, I know that you will lead the way."

There were mumbles of surprise, skepticism which the old man ignored.

"Thirty hands of men will attack the accursed wall, and thirty of those will journey to the Gods. Those who stay upon this world will take with them great treasure and much grain, enough to store against the winter."

The sweet green grass, now the whip… "The Gods will be watching."

The old man fell silent. The earthly eye and the seeing one closed as though he were listening to some voice deep inside. His listeners held their breath, their need for air forgotten until, at last the seer looked about him again. There was a collective sigh from grateful lungs as the old man continued.

"Afterward, three crows will show the way to your homes. Those who do not see the crows will be scattered like chaff upon the wind; they will neither sit with the Gods nor lay with their women.

"This is what I know."

"How many will return to the Clan?"

"Dag Liogh, I have told you what I know. Do you have another's blood to spill?" Several shook their heads.

"Let me be gone then. I have others to see before the night is done."

And as they left, the watcher waited for the forest sounds to return before clambering stiffly from his perch to the ground.

Dag Liogh, son of the Chief and Manon, his younger brother. As an agent of the Roman army, Marcus had traded with the tribe though no trader was ever invited to the home village. Hitherto the Clan Liogh had been a secretive tribe, but now they were in the forefront of whatever trouble was brewing.

Marcus made his way back to his horse, treading as carefully as before. He had known for days that something was in the offing; there had been a tension in the air—like the feeling just before a lightning strike.

An attack by the river, Marcus thought, and he could think of three which passed through the Wall within half a day's ride. *Which one did they mean? And when? There was so much I couldn't make out properly.* Marcus paused in mid-stride. *An attack from the Brythonic side—is that what the seer told them?* He continued on, Vircovicium was several hours ride away. *Perhaps there will be others there; maybe they will have information to add to mine.* No matter; he still had to report in to the senior Centurion, Aemilius Karras. *Let him think about it and make up his own mind.*

⚜

VIRCOVICIUM

Cassius Aurelius Pintus relaxed in his bathhouse. It still smelled of mortar, and there were places where the plasterwork needed refinishing, but all in all, his new command pleased him. Vircovicium—*Housesteads*—was one of the new stone built forts along the line of the wall and Aurelius sacrificed to Jupiter daily to show his gratitude in being appointed its Commandant.

As time went on Aurelius had managed more and more, to convince himself that it was due to his own merits that he had secured the post. In his more pragmatic moments, however, he might pour a libation to the sister who had married an older Senator. His brother-in-law made a point of elevating his relatives whenever possible on the principle that powerful and grateful kin were useful even to senators.

That particular *quid pro quo* was over a year old now, but had only just borne fruit. The present appointment was good for a year; he might let it go for another half year before returning to Rome and a more comfortable post but out here, on the frontier, battling against the barbarian… Aurelius chuckled. A handful of filthy savages. It was all good propaganda at home—keeping the frontier safe, guarding civilization.

Aurelius clapped his hands, and when the slave brought the oil, he rolled over onto his stomach for the boy to begin the massage.

One week. He had arrived just seven days ago with a hundred and sixty men. His wife had complained all the way from Eboracum—*York*; she had bored the head off the commandant at Cataractonium—*Catterick*—and again at Corstopitum—*Corbridge*, and would doubtless do so to anyone who would listen to her tonight at the party. He counted himself fortunate that he had been expected to ride with his two centuries rather than share the ox-drawn carriage with his wife and her own little retinue.

Aurelius had loved the place as soon as he had set eyes on it. It had been a sun-filled day—a rarity this year—and the grey stone had stood out against the hillside where raw earth and bare rock still testified to its newness. Perhaps it was the position it occupied, high up on the crest with panoramic views to north and south; it certainly reminded him of his family's home in the mountains two hundred miles north of Rome. The fort itself also reminded him of his first tour of duty at Rhaetia, that had been new too, and he had his first heady taste of command, where whatever he said was instantly transmuted into action.

Vircovicium was no different than hundreds or thousands of other forts all over the Empire. It was the same rectangular area enclosed within stout walls, turrets along the walls and at the rounded corners, and heavily fortified gates to each of the cardinal compass points. There was accommodation for a cohort of infantry and the Praetorium, or Commandant's house, was built close to the southern gate with a quite astounding view down into the valley.

The big difference though was the fact that this was *his.* This was his passport to an appointment of influence back in Rome when his tour of military duty was finished.

There was a gentle knock at the door. "Master?"

"Well?"

"The Lady Aelia wishes me to inform you that there are still no swans for the dinner table tonight."

Aurelius could just imagine his wife's strident voice. *Tell my husband my patience is close to an end...*, but the young man was speaking again.

"The menu is already fixed. My Lady requests your decision."

*Aelia demands that he do something about it, h*e paraphrased to himself. Aurelius' wife was a pretty woman and in all fairness, she always presented herself to the outside world impeccably. She had kept her figure throughout their marriage, and she was more inventive in bed than a Roman whorehouse fed on oysters for a week. But Aelia's voice had a distinct likeness to the whine of an angry hornet. The slaves certainly respected that shrill voice. If its demands were not met, there would be trouble, serious trouble.

"Very well. Tell your mistress that I shall see to it immediately, and tell Ursio to attend me. I shall be wearing dress armor tonight, but I want something practical at the moment."

By evening, the courtyard and adjoining rooms of the Praetorian were overflowing with people.

Severus had arrived with upwards of forty friends and hangers-on and was stealing the scene, as Aurelius had feared. He had dragged a chair away from the wall and placed it near the center of the main room, which was open to the courtyard. His attitude was quietly heroic and just now, he was holding forth on some minor punitive expedition. One might think he had personally subdued the whole of northern Britannia himself, still; Aurelius smiled wryly. The man *was* Governor and had always been good at putting down rebellion. People passed him by, kissing the be-ringed fingers on their way or stayed to listen and offer sage nods and attentive expressions.

Aurelius tried to keep his own expression neutral, as there were rumors that Sextus Lulius Severus was about to be recalled and posted to the Eastern protectorates. But rumors gathered about Severus like crows at a battlefield.

Aurelius arrived late at his own party, as the business of the swans had delayed him considerably. The butcher's shop in the vicus had a pair of grey geese; they would have to serve in place of the swans. That in turn meant that he had dressed rather hurriedly and was not certain that he cut as brave a figure as he might.

Aurelius maneuvered himself into the conversation and succeeded in drawing considerable attention when a centurion in full dress uniform appeared. A few minutes more and Severus would have been in retreat, but when the officer nodded and obviously needed to speak to him, there was no way out.

"Yes, Centurion?"

Aemilius Karrus was one of the *primi ordines*, the Legion's five top centurions, a thick-set man of forty-eight years with candid brown eyes; he had seen service under Emperor Trajan. If he interrupted something, it was a necessary interruption. Aurelius knew that the matter must be important.

"Commandant." The Centurion's eyes swept the group of nobles and notables before returning to Aurelius' face. "I would like to introduce Beneficiarius Marcus Uffin Gellorix to you." A fellow appeared at Karrus' shoulder as if magic had been employed. "He was appointed by your predecessor and controls the Speculators."

"Speculators?" Aurelius looked the other up and down and frowned slightly. Uffin was a Brigantine name, as was Gellorix. Brigantes were the largest tribe in Britain, occupying the North West "Ah, the group operating out of Vindolanda."

"Exactly. Now of course, they are being transferred here."

Now it came to Pintus, Quintus Aelius Mansustus' bastard. Back in Rome the former legate was a senator with a fair amount of weight to his arm, and the new Commandant had been well briefed. *So here is the fruit of that particular union with the Brigantine woman; no wonder the Senator's wife was so tight lipped about their time here.*

"So you're our spy then, young man?" Aurelius scowled. The young man took a step forward. Aurelius thought that he had insolent eyes, and being taller than the average Roman gave the man an unfair advantage.

"I prefer the official status. *Areane*. A scout," he said.

Godless little upstart with mixed names. Aurelius' dislike increased. And wearing a toga. "And just what is it you *scout* for?" Despite his dislike of half breeds, Aurelius had to admit that the young man's Latin was flawless and even to a man like himself, his manner was quite disarming. *The white samite of the toga and those copper highlights in his fair hair must grant him instant success with women. If he ever chose the couch-and-matron route to the top, he would enjoy a great deal of success.*

"Information. I can pass quite readily as a native. It's a useful gift."

Aurelius nodded. He remembered hearing tales that the man's father maintained contact with him, too. There could be a lot of influence here; he was someone to make use of rather than to fall out with.

Marcus Gellorix's face became serious. "This is why I came tonight. Your party is no secret north of the Wall—the Callatae have known about it for days."

"Callatae?" Aurelius frowned. "I tutored myself concerning these barbarians, but this tribe escapes my memory."

"They are less known than some. They have been in the area a generation or two, since the rout of Mona."

"Aha. Since we wiped out the nest of Druids. So, what does it matter? We have two cohorts of Roman legionaries here..."

The Romano-Brigante shook his head. "That is not what I'm telling you. There is something else you need to be ready for, something is being planned."

"How do you know? Hmm? You look like a native and they open their hearts to you. Is that how it goes?" Aurelius' words oozed sarcasm.

"To some extent, yes. I've only just returned from out there. I've seen Cruaghs and Barribyns on Liogh land." Marcus smiled disarmingly.

"Explain to me the significance of these barbarians visiting each other. No, don't bother. I've enough to do tonight. Tell the Centurion."

Aemilius Karrus took hold of Aurelius' elbow. Though junior in rank, he was still a senior officer with more experience in the field than any tribune or legate was ever going to accumulate. Even legates listened to senior centurions.

"Please listen to Gellorix, Sir. What he describes is as unlikely as a civilian entering your private bedroom. You see, these people are tribal. Territory is marked out in the same way wild animals stake out their domains. A tribesman crossing the line between territories would normally be killed out of hand."

Aurelius recognized when he misunderstood a situation, and he knew that to ignore his mistake would be far more foolish than to admit it.

He nodded and looked at Marcus. "These tribes have made some sort of pact?"

"Indeed. There is no other explanation."

"And what is it you propose we should do? You haven't told us yet what is behind the pact so I presume that you don't know?"

"No, I don't. Not yet. What I would suggest, Sir, is that all centurions should be informed of the situation, and extra vigilance should be maintained until we *do* find out what is going on. I shall also inform other Commandants in the area."

"It seems a reasonable thing to do." Aurelius smiled, a not too pleasant expression. "By all means—pass your information to the other commanders; though as we have several here tonight, of course, I can pass on your information myself. Let me see if I can pick them out, oh and Centurion."

"Sir?"

"Alert your fellow officers as the Benificiarius suggests." Aurelius turned and left them as though they were a part of the furnishings.

Aemilius Karrus frowned for a moment and then shrugged. "It's a menagerie, Marcus, a menagerie; can you imagine these people planning a campaign? Well you've done a good job, anyhow. Off to see your mother now—or drink away your worries?"

Marcus shook his head. "No, the drink can wait; my mother can't. Time weighs heavily with her nowadays. Since Father returned to Rome, she has few friends. I'd better call in at the guard house and see if there're any reports in from other scouts." Marcus hooked a thumb in the Commandant's direction. "I suppose he'll take the credit for warning the other commandants?" Marcus gave a pained grimace.

Aemilius Karrus grimaced. "Undoubtedly. That's his job isn't it? We do the work; he carries the weight of responsibility."

Marcus laughed. "And if a Cruagh cuts the Old Man's head off to hang on his belt, it'll be a little less weight for him to carry!"

"Well the Cruagh'll carry it for him, won't he? At his belt." Karrus chuckled at his own wit and clapped the other on the shoulder. "You've come a long way since I pulled you out of the way of that horse, all that time ago. How long has it been?"

"That runaway? Four years, Sir. Seems an age, though."

The centurion gave a conspiratorial chuckle. "Wait until you can say you've got 28 years in. *Then* you can say you've done some soldiering. Greet your mother for me."

In answer to Marcus' question, the Optio at the North Gate guardhouse nodded towards the inner room. "Arras came in an hour ago; he's still warming himself, so he says."

Marcus nodded and stepped past the officer. An oldish man sat beside the corner brazier nursing a mug of ale. He looked up with a start as Marcus came through the door. It was Arras Megorix, a trusted scout who had worked for Marcus for almost three years.

"Warm enough now?"

"Thereabouts." Arras took a short poker from the hot coals and dipped it into the beer. It bubbled briefly and a cloud of aromatic steam rose from the mug.

"Where've you come in from? North and West?"

"Briogix actually."

"And? What goes on at Briogix?"

"Why that old devil Caratac is there, surrounded by a bevy of Druids. Whipping the young bloods of the Selgovae to a fever pitch. Lot of men bearing swords instead of kindling"

"War?"

"One tribe? I'd think border nuisance more likely."

Marcus shook his head. "I've heard more. I'm certain the Druids are stirring something up, something more than a few border skirmishes, but I've been out there for the better part of two months and I still don't have a definite idea about what's going on."

Arras shrugged, and Marcus copied the gesture as the other swallowed half his beer.

"It's time I saw my mother. I'll talk to Aemilius and I'm away. May the Gods smile on you."

"And you."

Marcus took his own horse from the stable and walked it down through the South Gate. He mounted there and rode quietly down to the Vallum, following the military way for a few miles.

Aemilius Karrus' lead scout was not the only one to leave the fort before the partying was done. Iavolena was the wife of Vibeus Gaius Septimus, the Commandant of Throp. It was a small fort off to the west; a sometime marching camp and temporary quarters for the most part for garrisons on the move. Iavolena had a young surveyor in tow. He was 15 years younger than her perpetually worried husband and the only favors that interested Titus were those that Iavolena was eager to bestow.

She found her husband in the outer fringes of the crowd, which danced moth-like around Vircovicum's new Commandant.

"Vibius. This wretched headache has grown steadily worse." She screwed her features up until she felt they indicated the appropriate level of pain. "I simply have to return home."

Septimus was clearly alarmed. He put the empty glass down and wrung his hands. "We can't go yet, I haven't been introduced to the new Commandant and the Governor's here. I want to meet him too."

"Oh, don't worry yourself. Cerea's with me."

"What good's a female companion going to be if you're set upon by thieves, eh?"

"This close to the Wall? This is Rome, Vibius. Everything between the Wall and the Stanegate counts as Rome. Oh, all right..." she threw up her hands. "Titus is still here—he'll come with us, all right?"

"Titus who?"

"Titus Severius, Vibius. You met with him the other day, the surveyor. He has no reason to stay for the backslapping." Septimus winced a little and filled his goblet.

"Oh, yes. Yes, fine but even so, just a man and a girl. No, I'll have a couple of legionaries accompany you; tell Tetricus I've ordered it. Yes, you trot along now, hope it gets better. Um, it will probably be the small hours before I get back, you know."

"Don't worry. I'll sleep in my own chambers, you won't waken me."

Iavolena turned away and went back to the doors where her voluptuous form was outlined against the light of flambeaux in the courtyard. A man's silhouette joined hers and both disappeared. Septimus turned back to his companion, but Lestus had already gone.

"I told him I'd be quite all right, but I thought the old fool was going to get all protective and insist that I stay here." Iavolena looked across from the light carriage to where Titus kept pace on his horse. "Anyway, he won't be back before dawn; he's bound to be last in the lineup."

"Hush. Our honor guard will hear you."

She chuckled. "Vibius insisted on them, but they're staying well back, out of earshot." Iavolena pulled her wrap away from her hair and faced into the cooler air. "Do you know, I think it's going to rain? I may get very wet and you'll have to help me bathe and warm myself." She reached across, stretching out her hand for Titus to hold. "We have the whole of the night to ourselves, Titus darling. I know you leave at first light, but you'll be back soon, won't you?"

Titus was a dark, good looking man a few years older than Iavolena's 22. "I have to lay out a villa near Luguvallium—*Carlisle*—for the Tribune Valerius. It depends on what he wants, really. A month, three months, men of this sort don't care about the likes of you or me."

She expelled her breath noisily. "If only there was some way we could pretend to be man and wife. Perhaps I could tell Vibius I simply must have a holiday."

"Vibius isn't going to allow that. He knows he has a beautiful wife; it's only the sight of you that gets him invited to parties like tonight's."

Iavolena giggled at the compliment.

"Perhaps the barbarians will kill him off on the way home."

"I doubt it." The road narrowed a trifle and Titus let go of her hand as he rode on in front. "Fortune doesn't run like that."

⁂

WILLOWFORD

Sheer walls of red clay fell more than 12 times the height of a man to the shallow river. It had been a cold dry summer thus far and the water was far below its normal level for the season. For countless thousands of years the river had meandered backwards and forwards across the valley floor, laying down sediment and carving new pathways across the flat meadows. Apart from occasional boulders embedded in the clay, there was no rock in the area; year by year, the river slowly carved the valley wider and wider.

At this moment in its long lifetime, the river flowed along the foot of the northern cliffs before taking an acute turn to the left to flow through the latest barrier to its progress—a high and wide stone wall along the valley center. It crossed the course of the river with a series of sluices and climbed the steep hillside to the west.

The four sluices in the wall were normally underwater. They were half as high as a man and perhaps, three spans wide; logs and debris brought down by the river had to be cleared frequently, a duty which the Roman legionaries hated for the waters were icy, Northern Briton was a cold and miserable place.

They much preferred to stand above and urinate from the bridge turret, taking bets on which of them could reach the farthest of the sluices. Sometimes, they defecated into the water further up, gambling on the results of the race which took their motions into the carefully designed bridgeworks.

The Roman engineers had done their best. Faced with the task of building a wall eighty miles long in order to separate the barbarians from civilization, they had not chosen the easy route. The line of the wall went up and down hillsides, along the edge of windswept crags, across rivers and bogs; always with one object in mind—to control the movement of the savages.

Every seven miles or so, there was a fort garrisoned with men from Germania, from the Low Countries, from Lusitania. There was a sprinkling of local men—often the product of union with the Britons but by and large, the Romans garrisoned the Empire's borders with men who had no loyalty to the local area. Every mile was a smaller fort at which twenty or more men might be barracked and at every third of a mile was a turret where two or three legionaries stood guard and walked their section of wall.

The turret at Willowford stood on the eastern bridge abutment and to the west, across the river, once the wall had breasted the rise, was a mile castle. Beyond that, the turf wall had not yet been rebuilt in stone. A lack of local material had held up the replacement; both good construction stone and limestone for mortar had to be brought in by the painfully slow ox carts over difficult terrain.

Racellus looked up at the hillside beyond the bridge. This was a bad spot despite its being somewhat sheltered from the wind. The steep flight of steps made it impossible to hurry up to or down from the mile castle which was virtually invisible beyond the top of the bank and in fact, the mile castle was quite out of sight of the main fort at Banna. The turret to the east looked out over the Selgovae lands to the north and across to the next turret along the wall to the mile castle at Poltross Burn.

Two hundred paces from the bridge and on the north side of the river, a stream had made a steep cut into the clay face. It had long ago run dry and was now choked with brush and its way marked with scrub oak and dense alder. Thirty dark shapes moved slowly down its precipitous length, careful not to make any sound which might be heard from the wall. As foreseen, the wind carried a cloud of mist like fine rain from the west.

Dag felt it begin as he led his men out along the narrow shelf between river and cliff. He grinned, for it would cloak both movement and sound. Equally, of course, it hid the wall from his own eyes, but his several days of surveillance had given him a mental picture of the area sufficiently detailed for him to describe every bit of strategic cover.

With a gesture, he gathered the men about him and gave orders in a whisper.

"The sun is gone. Soon it will be dark enough for our purpose. I shall tap Verrick here on the shoulder when I go, the rest of you follow in turn. Tell your fingers as we decided, hm? Ten hands between each man?"

The others nodded to show they understood, some gathered pebbles to help them count. Dag nodded back, checked the roll of goat skin which contained his weapons and prevented them from rattling. Soon they would be drinking the good red blood of the invader. *If the Gods so willed*, he added to his mental deliberations.

Darkness was now almost total. Dag Liogh lowered himself into the water, no more than knee high here though its depth would double and triple when he reached the point where it made its sharp turn toward the bridge.

He moved carefully, testing each footing before committing himself, cursing slowly and steadily. This sort of thing was alien to him, creeping along like a young lad out to steal a grass bracelet from a girl. Far sooner, Dag would have raced along the length of the wall in his wicker chariot, hurling javelins at the guards. That was skill and courage, that was worth showing to the invaders. Ceremonious chanting of curses and screaming insults like his forebears; that showed a man's worth, not this cowering in a river bed.

Nevertheless, times changed. His foes wore a second skin of metal plates; they carried long spears to prevent personal combat and built huge walls of stone to hide behind. Well, the Druids evidently agreed with him, it was time for the Liogh kinsmen to show that they would still go where they wished.

Staying close to the north bank, he drew near to the bend. His upper body was smeared with the same red clay that made up the cliffs; he was practically invisible to any-one more than two or three paces away. As he entered the deeper water, Dag became one with the elements, a ripple in the river, a gurgle of water against the bank.

Dag pushed the bundle ahead of him as the water's speed increased near the sluices. He looked up at the turret, the crenellated rampart, the walkway over the water—deserted. He was swept towards the right hand side and he swam strongly with his legs to put him-self nearer the center. He approached the right hand sluiceway and turning on his side, he aimed for its center.

There was an obstruction, a branch had caught crosswise on to the opening and its several smaller branches had picked up twigs and weeds. He would have to cross to another sluice. There was a splash. A clearing of the throat and another as a Roman legion-ary spat a bolus of phlegm into the water.

Dag Liogh froze. The Roman seemed to look straight at him, he lifted the spear and Liogh waited for the killing stroke. He closed his eyes; in the cold, near freezing water, he sweated. There was a thump as the other grounded his spear butt, another cough, another splash next to Dag's ear.

A moment later, the Roman turned and climbed the steps to the ramparts. Dag's sight turned black, reality wavered, he all but fainted with relief. His senses returned and even though no one else would ever know, he was shamed by the private fear that had so paralyzed him.

It had seemed interminable, but the whole episode had lasted no longer than a handful of heart beats. Dag tore at the branch which obstructed his passage; it moved aside and caught on an iron bracket leaving the way free. The bundle entered the recess; Dag let the water carry him into the entrance and sweep him through, the stone piers scraping him back and front as he went.

Against the blackness under the bridge, the far end of the tunnel was a square of lighter black. It grew larger; he was swept out into the water on the south side, the lands of the Carventii.

Dag lay on his back, letting the rush of water take him away from the wall and towards a narrow beach further along, a phosphorescent glimmer of pale sand. The top of the wall was visible where it cut off the stars, he swept his gaze along the invisible line but there was still no movement up there. A small glow to the east told him the position of the little box where the invaders rested; another, closer to hand showed him the one on the bridge. A lone figure paced slowly along the rampart, away from the river.

He crawled out of the water, the night air almost warm after the icy cold of the river. Well, he had no need to see the invaders. He knew where they were, soon they would know where *he* was, but too late if all went to plan.

⁂

The wind drove the rain down Racellus' left side. He pulled the woolen cloak closer despite its being wet and leaned his pilum (spear) against a crenellation.

He could have turned and gazed off to the south, he would take the wind on his right hand side and give the other one time to thaw out, but no one was going to attack from there.

My decurion is not going to come out in this weather, he told himself, *he'd not venture out of the warm little turret before dawn.* However, Racellus had an irrational fear of being caught, he would be put on rye bread rations for a month and have his pay docked. It did not appeal.

So Racellus cursed the rain and the wind and everything else he could think of about this benighted land including his luck in being posted here. He gazed blindly out over the little river, remembering his recent past.

He had been here little more than a month, in fact, it was only three months after his eighteenth birthday when he had been posted to VI Victrix along with three score or more replacements. For two weeks he had trained within the military area bounded by the wall and by the fort at Throp on the Stanegate where the small contingent of new recruits was stationed. Two weeks of swinging a double weighted wooden sword and overly heavy shield; there had been digging and building temporary camps, forced marches with full gear and field rations. Racellus had thought his arms would drop out of their sockets and his stomach would never digest another meal.

Then there had been a further two weeks of sentry duty along the wall to get to know the neighborhood. On the morrow, he would be up towards Banna, shifting stone and carrying buckets of lime. It was planned to rebuild the rest of the turf wall in stone by the next year at this season.

Racellus was lonely. He came from Tarreconensis, from Sellae where the grapes grew all year round and a frost in winter became folklore for a generation. His companions were mainly from Belgica and Germania Superior and had it not been for the smattering of Latin that all legionaries had to learn, they would have no way of communicating at all.

The Iberian sighed and made an attempt to penetrate the mist and check that the Roman Empire was not about to fall. Balmy summer evenings, drinking with friends, the girls with their flashing eyes and dark skins that smelled of orange blossom and grapes…

What on Earth had made him join the Legion? The idea of travel across the Empire had been tempting. His own excellence with the javelin had been another reason; his winning the local tournaments had brought him to the notice of the garrison and the suggestion of his joining.

Racellus turned and walked slowly towards the next turret. Idle thoughts on an idle afternoon, look where they had got him; all the way to a narrow parapet overlooking a forested wilderness supposedly filled with naked savages which whom he had yet to see any sign of. By all accounts, there were also tattooed half men who skulked through the dark forest aisles like rats through drains.

He counted his paces. One hundred fifty, half way, almost. He turned about and started back. There had been stories told the new recruits by the older seasoned legionaries; ostentatious displays, dancing and sword work, incomprehensible ranting and screaming. The natives were, he had heard, incredible horse riders and skilled charioteers. In various skirmishes, they had succeeded in using them against the might of Rome, driving the light wicker carts at breakneck pace with their small horses. Only the fact that they lacked sufficient organization had saved the Romans from humiliating defeat at times.

Why? Racellus wondered. Rome had brought civilization and order to the whole world. How long would it take these Galae to realize which way the Fates pointed?

At the bridge he stopped once more, pressing into the lee of the turret. He pulled the cloak about him again and held his scutum (Shield) away to stop it rattling against the wall as he leaned over and looked from right to left. The water rushed into the sluice ways and suddenly the sound of the running water made his need to urinate unbearable. Racellus walked quickly along the back walkway and out onto the bridge. He shivered as he lifted the cloak and hardly felt the sword take him through the throat.

Racellus of Sellae died on the bridge that crossed the Irthing as he cursed the miserable weather as the wind tugging at the cloak they had given to him in Iberia. It was the twentieth day of August of a miserable summer; he had never experienced a Brythonic winter.

Dag Liogh pulled his sword free and the legionary's body slumped against the wall and slipped to the floor. He pulled the cloak from under the corpse and the helmet from its head, holding them as several of his own men climbed up to join him. He handed the cloak and helmet to the first man up.

"Time to change sides, Manon, my brother."

Manon grinned and donned the gear. He picked up the fallen pilum, started across the river and up the steps, six others followed him. And six more went to take out the turrets between the bridge and Poltross Burn.

Dag Liogh and Verrick reached the mile castle beyond the crest of the cliff. Minutes crawled by. They waited stoically and presently came the sound of a tawny owl from back along the wall. So realistic was it that but for the expected pattern of calls, Dag could picture it swooping down upon its prey. True in its way, for any soldiers at the two turrets east of the river were now dead. The killing had been as silent as an owl's kill. No sound, no alarms.

The main group was still outside the wall, which separated them from the Britons; they too had moved quietly, purposefully up the hill. They came to the main ditch which ran along the north side of the wall with its nasty little ankle breaker channel at the bottom. Further on, where the causeway spanned the ditch to the mile castle gateway the wall was built in stone. It was the same at each of the turrets, a few paces of curtain wall in stone with the main part of the wall built up from turves all the way from the river Irthing to the western coast.

Dag waited on the rampart and watched, as one by one, his men thrust swords into the turf until they had formed a ladder. Up they came, a few minutes and the whole force was on the rampart. They had done this before, the result of much practice, but this time it was different, this was a part of a greater plan; not chickens and sacks of grain this time—not *just* chickens and sacks of grain. This time they were going to raze the invaders' buildings at Throp. This time…

This time, Dag Liogh had told them, they were going to burn every turret and mile castle between Banna and Vircovicium. Dag had told them this, but there was more that he had not told. Three hundred men would follow his orders; a sign which the Druids hoped would unite the tribes to eventually tear down the wall forever.

The mile castle was perched at the top of the bluff called Harrow's Scar a hundred fifty paces beyond the now silent and empty bridge turret above the river. Two small barracks occupied most of the space inside the rectangular enclosure and could house upwards of thirty legionaries.

Dag had watched the comings and goings through several days, and knew the routine well. Soldiers coming off the wall at night would wake their replacements or if already awake, would often spend a few minutes talking in the yard below before the new men went up to the rampart. Tallying the numbers reported to him, Dag calculated that at least twelve of the fortlet's complement were dead. At most, there would be fifteen to be reckoned with. Three hands, a small matter.

He looked around at his own men, nodded, and went down the steps. They divided into two groups, one to each barracks. He had not, of course, been inside this or any other Roman construction before and was a little nonplussed at what he saw. A hearth holding glowing coals gave more than enough illumination for his dark adapted sight, eight double bunk beds were ranged along one wall; there were seven or eight men asleep or at least, resting and taking no notice of the small sounds he had made at the doorway.

Pila stood in a rack next to the door; beyond, a small altar bore a stone figure and a bowl of oil with a lighted wick floating in it.

Dag grinned and plucked a pilum from the rack as he entered the long room, his kin came behind and each one took one of the Roman weapons. Three legionaries died instantly, skewered on their own weapons while they slept, a fourth and a fifth had been awake and were groping for their scutae as the wicked spear points took them through the ribs. The sixth turned in his sleep as the spear point hurtled towards him and caught him in the arm, bouncing off the humerus, breaking it and waking the man to a pain filled world. There had been so much force in the thrust that it had carried on, flying across the convulsing body into an already dead soldier in a farther bunk.

The sight of several near naked men, tattooed, smeared with mud and with hair dyed red from goat's fat and beech ashes convinced him that he was already dead and in some unholy vision of Hades. He was not so lucky, one of them held aloft a flaming torch and as he tried to raise his arms to beg for mercy, so three pila smashed through his ribs and tore open his stomach.

Outside, they rejoined the others, all the Romans were dead, none had got away to Banna; the main fort was unaware of anything amiss. The torches were tossed into the barracks, in a few minutes the place would be an inferno.

Dag cupped his hands to his mouth and vented a shrill screech. They climbed to the rampart and back toward the river, descending the steps to the bridge. Tongues of flame were already rising from each of the turrets beyond the river.

Dag Liogh felt the rising tide of elation coursing through him—the killing rage always left him feeling this way, invincible, unstoppable, immortal. *Now, they had their diversion.*

They crossed the river and left the military area, heading for the woodlands south of the wall. Although most of the trees and brush had been cleared, the terrain at Willowford was uneven; the river cut through a deep and steep sided valley. Dag led his band up a gully and then, like dark shadows, they slipped into the cover of the woods.

Dag was the last into the darkness beneath the trees, holding back to be sure that every man of his tribe was with them. One last look around and ready to follow the rest, he saw a loan man walking his horse with casual haste along a faintly discernible pathway. For a few brief moments, Dag stood and watched the other. *Roman? Carvetian?* He slipped between the trees. *What did it matter?*

Unaware of the scrutiny, Marcus Gellorix went on his way. The path would take him to the Stanegate within a matter of minutes and once on the paved military road he could ride on with some speed.

CHAPTER TWO

THROP

SCORES, PERHAPS HUNDREDS, OF TORCHES WERE ON THE MOVE. Their rufus light tended to defeat that shed by the half moon so that spaces within the walls of the fort were simply black expanses punctuated by the burning brands.

Along the valley however, the moonlight was quite bright enough to see runners along the road from the wall to the North. The line of the wall itself was, of course, out of sight but the individual glows from the burning turrets and the larger one from the fortlet at Harrow's Scar, stood out.

Dag Liogh squatted in the shadows of a low alder bush. He knew what was about to happen and grinned into the darkness as he went over his own plans. Throp was not a large fort nor was it well defended; it lay to the south of the Wall and was used as a way station for the foreign troops who spent so much time in marching from one place to another. Soon, its small garrison would be gone leaving behind a token force to man the gates and signal braziers.

Despite the clarity of the moonlight, the wind still blew steadily, driving frequent showers of fine rain into the faces of the soldiers who were now leaving the gate and heading north and westward towards the fires that the Lioghs had set.

From the fort at Banna where the Wall was still built of turves a small relief detachment of legionaries was marching towards Harrow's Scar. On a clearer night, they would have realized that something was amiss almost immediately but on this occasion, a squall of rain was ahead of them. It was not until they crested the small ridge which hid the mile castle from them that they saw the flames blurred by the rain.

At a word from their decurion, they broke into an orderly run and arrived at the outer gate minutes ahead of the breathless runner who had just climbed the steep bluff from the river bridge. One of the original party immediately turned to retrace his footsteps to Banna; a moment later however, he paused, seized a burning pole and climbed to the wall rampart and continued to the top of the hill. If he could attract attention through the obscuring rain, it would save his traversing most of the mile back to the fort.

Banna's Commandant was attending the party at Vircovicium and would not hear about this for more than two hours. His senior centurion was at the scene within a quarter hour, however.

"Vetris' Beard." He stood beside the decurion who had left the relief party and shook his head. "Unbelievable. Have the Gods dropped a thunderbolt on it?"

"They'll be dropping one on you if they hear you swearing on the name of a local god."

A sword had once laid open his face from the corner of his mouth to the ear; Antistius Adventus smiled bleakly, the old scar turning it into a leer. He had learned through a long career to propitiate many gods and local gods were as good as any to swear by. "It won't matter much; the Big Man is going to have my balls for this."

"You? Look at the lie of the land. How often have we said that the Godless place is out of sight from Banna? Hmm. If the engineers had used a bit more thought and a little less rank, they'd have put the mile castle on the top of the ridge."

"I've no doubt you're right, Melanos. Let us hope that I can convince the enquiry of the fact."

"An enquiry? We need an observation tower, not an enquiry."

There were close to one thousand legionaries in the stretch between Borcovicio and Banna. They were from the First Tungrorum Milliari at Banna and the VI Nerviorum, the latter called in from Aesica where they had been awaiting permanent disposition. They found nothing except the evidence already available in the form of fifty eight Legionaries dead and the smoldering remains of the torched turrets and mile castle.

Of the perpetrators, there was no sign—not at least in the area in which they were searching. None of the Roman officers thought to turn round and look behind them; no Albyn was going to be skulking around to the south, watching and waiting.

Shadows moved along the sides of the old wooden fort, hands touched the mildewed and even rotting boards as they passed single file above the ditch which was almost filled in, in some places, with rubble and kitchen rubbish.

Five men of the Lioghs stood along the turf incline below the north eastern corner turret. They carried long poles; they stood ten paces apart, hidden in the gloom at the foot of the timber ramparts.

Five hands of mixed Liogh and Cruagh fighting men stood similarly hidden along the south wall, although, here they carried long metal spikes and swords loosely strung through belts or loops.

Three times this number stood off from the walls, within the cleared area which surrounded every Roman fort to the length of a bow shot. They were hidden as far as possible by small bushes, a pile of building stone, an ox cart and other reminders of a relatively peaceful existence to the south of Emperor Hadrian's Wall. They held powerful native bows, each one with an arrow already notched to the string.

A cloud crossed the bright face of the moon bringing shadow and a flurry of rain. An awesome thunder broke out, booming and clattering and terrifying anyone unprepared for it, sentries atop the walls rushed to the north and east walls convinced that a major conflict was already joined out there in the darkness. Several shot arrows or hurled javelins at half seen shapes but there were no answering cries of pain to reassure them that their foe was mortal.

Dag waited with those along the south wall, cold and hungry, shivering—from the cold he told himself and doubtless, this was so. As the noise from the north side drew the sentries away he and all the others there, lifted a stone and hammered a spike into the wall, the stratagem had served the smaller band at Harrow's Scar, and it served them now. Each man climbed up and stood on the spike and repeated the action.

The men had been chosen for height so everyone was within reach of the crenellations along the stockade. Giving himself no time to think about it, Dag pulled himself upward; he seized hold of the upper edge of the crenellation and jumped through the gap.

Only now, as fifty warriors of the Callatae stood upon the inner walkway did the puzzled sentries realize that it had been a deception. As Dag Liogh led his band towards them, a cloud of arrows swept across the ramparts, carrying many of the defenders to the nether world. So fast had events followed on the heels of the distraction that many of the Romans died without knowing who it was they were fighting.

The screams of dying men had already warned the rest of the fort's occupants and silence was no longer an ally of the Callatae, they screamed and roared their hatred and defiance, unnerving the Romans who paused too long before striking at the native warriors.

Dag roared as loudly as any, his blade scything into those who came against him. He sent them spinning to the courtyard below with blood spurting from neck, from belly; with arm or leg severed, but even in the midst of the blood lust that had come upon him, Dag wondered how long this could last.

Roman archers had reached the corner turrets and were beginning to pick his men off without exposing themselves to the barbarian bowmen outside the fort. Reinforcements were rushing from the barracks buckling on armor as they came. Many of the defenders were not fully awake; they were newly out of their bunks or drowsy from drinking wine at a hearthside. Yet these men were Romans, trained professionals with fighting instincts honed to sharpness every day. They fought by reflex: stab, parry, advance, strike, retreat and warrior after warrior was cut down.

The toll of Callatae dead and that of their Selgovae allies began to rise and Dag saw many of his kin go to meet their ancestors. But the Romans were outnumbered, some of them still not conscious enough to realize they were dead men. Bravely they fought as individuals, but disorganized, the Roman's group tactics were unusable; it was only a matter of time before the defenders were overrun.

Down in the fort itself, a small detachment of Thracian auxiliaries boiled out of another barracks. They were light cavalry troops used to fighting from the backs of responsive horses and not accustomed to close combat in confined spaces.

Dag Liogh led five of his men at a run and met them head on. The interior of the fort was filled with bunkrooms and storehouses between which the narrow passageways were more suited to sly knife work than to the slashing cut of the horseman. All six reached the gate without serious casualty and as four of the Albyns held the Roman troops at bay, two lifted the bars from the heavy doors which swung inward under pressure from outside.

A body of the small, but solid northern warriors poured through the gates overrunning the defenders by sheer weight of numbers. The fighting lasted little more than half an hour. The defending force was outnumbered three to one and while many died on both sides; the odds steadily rose in favor of the Lioghs and the Cruaghs.

At the end, half of them remained in the fort, looting weapons and provisions. Dag moved the rest of them out and down the hill to the vicus outside the west gate. Anxious faces at windows and behind barred doors had their worst fears confirmed.

Fort Throp's present purpose was to provide accommodation for units moving along the Stanegate military road. Larger detachments would camp outside the fort on sites set aside for military use while their officers would be accommodated within the fort or, depending on relative rank, at the Mansio the official hotel in the vicus.

This civil settlement had grown during recent years with the building and rebuilding of the Wall. Its mansio had been extended several times to meet the demands of travelers to the area; shops and workshops had sprung up to house a dozen or more trades and services. Military money flowed more freely than the local currency and as soldiers retired, they often settled close to their last posting to marry local women with whom they had formed lasting relationships.

So it was at Throp, though none of this meant anything to the Selgovae and the Callatae warriors who swept through the vicus killing anyone who stood in their way or attempted to protect what they owned. Weaponry, trinkets, poultry, grain… anything portable and of reasonable value.

Dag had six swords strapped to his back, three of the shorter Roman pattern and three of heavy Carvetian make, he carried several iron pila heads broken off the shafts. He left six men dead behind him and now that the bloodlust was dying, he waited for his closest kin to join him and wished that he had been able to take some horses with them. They could have taken their pick from the stables, but getting them through the Wall was not, of course, possible.

No. He shook his head to dismiss the thought and raised his right hand to his mouth. Once, twice, thrice, he gave the call of the screech owl and his men returned one by one, laden down with looted goods that would make good barter later.

"Which way do we go then? Have you seen the sign?"

"Oh come on, Manon," he cried when he saw what his brother had picked up. "What use is *she* going to be while we're getting across the wall, eh? And no, I have not seen the sign yet. The invaders go *that* way though," he pointed to the west, "so we go the other way. Dawn is close so we must move fast." He raised his voice to make sure that all heard him. "Carry only what you can without faltering, we must leave here *now*."

To the east, woodland grew densely for many miles towards Borcovicio. It had been cleared along the Stanegate and along the line of the Wall, but offered excellent cover to the Liogh kinsman. They moved through this sort of country as effortlessly as the boars and small deer whose paths they used.

They came to the northern edge of the woodland; some one hundred paces beyond was the wall with a two storey turret almost opposite their position. There had been neither sight nor sound of other Callatae nor of Selgovae in the area although this was only to be expected of warriors who naturally fought alone or at most, in small roving bands.

"What do we do now, Dag?"

"We wait. We wait in silence, Manon, my brother."

So they waited as the east became grey with the false dawn and the sound of marching feet and the clink of metal accoutrements warned them of the presence of Roman legionaries.

Dag soon became tired of waiting and was contemplating ordering a dash to the turret where steps would take them up to the ramparts. *Should I wait longer, should they go now?* And his question was answered. Another band further along broke cover; yelling and screaming at the top of their lungs, they dashed forward. A second group followed the first and startled a flock of starlings into the air.

"Now, Dag Liogh. Let us..."

But Dag's hand was firm on his brother's arm. With the other, he pointed. Three crows, their cries almost drowned out by the raucous calls of the starlings had also been driven from their roosts by the charge of the Albyns. They fled eastward, bundles of black rags against the coming dawn.

"There. That is the way we go. Stay low, the light is deceitful and we shall be hidden against the trees." And they ran, bent under the weight of booty. The crows, not natural night fliers, flapped slowly away ahead of them.

Behind Dag Liogh and his kin, more and more warriors from the north—upward of two hundred—were fighting a knot of Romans at the top of the turret steps. The Wall was quite heavily patrolled after the night of activity and the Roman presence around the turret was growing quickly as legionaries ran towards the sound of fighting. Almost without thought, they brought to bear the tactics which they practiced daily. Small squares at first with their oblong shields overlapping and protecting each soldier's body; the squares grew as patrol units joined together into mobile rectangles with a line of pila thrusting through the gaps.

Scream and roar as they might, the tribesmen could not get near enough to employ their long swords. Roman javelins pierced the skin covered shields; the javelins were barbed, they bent, becoming impossible to remove and made the shields useless. The raiders had little choice but to drop them along with their plunder and fight on unprotected with swords and clubs.

It was a rout. Men climbed the wall, finding secure foot and hand holds in the roughly dressed stone though few made it to the top. Fewer still leaped down to crawl across the ditch and dodged Syrian arrows in the misty morning to the north of the Wall.

Dag's party saw none of this. When the crows found new roosts in willows along the course of a stream, they followed the watercourse to the culvert which brought it under the Wall. There were no patrols at this point. Every legionary from Poltross Burn to Willowford was busy seeking revenge for the night of mayhem and murder that had been inflicted. Dag's twenty-three kinsmen pushed and pulled each other up to the rampart and as carefully, climbed down the other side. Within minutes, they were lost in the Selgovae woods again, each composing their tale of heroism.

Many more cursed the Druids and wondered what twisted game they played to have persuaded so many Cruaghs and Lioghs into giving their lives to the Gods. What booty there was, was no consolation for the loss of kinsman with so little honor gained.

⁂

VIRCOVICIUM

Legate Gaius Marcellus Flavius was just thirty years of age, a slim young man, prematurely grey and with a commission from Hadrian himself. He had been one of Severus' several Deputy Governors of Britannia for almost nine months; the whole of the last bitter winter, the sick joke of a spring and the recent apology for a summer.

Unlike most administrators of the Roman Empire, Marcellus had previous military experience. In Dacia he had distinguished himself in action against the Sarmation tribes receiving the *Corona Vallaris* for being the first officer over the enemy ramparts. He was, too, an able executive, stepping adroitly through the politics and avoiding the daggers aimed at his back. He enjoyed the social life and if it was a little less flamboyant than that which he had been used to closer to Rome, then at least here, he was a bigger fish in a smaller pond. If he had a reputation for impetuosity then that only endeared him to his command.

"Silence," he shouted and winced. *If I'm ever going to make General, I'm going to have to learn drink more wisely.* Without that promotion, he stood little chance of realizing his ultimate ambition in the Senate.

"Now. Choose a spokesman and tell me again, slowly, without interruptions."

Aurelius Pintus saw himself as the ranking Commandant here. He had been at Vircovicium a scant week, but this was home ground; it had been his party even with Governor Lulius Severus there. "It seems that the barbarians somehow got through our defenses."

"That much is quite obvious. What I'd like to know, is how?"

The Commandant shook his head. "We don't know. Not yet, but we will, Jupiter's fist, we will."

"Yes, yes." Flavius waved a languid hand and closed his eyes. "What did these barbarians do?"

"Well, it appears that they burned several turrets on the Wall and a mile castle. We assume that this was just a feint because as soon as all the unassigned forces had gone to investigate, they hit Fort Throp. There was no great damage there; they seem just to have looted what they could carry and set light to one or two barracks."

"And that's it? What were our forces doing while all this was going on?"

"There was quite a lot of fighting, Sir. We lost a hundred men."

"A hundred?" Flavius' coloring was already high, but now it started to shade through beetroot red to purple. "A hundred? And how many of these miserable barbarians did it take to do that? Hmm? A thousand?"

"Several hundred at least, Sir. We've counted a hundred and sixty killed already." Aurelius Pintus frowned and then added, "Many, many prisoners too. They can be put in the mines or the building parties or even sold in the South as slaves. You have my assurance that very few made it back to the North. Very few, if any."

Flavius saw a glimmer of light at the end of his tunnel. "So it *could* be said that we have fought and won a major battle here? Put down a major uprising?"

A lot of shit could be seen ahead, Pintus trod carefully. "You could say that, Sir."

I might just come out of this smelling very sweet, Flavius said to himself. If Severus is still snoring his head off in that whore's bed. "Is there anything else you think I should know?"

Pintus nodded to Septimus who reluctantly stepped closer.

"Vibius Gaius Septimus, Sir. Commandant at Throp." He faltered, Flavius' eyes swept over him as though he were a piece of offal. Septimus could feel the tremble in his bones begin. "It would not have happened if I'd been there, Sir, but I was called to the festivities here."

Flavius rolled his eyes up. "Yes?" He sighed, letting his world-weary gaze rest heavily on the older man with his over large nose.

"I'd have been there to rally my men, provide proper leadership..." He could see that this was not going down so well. *Why did I never have the self-confidence of these other...?*

"But this is more important than a few chickens and swords taken for booty, Sir. My wife... my wife has been taken. She's the youngest sister of Senator Vexillium, you know. Both her and her companion, the lady Cerea, have gone missing in the attack."

Marcellus Flavius beamed.

"Well now. This alters things, hmm? No one escaped, you said Pintus, no one. Yet we have two women taken. Well born women, eh?"

Flavius' complexion was almost back to normal. His headache was evaporating. He prodded Pintus in the chest in time to his words.

"A major uprising, Pintus. Examples must be made. Punitive measures. Search parties. Do I make myself clear? Major issues are at stake."

"I'll see to it immediately, Sir." Pintus suddenly realized what he was being ordered to do. He was a newcomer, only just taken up his command and here was his first opportunity to shine. "At once."

"See to it. Oh, and Pintus..."

"Sir?"

"Don't disturb Governor Severus. He's had a busy night." Flavius liked making instant decisions, it made him feel alive.

"Right, Sir." But Aurelius Pintus was already ticking off items on a mental list. First he wanted the bastard, what was his name? Gellus? Gellorix, Marcus Gellorix, that was the one.

WHITE TARN

Marcus knew nothing of the events of the previous evening and night. He had left the party after passing on his warning. He had been away from the family home for a month now, far too long for his mother to look after everything.

He realized, of course that it was his father's influence that had brought him his present rank in the Roman army and indeed, Roman money had rebuilt the farm where he lived with his mother. He knew, too, that the education he had received was out of the ordinary, even for well favored though out-of-wedlock sons of Roman officers.

The Romano-Brigante had old memories of sitting on his father's knee. He could recall playing with his brass-chased helmet and silver torque and as a toddler, his Roman father had made him a toy sword and shield from wood.

These things happened. Marriage with local women was out of the question before discharge and such disjointed family groups as his were not uncommon. A lower ranking officer than his father might expect to stay in Briton until the end of his career, but not so Aelius Mansustus. The almost inevitable recall to Rome came in Marcus' twelfth year, an event that even knowing it was not his father's fault, Marcus could not forgive him for.

Aelius had, after all, entered into a relationship which he knew to be doomed. He had sired a child. He had accustomed his barbarian family to a standard of living which he knew could not be maintained once he had left.

Still, Aelius tried. Even after nine years, parcels came twice a year from Rome. Strong boxes of coin, a bolt of silk perhaps, ivory figures, spices, wine. Once there had been a complete set of Samian kitchenware from somewhere in Gaul where he had been stationed for a few months. Yes, his father did not forget them.

And he had taught the young Marcus Latin, he had paid a well-tutored officer to spend a few months drilling some Greek into his son as well as a smattering of philosophy and some of the plays.

Marcus had written occasionally although he had no way of knowing if the thin wooden boards ever reached their destination. He had told his father how his mother's health had failed after his leaving, how she had cried herself through the nights. How, in the early days they had been treated as outsiders by both the Brigantes and the Romans and how his bastardy was looked on by his father's erstwhile companions.

Aelius had much unhappiness to answer for.

Marcus guided his horse through the dense woodland. Deadfalls kept the native fires burning throughout the year with no need of cutting, and game was so plentiful that meat was never a luxury—so long as there was a man in the household. For a month, there had been none and it was with anxious eyes that he scanned his mother's home as he slid from the saddle and made fast the rein.

It was a house like no other that Marcus had ever seen. Initially, it had been a traditional round house, its walls being willow woven through the supporting uprights and covered with daub. His father had had rectangular extensions built to either side with their pitched roofs joining the original conical thatch. In addition to the central room for all purposes, there was now a bath house to the west, next to the mere and a pair of bedrooms to the east.

He saw that the water trough held enough for his mount and collected a double handful of hay from the small sheaf before crossing the clearing to the main door.

Inside, his mother sat near a window overlooking the small pond, her favorite place in the single circular room. She was twisting thread from flax, watching the spindle near-sightedly when he entered and failed to hear his footsteps until he was quite near.

"Mother."

She jumped at the sound and smiled for she recognized her son's voice moments before her eyes refocused on his face. Marcus' features held more than a touch of his father in the strong nose and brows, in the curl of his hair. Yet his build was Brigantean, from his grandfather; large, big boned.

Marcus smiled too, the dimples in his cheeks as he bent to kiss her, clearly came from herself. The best of two worlds she told herself every time he came back.

"Meat?" he asked. "Do we have meat in the pot?"

Avorocoeu shook her head. "It does not always agree with me," he knew the excuse to be a lie, "there's honey and bread if you're hungry."

"It will do for breaking my fast, but I'll hunt today, bring back something tasty, something juicy. Hm? Boar or some venison? Tonight we'll feast."

"Whatever you want, my son."

He was about to kiss her once more on the forehead when the sound of a horse coming through the ling somehow destroyed the mood.

Marcus recognized the man at once. An *immune* who worked mainly as a messenger, a feeling of disquiet came over Marcus. The messenger didn't dismount, speaking from the saddle as Marcus waited just outside the door.

"Commandant Pintus wants you back at Vircovicium. Last night—or was it the night before? I've lost track of time since leaving Vircovicium. Um, what was I saying?" He swayed and pulled himself upright again.

The man was plainly exhausted; it was as much as he could do to sit his horse.

"Come inside, Lucius." He helped him down from the saddle. "Come and sit down and take a cup of ale. I'll see to your horse and you can tell me what you came to tell me."

Marcus half supported him inside and pushed him down onto a bench. "Mother, get this fellow something to eat and drink, will you? I'll see to his horse meanwhile and to mine as well."

Later, he returned to find the fellow looking somewhat more alert.

"Better?"

"Much better, thanks. Sorry to be in such a state."

Marcus shrugged. "Forget it. Comes to us all. Now what does Aurelius Pintus want with me so soon?"

Piece by piece, the happenings at the Wall were related to him and Marcus' expression became grave. All he had learned and passed to the Romans had been for nothing. *Too late, they had acted too late although...* He thought about it and worked out what had happened when. In fact it was as much his own fault as anyone's, the raid must have occurred almost as soon as he had issued the warning, there simply hadn't been time to do anything.

There was nothing else to be done; he would have to cut his visit short and return as ordered—for what, he didn't know.

However, once Lucius, the messenger, had left, Marcus set about cutting wood and mending the broken shutter and ... and a dozen other small chores.

It was little enough he could do and even though she smiled, Marcus knew Avorocoeu wept inwardly to see him go so quickly.

"I'm sorry Mother. You know I've no choice in the matter, don't you?"

She nodded, but remained silent.

"Well, I can leave in the morning and still be there soon enough. I shall travel faster than Lucius; he's still asleep on his feet...

"Anyway, I have something for you, at least let me give you this." He reached into his pouch and took a brooch of cast bronze which showed a snake twined into a knot. It had been enameled in green with two minute garnets for its eyes.

"There. Is that not beautiful? I bought it from a Votadinian craftsman of rare skill." He reached forward and pinned it to the shawl around her shoulders and she moved so that the window light sparkled on the enamel.

Avorocoeu was still a beautiful and striking woman and for a moment, Marcus just watched her. Then, "a trifling present of beauty to one who's beauty holds no compare." He spoke in his native tongue, two lines from an old ballad, slightly misquoted to suit the occasion. Marcus didn't go hunting that day, nevertheless, they ate well at the table he had built many years before.

"I thought you said you had no meat, Mother. Who trapped the hare and the grouse?"

"Why I had forgotten them. It was Gellatorea, of course." She smiled and the skin wrinkled into a lacework of tiny laugh lines around her eyes. "He has loved me for all these years even though I chose your father. He'll not come when you're here, but he is never far away."

Marcus nodded. "I dare say you forgot about the game because you know what I would say if I'd been reminded of Gellatorea."

His mother chuckled. "Nonsense. I don't know what you're talking about."

"I'm talking about your poor suitor, Mother. Invite him here. You know as well as I do that Father can never come back."

Avorocoeu's lips tightened and she looked away.

"Your father was the only man that I have lain with. It will remain so until I die." She turned back to Marcus. "I like Gellatorea well enough. I make him clothes for the winter and mend them and he sees to it that I do not go short of the things that are needful." She turned away again. "But he will never know me as Aelius did; Gellatorea realizes this.

"The bracken on my bed stays softer when I am the only one to lie on it."

"Well. It is a pity. A waste beside." He reached across the board and took his mother's hand. "These are not the best of times for families, ours especially. I have to travel; I cannot stay to look after you as a son should, but I have this to say.

"Wherever I go and however long I'm away, you are always in my heart; my thoughts are ever with you."

Marcus yawned then and chuckled, changing the mood. "I can ride as long and as far as the next man, but I must take to my bed soon if I am to return to the Wall in the morning. Will you forgive me for leaving you so early?"

"Of course, my dear. When you say things like that, you sound much like your father and he could talk the thrushes out of the trees." She patted his hand. "And you have something of your grandfather about you too. My own father, gone to his ancestors these many years. He might have been King of the Brigantes."

Marcus pushed himself to his feet. "If Venutius had not divorced his southern wife, perhaps; if he had not chosen to oppose the Romans, perhaps. Anyway, there'll be no more Kings in Britannia; anyone calling himself King is going to get knocked down very quickly. Even those north of the Wall, their days are numbered.

"Be proud of our heritage Mother, that is what is sacred."

He kissed her and went to his room. Behind him, Avorocoeu nodded her acceptance of the truth though it failed to prevent her weeping for those memories of the past.

⁂

The next morning, Marcus was awake at sunrise. His mother had left a big stoneware bowl full of water next to the fire, it was pleasantly warm and he carried it outside to scrub himself with ashes and Roman oils before scraping the layer away with a copper strigil. A minute later, he plunged into the cold waters of the pond and swam to the center and back again.

On an impulse and aware that it would make his departure later than he had intended, Marcus leaned through the window of his bedchamber and took three slender iron tipped spears from a wall rack. He went to the far side of the little lake and waited. Three times he struck, freezing as motionless as a statue between times and when the sun had cleared the tree line, there was a silver fish wriggling on the end of each of the spears.

Back in the house, Marcus quickly gutted them and filled the empty bellies with a little dried sage. A handful of beech nuts on the dull coals of last night's fire quickly burst into fragrant flame, he baked them and laid them on plantain leaves.

The aroma brought Avorocoeu from her couch and delighted that her son had not left before she woke, she joined him in a silent and companionable breakfast. Goat's milk laced with honey finished the meal off and he made his preparations.

Marcus could delay no longer and gathered his riding gear together.

"Take care, my son." she said as she embraced him. "I've heard the Selgovae are arming themselves."

"Even in this quiet place, you've heard of that, eh?"

Avorocoeu drew back a little and looked at Marcus. "*You* know too? Gellatorea brought me the news, even this quiet place is awash with rumor."

As he rode towards the north east through Carvetian country, the sun died and cloud hid the pale sky of early morning; there was an occasional glimpse of blue, a flash of sunlight then the threat of rain again. The weather exactly suited his mood: uncertain, changeable, morose. He lived in uncertain times, walked an uncharted path.

His Roman friends and his superiors wanted him to be Roman, to think Roman—with just enough *barbarian* to make him useful. His mother and those Brigantes he could still call friends expected him to be Brigantean, with just enough Roman ways to be able to secure small favors from the occupying armies of Rome.

Marcus enjoyed his job. The danger in what he did was a constant companion but the sense of excitement was a stimulant he had come to crave; only the rush of adrenaline seemed to make him feel alive these days.

He entered the thickest part of the forest, bending low in the saddle below the gnarled boughs of trees along the secret ways of his people.

VIRCOVICIUM

Twenty four hours and the place was transformed. Severus had departed in the early morning before sun up and had left his Legate to get on with things as he saw fit. Already the word of Gaius Marcellus Flavius had worked wonders; Commandant Pintus wondered if the whole of the Britannia occupation forces had been ordered to gather outside Vircovicium's southern gate.

Three cohorts, twelve hundred men squatted around little fires which provided more cheer than real warmth. A few leather tents had been put up and pila stuck in the ground to hang helmets and cooking pots on. There were Syrian Archers, Frisian cavalry, infantry, engineers and pioneers. A *numerus* of native soldiers carrying sling shots and clubs kept to themselves down where the approach road bridged the stream.

A squad of military slaves hauled a catapult and a ballista up the steep slope around the south west corner to the western gate. More slaves hauled baggage and supplies to ox carts and moved these into position behind the engines.

Nearby forts had been stripped to their minimum establishment in order to put this expedition together. Truly, this was a Legion preparing for war.

In the Headquarters building with the Legion's eagles as a suitable background, Pintus sat back in his carved oak chair. Before him stood his key officers.

He was already familiar with the centurions including the chief centurion, the *primus pilus* of the Legion who had accompanied him from Eboracum. That officer was due to return there, to the Legionary fortress, where his main duties lay.

The Praefector of cavalry from Lugovallum and the three Tribunes commanding the infantry, the engineers and the *numerus* were new to him and he watched them carefully, to gauge their caliber.

"Our best information," he was saying, "comes from our scouts. They say that the barbarians came from as far beyond the wall as fifteen or twenty miles, maybe even more. The tribes of some of the dead have been identified from that blue dye they use, the patterns are quite traditional."

"I thought the business had died out." This from one of the centurions who had recently arrived with Pintus.

"The word? Apparently so, except with these Callatae. However, it tells us where to look for these, er, ladies. They must be found and returned unharmed."

"If we're not already too late," said the same officer as before.

"Indeed. If we are, it will be unfortunate though mostly unfortunate for these tribesmen. They will have signed their own death warrants if that *is* the case."

Aemilius Karrus, a senior centurion, spoke. "Are we absolutely certain that the barbarians have taken them?" It was the reservation which had occurred to many of the officers though few would have dared to voice it. "You see, Sir, from what I've heard, these Barbarians were pretty well scattered at the end. It would have needed a measure of organization to take two women back with them."

Pintus felt like shouting at the man. *Where else are they then? Every inch of the way from here to Throp has been searched, every room and passage at Throp.* No one talked down to an officer of Aemilius' experience and rank though. Pintus controlled himself.

"It must be said that we are not absolutely certain. But two pretty women were riding back to Throp at the time of the raid—which does appear to have been exceptionally well organized and there is no sign of them anywhere else. Logic demands that there is a better than even chance that the barbarians have taken them."

The grizzled centurion nodded. "Better than evens. Thank you Sir."

"Any other questions?"

"Sir. What's our total strength going to be?" It was one of the Tribunes. *Infantry,* thought Pintus.

"Close to sixteen hundred, Tribune. Nearly a third of a legion all told. And *I* shall be in command." He looked at the other faces there. "Anything else? No? Very well. We march at tomorrow's dawn."

When the officers had marched out, some touching the small statue of Jupiter near the entrance, Aurelius Pintus beckoned an aide forward. "Any sign of that Marcus Gellorix yet?"

"Not as yet, Sir. The Beneficiarius was north of the Wall for five weeks and I'm told he went to visit his mother after he returned. A messenger has gone after him, but it's more than a good day's ride."

"I hope he was told a good night's ride will get him just as far."

"Actually, he did expect to ride through the night, Sir. I'll inform you just as soon as there's news."

"Ah well. Does he know we'll soon be at war?"

"Gellorix? Not until the messenger catches up with him, Sir. If you remember his speaking with you at the party, he left immediately afterwards."

"Nice piece of luck, hey? A man with a more suspicious mind than mine might think it too much of a coincidence."

"Commandant Lestus of Vindolanda always thought highly of him, Sir and the centurions always take his information seriously. A most reliable scout by all accounts."

"Well, we shall see, Garius. We shall see."

As Aurelius Pintus had decreed, the army marched at dawn.

Assembly beyond the west gate started at the fifth hour and went on until Pintus left his house by a rear entrance and flanked by two centurions, crossed a pathway where dew dripped from the eaves in the darkness. The Quintana had more light, illumination coming from the open windows of the main workshop.

They turned onto the well lit *Via Decumana* which led to the west gate and out onto the one piece of ground level enough for parades and the assembling of punitive expeditions. At the front of the line was the *numerus* of Mauritanians, they were followed by cavalry then infantry, engineers and pioneers. Then came the baggage wagons and the wheeled equipment drawn by complaining oxen.

A space had been left for the Commandant's staff which Pintus now joined, mounting his horse from a portable block. Behind him came more cavalry, more infantry and finally the Legionaries, Rome's crack troops, the backbone of her war machine.

Pintus took his horse forward and spoke to the Tribune leading the Numerus.

"You know the procedure, Tribune. Your men will lead well in advance. I want any prisoners you brought back for questioning when we make camp."

The Tribune nodded, saluted with fist across his chest armor and Pintus walked his mount back to his position.

Pintus tucked his purple cape around in front and nodded to the Senior Centurion, Aemilius Karrus. The nod was passed on to a lesser centurion who in turn relayed it to a decurion to start the marching cadence. The sound of the *cornua* signaled the legion to march; the pace was slow and because of the ground plan at Vircovicium, they marched around the ramparts to the south gate and then north along the *Via Principalis* to pass through the Wall itself.

It was always an unsettling thought when it occurred to Pintus. The Roman army marched at a pace set by the oxen. To march faster meant leaving behind the major supply of weapons and rations.

As they cleared the gateway, flags were unfurled, the signifers the (horn blowers) marched out, the aquilifer carried the Legions golden eagle standard alongside Commandant Pintus himself—it was the most coveted position in the legion.

An hour later, the last rank passed through the northern entrance and the gateway was closed.

The Sixth was off to war.

CHAPTER THREE

VIRCOVICIUM

WHEN MARCUS PASSED THROUGH THE GATE AT VIRCOVICIUM, the general state of desertion astonished him.

"Ha! They've invaded the barbarian lands," the officer replied and spat into a puddle of rainwater. Succinctly, he described the pomp and splendor of the early morning departure.

"You'd better tone down that expression," he advised, "it looks like most of us feel."

"Incredulous?"

"That's the word."

Garius Mellius was one of several aides to Commandant Pintus and like Marcus himself, a *benificiarius*. He smiled and beckoned Marcus through the atrium. "Follow me, Marcus. May I call you Marcus? I've an office on the south wall and two rooms. I've just had some wine delivered; give me your opinion on it while we enjoy the view."

Marcus grinned and his brown eyes became nested in laughter lines. He could have done with a nap, but this was the way Romans worked—a glass of wine, a chat, a few minutes' gossip before getting down to business.

"Isn't that breathtaking? I'm originally from the Low Lands; I never saw this sort of country before being posted up here."

"Well it's a bright morning. It can be a bit bleak when it's raining, or snowing."

"Oh I'm sure. Pintus has only been here a little more than a week; we came up from Cataractonium and it just got better and better. Now that wine I mentioned."

Garius poured a goblet and passed it across and then filled one for himself.

"Still in touch with your father?"

Marcus tried not to let the pause of surprise drag on too long. For a new boy, Garius must have had his ear to the ground damn quickly.

"Yes. We write fairly often." He chose to say no more knowing how easily words became corrupted with repetition.

"Nice fellow. Met him in Durobrivae when I first came to Briton." Rather than the more usual Roman name of *Britannia,* Garius had used the native word, perhaps in deference to Marcus' parentage. "How's the wine?"

"Very fine. Fruity." Marcus sat down and gazed out of the window and across the wide valley between the fort and the scarp to the south. The valley itself was heavily wooded, but the rocky outcrops on the upper hillsides made him think of the bare bones of the earth poking through its worn out skin. Perhaps there were places where it was so worn out that the *Underworld* might be glimpsed through cracks and faults.

Of a sudden, the urbane ways of Rome seemed tiresome.

"Yes. Excellent wine, Garius. Now tell me something. I know a third of a legion has left through the northern gate—by all the Gods, why? I can't believe it is purely retaliation. Rome doesn't react in haste like this."

Garius looked at his visitor for several seconds. He weighed his words and spoke slowly. "You are quite correct, of course. Pintus is acting quickly because it is, in part anyway, a rescue mission."

Marcus frowned. "Go on."

"You know Praefector Vibius Septimus?"

Marcus nodded. "Throp?"

"The same, apparently—his wife was lost, presumed carried off in the raid of three nights ago. She and a lady companion—a fairly well born girl—were at the party given by our Commandant. You were here, I believe."

"Yes. Yes I was. Not for long though. I had some information to pass on and then I left."

"I'm with you." Garius chuckled. "I really can't stand the fawning that goes on at these things. At least with my antecedents, I *know* I shan't go very far in terms of promotion; I don't *have* to join in. Well, where was I?"

"Vibius Septimus' lady."

"The fair Iavolena. Iavolena felt ill or faint or whatever they feel. She left the party early with her companion and one or two others. They were waylaid, or so it would seem."

"And none of them reached their destination?"

"Of that I'm unsure. You'd have to visit the fort at Throp, but I have to pass on your orders and they say you are to follow the Legion and report to Pintus as soon as you catch up."

"Mm." Marcus folded his hand and leaned his chin on the fist. Two missing women, he mused. An abduction by the Selgovae seemed an unusual event. Not impossible, but unusual unless there had been some sort of price put on the women's heads. Unlikely in itself. Children would be more likely to be taken, in order to raise them as tribal slaves but metal, weapons, fowl or game even; these would be of more interest than women.

Was the Legion chasing a fantasy? He looked up at Garius.

"What sort of man is Pintus? Between ourselves, now. It'll go no further, I promise."

Garius ran a hand through his grey and thinning hair. "Brave, bold. He's a seasoned cavalry officer, one that men will follow—he has the, er, the charisma to lead them, you know?"

Marcus nodded.

"I shouldn't say this, but he's one who follows his heart, not his head. Not that it has done him any harm though. He'll see a few seasons out as Commandant here, then back to some warmer clime with a good promotion."

"Well thank you for your honesty. Still though, you're his aide; why did he leave you behind?" Garius gave Marcus a grin filled with chagrin. He was still wearing a cloak and moving it aside, he extended his leg so that it could be seen clearly. The cleverly designed sandal contained only half a foot.

"I killed a man in battle, a Cartavellauni. He fell dead, but his hand still held the sword as though he would take it with him to the next world. It cleaved my foot in two, an accident. That was—hm, fifteen years ago; I was with the Twentieth. Too young to be pensioned off so they retained me as a scribe."

Garius chuckled to lighten the atmosphere. "Been benificiarius to five officers of high rank since then, all of them career officers, all of them stay two or three years and then on to something bigger and better. Well, I'm good at my job; I'm trusted with the keys to the treasury."

Marcus smiled. "Well..."

"Well, marching and fighting are beyond me now. I dare say that if some young savage, some Brigantean, say, were to attack me; well, I could try and hold him off with a quill." Garius grinned.

At least, thought Marcus, he has come to terms with it.

"I don't limp, you didn't notice, did you?"

Marcus shook his head.

"No, I don't limp. I just fall over if I try to move too fast."

"You're a brave man, Garius." Marcus tilted his head to one side and looked at the other. "Bravery doesn't have to be measured by the sword although these are times when that isn't appreciated.

"Now, I'll tell you what I intend to do. Just in case Pintus checks with you when he returns, I want you to forget the time of day I arrived here. A few hours delay in going north won't make any difference with the speed at which the army will travel. You see, there is something else I should do first..."

⚜

THROP

Marcus rode a fresh horse slowly along the Stanegate from Vircovicium to Throp. He kept to the edge to avoid the almost continuous stream of ox carts and small squads of legionaries. There were other travelers too, both mounted and on foot. It was a busy day.

He did his best to ignore the others, trying instead to visualize how it would have been for a small group three nights earlier, riding in the dark.

Would there have been laughter? Jests? Perhaps one of them had told tales of night-time spirits to chill the women's blood. Still, Septimus' wife had been ill, hadn't she? Maybe they were hurrying to get her back to her quarters. Maybe she had recovered, women were like that …

Did they eventually reach the Fort at Throp?

The gates loomed before him, wooden but huge, heavy, made from native oak. Marcus did not have the day's watch word and thus, could not enter immediately; after the attack, he could not blame their caution. It took a few minutes to fetch someone to establish his identity and as he waited, he noted the fresh damage wrought by sword or axe on the timbers.

Finally, he was allowed in and conducted to the small stone villa. It was the only stone built structure in the place; it seemed to be the only one without visible marks of fire on it.

The entrance was four square and plain. It was laid with red quarry tiles and its walls were rough plastered and lime washed. It led onward into an L-shaped passage with windows on the left hand wall and doorways to the right. It skirted the small and rather cramped villa along two outer walls.

The aide preceded him and fairly rushed him along; so much so, that Marcus nearly tripped over the raised edge of a crack which spanned the corridor. A moment later they stopped, the aide tapped on a door and ushered the Scout through.

Vibius Septimus, though welcoming him, was visibly distressed. Marcus had to believe the man held his wife in great esteem.

Such was not always the case. Politically advantageous marriages were frequent although this did not necessarily rule out affection or even love.

Septimus was in his forties, his black hair liberally flecked with grey. He was quite tall, a fact hidden by his somewhat stooped posture which gave him a clerkish look; his fingers fidgeted constantly, as though they were playing with an invisible stone and this made him seem nervous, apprehensive.

"Welcome, welcome. Marcus Gellorix? That the name? I'd have thought you would be off with Pintus, scouring the northern lands."

Septimus indicated a couch and a trifle abruptly, sat down himself. Marcus wondered if he had been drinking, perhaps this was the root of his agitation.

"I should be out there myself instead of sitting here, worrying. Oh..." Septimus started as a servant appeared with a tray bearing goblets and a jug. "Ah. Some wine. I'll join you in a draught if I may."

"Go ahead, please Sir. For myself, I'd prefer some water if it's no trouble. I've been riding for a considerable time and I still have to catch up with Pintus. Wine will probably put me to sleep."

"Of course, a wise choice." Septimus clapped his hands and the servant returned. "Water. Water for us both."

When the water had been brought and a goblet filled for Marcus, Septimus mixed a little with his wine and drank half at one swallow.

"A hundred of my men are dead," he started. "Killed by these same swine who have taken my Iavolena." His voice broke and he took another mouthful of wine, topping it up from the jug. "I'll not rest until the Gods have seen fit to give me vengeance for those men and for my dearest wife."

"Well, this is what I came to see you about, Sir. I want to know about the group she left Vircovicium with. Do you recall who they were? Their names?"

For a long moment Septimus looked blank, but then evidently got his mind into motion. "Cerea, of course. Cerea, her companion. There was the surveyor; hmm. Titus Severius was his name."

"Anyone else?"

"Two cavalrymen. Vanus and Cobius, I imagine. They came with us on the outward journey; they weren't with me when I returned."

"And they are all accounted for?"

"Pardon?"

"Are any missing—besides the two ladies?"

"No, no. Both Vanus and Cobius have been counted among the dead. They," Septimus screwed his eyes up, perhaps visualizing a report, "their bodies were found outside the south gate among those who were fighting the savages."

"And Titus Severius, the surveyor?"

Septimus shook his head. "No idea. He was due to leave that morning I understand. A job at... at Luguvallium, I think. He probably left the *mansio* after seeing the women back."

"That's a little strange, don't you think. If the party was back here early enough to fight, one would think Severius would have been among the defenders, alive or dead. He was a surveyor, of course but he was a legionary first."

"Perhaps they couldn't get through the gates; perhaps the fighting had already started when they reached here."

"Perhaps. In which case, maybe the surveyor tried to help the women, perhaps he hid them—in the *mansio*, conceivably—or he has taken them further, away from the trouble."

Septimus looked up. "What are you telling me?"

"Just that your wife and her companion may not have been abducted. They may be somewhere safe."

Septimus wanted to believe, but could not yet take the step. "But surely they would have returned by now? It's been two full days, don't you see that?"

A new idea was hovering at the back of Marcus' mind. It was not clear yet but... *Not if they didn't want to return*, he thought. He made a dismissive gesture. "You are probably correct, Sir, but... suppose he has taken them on to Luguvallium? That's where he was going. That's thirty miles. Has anyone been sent to enquire at the garrison there?"

"No," Septimus replied slowly. "No, nobody."

"Well anyway, could you give me a detailed description of the lady? Her apparel on that night, jewelry, had she any identifying marks?"

"Marks?"

"Moles, birthmarks."

"Why would you want to know that?" But Septimus had already worked it out and didn't like what he saw. "In case she is dead? Oh no. That's not possible. They wouldn't, not my Iavolena. She's beautiful, Gellorix, beautiful, gentle. Nobody would kill her. Besides, I'd know if..." Septimus' eyes brimmed with bright water, overflowed.

Marcus found himself at a loss. He seldom had to deal with officers who allowed themselves such a show of private emotion. "Well, anyway unlikely as it may be..." He leaned forward and put a hand on the other's shoulder. "It's just routine you know. A precaution."

Septimus nodded and visibly pulled himself together. "You're right, young man. Quite right." He answered Marcus' questions steadily and eventually took the benificiarius into his study. "Here, you see? This is my Iavolena." He gestured towards a sculpture which stood before the main window.

Marcus regarded the life-size bust. The woman certainly was beautiful. The high cheek bones and a delicate chin with slightly almond shaped eyes gave her an elfin look which he would easily remember. The morning light sparkled on a decoration cut into the folds of the marble robe about the shoulders of the likeness.

"What is this?" asked Marcus bending nearer. "A sea shell?"

"A brooch. I don't recall where... oh yes, Yes. It's a sort of sea shell. One of those that they chip out of sandstone. Got it from an officer who took it from one of the local shamans."

"What, a druid?"

"Mm. That's right. Druid."

"It's quite unusual isn't it? For an ornament, I mean. Is it here, among her jewelry?"

Marcus followed Septimus from the study and along an oak paneled passage to the rear of the small accommodation. There had been a roof leak at some time recently and a green stain showed where moss or mold had taken advantage of the damp. He had noticed other signs of neglect, too: a crack in a window pane, a corner where the mortar needed re-pointing, a worn out patch of floor mosaic, threadbare rugs. Throp was an unimportant marching fort and the newer Wall fortifications had the best of the artisans and most of the money.

They entered Iavolena's bed chamber, a small, but well lit room furnished in a very feminine style with patterned wall hangings and pastel colors. Shelves carried rows of bottles and pots of make-up and skin lotions with here and there the odd gap in the line.

Septimus went to a chest which rested on a carved teakwood table, the top was inlaid with mother of pearl flowers and the sides with a frieze of stylized animals also cut from mother-of-pearl. He opened the lid and lifted out a tray which carried a score or more finger rings, ear ornaments and hair slides. The base of the chest held gold and silver items, some jet and precious stones and several heavy dress brooches.

"No. The shell thing isn't here. Hmm." Septimus frowned. "I don't remember her wearing it to Vircovicium, but er, it's not surprising, I had other things on my mind."

"Other things?"

"Cassius Aurelius Pintus."

"Ah."

"You'll have met him. Ambitious, political. He has responsibility for this forward area."

"Oh Yes. I have met him and in fact, it's time I rode out to meet with him. Could you do something for me?"

"Of course, if it's in my power."

"The surveyor you mentioned."

"Severius?"

"Send a messenger to Luguvallium and check that he arrived safely. I'll come by for the answer when I get back from Albyn."

"The jewelry." Marcus turned back to the open chest. "Anything else missing?"

Septimus looked through the items. "It's difficult to be certain you know. I seem to remember a ruby brooch that I bought her a few years ago, I can't see it here. There was a sapphire cluster too, went very well with her eyes you know, did I mention she had blue eyes? Very blue, quite brilliant." For a moment, Septimus fell silent and took a deep breath. "That isn't here. I suppose she may have put them in the strong room. I'd better check on that because there don't seem to be quite so many things here as I'd have thought there should be."

Marcus left Throp and headed for the Wall. The items of jewelry that Septimus had mentioned had not been found when they had gone to the headquarters building and down to the strong room. The several small gaps in the containers in Iavolena's bed chamber also made him think. There were several explanations he could think of, but were they the right ones?

Marcus passed through the Wall at Harrow's Scar and stopped for a few minutes to inspect the burned out shells of the two barracks. Then, he went on and settled down for a long and tiring ride along trails leading north and east, to where he estimated the Sixth Legion would be.

SELGOVANTIA

Lug Mlorug, eldest son of Elig, the head of the Mlorugs knelt beside a large rock outcropping, squinting down the hillside at the men and equipment passing by below him.

Lug had seen Romans before, small bands, a handful at a time, but not like these and not in such uncountable numbers. Even thinking about so many made him dizzy. Those which had caught his attention were stranger than most he had seen; they were dressed in metal studded leather body harnesses with metal helmets the same shape as the domed huts of his own family. Like himself, they wore animal skins, but as short cloaks about their shoulders.

Hunters! Now he noticed the quick and silent movements which took them across the heath and the ever vigilant glances from their black eyes. Those hawk nosed faces though, the droopy moustaches and night black hair... *strangers and what were they here for?*

Lug shrugged and backed away until he was below the ridge. A crevice ran down the slope becoming a stream bed a hundred paces lower. He ran down it until he came to the spring which fed the stream and stood up. Cupping his hands about his mouth, Lug gave the cry of the rock eagle and waited a few moments.

There was movement across the valley, a figure made tiny and indistinct by distance though his answering call was clear enough. Lug made another call; this time, the call of a blackbird in distress to signal intruders. When the call had again been repeated and the far figure had disappeared, Lug bent to drink at the moss lined spring and returned to his post to learn more.

The *Numeri* came from Mauritania and as well as their usual weapons of a long curved sword and a spear, they carried small wooden shields, round and embossed with metal. They had slingshots too, with a pouch of lead ammunition. One of their own officers had been briefed and his orders in their native language had been explicit: any man, woman or child they encountered was to be killed or captured, no one was to be left to carry news back to their villages.

Consequently, they scouted the ground carefully. But the country they came from was hot, its lands composed of sand and bare rock. Lakes and forest and spreading brush were all new to them and despite their adapting quickly to the new conditions, the solitary and concealed lookouts went unnoticed.

The Mauritanians were natural hunters and killers; they enjoyed the sort of work the Romans put their way. They were often out of sight of each other, but their limited contacts with the local tribesmen had given them confidence; they thought of them as pathetic savages. What was there to fear when a sword hilt banged against a shield would bring a dozen warriors inside a few heartbeats?

The Romans made good use of them, too. They covered an area quickly and completely. They had fought the Numidians and the Baeticans for centuries and those were noble warriors. Now, warfare was second nature to the Mauritanian, a born instinct. A Roman officer who knew his profession was often thankful that the Mauritanians fought for and not against them.

This time, Pintus had sweetened the pill even more than usual. He had promised them that success would mean employment as auxiliaries in the future: uniforms, equipment and regular Roman money.

Lug, still astonished by the little men in their metal hats who carried those almost delicate swords was now dumbfounded. Rank after rank of soldiers, terrible engines, more soldiers, officers in gleaming brass and iron marched by in their hundreds. A glittering panoply which hurt the eye to watch. Would it ever end?

It *did* end eventually. And some time later, Lug picked up the little pile of stones he had used as counters, one for every body of men who had passed him. He returned to the spring again to refresh himself and then set off at a fast trot through the forest which lined the lower parts of the valley.

Despite the fact that the Mauritanians had scoured every part of the route, checked every suspicious shadow and found no one, it would not be long before every chief and every fighting man in the land of the Selgovae would know of this incursion.

At the hill fort of Briogix, some twenty miles north west of Lug's sighting, forty six heads of families and their retainers had gathered. These were the first, the nearest and while the Druids' messengers had still to reach the more distant villages of Albyn and even one or two in northern Briton, they had no intention of missing the excuse for a feast or the nightly tales of heroes and gods from the Druids. Thus cooking pots steamed and bubbled, carcasses of boar and deer roasted over fire pits, ale and mead were poured and drunk.

That night, the forty-six gathered and sat in a circle. Those of more lowly status stood outside and listened as the sun set and the first stars glittered. Byrrig Mellaurig was chief at Briogix and nominal host to the gathering. He acted as mediator and signaled Anig Mlorug to speak.

Anig Mlorug was a grizzled figure of a man, fifty seasons lay behind him, his back was bent and his right hand hung useless since a boar had bitten the sinews in his forearm. Still no other, no younger man had seen fit to challenge his authority for his wisdom was respected as were the honors gained in earlier years, honors which the bards still sang about.

"My son keeps watch from the Crags which overlook the Assorign Pass." He told the assembly. "He has sent word of warriors there, stranger even than the Romans, heavily armed they were and searching the countryside bush by bush, stone by stone."

"A foraging party," suggested someone and immediately fell silent when Chief Mel-laurig turned to him.

"Perhaps they forage for human meat," replied Mlorug allowing his glare to rest on the one who had spoken out of turn. Mlorug scratched at the coarse hair which covered his chest, still red and thick despite his age. "Aye, two legged meat. For behind came Romans, an army too large to be counted. Foot soldiers, horsemen, great wooden engines on wagon wheels."

Mlorug breathed a moment and took a pace inwards from the circle's edge to show that he had not yet finished. He wet his lips and swallowed. "There were oxen pulling carts filled with supplies and then came more soldiers and more horsemen. They were headed towards the ford up at Cartelmaugh but slowly. As fast as the oxen can walk, no more."

Now he relinquished the floor, bent his knee and sat down. Byrrig held out his arms, inviting questions and the wind blew the smoke from cooking fires across the glen.

"How many? Hmm? How many soldiers?"

In answer, Mlorug called to one of his men. The fellow brought a leather bag and poured out the contents, a small pile of stones.

"Each stone is for a band of soldiers. Each stone stands for two hands of men."

Someone else reckoned the pebbles. "Ten," he said. "And ten and ten and..." When he had finished there were seven piles of ten and three solitary stones. Fourteen hundred and sixty men, if Lug's estimate was to be believed. The news caused a stir, everyone—both those in the circle and the ones who stood without had something to tell or to ask of his neighbor. Byrrig allowed the noise to continue for some while before repeatedly banging his fist against a shield to attract attention.

"Why are they here?" he said. "This is the question we must answer. In all my years such an invasion of our lands has not been seen in these lands given to us by the Gods. Not since the time of Calgacus has there been so many. Why? Why have they come?"

Fellur Cruagh stood and waited for recognition. He was a tall and wiry individual with blond hair and a huge crag-like nose which jutted out over his moustaches.

"They have come to seek revenge for the attack that our sons made not four days gone. Their dead are restless in their graves."

Byrrig scowled and spat. "What men are these who fail to respect the time of mourning? Our dead also demand vengeance yet there is a proper time."

"They are not men," offered Dag Liogh whose elderly father had died during the night of that same raid. "They hide behind stone walls; they bind hard metal about their bodies and skulk behind shields big enough to cover two men." Liogh too, hawked and spat and scorn dripped as thick as the spittle. "They make themselves like a hedgehog with their long spears and dare not fight a man to his face. They have no spirit; no one has taught them how to fight like men."

Byrrig nodded. "There are more questions here than we can answer, I think." Byrrig nodded to a kinsman who stood at the door of the *Broch*, the kinsman knocked upon the door frame and presently, an angular figure wrapped in somber grey robes stepped from the narrow door. He wore a cap against the night's chill and from its sides and back there burst a mass of shoulder-length white curly hair which matched the beard and moustache that covered his face.

One of the oldest of the Chiefs who was standing took an involuntary step backward. "Carotach." He breathed. "Chief of the Druids. Here at Briogix and him the wisest man in the free world."

"I thought," observed someone else, "that he never left the shrine at Medionemeton"

"Well now he has..."

Such comments were made on all sides although none expected them to be answered; the remarks died as Carotach entered the circle between two men who hastily parted company to make a way. The elder among the chieftains bent and touched their heads to the floor; others, younger and less respectful followed suit more slowly.

For many long seconds the Druid remained silent, turning and turning and staring at his audience, letting the tension build. "The stars move through the heavens," he said at last, his voice mild, matter of fact. "Their positions tell me of a period of changes. Some of these changes will happen come what may, others there are which we must make for ourselves. Strangers come, strangers go and all is foreseen."

Again he fell silent and darted glances at various of the men. "Squirrels searched the woods before the nuts had fallen and thus I knew that the Romans would be searching, too. This morning, two does crossed a river when a bridge lay not ten paces from them and so I know that the Romans search for two women of their kind. Their search will continue until they find disappointment. All is clear."

Evidently, the Druid had said all that he was going to and the boldest of the Clansmen ventured questions.

"Should we fight them?"

"How long will they remain?"

These and many variations came thick and fast at last.

Carotach held up his hand and the voices ceased as if so many throats had been cut.

"Does the fox lay with the goose? Hm? Or the dog with the hare? Does water mix with fire and will the sun not rise on the morrow? There is not sufficient time to find so many answers for soon I shall journey to the Halls of the Gods. I know what I know, which is this: the strangers came before, where the sun rises over the sea and then they left. They will come again because their Gods have decreed it and our own Gods have permitted it.

"I will not counsel war for it is not the way of the Druids. I will remind you of this, however. The spirits of the departed return to live within us all; listen to what *they* tell you in the darkest part of the night when you are alone. Listen and *they* will surely counsel you."

Carotach spoke to Byrrig. "Have them make up the fire." And when it was done and the flames cast a bright and shifting light, the Druid brought his hands from beneath his cloak. Two wrens took flight from his opened hands, lifting and tumbling in circles around the tall and enigmatic figure. At last, they perched on the Druid's shoulder, their eyes glinting in the firelight like amber beads.

"Our souls are eternal," he shouted. "Eternal. They fly from our bodies at death and fortunate is the man who shelters one, for his own life is made the richer."

⁂

Chaos. To the untutored eyes of the Selgovae and Callatae, the scene was pure and simple chaos. Yet over the space of half an hour, order came out of the confusion in the shape of a Roman marching fort.

Each yard of perimeter wall was the responsibility of a single legionary. Three stakes were driven into the ground, a yard of ditch excavated and the spoil thrown up to form a defensive mound.

While the barricade was being erected, other soldiers were pitching leather tents, digging cooking pits, setting up the commanding officer's quarters.

At the end of an hour the work was almost complete; food and drink were being prepared while the animals were being settled and guard rosters set for the night.

In the officers' tent, Pintus examined the prisoners brought back by the numeri. They were a sorry bunch, three old men, a fat woman with well faded charms and an even older woman who seemed to be in her dotage. There was a boy too, who sat quietly in a corner where a soldier had thrust him. Pintus took a long drink of wine from his goblet and shook his head.

He had asked the officer in charge why they had not caught any younger men. The Mauretanian had shrugged. "There *were* none—or almost none. We cornered two, but they would not surrender, they fought to the death."

Pintus nodded at one of the old men. "Bring him here."

Two legionaries pulled the fellow erect and marched him forward.

"You there," said Pintus, using a bluff and friendly tone. "Tell us where your villages are. And where are all your..."

The old man bowed and made some inexplicable sign with his fingers. Pintus shook his head in disgust. "They don't understand a word, do they? I've been brought a bunch of deaf and dumb fools."

He lifted his foot and placed it on the man's bent head, one good shove and the fellow was bowled over backwards into the dirt; there was a thud when his head struck a tent pole. Blood streamed from the wound and seemed to briefly galvanize the oldest woman into sanity. She screamed something unintelligible and ran at Pintus with her fingers crooked to scratch and tear. A guard tripped her and dragged her back.

There were seven centurions in the tent, two tribunes and the Praefector of the cavalry regiment. Stony faced, all of them witnessed Pintus' act.

Bellus Ruis shook his head; he was a senior centurion. *Pintus was tired and angry, but did he really expect them to speak Latin?* "We need one of the scouts to translate, Commandant. They simply don't speak Latin." Like many of the military who had been here a long time, Ruis could speak and understand the native language, but out here, so far from the Wall, dialect made it difficult to understand.

"Scouts?" Pintus' expression was angry, his face suffused with blood. "Brythonic spies with no loyalty to the Empire. What version of the truth will they tell us?" He cast the cup aside, the dregs splashing across the centurion's sandal. "None of them are to be trusted."

"We could wait for Gellorix, Sir. He has Roman blood in his veins."

"Gellorix! Yes Gellorix the Bastard, I'd forgotten him. Where is he? Fighting his own little war somewhere? He should be with us by now, half a Citizen that he is"

Bellus Ruis had been posted to Briton from his native Narbonensis and had known Aelius Mansustus, the father of Marcus Gellorix, the half Roman boy since his arrival. He resented the new Commandant's attitude, but of course, could do little to right the injustice. He tried though.

"It would have taken the messenger a night and a day to have reached him at his home, Sir. Had the Beneficiarius been able to return immediately, he would still be a day behind us. I can vouch for his loyalty too, Sir. His information has saved the lives of many a *citizen*." Ruis came close to insolence in his tone with the final word, but Pintus either did not or chose not to notice.

"Well, I'm sure the Beneficiarius has good reason for doing whatever he may be doing. However, we are here in this God forsaken wilderness and he is not. Is there anyone else who can speak with these people?"

The officers conferred and ordered a certain slave brought in. The slave was a Carvetian who had fought with a Roman legionary and now labored with the oxen which pulled the wagons. His health was failing; he would probably not see another season through, but he was offered the chance of food and a lighter job in return for his co-operation.

Information of a sort was gleaned.

Three questions were asked.

Had armed warriors returned north across these hills in the past two days? Had any of them seen two strange women, Roman women? Where was the nearest major settlement?

Each of the prisoners shook their heads emphatically. No one knew anything.

Pintus tried a different tack. Who could answer these questions? No one knew except for the boy who innocently suggested that they ask Chief Mellaurig at Briogix.

"Ha, ha." Pintus' face creased into a smile. "Take them all away. Except the boy. Bring me a sweetmeat of some kind and a cushion."

A few minutes later, the young boy—perhaps eight or ten years—was sitting on a soft cushion placed on a stool next to Pintus' campaign chair. He was eating a long roll of honeyed pastry. Pintus beckoned the Carvetian slave nearer.

"Ask him what is Briogix?"

"A huge place with fine stone buildings with reed thatched roofs and many cooking pits."

The Roman was not certain that the slave had translated correctly in either direction, but he persisted.

"And where is this huge Briogix?"

"At the top of a hill on the far side of Raven's Crag."

"And Raven's Crag?"

"From here to where the sun sets."

"How many people live there? How many warriors?"

"Many. Many."

"Well, well. We have a little information despite the tardiness of our good Beneficiarius."

"Yes, Commandant. My congratulations. What shall we do with the prisoners?"

"Hmm. Kill them, Centurion. They're of no further use to us and we don't want words of warning getting out."

"The boy, too?"

But when they looked, the boy had already gone.

⁂

ABALAVA

Iavolena, wife of Vibius Septimus, looked down on the slow waters of the river which wound through the small town they had come to, west of Luguvallium, and called Abalava. Some people named it Avalena which was quaintly like her own name. A good omen? Iavolena thought so. The vicus was on the Stanegate, but the place that Severius had found was a new wing for a farm house some way from the road. The owner, a Romanophile Carvetian, was away on business and extensions to his Romanesque villa had been put in hand before he left.

She felt that happiness had come at last for now she had a new lover, a vigorous man with a sexual appetite which astounded her. He had found her a new and luxurious home; he seemed to dote upon her. Iavolena had married Septimus when she was eighteen and he thirty six; she had expected an experienced lover, a man who knew how to treat a woman of some nobility. In this, as in so many things, she had been disappointed. Vibius doted on her, bought her jewelry, fine fabrics; he stocked the best vintages he could come by, gave parties, hired actors... but none of it really satisfied her.

Well, he had placed her on a pedestal, she had thought to herself, rationalizing her actions. If she was then out of his reach, it was his own doing. Out here on the far frontier, temptation beckoned. Vibius preferred the jug to a tumble and there was a surprising number of officers willing to risk their careers and share her bed, Carvetian too sometimes... Iavolena chuckled at a memory.

"Mistress Livane... Perhaps you would care to inspect your accommodation now?"

Iavolena started at the sound. Belatedly, she realized that Livane was the new name she had chosen for herself, a new name like the new copper hair color, a new woman. Iavolena was gone.

The building was constructed in the early Greek style with four slim Doric columns supporting a shallow triangular entablature. Double doors of seasoned oak opened into a hallway leading through to a small atrium. The architect who had been hired to make the extensions did not take her this way however, he led her to the left, to the west where a smaller pair of matching doors gave entrance to a lobby with a high ceiling and a floor covered in a marble mosaic depicting Minerva at the waterside.

Malovius the architect led her inside where six doors opened to sleeping chambers, bathrooms and a large lounging chamber: the new guest wing. Malovius took her to the main sleeping chamber and left her there. Iavolena, now Livane, was delighted. The room was on the outside, the window opening over the wide mouth of the Ituna estuary where flocks of seabirds turned the grey mud banks white with their plumage.

Titus Severius had engaged a local girl to act as her chamber maid. The girl, Vetia, would be coming shortly and Iavolena, as Livane, looked forward to luxuriating in her first bath in such fine surroundings.

Tomorrow, too, was a time to look forward to.

She had been careful to bring with her only those jewels which Vibius had known nothing about or that she felt were old enough for him not to notice their absence. Tomorrow, she would go into Luguvallium to trade a few of them into coin and buy cloth for a new wardrobe. It would take a few days to be made up into clothing and then she could begin to shine.

Vetia arrived, shown through to Iavolena's quarters by a member of the gentleman farmer's household. Iavolena took her bath, enjoying the thick towels, the scented unguents and creams loaned to her by the Carvetian mistress of the house.

Her maid was dark and sloe eyed, a beautiful girl with a quiet and unassuming manner which suited Iavolena well. She wondered though, if she should seek someone a little more plain in appearance. Men were, after all, easy to lead astray. In the quiet of the bathroom, she heard the outer door open and close. Heard his sandals cross the mosaic.

"Livane."

"In here, my love." Not quite dried, she rose from the couch where Vetia had been massaging her shoulders and dismissed the girl. Apart from a scarf which tied her hair up to keep it out of the water, she stood there naked as he opened the door.

Severius stopped as he saw her body outlined against the window. Every delightful curve; the rounded buttock, the full breasts were silhouetted against the pearly radiance.

Severius could no more stop his reactions than prevent the passing of time. His loins stirred and he crossed the room as she turned away and bent to pick up a towel. He held her waist to prevent her straightening up and a moment later, he entered her.

Iavolena's almost instinctive response was to stiffen, to prevent his ingress. She preferred to be in control, to dictate what was to happen and when, but then she realized that she was, already, in control. Titus' every action was governed by her, he was her lover and would do whatever she wanted.

She softened, acquiesced, relaxed as she realized her power and moved back and forward, back and forward to enjoy her own sensations. Iavolena heard him moaning and she stilled, drawing out the sweet moments, controlling the pace.

Now, who dominated who? Iavolena had the smile on a cat's face when it plays with a bird. It was all so easy. So easy.

CHAPTER FOUR

SELGOVANTIA

MARCUS HAD LEFT THE CHARRED REMAINS OF HARROW'S SCAR an hour before. He had ridden on until well north of the great ridge of the Win Sil with its crags and cliffs; then he turned eastward taking the paths which threaded the woodland covering much of the Selgovae lands.

Presently he came upon the path taken by the Sixth. The ground had been trampled and rutted, small bushes uprooted or flattened; a blind man could have followed it.

Marcus shook his head and let his horse pick its own way along the trail. He would like to have given more thought to the disappearance of Iavolena, but whenever he tried to concentrate, his mind wandered on to the matter of this apparently stupid foray into Albyn.

The brown and off-white homespun that he wore was almost universal among the native tribes. These and the hood to cover his short Roman style hair were enough to shield his identity from the several lookouts he passed. It was a disguise which he had used many times, a character he had grown into. No one that he saw this close to the Wall gave the lone trader with his two small horses as much as a second glance.

Soft rain blew gently against his back as he traversed the downward slope towards the tree line, and shortly the trees, sycamore, beech, birch gave him some shelter, the trees would soon be wearing their fall colors, reds and browns among the olive green of the conifers. The air smelled sweet and clean to Marcus who had been born and raised in this sort of country, it was a soft and mild season of forest fruitfulness, the last beautiful month before the harshness of winter.

Eventually the trees gave way to open moor land, purple heather cloaked the hillsides and the sound of brooks and streams was everywhere. His earlier despondency evaporated and he was able to focus on the task of catching up with Pintus and the Sixth. The matter of the disappearance of Septimus' wife drifted to the back of his mind as it became more urgent to keep his wits about him. This could be dangerous territory for a lone traveler, his two horses were a valuable prize for an opportunist thief and the fact that he was a double agent only added to the danger. Vigilance must be his watchword.

He was left alone, however. Only once did he see anyone else, someone obviously on lookout duty and just as obviously alone. Marcus' presence would be noted and reported, nothing more.

The passage of the Legion was still plain to see. In marshy areas the wheel ruts and the hoof marks of the oxen were still deeply impressed in the mud. The footprints of legionaries were also evident where they had pulled and pushed the heavy wagons through the soft ground. Marcus snorted with amusement, he had spotted a sandal still stuck in the mud and wondered what its owner had done afterwards.

Within a day or two, most of the damage would have been repaired by nature, a nature which all but ignored the Romans' intrusion. His horse shied as a hare shot out of the remains of a trampled bush at its feet and disappeared into the heather a few feet away.

The ground climbed a little and became firmer; Marcus was able to urge the horses to a canter for a few minutes. Five magpies wheeled across the clouded sky, and a moment later, a sixth followed, three pairs—a good omen. Alone, Marcus felt at peace with the world and his attentiveness relaxed a little.

Why had Pintus led this absurd invasion into a land with which he was so unfamiliar? Had he consulted with the other scouts? The worries returned, catching him unawares.

⁂

Just before dawn, Byrrig Mellaurig stirred upon his bed of bracken. Memory of yesterday's events came back to him slowly. His initial impulse was to rise and to call for action from the various chiefs to whom he was host. But hard on his first thought came a second, to lay still and put his mind to work instead.

Many years before, impetuosity had led Byrrig's father, Gullan, to drive his war chariot directly at a detachment of Roman legionaries. Instead of admiration for the maneuver and personal combat, Gullan's reward had been a callous javelin through the heart. It was a harsh lesson and one which Byrrig sometimes remembered to heed.

Impulsive actions were applauded by his fellows, but all too often, the applause was posthumous.

Byrrig had no wish to meet his Gods before the appointed time. Life as Chief was good; others deferred to him, listened to his views, the best meat was brought to him, there were always plump young women to warm his bed.

Thought was not an easy process though and it was not until his empty stomach reminded him of breakfast that an idea surfaced. A sly grin came to his lips.

It went without saying that there would have to be an offensive against the Roman incursion. Why not let the Callatae lead that offensive? These Callatae still painted themselves in the old ways, since settling in the northern territories after leaving Mona, they had scarcely changed their ways at all. The Druids had favored them, had persuaded them into leading the raid on Throp… It went against the grain to stand off-center, but Byrrig would do it, let the Callatae face the consequences of that campaign.

He grinned into the darkness again and prodded his sleeping companion in the ribs. "Up with you, woman. Bring me some food before the day is wasted."

Now, how to say the words which would bring this about…

⁂

The Romans had been tracked every step of the way. The column of men and materiel was so long that most of the local lookouts had left their posts, and were following the progress of the incursion.

The last Roman camp was still a day's march from Briogix which was partially surrounded by an arc of protecting crags. As the chiefs were gathering at the center of the stronghold, final intelligence was all but complete. A rough map of the area had been constructed of sand, pebbles and rocks to show the Romans' position.

"Here," Byrrig told them, "is the way they must come to reach Briogix." He pointed to a furrow drawn in the sand. "Going by our secret ways, we can have a mounted force above them before the sun is at its highest."

Several conversations started and an argument. The Callatae, distinct from their Selgovae cousins by virtue of their tattooed bodies, were fingering the naked blades of their swords. Byrrig Mellaurig raised his hands to recover their attention. He spoke quickly, his voice loud. "I would claim the right to lead our warriors, but the invaders are encamped on land ceded to our Callatae brothers. Perhaps their chief would prefer that honor?"

The offer was greeted by silence. To make such an offer to another was either craven hearted or great gallantry, which was this? Everybody knew that Old Liogh had died and a new leader had not yet been elected; the old man's son occupied the position by default and on sufferance.

The silence stretched on until someone said quite quietly: "Dag, Dag Liogh." And it grew, first one then another voice took up the words. "Dag Liogh, Dag Liogh, Dag Liogh..."

The chant gathered momentum until both Callatae and Selgovae were shouting his name, clashing swords against shields.

Dag Liogh walked to the front, into the circle and turned to face his tribe, some of them only just arrived from outlying areas.

"Is this truly your wish?" he shouted. "Is there any one of you who believes me unworthy of my father's cloak? Let him say so now and face *Broadwand* here." He lifted the huge sword aloft and large as it was with its long curved blade and cast bronze hilt and handle, the arm which lofted it made it look prosaic.

"Is there such a man?"

Silence was his only answer.

"Then I swear on the soul of my father that I shall be a good and a just Chief. I shall defend our lands and bring honor to the name of the Callatae."

He let the sword drop and grounded the point at his feet.

"Callatae, ready yourselves. We ride at tomorrow's dawn. Selgovae brothers, will you ride with us?"

"Aye!"

Every throat roared the affirmation and Byrrig Mellaurig, who had schemed to avoid being in the van, shouted the word as loudly as any and then hoped that he would not regret it later.

"So what do you have in mind, Dag Liogh?" he asked as the warriors made ready.

"Perhaps the same as yourself, Byrrig. Look at your map." Dag used a twig to point out the features. "Here, the Romans must pass through Goat's Gap pass which brings them down below the Sand Crags. Now, I will lead my men on the side of the rising sun. Will you take yours along the opposite side? Between us, we can attack from above or ride down upon them. They outnumber us, but we have a greater number of horsemen, and their surprise will favor us."

"Hmm." Byrrig scratched at his beard. The strategy was good, he could not fault it, but too ready an acquiescence was a bad thing.

"If the battle does not go our way, we can ride off to Crolligh's Bog and let them follow us there..." He winked. "All that metal plate they wear, they'll sink right through to the Underworld."

Byrrig Mellaurig nodded. "Yes. I like it, Dag. I'm with you." *After all*, he thought, *I shall stay on the heights and direct the Selgovae from there.*

⁂

The Roman force had a harder day than they had anticipated. Rather than the four miles an hour that was the usual pace of an army on the move, they had barely managed to keep moving in places. Fallen trees to move, marsh and bog to be skirted or crossed on bundles of reed, and heather, steep and rocky inclines where the wagons had to be man-handled up or down—all these meant lost time and fraying tempers.

The scouts had found a barely large enough piece of ground for the overnight marching camp and marked it out, not that the markers were a great deal of use for dusk was far advanced by the time the major part of the force had arrived.

Pintus, choleric by nature, was fuming. He had planned to be at this barbarian stronghold that afternoon and had expected to over-run it on the morrow. Each delay had seen his anger mount and by evening, he was snapping at his immediate subordinates and openly contemptuous of the centurions. When told that supper would be delayed while kindling and firewood were searched for in the near-dark, he was half berserk with rage.

Bellus Ruis took the brunt of both Pintus' wrath and the dissatisfaction of the rank and file. His mouth was compressed to a single thin line and he kept it firmly closed while Pintus called him all kinds of incompetent fool. Ruis held responsibility for his men and their performance; he also passed down the sometimes unreasonable demands of the Commandant and Tribunes. He did not have to like it, but that was what he was there for.

So he did not point out that the cooks, like everyone else, had had their shoulders against the wagons and that the small number of slaves and non-military personnel had been pulling the oxen out of the mud as much as the wagons. In the twenty years he had been a career soldier, Ruis had served under all manner of officers and Pintus was neither better nor worse than most. To all appearances, he took the tongue lashing calmly, inwardly though; he seethed for he suspected that he was being repaid for standing up for the still absent Marcus Gellorix.

At last Pintus fell silent. Ruis felt able to salute and leave the headquarters tent which was still flapping in the wind as stakes were laboriously set in the darkness.

Ruis walked down the small slope where enough fuel had been found for a few small fires. The cold evening air cooled him down and he felt his anger departing. A soldier, he felt, should not be angry, it was unprofessional. The fires gave a little light, enough to see what was happening—men rushing around erecting the leather tents, carrying shovels and the stakes for temporary palisading out to the perimeter.

The centurion strode up to where the wagons had been drawn up into a U-shape to give a little shelter from the prevailing wind.

"You," he shouted, pointing to the nearest legionary. "And you and you." He indicated two more. "Get those stools off the wagons and anything else that's burnable and looks as though it can be spared. Break them up for firewood; I want those pots on the boil before I come back this way again. Right?"

"Right Sir."

The men were dumbfounded at the sudden change in their officer's character. *Perhaps he was not as calm as he had thought,* Ruis wondered. Deliberately, he grinned. "Anyone who wants to sit can stick their thumbs up their backsides and sit on their elbows. Right?"

"Yes. Right Sir."

"Except for the Commandant's chair, if that's still there, for Jupiter's sake, get it up to his tent."

That done, he felt better. By the time he'd walked the perimeter, the cooks might have got something warmed up; he was getting damned hungry.

⁂

HIGH SIL

Marcus, still following the tracks left by the Legion, came to the point where they had chosen to veer to the east around the hills ahead. The Scout had presumed that they were making for Briogix, but this route didn't seem to make any sense whatever. Did Pintus know something he, Marcus, did not or were there no scouts with him?

Whatever the answer Marcus knew that the ground ahead was fraught with difficulties for a military column with ox-drawn wagons. He thought for a moment; there was no point in trying to reach the Legion and offer advice tonight. By the time he got to them, they would be in the throes of making camp. There were, perhaps, two hours before full dark and an old customer who had become a friend lived hereabouts. He would visit Callog Regor tonight and catch up with Pintus before tomorrow's midday.

Callog's dwelling was high on the side of a hill where a spring brought him water and a narrow path along a saddle ridge gave him a clear view of whoever might come calling.

He kept a few sheep for meat and wool and would trade dried meat every now and then for knives and such things as Marcus brought with him.

Marcus was by now, riding the second of his horses and both he and they were in need of food… *and good company would not come amiss, either.*

The wind was blowing at his back and the dogs started barking before Marcus set foot on the ridge with still most of a mile to go. He led the horses along the narrow pathway and before he came abreast of the stunted trees which flanked it at the end of the saddle, the dogs stopped their uproar and a voice hailed him.

"Is that you, Uffin?"

Marcus naturally used his Brigantean name in his guise of trader. He called back, "Aye, Callog. Has your wife any of that stew left from last time I was here?"

"I dare say so," said Callog. "I dare say, for she never empties the pot. Liggy fills it to the brim every day." His tone changed good cheer to serious. "So what brings you back so soon? It can't be more than a ten-day since."

Marcus hooked a thumb at the two horses he was leading. "These two little beauties. I sold them sight unseen when I was here before. Had to bring them for the rest of the money, paying me in… "Marcus lowered his voice to conspiratorial levels, "in Roman coin."

Callog raised one eyebrow and then the other. "Been a deal of too-ing- and fro-ing these last few days. Men going south, Romans coming back. Give you any trouble?"

Marcus shook his head. "Been following their tracks, haven't I. Easier going, that way."

"What're they here for then? Do you know that?"

Marcus chuckled and began to lead his horses forward. "Heard they're looking for two women."

"Two! By the Gods, Uffin, I'd have thought they were after hundreds. Don't they have enough of their own?" He poked Marcus in the ribs. "Carvetian women not good enough, eh? Brigantean either"

"Roman women, Callog. Two Roman women. They think some of your tribe—or maybe the Callatae, took them in that raid."

By this time, they were standing outside the hut that Callog called home. "We've more than enough women without having to steal the Romans'. Who'd take women? Now iron perhaps, that would make sense, a good sword, but women?"

Marcus led the horses into a lean-to, pulled the bridles off, and found a basket of hay for them before following Callog into his house. They were met by four huge raw-boned hounds with coarse fur and large mouths. Behind these were three young girls ranging from six to fifteen, and a woman with plump pleasant features and bright eyes.

Despite there being only a pair of rush lights, Marcus found himself shielding his eyes. There was more light than there had been outside where evening was turning to full night. Callog had always seemed ageless to Marcus. He had one of those faces which seemed to glow with health and vigor, dark hair though he must be in his fourth decade and bright blue eyes that were never still. An exuberant beard covered the lower face and through this, ever and again, his teeth would gleam in a smile.

All this was but a moment's thought for wet tongues washed around Marcus' neck as the dogs, now aware of the visitor's identity, jumped up at him. A word from Callog sent them scurrying to a corner and then it was the girls who rushed to him.

The two youngest clung to legs and waist.

"Have you brought us something, Uffin," they chorused. "Have you?"

Marcus was ready for this; a good many of the people he visited had young children who reacted in just the same way both north and south of the Wall.

"Well, let me see now." He pretended to think and then plunged a hand into a capacious pocket. "Here, do you like these?" He pulled out a pair of apples which had hung upon the tree at his mother's home less than two days before.

"Apples—are they sweet?"

"Sweet? Of course. Would I bring you sour apples?"

"What do you have to say to my friend?" Callog broke in. "Hmm?"

"Thank you, Uffin."

"Thank you."

The eldest of the girls had hung back; she looked sideways at Marcus, pretending her interest was elsewhere, her hands twisting the ends of the shawl which hung across her shoulders. Marcus smiled at the shy girl, then reaching down to the youngest girl, picked her up and then the second. He whirled them around, sending them into fits of shrieks and laughter before setting them down.

"Now Asel," he said, turning to the third daughter, "don't I get a hug anymore?"

Asel was on the verge of womanhood. Her young breasts beneath the night shift were firm and the nipples stood as proud as acorns. Shy though she was; it was obvious that she found Marcus attractive.

Callog chuckled. "Our little Asel is growing up, Uffin. Maybe she sees you as a husband, eh?"

"Ah, Callog. You great bumbling bear. Uffin doesn't want to know about that sort of thing."

But despite Liggy's cutting her husband off, Asel was fuming at his words. Even in the dim light, her eyes were bright with anger and she busied herself at the darker end of the room, turning her back on family and guest.

Callog winked at Marcus but otherwise ignored the embarrassment he had caused. He turned to Liggy. "Man here wants to know if there's anything left in the pot?"

"And when has there ever not been?" Liggy demanded. "And when hasn't there been wild onions and millet and fat hen with the meat? Eh?" She pointed up into the dim recesses of the roof. "A leg of smoked pork came down from there today and its been simmering since the early morning."

Marcus looked up at the array of joints of meat hanging in the smoky roof space to cure. "Reckon those dogs of yours have done you proud."

"Oh, they've done their share and they'll get their share as well." Callog went to the pot and held up the ladle to sniff it. "What else is in here then, hmm?"

Liggy frowned. "There's fat hen and emmer and there's *golden of pleasure*. Now that all goes to make it a feast and I tell you this, Asel's as good a cook as her ma."

Callog dropped the ladle back into the pot and rubbed his beard. "Let's you and me have a cup of ale while Liggy brings this stew up to the boil." And while the two youngest daughters sat on Marcus' knees and crunched their apples, Callog brought them a pair of leathern cups filled with his own brew of ale.

Presently, Liggy brought bowls of carved white sycamore filled with hot stew and since the women retired to the kitchen end of the dwelling to eat, Asel was persuaded to leave her bed and take her meal. Even so, she was remarkably quiet and cast a deal of sideways glances in Marcus' direction. A fact that Marcus was well aware of and one which he pretended to ignore.

Afterwards, Callog dozed in his chair, and Marcus rested, too. He was grateful for the shadows for Asel's attentions were becoming as disconcerting as her father's ill-judged jest had been to the girl.

Marcus was well past his twenty second birthday, but as old as he was, he was unusually naive in the matter of women. Until joining the Legion at eighteen, he had met few who were unmarried or who were his own age. This had been due to both the relative isolation of his mother's house and the education his father had insisted upon.

Since joining the Legion, his unique position of not-quite-acceptance by both Romans and Britons had conspired to keep him surprisingly ignorant of the practicalities of sex. Most of his fellows visited the brothels which were to be found in every vicus, but Marcus avoided them and declined invitations. Women made him nervous and he used his father's admonitions to shun the brothels as a convenient excuse to continue his abstention. In his own mind, the pains and anguish of adolescent passion had only served to prove him right. The Legion and his stressful profession became his life, a not infrequent choice among career officers.

Still, the sight of Asel in that too revealing shift made him wonder what it would be like to touch those rounded breasts, feel the hard nipples against his face, his lips…

That was enough, he thought and gave himself a mental slap. He stood up and stretched. "Best to turn in, I think."

"What?" asked Callog. "Turning in? Liggy…"

"I'll sleep with the horses," Marcus said. "Got an early start in the morning. I'll call on my way back if I have the time."

As Callog woke all the way up and started to stand up, Marcus took something from his pocket. It was wrapped in a narrow strip of oiled homespun; he offered it to Callog. "A token, old friend."

Callog took the bundle and unwrapped it.

"May it keep its edge through all of your days."

"A token, Uffin? This is too much for a bowl of stew."

Marcus laughed. "And for the company. Now what price can you put on that?"

Callog shook his head. "Well, my thanks." He lowered his voice. "And when you think of taking a wife..."

Outside he pulled a blanket from his pack and settled himself down in the lean-too. The thatch was thin in places and stars gleamed through, but it protected him from the light rain which was still falling and presently he was sound asleep.

⁂

SAND CRAGS

In the far off days when the World and the Gods were young, when Albyn and Briton were still joined with the rest of the World, the mountains were new, with sharp and jagged edges to them. Rains washed them, earthquakes tumbled them and ice split them apart. There were cataclysms and eruptions of fire from beneath the earth. Erin parted from Briton, a huge crack ran the width of Albyn and the sea ran in to it and made the lakes which now separated Caledone and Creone lands from each other.

But the Earth was not yet done and spewed out enough fire and rock to build yet more mountains. The ground heaved up so that what once had been plains were now hills and where rivers had once flowed, their dried up courses became high mountain passes.

At one time the soft and crumbling Sand Crags had been dunes along a sea shore, but time had left it far inland and the elements had hardened its surface into a false rock. But time had been insufficient, the hard rock was only a skin and even this became soft again when the rains came. Soft and unstable and treacherous.

"This is the place, Manon." Dag dug the heel of his foot into the surface as he looked down slope. "It will take our weight going down, but no Roman is going to come up there at us." He turned to look back across the almost level expanse of barren sandstone to where the four hundred or so Callatae warriors sat their horses. "Tell them to secure the horses to a slip line, unbundle the throwing spears and wait for me."

Dag Liogh lay down so that only his head was visible above the skyline and that hidden by one of the infrequent tufts of grass. The pass below him had been cut into the rotten sandstone by a small stream which ran through the defile spreading out in a wide shallow sheet of water with here and there, an unsuspected deeper hole. The farther side was the same decaying sandstone, it was a steeper slope and the water had undercut it drastically.

Intelligence confirmed that the Roman column was making for this pass, the only one their scouts would find on this side of the range they had chosen to skirt.

A sudden sound made him turn. "Get down man, I told you to stay back."

Manon lowered his tattooed body to the ground. "There are men coming, Dag. Strange men with those little round hats like they saw the day before yesterday. They're coming up the lower slopes like dogs harrying game."

"Mm. How many?"

"We can't say. They are still in the woods and scattered."

"On foot or mounted? How near?"

"On foot and near enough to shout at."

"Take ten hands of men with you with bows and knives. Kill them, without noise if you can. If you cannot deal with them all, let a few of our brothers lead those who remain away from here."

The interruption had broken his concentration and he turned back to the pass and attempted to rebuild his mental picture of what he expected to happen. He looked across to the opposite slope, if Byrrig Mellaurig was across the other side, then he was keeping very low.

A sound from below brought his attention to the entrance where the stream had widened and deepened at the edge of the sandstone. Several of the men that Manon had described were there, black haired with round helmets and leather harnesses. Their movements were quick and agile, as surefooted as a deer; they carried round wooden shields and swords of similar size to his own although of a somewhat different shape.

There were four of them; no, a fifth followed on behind, looking behind him. They had obviously got away from Manon's force and not been successfully led astray. The five of them went through the pass, Dag left them alone.

Pintus was still in a foul mood and this probably affected his thinking when he rode to the head of the column where it had halted, where the valley floor became a gradual incline. "What now?" he shouted, but fell quiet as he saw for himself what the problem was. The floor of the shallow valley was covered in fine mud which had washed down from either side and accumulated over the years. As each foot came out of the mud, it revealed a black ooze beneath the coarser sand and released a stink of decay.

"Well, get them across as fast as you can," he said tiredly. He wheeled his horse around and was about to return to his place further back when the first spears fell. His horse took one of the first in its haunch and reared, screaming; Pintus was unseated even as he saw man after man transfixed with the bloodied javelins.

Centurions shouted orders, horses milled and the world tilted at an alarming angle as he hit the silt and it was long moments before his shocked mind realized that his horse was gone and that he was lying in the churned and stinking mud.

Pintus shook his head to clear it and pushed his helmet into place as he regained his feet. "Where are they? Who is attacking us?" The questions fell on deaf ears as around him, the legionaries tried to huddle behind their shields as the deadly rain of spears came at them from a multitude of angles.

Byrrig Mellaurig rode through the secret pathways which traversed the dense scrub along the western flanks of the crag and watched the spears decimating the army below.

He had not thought of using such a tactic and felt a short-lived shame at being shown up by such a younger man. The chagrin was quickly followed by a grin and a feeling of elation for here was their bitter enemy being humbled.

Gone were his earlier thoughts of leaving the glory to the Lioghs and playing safe. With a shout of pure, unadulterated joy he urged his stallion forward to the edge of the steep western slope of the pass.

"Selgovae," he screamed as the blood coursed through his veins and the battle rage rose in him consuming all reason. Byrrig led the five hundred of his tribe out onto the bare sandstone and down the slope to where the Romans floundered in blood and mud.

In places, the sandstone shell was thick; in others it was as delicate as an eggshell. Many horses skidded and kicked their way down in a more or less controlled descent while others sank into the softer stuff, breaking their legs and hurling their riders forward to plunge into the milling Romans below.

One falling horse might take fifteen or twenty legionaries with it, knocking them unconscious, maiming, killing. A man with a flailing sword in his hand might take two or three before he hit the mud and injured himself. Those who managed to reach the bottom in control so bewildered the Romans that killing the invaders was like knocking pigeons out of a bush.

Byrrig Mellaurig's horse scrabbled for purchase on the slick surface, its hooves gouging long grooves into the sandstone. It was not the most dignified charge that the Chief had ever made, but majesty was far from his mind. He screamed curses and vilifications as the horse careened down the slope and sprang from the very edge into the throng below. Mellaurig's blade whirled about his shoulders, cutting a swathe of dead and dying legionaries as he urged the animal forward. There, he could see the scarlet cape worn by the Roman leader; Mellaurig dug his boots into the horse's ribs and goaded it forward through the press of fighting men.

An iron tipped spear struck the warrior's shield, almost tearing it from his grasp. The cursed thing was barbed and he could not shake it loose. In the end, he had to toss the shield away so that he could still wield the huge sword effectively. A moment later, a second spear took him in the now unprotected arm and the impetus simply swept Mellaurig from his horse.

Now, he was down among the foot soldiers and those of his own men who had been unhorsed. Three of them came to his aid, protecting him while he struggled to disentangle the spear from his mutilated arm. A few moments later, he struggled to his knees and from there to his feet. He swayed a little, blood was running thickly from the wound, but his right arm still worked, still raised Broadwand high and he led the three who had covered him in a killing spree which his tribe would sing about for the rest of his... life.

The fatal blow came from a Legionary who had risen from behind a dead horse. The short Roman sword slipped upward into his rib cage from the side, slicing vital organs apart and piercing his right hand lung.

Mellaurig fell to the ground and smiled weakly as his comrades formed a triangular defense around their Chief. *If only he had heeded his own counsel but, then, the time of everyone's journey to the Otherworld was fixed at birth.* Byrrig Mellaurig's soul fought free of its fleshly prison, the golden cord snapped. *The Gods might grant me time to watch the battle won or lost.*

With the main attack apparently coming from the western slope, it was inevitable that the few legionaries who established some sort of order would retreat up the eastern side, but it became a terrible slog through the sludge and Dag Liogh's men met them singly and in twos and threes. Long curved swords sliced the heads from pila and Romans alike.

Blood ran down the sandstone in rivers to dye the churning stream vermilion.

Upon this scene came Marcus, he had traveled along the eastern side of Sand Crags since leaving the Callog place and had met no one during the two hour ride. The sounds of fighting had reached him a mile away and while he was fully alerted, he was quite unprepared for the degree of carnage which met his horrified eyes.

Whatever had happened? There was no answer, but his duty was near instinctive; automatically he was guiding his horse down to the scene of the fighting, letting it pick its own way until it stood fetlock deep in the red froth and mud. Once there, he urged it forward, towards the Legion's Eagle.

Dag Liogh had watched disaster overtake a third or more of Byrrig Mellaurig's heroes. He ached to be down there, fighting hand to hand, but he was cool enough and pragmatic enough to know that it would be courting catastrophe to join the Selgovae. Without their horses, his men would not be sufficiently mobile—with them, they would suffer the same misfortunes as their allies.

He had never expected total victory of course. Dag knew that the best that could be hoped for was to make it too uncomfortable, too *expensive* for the Romans to stay.

He passed his orders along the ranks. "Pick your targets; make every spear and arrow count. We are here to close this flank against the Romans' escape."

Bellus Ruis had seen Pintus unhorsed and rode through the press towards his Commandant. He had to dismount and lead his horse when a tangle of bodies—both human and equine—came tumbling down the slope and Pintus was on his feet by the time he arrived.

"Ruis, Commandant. Take my horse, Sir; get out of here." But even as he spoke, a javelin struck his mount in the neck. Its front legs buckled and the beast went down coughing bloody froth.

Pintus clapped the Centurion's shoulder. "Thank you, the thought was a noble one."

Ruis deflected a blow from a Selgovae warrior and stepped inside the other's guard to dispatch him. It took three blows of his shorter sword and taught him a lesson in respect.

"Back to back, then Commandant. We'll hold these hounds off until we can fall back in good order."

"Aye Ruis. A taste of Roman steel." And they gave battle, each protecting the other as, step by step, they cut their way back towards the end of the pass.

"I swear to you, Ruis." Pintus gasped the words between thrust and parry. "The wine in my house… will always… flow for you."

It was several long moments before the Commandant realized that he was speaking to a dead man. Ruis died without knowing that an arrow had found the one space between helmet and shoulder plate.

"Bellus Ruis… Must you… leave me now?" Pintus shouted the words in time to the thrust of his sword, three Selgovae died making his punctuation marks and as they fell he was confronted by a horseman sliding off the treacherous slope above them. The horse caught a back foot in the soft surface and its rider shot over its neck straight towards Pintus. In seeming slow motion, Pintus saw the rider's spear sweep towards him, as unerringly as if mighty Zeus himself grasped the shaft; it plunged between his ribs with the full weight of the barbarian behind it.

Marcus had almost closed with the Commandant, was on the point of pulling Pintus up onto his own mount when the spear struck home. With a cry of rage, he flung himself on to the Selgovae's back and struck him unconscious with the heavy hilt of his sword.

He pulled the dead weight of the Commandant's assailant aside and bent to look at the wound which was grievous. He took hold of the now-broken shaft and wondered if it could be wrenched out of Pintus' body. Even though he knew it was far too late, he tried and failed to see the group of Romans who had fought through to their Commander.

The blow was heavy enough to have killed him, but some accident of fate, the sword's turning at the last instant, his own movement, perhaps, saved Marcus' life.

At last, the tide of battle was turning. Some semblance of order among the Roman legionaries was being restored. Pintus' body and Marcus Uffin were carried off the field as the last of the Selgovae retreated northward.

"Well done, kinsman." Dag signaled them to fall back. "We live to fight them again. We have no trophies today, but tomorrow we shall harry these Romans back to their wall, the pickings will be rich ones, I promise you. We return to Briogix and honor our Selgovae brothers for to them, go this day's honors."

"Some of us already have our trophies."

Manon had returned with the band of men who had taken on the Roman advance guard. They carried with them swords and shields and the conical hats of the Mauritanians and many of them carried a head taken from the dead.

Dag Liogh grinned. The heads would become honored mementos and stories of their acquisition would be told and retold, polished just as much as the skulls of these gallant little fighters. From every skull, a draught of good strong ale would be drunk to the honor of their erstwhile owners.

The Sixth licked its wounds and counted their dead. In fact, they had lost a quarter of the expedition although among that number were the Commandant himself, a praefector, four tribunes and six centurions.

Had the natives not run away as the Legion was coming to terms with the ambush, the Romans would almost certainly have won the battle with great cost to their enemy. As it was, they had now to return to Vircovicium; a full report would have to be presented and whatever the consequences were, they would have to be accepted.

The only good thing to come out of it, thought Aemilius Karrus, was the perpetrator being caught. He could be made to carry a lot of blame.

⚜

HIGH SIL

Callog's daughter sat at the edge of a spring-fed pool of clear water.

Asel watched her reflection as she combed her corn-colored hair. Two bright blue eyes gazed up at her, but she was looking beyond her own image. In her imagination, Uffin's face lay amongst the pebbles which covered the bottom of the pool and it was his eyes which stared back at her.

If her da continued his jokes at her expense, she would speak to Uffin herself.

CHAPTER FIVE

VIRCOVICIUM

THE DEMORALIZED SIXTH RETURNED TO VIRCOVICIUM TWO hours after dawn with Aemilius Karrus, the highest ranking officer left, riding out in front. Every man was haggard and weary, it took an effort of will to place one foot in front of the other.

Karrus had forced marched them most of the way with driving rain obscuring their vision and clinging mud grasping at tired legs. They had marched and rested, marched and rested, two hours slog with a quarter hour leaning against rocks, trees, each other. On the second night, he had allowed them two hours rest before resuming the grueling trek with smoky torches to help them on their way.

That final day, Karrus had let the more bellicose of the legionaries to form a group and scout both east and west. They had captured a number of Selgovae natives off guard and brought them back for slavery. There had been some losses among the Romans too, not all of them returned from these forays.

From the north on a good day, Vircovicium was visible for fifteen or twenty miles wherever the ground was open enough to give a view. With the rain still lashing them that morning, they were less than five miles away when someone glimpsed the fortification and raised a thin cheer. Even in their exhausted state, the men picked up their pace a little.

As they entered the north gate, Aemilius Karrus pulled his horse to one side and remained there, mounted, as the full column marched through and past him. Only when the last man was within the fort did he climb stiffly from his mount and patting the animal's neck, call to a legionary.

"See to him, will you? Like the rest of us, he's been through a lot."

The man nodded and led the animal away.

"And round up whatever able bodied men you can find, use my authority. Get them to help with the wagons, feed the horses and the oxen."

Karrus walked down the slope towards the headquarters building. The rest of them could sleep where they dropped for all he cared, but for himself there would be reports to make, explanations, several more hours before he could retire.

He came to the entrance and rubbed his gritty eyes before climbing the steps one by one and feeling every year of his forty six. There was a pulled muscle and perhaps a cracked rib which he had long since grown used to on horseback, but now that he was on his own feet. They began a whole new orchestra of aches and pains.

A legionary on guard duty saluted him smartly as he entered the building. His fingers had been holding on to the horse's reins for so long that it was all he could do to fist his right hand to return the gesture.

Perhaps it was time to seek retirement from the army, he wondered and wondered, too, whether the discharge ceremony which was held every other year came this year or next. Suddenly, a pension from Rome and a marriage to Marra, the Brythonic woman whom he'd visited and supported for years seemed very attractive. *Raising pigs and growing vegetables—could be worse ways to pass the time.*

Ah well. Time to see the Legate... first things first. And he unconsciously tugged at his *lorica* to straighten it up. The brass segments over the left ribcage were bent or missing over an area as big as his hand, that was where his ribs hurt. He had no idea what had struck him, but Karrus guessed that he would have been dead without the protective covering of mail.

Marcellus Flavius knew two things before Karrus knocked on the door. First, it was obvious that things had not gone well—the state of exhaustion exhibited by every man of the returning force spoke of this. Secondly, he knew that he could not lay the blame against Aemilius Karrus, Karrus and men like him carried out their orders to the letter even though those orders might make little sense without a knowledge of the full picture. No, without officers of Karrus' proven ability, no Legion would function, certainly not with the efficiency and precision which were bywords for the Roman military machine.

"Enter." Flavius remained calm and patient as the Centurion closed the door behind him.

Karrus, weather-stained, unshaven, limping, stood to attention and brought his right fist smartly across his chest.

"Senior Centurion Karrus, Sir. Senior Officer of the expedition."

Flavius had seen the fellow arrive, had watched him all but stumble down the slope; now he saw him at firsthand, fatigue etched into every line of the officer's face.

"Sit down, man, for pity's sake. Aemilius, isn't it? A glass of wine, perhaps, some bread?" Flavius was dismayed at the officer's appearance. The deep lines were new, the grey hair seemed paler than before and Karrus' weary eyes expressed pain. This man had been to Hades and back.

Karrus pulled a stool away from the wall and sank onto the seat.

"Thank you, Sir." He shook his head. "Just some water please, Sir."

"I guess you didn't make camp last night."

"We stopped for two hours, Sir. We stationed guards and took the weight off our feet—as much to water and rest the animals, Sir, as for the men."

A few minutes later, an aide brought a tray with a pitcher of fresh water and a terracotta beaker. Karrus drank deeply and wiped his mouth with the back of his hand, the rasp of fingers against stubble loud in the quiet office.

He began his report. The search for informers, the journey and the ambush, the retreat and the loss of men and equipment. Karrus added his own observations in a voice devoid of emotion.

"The Mauritanians brought us wrong information, Sir. They were in unfamiliar country against unfamiliar forces and they read the signs wrongly. Commandant Pintus... They were sent out to scout mountainous terrain when they were used to desert and steppes, they... It was a mistake."

Flavius nodded and made some notes on a wax tablet. "The ambush?"

Karrus shrugged. "We should have been more informed about the route. The Mauritanians, again; I believe they were ambushed themselves, or led astray perhaps and picked off. Only a few returned, three or four."

"What about the local scouts? They should have known."

Karrus frowned. "They were not consulted or their information was not used."

"He didn't trust them? Their information has always proved good before."

The Centurion shrugged and looked at his hands, fingering a half healed cut across the left wrist. "The Commandant had taken a dislike to the Beneficiarius, Gellorix. He was late to report and Commandant Pintus seemed to think that he was taking pay from two masters."

"Gellorix, eh? Go on."

"When the Commandant was unhorsed in the ambush and cut off, we—well a squad of legionaries—caught Gellorix just as he plunged the spear into the Commandant."

Flavius was dumbstruck. "Gellorix... assassinated..." He tried again. "He's half Roman, Mansustus' son. I'll have to think about this later, Karrus... Aemilius, it's too much to take in all at once, it's... it's a bucket of horse shit though; every commandant who has any locals working in this sort of position is going to have to think about it too."

"Carry on with your report. The ambush."

"Yes Sir. As you may have guessed, we were taken totally by surprise. The pass was very narrow and waterlogged, the regulars had no real opportunity to fight; there were these wild men on horses careering down on us from one side, and blue painted warriors on the other laying down a barrage of javelins and arrows. Without a lie, Sir, about half our dead were killed by being crushed beneath falling horses the other half dead from arrows and spears. Very few were actually killed in combat. When we did get organized, there was very little these barbarians could do but slink away but our initial losses were appalling."

"And they were..?"

"Eleven officers, Sir and the Commandant. Over one hundred regulars and over two hundred auxiliaries and numeri. The numeri losses were almost total."

Karrus was set to continue, but realized that he'd said enough. The thin lips were drawn together in a hard line. Flavius' nose was almost white and a finger was tapping an irregular rhythm on the table.

"There are a lot of barbarians who won't bother us again, Sir," he said, looking for positive facts to give the Legate. "Two hundred dead, a hundred or so prisoners that we took at the scene of the battle and some on the way back. We can torture quite a bit of information out of them."

"And the assassin, Karrus?"

"Oh, we have him, Sir. We have him."

For a moment, Flavius smiled. "Let us be pleased when the Gods bestow small favors. What of the women? This whole thing was to recover two women."

"We tortured several of the prisoners, Sir. They knew nothing. They died protesting they knew nothing. I, er, may I express my own opinion, Sir?"

"Of course." Flavius had regained control of himself.

"I'm not sure that they were taken north of the Wall, Sir. Those who we interrogated could hardly take us seriously until the irons began to burn."

Flavius was quite silent for some time until evidently, his thoughts passed on to other subjects. "Blue, Aemilius. You mentioned men being painted blue, on the eastern side of the pass."

"Yes Sir. I understand that they are of the Callatae, a tribe from further north than usual who seem to be allied with the Selgovae. Their Chief, incidentally, was killed in the attack. The Selgovae Chief."

"Hm. Blue. There were many among the dead in that raid on Throp who were painted with blue patterns." Flavius scratched his head. "Well, small favors, Aemilius, small favors. We have a Chief who will lead no more raids against us; we have a man to try for murder. Did anyone interrogate this Gellorix? Why did he do it?"

Karrus shook his head. "It's understandable, but the soldiers who pulled him off the Commandant nearly kicked him to death. I doubt his own mother would recognize him and he's still unconscious."

"After two days, Aemilius? He'd better not die on us, not before he's tried. Oh well. Get some sleep Centurion, I'll decide what to do for the best."

Karrus stood up and saluted. He managed a pretty crisp about-turn and marched to the door. Flavius watched him sag just before the door shut behind him.

So, he thought, *Mansustus' boy.* The result of a liaison between Rome and Briton, of the carnal sort—should he deal with the business himself or pass it on to Governor Severus? Mansustus was not his sponsor, his patron was Hadrian himself, with a little care he might keep the Emperor happy, Severus happy but Mansustus...?

Flavius rose and went to the window. He pushed it open and was rewarded by a beam of sunshine. It had rained solidly for four days and suddenly the sun shone down. *It was a weird country and no mistake.* Karrus, he saw, was heading for the south gate.

If he could keep all those clubs in the air at once, he might even make General a bit earlier. Just before he reached the gate, Karrus turned left and was lost to sight.

The Centurion was going to the bath house. Flavius nodded to himself and returned to the table. He picked up the stylus and began to make notes about his ideas before he forgot them.

⁂

MEDIONEMETON

Medionemeton lay many miles to the north, as far north of Briogix as that stronghold lay north of the Wall. Mandeltua, heir designate to the position of High Druid clutched at the stone which hung from a cord around his neck.

Samhain was approaching and the boundaries between this world and the Otherworld began to overlap. The barriers grew thin and indistinct. Samhain was a time of prophecy and Mandeltua could feel the presence of the Gods more clearly with each day that passed.

He muttered a prayer to the Caelleach as his little finger traced the spiral in the stone.

The Druid looked at the stone, at the segments of glittering crystal on the reverse and the polished convolutions of the obverse. He let his mind follow the vanishing pattern; he closed his eyes and followed the spiral down to its microscopic vanishing point.

Visions filled his inner sight. He watched the water wash through the sandy pass and the Romans marching stolidly forward. He saw the first javelin strike the first legionary and the first horse slide on its haunches into the melee below.

Uffin arrived and tried to remove the fatal spear from the Roman's body. Mandeltua's eyelids flickered as he saw Uffin's fate.

⁂

VIRCOVICIUM

After steeping gently for half an hour in the warm bath, Karrus stood up and went to the frigidarium where he stood at the side of the bath and debated about taking a cold plunge.

I'm getting old. There's no doubt about it, he said to himself and skirting the bath, he made his way back to the dressing room. A few minutes later, he climbed the hill to his barracks and threw himself down on the pallet. Officers of Aemilius Karrus' standing had their own private rooms within the barracks, a fact for which he was often grateful; he was asleep before he remembered to take his sandals off.

Karrus slept for about three hours before waking and gradually becoming aware of a conversation in the common area outside his door.

"… seems unlikely. I spoke with him at some length before he left."

That was, hm, the aide to Commandant Pintus. The lame fellow. Mellius Garius.

"I've never had cause to doubt Marcus' loyalty and that's a fact."

"Took his duties very seriously, I think."

The conversation continued. Each of the speakers trying to make sense of Gellorix' murder of Pintus. Karrus listened without any feeling of being an eavesdropper; he, too, had been surprised by the facts reported to him.

"I think I'll talk to the fellow myself. At least see what he has to say," Karrus muttered to himself as he rose and started to change into his parade uniform. "I owe him that at least. First things first though." He took down the brass helmet with its crest of scarlet horse hair and cradling it on his left arm, passed into the main part of the barracks.

"Sir," said Garius and stood to salute followed a moment later by the decurion who had been talking with him.

"At ease, legionary."

The weather was holding, a mild breeze blew the scent of newly cut grass from the stables and chased a cloud of golden leaves until they landed in a water cistern, carpeting the surface. An early fall was coming, tree by tree.

The *Praetorium*, the Commandant's villa, was downhill, but still high enough to see over the south wall and across the military road, the *Stanegate*, and the valley beyond. Karrus followed the covered colonnade around to the main entrance and knocked on the open door. A houseboy appeared.

"Senior Centurion Aemilius Karrus," he stated. "I wish to see the Lady Aelia."

The boy nodded and ushered him through to the atrium while he vanished in search of his mistress. A few minutes later Aelia, wife to the late Cassius Aurelius Pintus, entered the room.

"Centurion." Aelia was pale, her eyes were reddened and neither her makeup nor her hair were as flawlessly arranged as was usually the case.

"Lady, may I present my sympathy? Your husband was a respected officer and the Sixth Legion mourns his loss."

Aelia nodded. She fixed Karrus with a gaze whose intensity he found quite uncomfortable. Eventually, he found himself trying to think of something to say.

"If there is anything I can do, Lady..."

"I think you have already done too much, Centurion."

"Lady..?"

"You let him have his own way, Centurion. You could have argued him out of this foolishness; you career officers are supposed to hold your Commandant's hand so that this sort of thing doesn't happen, but you let him have his head, didn't you?"

"My Lady, I..."

But once started Aelia was not about to stop. She walked around her visitor so that he had to keep turning his head and then shuffling his feet to stay facing her.

"A Commandant is a political appointment, Centurion. Aurelius didn't know one end of a ballista from another." Some color had returned to her cheeks and she stabbed Karrus on the chest with her finger.

"Really, Lady, Commandant Pintus was not as ignorant as..."

"As some? Perhaps not. But you and your fellows knew that this was a stupid undertaking, a waste of time. I hear what's said you know. That slut of a wife to Septimus, her stupid companion, and a third of a legion goes in search of them. Who was riding with my husband? Were you? Who was supposed to look after him and protect him?"

The tongue lashing lasted several more minutes, becoming more and more vitriolic. Conceivably, it made Aelia feel better, but Karrus could do nothing but listen to her and take the insults. He sweated. He eased the leather tunic and felt the perspiration pool and run down his back. Towards the end, the arm which held his helmet was shaking. Both honor and courtesy demanded that he did not tarnish the dead officer's name in order to protect his own, but it was no easy matter.

When the Lady Aelia more or less dismissed him, Karrus did not trust himself to speak. He nodded and stumped woodenly out of the villa and back to the Barracks.

Confound Gellorix. Hades take him. Karrus could think of no reason, no extenuating circumstances that would make sense of Gellorix's act. *Twenty men or more had seen him, testified to the assassination.* The Centurion shook his head. *I will have to leave the matter to Marcellus Flavius, it was the Legate's responsibility, anyhow.*

Marcus lay on the stone floor of a store room and shivered. Consciousness returned in little packets of pain and misery so that he could not distinguish reality from dreams. Was the agony nightmare or fact? Whichever, he begrudged the moments spared from the blessed numbness even though he had to watch the blue faces of the Callatae and the berserk rage of the Selgovae. Even the moment of Pintus' death, although it grew more grotesque at every repetition, was peace compared with the times when his left eye seemed on fire and the broken ends of his ribs seemed to grate on the hard floor with every breath.

But all things pass. Even the silent parade of dead faces and the blows of the Roman legionaries as they kicked his unfeeling body, even these passed and he came to a dark place, still and vast. A face coalesced from the black vapors which swirled at every hand. It was neither a kind face nor a cruel one, neither young nor old and the mouth opened and spoke words to him in a strange and primitive language. Though he felt perfectly familiar with both the face and the tongue, Marcus felt certain he had known neither of them before this moment.

The words were truth, so certain, so undeniable that they appeared to Marcus like stone tablets inscribed with runes of ancient power.

"Your destiny awaits you Uffin Gellorix. Soon, you will follow the bright star and join me."

That was all. The face returned to the black mists and Marcus lay like one dead.

And at length, even this passed.

He woke to reality. An ocean of pain washed over him leaving him sweating and gasping for breath as the shock wore off. Tentatively, moving slowly, Marcus explored his body, first with his mind and then with his hands.

It was difficult to breathe and his fingers, swollen and unresponsive, found lumps and contusions scabbed with dried blood. He could not see—was he blind or was the place in darkness? He traced his features, swellings and half-healed scars had turned them into the face of a stranger. His left eye was caked in what he assumed was blood, the lids of his right eye were gummed together with more blood. Marcus was sure that his nose was broken and that he had lost some teeth and his jaw simply would not work, but his fingers were such dubious tools that they told him nothing useful.

What had happened? Marcus tried to recall the immediate past. Had one of those Selgovae horses fallen on him? What had the legionaries, that he'd seen in his dreams, been doing? It seemed that they had inflicted his injuries, but it was hardly a rational memory; it could not be right.

Time went by and the cold seeped into his bones. He had to move, had to do something or he was going to die of the cold.

Gingerly and very slowly, Marcus tried to separate his right side eyelids. They parted gradually and the Stygian blackness became a dark and indistinct grey in which black amorphous objects loomed.

Carefully, he turned over and began to get his knees under him. Something clanked. Shackles? Who had shackled him and why? The floor was stone, the way that the iron shackles struck it told him that much. Had he been captured by the Selgovae or the Callatae and imprisoned in a broch.

With time, he was able to ignore the worst of the pain and think about his plight. Somewhere there was an answer and only by finding that answer could he do something about extricating himself from this predicament.

He tested the shackles. They were secured only about his ankles and thus he was free to crawl about his prison. The enclosure measured about three lengths of his body, two in width—too small to be a broch despite the stone floor, nor was it round. This had to be a store room of some sort, but where? The walls were of stone and there was a solid sounding door in one wall. In one corner the floor was damp and a sudden drop of water from above felt like a slingshot against the back of his head. Nevertheless, he laboriously turned over on to his back and lay under it, letting the water fall on his bruised lips and fill his mouth. A slow but very much needed drink.

After the constant pain, the cold was the most insistent sensation and then came hunger. After that, Marcus was frightened, frightened of not knowing where he was or what had happened to him. His career had been built on knowledge and a lack of it threatened his job and himself.

Knowledge. He was in Roman hands, he had proved that he was not in a broch, a Roman built structure was the only other place to find a stone floor. But why shackle him? He'd been late in meeting up with the Sixth, but that did not warrant this sort of punishment nor did it explain his injuries.

Marcus pulled the rough woolen cloth closer about him and tried to find a more comfortable position. At least he was in Roman hands, if there had been some sort of mix… perhaps they had simply not recognized him, perhaps he had been set upon by a band of local warriors and the Romans didn't realize who he was. And despite the abuse his body had been subjected to, Marcus fell asleep.

A boot in the side brought him rudely back to wakefulness. Rough hands seized hold of him and hauled him to his feet. Marcus tried to protest, but could hardly utter a sound and his jaw was still too stiff to move. He was manhandled outside into the daylight and the brightness blinded his one good eye for several minutes. He felt the smooth stone of a roadway under his stumbling feet and heard the familiar jingle of weapons and lorica. Through a haze of tears, he recognized Vircovicium. His own fort, with a sob of thankfulness, he let himself be led up the steps of the headquarters building. Now he would be able to explain who he was.

The Legate, Marcellus Flavius sat behind a broad oak table in the main briefing room. He was dressed in his full uniform, he was present in his capacity as Governor of Briton Inferior and behind and to one side were a Tribune and several Centurions, Marcus knew most of them, had worked with some. Today, they wore dress uniform, carried parade helmets in the crooks of their arms; they looked straight ahead, ignoring his presence. He looked for Karrus, a friend of some standing, but he was not there. It was then that he feared the worst.

The two men—legionaries, he presumed—who supported him at either side marched him forward to the front of the table.

"Ave," he said although nothing but a croak issued from his mouth. He felt sick and the room danced around him.

Flavius was quite shocked at Marcus' appearance, but ignored it for the time being. He coughed to gain the attention of the officers present.

"Beneficiarius Gellorix. You are brought before me today to receive sentence for the act of murder. I have decided, out of respect for your father, to have you sent to the mines. Understand this, had it not been for your father's rank and standing in Rome, your sentence would have been crucifixion. A lot of effort has been invested in you, young man; at least this way, you'll pay some of it back."

Flavius fell silent. Thoughts came and went. He leaned forward.

"Tell me Gellorix, did the barbarians pay you to kill Pintus or was it because of some petty injustice he'd done you?"

Marcus's mind reeled from the impact of his supposed act of murder. He hardly understood the question and tried to protest at the mistake, but his injured jaw just wouldn't move. Everything he tried to say sounded the same, a string of inarticulate croaks.

Flavius lifted both his hands, palms forward.

"Don't bother. I don't think I want to listen to your reasons. You'll have plenty of time to ponder your actions at Evenhope. Grassus." Flavius leaned back and turned to the scribe who was sitting under a window for the light. "Record this." He turned back to Marcus. "The name of Marcus Uffin Gellorix is to be struck from the Legion's roster. Senator Mansustus is to be informed of his son's actions and of my decision."

The scribe wrote with a pen nib made of iron wire dipped in an ink of gall and sloe berries on a thin shaving of Birchwood. The facts as Marcellus Flavius knew them had become a part of history.

Marcus was taken through the back door and chained to the last man in a long file of prisoners. The destination for all of them was the same, the mines at Evenhope, some twenty miles south of Vindolanda.

Aemilius Karrus watched the young man out of sight with mixed emotions. He had thought that he had known him, had counted him a friend for despite the difference in years there had seemed to be a bond of understanding between them.

For a moment, Karrus wondered if he should have attended the hearing. No. He had no evidence to give except as a character witness and even in this, Karrus felt himself to be on unsound ground. What Gellorix's motivations had been would remain a mystery; it was unlikely that their paths would ever cross again.

⚜

ABALAVA

When she first realized that a piece of her jewelry was missing, Iavolena turned the place upside down. She questioned Vetia for the best part of an hour and eventually wondered if the girl could be as guileless as she appeared to be—theft seemed to be something that had simply never crossed the servant's mind.

After the second piece went missing, Iavolena laid a trap. She placed a pendant brooch to one side of her jewelry chest and partly under a bowl, so that it looked as though she had missed it and perhaps, forgotten it.

She checked its continued presence whenever someone else had been in the west wing of the house. The farmer's daughter, a messenger from the dressmaker's, the baker, Vetia, a workman come to mend one of the lead-lined cisterns which collected rainwater. And Titus Severius, of course.

The brooch remained where it was all of that first day, most of the next. Vetia had gone to Iavolena's chamber to fetch the embroidery frame and work chest. Iavolena checked, the piece had vanished. She made the girl strip and inspected every garment, she pulled the girl's hair out of its braids and combed it through, she examined Vetia intimately; nothing.

But Vetia was not the only one who had had the opportunity, of course. Titus, her lover had come home when the evening had become too dark to work. He had changed and gone out again, down to the taverns, a habit he had formed over the past week or so.

Iavolena waited. Titus had explained that he had work to discuss with a new client, some income over and above his army pay, Iavolena had made her own guesses. He would normally return about midnight, happy with himself and smelling of cheap wine.

Tonight was no exception. He more or less staggered through the door and made for the bedchamber. He didn't notice Iavolena waiting for him until she spoke.

"Where is it?" she asked as soon as he was in the house.

Titus frowned and grinned at the same time. "A guessing game, my love? Why aren't you in bed awaiting my caresses? Hm? Like the last five or six nights."

The sarcasm was not lost on Iavolena; it added fuel to her fury. "Do you really think I want to lie with you in that state? I'd rather be bedded by a boar, at least its pizzle wouldn't droop the way yours does. You're a walking wine bottle, not a man fit for a woman."

Titus chuckled. "Walking wine bottle. That's good. I like it. Is the honeymoon over with then?"

"Over? It hardly started, did it? Forget it, I have. I just want my jewelry back, that's all. You stole it, didn't you?"

Titus nodded, sobering on the instant. "Yes."

Iavolena was taken aback, she had expected denials at least, not this. "Well, you'd better return it or I shall..."

"Yes? You'll what?" Titus put a hand to his ear. "*What* will you do or *who* will you tell? Your husband? Cerea? Oh no, she's dead isn't she, dead and wearing your clothes. I don't suppose she'll be interested."

Iavolena's face had turned white, a vein pumped visibly at her temple.

"You suggested it, you said it would throw them off the scent. *You* spoiled her face so they'd think it was me. Who do you think they'll believe when I tell Septimus that you killed her and abducted me?"

Titus' hand moved so fast that she felt the slap before she saw the hand. "Cow. Welcome to reality. How do you think we pay the rent on this place?

"Do you know what my salary is?"

Still unnerved by the blow, Iavolena shook her head.

"I get four hundred and fifty denarii a year. Now what does Septimus get paid? At least ten times as much. The food and the fuel costs ten denarii a week, the clothes you ordered last week came to over three hundred. Where do you think it all comes from, eh? If I'd had enough to pay, I wouldn't need to sell your jewelry, would I. think, woman, think."

And Iavolena *did* think. Money was something you used, she had never thought of its having to be earned, it seemed so... so *plebeian*. Septimus had just settled all the bills as they came in, he gave her everything she had asked for and more beside. If only he had treated her like a woman. "You could at least have told me, explained."

Titus Severius sensed victory, but the wine had affected his judgment. If he had stopped there... The insults came back, she had ridiculed his masculinity.

"Well, you'd prefer a boar though, wouldn't you? Wine doesn't make a boar's cock droop, does it? Well, let me tell *you* something." He tapped her chest quite forcibly, directly between the breasts. "It's not the wine that makes mine droop either and Marga has likened me to a stallion. She was quite delighted when I rose to the occasion three times tonight."

Iavolena lost all control then. She screamed every vile word she could think of, and hurled herself at Titus, clutching and scratching.

Titus took hold of her throat with one hand and shook her like a puppy with an old sandal. "You want the truth? Well I'll tell you the truth. You live in a make-believe world, you think the Gods put men on Earth just to feed and clothe and pamper you and to satisfy your carnal fancies, no wonder an old man like Septimus can't do anything for you. The whole of the Sixth Legion would have a hard time trying."

He pushed her away so that she backed up and tripped over a rug. She fell over the table where she had been embroidering and scattered everything including the lamp which, fortunately, went out. Iavolena herself, landed with a yelp of pain.

"It's about time you found out about men. We don't like to be at your beck and call. We like to choose the time and place; we like to take the initiative. Not all the time, maybe, but enough. You're like a leech—it takes burning to get you to let go."

All at once, Titus felt cleansed. He had got it all off his chest; he had put the woman in her place and could breathe freely once more. Time to be magnanimous.

"Now, you can go or you can stay, you're not a bad lay, but if you want to stay here in this," he swept his arm around to indicate the room, "this luxury, we do things my way from now on. For a start, the rest of your jewelry is going to be sold."

Titus sat on the edge of a couch. "Well? What do you say?"

Iavolena nodded. She sat up and looked up at Titus. "All right."

"Good." Titus stood up and stretched and then stepped around her and went into the bedchamber.

Iavolena, picked up the silks and the cloth, righted the table and after a few minutes, took her work box into the bedroom.

Titus Severius was sleeping on his side, snoring. Iavolena lay alongside of him and waited until he was sleeping heavily. She poised the long thin needle and thrust it in a single movement into his ear. He jerked once and stopped snoring.

⚜

VIRCOVICIUM

Karrus and Flavius were alone in the Commandant's house, the Lady Aelia having departed the fortress with her retinue at dawn that morning, bound for Rome.

Anger had completely replaced any grief she had felt for her husband's death; anger at the Roman army for not protecting him from his own folly, anger at the barbarians who had taken his life. She had even given Marcellus Flavius a dressing down at Pintus' cremation the previous evening. All in all, the fort was pleased to see her go. The ten legionaries and the decurion who had been detailed to escort her as far as Cataractonium were less pleased; they would spend the next two days cursing Karrus who had singled them out for the duty.

Flavius had already dispatched a message to Rome and another to Sextus Julius Severus, his superior and Governor of Briton. There had been rumors for six months or more that Severus was due to leave Briton, but there was no hard news. Certainly he had been here long enough and if he was about to pack his bags within a few months, he would be unwilling to take any decisions himself. The authorities in Rome would read the report in less than a month, but a definite reply to his queries and suggestions would have to wait on the Emperor's pleasure.

Karrus stood at ease in front of the huge table which Flavius had appropriated and waited for the other to break the silence which had developed.

"Well Aemilius, out with it. You look like a dog sniffing at a butcher's door."

Karrus grinned and ran fingers through thinning silver hair. "A number of things, Sir."

"Let's just drop the 'Sir' in private. Marcellus will do. Hm? Must say you're looking better this morning, feeling better? Anyway, what—*things*?"

"Yes S..." Karrus did not like senior officers to drop protocol and become over-familiar with their subordinates; there was not much he could do about it, however. "Much better, thanks, Marcellus."

Flavius, elbows on the table, steepled his fingers. "So?"

"It's a question of morale, Marcellus. The men don't like the way we had to leave the dead. I don't like it, if it comes to it, but at least I can see there was no alternative."

Flavius had read every detail of Karrus' report, but still he asked, "Why was no effort made to give them proper burial? You know how conservative the average legionary is about these things."

"There were several reasons. We had no way of knowing what the barbarians were going to do; they'd disappeared, true but could have returned with reinforcements and caught us out again. We had no scouts to send out to keep a watch on enemy movements. Secondly, there was not much timber up there. I'd guess it would have taken us more than a day to bring enough up for funeral pyres—we'd used everything burnable to cook with.

"And finally... Well, I just wanted to get the Legion back here. Better to leave three or four hundred dead back there than to risk the remaining twelve hundred. These were pretty demoralized men, Sir."

Flavius nodded. "I concur with everything you say, Aemilius. Your report does its best to show Pintus in a *reasonable* light, but I can read between the lines, Aemilius. Your hands were effectively tied.

"What do you say to this? We'll have the Legion raise a temple to Mars. It will give them something to do, something to occupy their minds and we'll hold a ceremony to honor our dead."

Karrus nodded. "Perhaps a second temple to Hercules, Marcellus. The foot soldiers revere Him highly."

"Splendid." Flavius put his hands on the table and levered himself up. "Been a long night," he said by way of explanation. "Spent a lot of time with Pintus' widow. She was not kind."

"Me too. Yesterday morning. She'd make..." Karrus was going to suggest using her as a secret weapon against Rome's enemies, but decided he might be stretching Flavius' camaraderie too far.

"Two temples then and in the meantime, we'll have the name of every dead legionary and officer recorded and we shall have to think how to reward the live ones."

"What about replacing our losses? All units have returned to their garrisons now and they're pretty thin in places."

"I've requested temporary strength from Eboracum, but—and this is confidential— I've asked Hadrian for reinforcements. The Ninth Legion has almost completed work on the Wall west and south of Luguvallium, two thousand men will bring them up to fighting strength."

Flavius went to stand by the window. "You see, I have a feeling that something is stirring up there, north of the Wall. Let us not put too fine a polish on the breastplate, Aemilius, we have taken a battering and the barbarians may well think that we are weakening after all these years.

"I propose to train the Ninth up to standard and go one better than Agricola. I'm going to take the whole of Albyn. What do you say to that?"

Karrus was speechless. He had been thinking seriously of retirement, had almost come to like the idea. *How could he apply for retirement with this in the offing? It could brand him a coward.*

The Centurion shook his head. "Brilliant, Marcellus. Brilliant."

Flavius lifted an eyebrow and smiled. "I thought you might like that piece of news. I'll tell you some more.

"I'm aware of course, that you can apply to Rome for discharge and your pension, it is almost thirty years, isn't it?"

Karrus nodded, not sure where all this was leading.

"I've read your record, Aemilius, exemplary. Your career both here and on the mainland has been quite exemplary. Now it's not in my power to make you Commandant, but it *is* in my power to promote you to the rank of Tribune."

"Well, I..." Karrus could not find the words to express his feelings.

"If Hadrian grants me permission to continue my plans here, I intend to appoint you Tribune in charge of the veterans, the *pilanii*. If not, then I'll find some other appointment. Make a bit of difference to your pension, eh?"

Karrus nodded again, still overwhelmed. *Had Flavius been reading my mind?* The matter of retirement was, for the moment, forgotten as he pictured himself in the uniform of a tribune. *After all these years, I'm finally going to make it.*

He smiled. "Thanks."

SELGOVANTIA

At dawn on the day after the Sixth Legion had retreated in disarray, the Callatae assembled in front of Dag Liogh's house. They were jubilant and boisterous; they rode their small ponies around in circles, in and out of the trees. Some of them stood up on the animals' hind quarters as they took the animals at a gallop around the village; others leaped from their galloping pony's back to the ground and up again time after time.

The shouts and cries of bravado grew progressively louder and the feats of horsemanship ever more dangerous until Dag emerged from the entrance to his hut. A gesture brought silence and grinning, his people gathered close to hear his words.

"My horse," he said and when this was brought to him. "The Sand Crags." And as if he had uttered some magical phrase, the Callatae were away, streaming after him with no regard for discipline and military order.

Nor were the Callatae the only ones abroad. Neither were they first. At the site of the battle, the Selgovae, greedy for spoils, were already picking over the Roman corpses.

At first, Dag Liogh was angry. Angry with himself for not being here earlier, angry at the Selgovae for beating him to the scene. However, the stench of battle—the bitter smell of blood, the sweet stink of entrails—and the presence of so many dead, both friend and enemy, tempered his resentment. Perhaps the Selgovae did have the right. It was, after all, they who had met the Romans in honorable combat while his men had fired arrows and flung spears from the heights.

But something must be said. The Callatae had expected a share in the booty and the uneasy peace between the two tribes would be easily broken if tempers flared like his own.

Dag rode up to the battle ground and grinned at the Selgovae warriors who looked back with hostile expressions.

"I am Dag Liogh, Chief of the Callatae. I am pleased to see our Selgovae cousins here to share the spoils of war. Where is Chief Mellaurig? We should discuss the division."

His words raised such a shout of anger from the Selgovae warriors that Dag was quite taken aback. A veritable giant of a man stood up and pushed his way towards Liogh, he stood in front of the Callatae Chief and glared up at him.

"If the Callatae had joined in the battle with us, they would know that Byrrig Mellaurig died gloriously yesterday. They would have been telling of his honors and his victories around their fires if they had been near enough to see our Chief go to meet the Gods."

The man's voice was quiet, but carrying; it spoke of anger only lightly restrained. He brushed back his long hair and spat at the hooves of Liogh's pony.

"As long as my name is Droghen, I'll not share anything with Callatae cowards except my own true sword, Heartseeker."

Dag Liogh noted the scars on the Selgovaen chest and arms and knew that here was a challenge that could not be refused. To back down after such an insult would mean his losing too much face and yet to kill him might mean war between the tribes and Rome was the enemy, not Selgovae or Callatae.

Dag freed his sword and swung his leg across in front of him, preparatory to dismounting. As he slid from the pony, he brought the heavy hilt of his sword down on the other's head; Droghen crumpled, he would take little interest for some time.

He lofted his sword and shouted, "Anyone who names a Callatae as a coward will answer to me, but I'll not kill this man for he has a brave heart and speaks only what many of you feel.

"If there are any who truly think that my tribe harbors cowards and is prepared to start a war between us, let him step forward and be the first to feel the kiss of Broadwand."

There was no rush among the Selgovae to step forward.

Dag shouted again, "Then let those among you who have a right to wear the cloak of chieftain come forward and we will discuss terms as sensible men should do. When all is done, we can celebrate this famous victory together."

This time, there was a small movement. Three warriors pushed between their companions and came to stand in front of Dag Liogh. Two were dark saturnine individuals, obviously born from the same womb, while the third was decidedly more cheerful and was thicker set. Despite his weight, this man walked like a cat, a cat who knew where all the fish heads were hidden.

All three of them, it transpired, were related to the late Chief Mellaurig. The brothers, Gorg and Drennan, were sons of the Chief's sister and Gavoc Mellaurig was the son of his brother. None of them had more than eighteen summers although all had attained their full growth.

Dag nodded, pretending to himself that this was just an ordinary occasion in the hope that his manner would therefore seem to be easy and composed.

"Welcome brothers. I'm sorry to hear of your uncle's death. I knew him and he was a brave man and an honorable one." Dag laid a slight stress on the word: honorable.

"He was a fool," said Gavoc, simply. "Had he not led us down the wall of the pass, there would be many more of my tribe here to celebrate."

The other two men looked uncomfortable at such stark words.

"I see that you have inherited more than bravery from your uncle. Nevertheless, his charge brought about the victory which we are about to celebrate and we must decide upon how to split the spoils between our tribes.

"I will say this to you. No Callatae will take a head. I decided that the wall of the pass was too steep to ride down and although our spears and arrows killed many, no Callatae were killed in personal combat. There is no honor for us in taking heads."

The three Selgovae nodded gravely, honor had been satisfied.

"My cousins and I have not yet discussed the issue of accession. It should be debated at our celebrations at Briogix so until then, we have no Chief to speak for our warriors."

Dag grinned. He liked this man—he was honest and more, his wide features and candid blue eyes appealed to him. Dag Liogh felt that they could do business together, with Gavoc Mellaurig; it might be possible to draw the links of unity between the tribes more tightly.

"Suppose that you three decide now, which of you should speak for your people. Then the discussion at your celebration will go more easily."

"A new chief is not always chosen from the heirs of the old one." This from Drennan.

"Perhaps not, but if there is an heir and he is strong enough, the discussion is a short one. Still, if the matter cannot be agreed, it will have to be fought over; it could as well be fought over now as tonight."

Gorg Mellaurig touched his brother on the shoulder and pulled him aside. They spoke quietly to each other for a few moments then more loudly to Gavoc. "We do not concede that you are in any way the better warrior, but we are agreed that your tongue is smoother than ours and that you are the cleverest of us. If you wish to claim the Chieftainship of the Selgovae tonight, we shall not contest your right."

Gavoc licked his lips and nodded. "My thanks, cousins. I shall so claim my uncle's seat, but only if both of you will sit by my side as my advisors."

The brothers nodded and ignoring Dag Liogh for the moment, Gavoc turned to the warriors who were waiting warily for the outcome of the discussion with the Callatae.

"I, Gavoc Mellaurig, shall claim the right to be elected Chief tonight. My cousins do not dispute this. I have agreed with the Chief of the Callatae that we shall take the heads of Romans killed by the sword. The rest will be burned for the right to their heads has not been earned. Spoils will be stripped from the bodies and heaped at one side until the Chief of the Callatae and I have decided the terms."

Dag Liogh admired the man. Not yet confirmed as chief, but already acting as one.

"Anyone who disagrees with this may challenge my decision. If there is no one," Gavoc waited for a space of ten heart beats, there was no challenge, "carry on."

Gavoc turned back to Dag Liogh and smiled.

"Well spoken and masterly too."

They embraced formally, a gesture which quite spontaneously became a real expression of friendship. Each pounded the other's back and at last, they drew apart, laughing. There was more here than a meeting of new Chiefs.

Picking over the bodies was a gruesome task. Limbs which but recently had been entwined in battle were now locked together in rigor mortis. In order to remove armor and leather harness, swords, money, the dead arms and legs had to be broken and there was no escape from the unseeing eyes of the dead.

Finally, though, it was done. The valuables—the weapons, armor—in short, the metal, was sorted into several piles and the few who had labored longer and taken leather shirts and linen vests, sandals or belts were allowed to retain possession.

While most of the warriors had been engaged, Dag and Manon and a few other Callatae, had ridden over the pass and explored beyond. They returned some time later leading seven horses which had strayed during the battle. The Callatae had found something else, a wagon which had been dragged over a small drop and overturned, the two oxen had died of blood loss after being hit and panicked by arrows. The wagon had been righted and emptied, three of the Callatae warriors were pulling it first up the far side of the pass and then easing it down the nearer side laden with the two dead oxen.

So much meat would turn the celebrations at Briogix into a feast of plenty. Gavoc, reckoned Dag Liogh, would have to invite the Callatae and the bond between the two tribes could only grow stronger.

⁂

MEDIONEMETON

Mandeltua was no longer a young man, nor even a man of middle years. The concentration needed to conjure visions brought its own pain, evident in the twisting of his hawkish features.

He kissed the stone, struck it against his forehead, pressed it against each temple but it remained as it had been—a strange and heavy seashell.

The Gods declined to speak with him today.

Mandeltua released the stone to swing on its leather thong about his neck and took up a bundle of holy sticks which he cast again and again onto the ground. At length, there appeared some sense to the configuration and he sighed with relief.

The sticks told him to leave Medionemeton for the south. He studied the sticks for several more minutes. Brigantea, that which he sought would be by the side of a lake between three hills. Gradually, the shape of the lake and of the hills against the sky became plain to him and he knew where to go.

CHAPTER SIX

EVENHOPE

A BACKBONE OF ANCIENT HILLS ROSE IN CENTRAL BRITON AND running northward, separated Britannia Inferior into two roughly equal areas. The northern end of the range was built from carboniferous limestone and here, the Romans had taken over several mining sites which had been in more or less continuous production for millennia.

Landslips and faults had uncovered strata where rich veins of minerals had once waited to be pried from the surrounding rock. Zinc, calamine, manganese, lead, coal: all there for the taking.

Now, after being worked for so long the intrusions had been cleared from the surface, the ore had to be dug out. Coal was mined for many of the nearby forts where it was used to heat the baths and the commandants' villas. Lead was an important mineral too, as well as being used locally to line cisterns and aqueducts and to make water pipes; it was exported and employed right across the mainland.

Evenhope was a busy establishment. Some hundreds of slaves were employed together with a smaller number of paid laborers. Roman staff managed the workforce and the kitchens and bathhouse; a single physician ran a small hospital. The slaves were housed in large rectangular wooden buildings and fed in an adjoining kitchen-refectory.

They waited outside of one of the dormitory buildings, a ragged line of exhausted men, women and older children. For two days they had been marched across country to the ring of ankle chains against rocky paths with their hands bound behind their backs. They had been fed—bread and a soup of cereal and boiled vegetables—and given water. For Marcus, the food was impossible to eat; his jaw was now set almost immovably and he could only ingest water and the liquid part of the soup through his clenched teeth.

The pain of Marcus' injuries was constant, flies buzzed around the dried blood which still caked his neck and head. His limp had raised blisters which had then burst and reduced his pace to an agonizing hobble. His whole being had become a single point of torment, to stand still and wait was a vast relief even though he swayed like a drunk, with willpower the only stick to support him.

The Optio in charge of the legionaries who shepherded the column of prisoners entered a hut leaning against the end of the dormitory. Several minutes later, he emerged behind a fat and balding civilian whose eyes seemed lost behind the puffy mounds of his cheeks. The fat man walked to one side and looked along the line of slaves; he raised his arms in silent supplication.

What have they sent me? The ill, the broken, the lame. The words were unspoken, but nevertheless clear for all to see. Aloud, he spoke in a thin reedy little voice with tones of resignation, "I suppose we had better see how many are fit enough to put in a day's work."

He waddled along the line, prodding, poking, feeling an arm here, a shoulder there and speaking his observations aloud for a scribe who followed him, to take notes on a tablet of much used and re-used wax.

"Name?" He addressed the prisoners in Latin or in the Carvetian tongue as seemed appropriate.

"Camm."

"Eh?"

"Camm."

"Furnaces."

"Name?" And so it went. "Coal heaver, mining, kitchens, mining, woodcutting…"

When all had been allocated, he addressed the prisoners as a whole. "You've been sent here for crimes committed against the State; *I* don't care what you've done or why you did it, what I *do* care about is the profitability of this mine. That's *all* I care about, right?

"A slave will live for eight years on the average, that's plenty of time to earn promotion through good work and respectful behavior. Promotion will double your life span, right?

"Work hard and you'll be fed twice a day; you'll get a sleeping pallet and a physician to cure the pox and to mend broken limbs. If, on the other hand, if you're lazy, insubordinate or fail to meet your quota, you'll be poled.

"Long life or short, you're here until you die. If anyone tries to escape, they'll be flayed; their hides'll be hung up for the birds and the flies."

He turned to walk away, but one of the prisoners, a woman, spoke up.

"We've been near starved for three days. Are you going to give us something to eat first or wait to see how many are left to be fed after a day's work?"

The fat man turned back again and laughed so that every fat wrinkle and roll of flesh shook with merriment.

"Oh, we'll feed you though why we bother I really can't say. The physician will take a look at each one of you first—we don't want you visiting the plague upon us, do we? After that, you'll get a meal and a place to rest. Tomorrow… tomorrow, my largesse runs out. Tomorrow you work.

"I'm Procurator Ellus, by the way, but I don't expect to see any of you again. If I do so, it'll be to order punishment so I don't think you'll want to see me either, will you?"

Just as the vast Ellus vanished inside his office, the world spiraled around Marcus and he passed out.

He awoke to the familiar sensation of pain and tried to remember where he was and what had happened to him. There was another sensation, the sharp smell of brimstone in his nostrils and this brought recent memories flooding back. He recalled the arrival at the mines and Ellus haranguing the prisoners, and then a veil was dropped across his memories.

Marcus was on his back and when he tried to raise himself, he found his hands tied at his sides.

"Don't move," said a voice, masculine, authoritative and speaking Latin. "Your jaw's broken and I'm doing my best."

Marcus forced his gummy eyelids apart and found a pair of grey eyes looking down into his. *Kind eyes*, he thought, *with still a little humor left in them.*

The eyes twinkled and the quizzical eyebrows rose. "You're restrained for your own safety," he said in Carvetian. "I've put two pieces of apple wood between your back teeth and I've bound your jaw tightly. You're going to chew nothing for several weeks, I'm afraid."

"I'm already used to it," Marcus tried to say, but only an indistinct mumble emerged.

"Yes, well. Water and broth. I've ordered some for you to eat before you leave. I'll check things out once a week and don't remove the bandage in between times. Right?"

"'Anks," said Marcus.

"And you're not going to talk much either, but it'll give your throat a rest. The rest of your injuries are bad, but they're mainly bruising and cuts, they'll heal. Now, I'll let you get up." The physician untied the bands which had held him to the table and Marcus struggled to his feet. The table he noticed had seen much use, blood stains and other less identifiable blemishes marked its surface.

"Sit over there." The physician indicated a bench and as Marcus hobbled towards it, a Carvetian slave brought a steaming bowl of soup into the room. Marcus' stomach rumbled and he took the vegetable broth eagerly and tilting his head up, contrived to pour the thick liquid through his just open lips.

The bowl was quite large and despite his continuing hunger, Marcus was unable to finish the contents.

"Is he finished?"

Marcus turned. He had not heard the newcomer arrive, a soldier and he had spoken in Latin with a guttural Germania accent.

"Yes, yes. I think so. You..." The physician nodded to Marcus. "Go now, but make sure you come back in seven days."

Marcus nodded and got tiredly to his feet. He crossed to the door and followed the auxiliary.

"And remember." The physician looked up from treating a young boy—Marcus had not noticed the new patient come in, either. "Don't take the bandage off or your jaw will set crooked."

The soldier took him across the site to one of the dormitory buildings. The interior was open with two rows of pillars supporting the thatched roof. The packed dirt floor was covered with bracken and Marcus realized that this would be where he slept. As he came in, there were scores of people sitting and talking around a dozen or so small hearths. He picked his way through the crowded room to a space near a fire and lay down. The atmosphere was rank with the smell of sweat and unwashed bodies mixed with smoke, he had endured worse and familiarity, he knew, would soon blunt his sense of smell.

Roman justice, tried and found guilty without a chance to speak against the charges. His attempt at removing the spear from Pintus' chest must have been misconstrued by the witnesses. It was poor comfort and there was little chance of proving his innocence now. Marcus corrected the thought. There was no chance of proving his innocence.

Just as he was falling asleep, Marcus had another thought. *What would happen to me if my fellow slaves found out I am a Roman legionary?* At least his bound jaw would prevent him from talking in his sleep.

⁂

ABALAVA

Iavolena rolled Severius' body off the bed onto a skin rug between the bed and the wall and wrapped it around him. She pushed the bed against the wall as far as it would go and methodically collected her belongings together. There were a few items which had belonged to Severius which she packed with the rest of her things; a wicked looking knife with a doubly curved blade, three silver wrist torques and a rather handsome brooch.

In the barn she found his horse still in harness and with a blanket on its back just as Titus had left him, too idle or too drunk to make the beast comfortable. Where was her own? Had Titus sold the animal along with her jewelry?

Iavolena shrugged to herself. It was too late to bother; in any case, it would save her the job of saddling and bridling the beast. She tied the largish bundle onto the harness and mounted the horse, taking it around the back of the house and out onto the narrow road which led through Abalava and on to Luguvallium.

The Fall was well and truly arrived now and this early in the morning with the sun scarcely above the horizon, the air was cold. Iavolena shivered and pulled the woolen cloak a little closer. The wind lifted brown leaves from the dirt road and blew them into her face; a gust, rather stronger than most tossed a handful of dust at the horse making it shy and Iavolena almost lost her things before getting it under control again.

She passed through a small copse which, for a few minutes, shielded her from the wind only to let it back later with renewed force. Tears from the cold air stung her eyes and blurred her vision, but the horse seemed to know its way for twenty minutes later the sounds of a busy *vicus* made her wipe her eyes and look about her. The short main street was lined on either side with timber framed houses, some of the buildings were finished with lime wash over the wattle and daub, others were built from turves, grass sprouting from each course the only decoration.

The place was crowded with people. Men leading donkeys piled high with late harvested cereal, others with a bundle of trapped hares all legs and ears. There were women with baskets of eggs, plucked birds, cakes of oatmeal and even one with a basket of black-berries picked the previous evening.

Children ran under foot making the horse nervous and skittish, children with legs like reeds and mop heads of flax, huge round eyes and snotty noses.

Iavolena, who had never considered bearing children—Septimus' children—turned away and looked straight into the eyes of a Briton who was listening to a companion. His gaze went from top to toe and then slowly back up to her face again. He grinned and transferred his attention to the horse. Beyond the two men who were dressed in heavy shirts and leather trousers were several Roman legionaries.

The horse, she thought. *They'll recognize it as military.* She dismounted and led the animal down an alley which led between a butchers and a wine merchants. Thick mud pulled at her sandals and she walked closer to the rough wall where it seemed dryer. Behind the row of shops was a low wall separating a narrow yard from more open ground; there were a few houses at some distance.

There was no one about. Iavolena led the horse through the nearest gate and untied her bundle. She left the horse there and returned to the main street, making sure the man in the leather trousers was no longer there before emerging.

She had two priorities: to find some lodging and to sell one or two pieces of jewelry. Once these had been attended to, she could begin to think of her future.

Turning left, Iavolena continued in the same direction she had been going before leaving the horse. Market stalls had been set up, temporary shops made of a plank resting across a pair of trestles or a small cart backed into a handy space. A potter's stall was piled high with gritty cream colored earthenware, a metalworker exhibited figures of the muses, of local gods and several small animals, all of them cast in lead or bronze.

Here, a cobbler squatted with a dozen pairs of wooden soled sandals hanging from a pole thrust into the ground; there, a glass blower showed off a row of small bowls while his boy built a small furnace on the edge of the road out of baked brick and soft wet clay.

Iavolena stopped to watch a juggler entertaining an encircling crowd of children and mothers before holding out his hat for a few sesterces and local coins. Moving off again, she almost tripped over a pile of baskets where a man was busily weaving willow and rushes together. "Watch where you're going, Mother." He grunted and bent over his work again.

She spoke Carvetian only slowly and it was some time before she realized what the man had said. "Mother indeed," she said, annoyed beyond all reason. "Pokey little place; where can I go?"

And as if in answer, she saw the mansio. The one place which catered to travelers without asking too many questions. She entered the doorway with some trepidation, not knowing what lay within or to whom she should speak to.

In the event, there was no problem. A woman was there, clearing up what was obviously the main room after the revelry of the previous evening.

"Um," she said and the woman, startled, gave a cry of surprise.

"Well and what can we do for you, Lady."

The woman, a native, had correctly sized up Iavolena and had spoken in broken Latin.

"A room. For several days," she said, eying the rough wooden tables and grubby layer of rushes on the floor. "My horse went lame, I've had to walk from the Ferrier's," she added by way of explanation.

"Room's three sesterces a night. Five if you want meals."

There was little choice and the room she was shown to did at least have a pallet of fresh smelling bracken and a small table. A jug of water stood on the sill in front of the open window, the air was fresh but chill.

Well, it would have to do, she thought. A few days, a week, perhaps two. Until I've sold some jewelry, raised some money.

Iavolena nodded and counted out thirty sesterces and handed them over. She looked at the empty hearth. "Can you lay a fire for tonight?"

The inn keeper's wife nodded. "At dusk." And she left to return to her cleaning.

Iavolena put her bundle on the table and opened it. The few clothes she had brought with her, she laid out on the mattress hoping that the creases would fall out. She hid most of her jewels and ornaments in the bedding—not all in the same place. Finally, three brooches and a pair of earrings in a leather bag at her waist, Iavolena left the mansio and retraced her steps along the street outside.

He was small, he was dark and wrinkled and wizened. He reminded her of a marmoset she had had as a child. In her memory, the monkey was a sad, fat little old-man figure sitting hunched over a piece of apple or chewing at its chain as it gazed out of the window at freedom. The craftsman, though, smelt of sweat and stale beer, the lines in his forehead were ingrained with dirt. His hands too, were like the monkey's, she noticed. Thin, quick, dexterous fingers.

He ignored her. He selected a ruddy stone from the scattered selection in front of him and matched it to the cavity in the silver eagle's wing he was holding. With a small forming tool, he bent the claws to hold the gem firmly in its setting and then looked up, a faint smile on his thin lips.

"My lady wishes to buy something? This, perhaps?" And he held up the newly finished brooch for her to inspect. His voice was like footsteps in gravel.

"No," said Iavolena, startled by his suddenly breaking the silence. "No, I wish to sell. I have some very good quality articles, I want the best price."

The jeweler snorted and spread his hands. "Such is always the case, Lady. So many come with no other purpose but to look, so few come to buy these days. Money is scarce— what would I pay you with?"

Iavolena was taken aback. She had not been prepared for such an eventuality. "You can't afford to buy anything from me?"

"Well, let me see what you are trying to sell. There's no harm in looking, is there?" He spread a piece of cloth over his work bench and gestured to it.

Iavolena opened her purse and put the five items down on the cloth. She watched the jeweler as he lifted each piece and held it close to his left eye.

"I can give you two hundred sesterces for the lot," he said blandly and taking up the eagle's wing clasp he had just finished, turned it over and over in his fingers.

Iavolena did not know whether to feel insulted or shamed. She picked up one of the brooches, a theatre mask carved from jet with the features depicted in tiny red stones which glittered in the strengthening sun light.

"That one cost a thousand denarii. I think you're trying to rob me and I think I'll call at the Roman garrison up the road and tell them."

The jeweler looked up at her, his eyes all but hidden behind his drooping eyelids. Blue eyes, a thin blue, like the water in a deep cistern. "I don't think you'll do that, my Lady. I'm not trying to rob anyone, I'm simply offering you what I can afford in the hope that you will agree. If times ever get better before I go to meet the Gods, I might be able to sell them on."

He gathered Iavolena's jewels together and handed them to her. "If you don't wish to take my offer, take your things and go. Go to the mansio tonight and try selling them there. The soldiers get drunk soon enough; I dare say one or two of them might be persuaded to buy something for their women."

Iavolena leaned forward and swept the jewelry from the old man's hands back into her purse. The pendant around her neck swung forward and caught his attention.

"That ornament around your neck," he said. "Where did you get that?"

Almost instinctively, Iavolena snatched it back out of his reach. She was about to tell him that her husband had bought it for her, but checked herself. "A gift," she said. "It was a gift."

"A sort of seashell, is it? One of those heavy, stony shells that are found in the rocks?" He cocked his head to one side. "I know of one who would wish to buy that. If you *do* wish to sell something, of course."

For a moment, a brief moment, Iavolena thought of parting with it, but her tongue was frozen, she could say nothing. Some sort of restraint held her immovably until she recognized the thoughts racing through her mind. *I can't sell it*, she told herself. *I mustn't lose it. Ever. It's mine, mine...* Her body grew less rigid, she regained control of herself.

"No," she said. "No, I can't sell it." She whirled about and left the workshop.

The jeweler raised his eyebrows and slowly lowered them. "As you wish, my Lady. As you wish." He heaved himself to his feet and went to the doorway, blinking in the brighter light of outside. He watched the woman almost running up the street; he saw her enter the inn. He nodded and went back inside and pulled a roll of thin birch bark from a shelf.

The jeweler sat down and unrolled the cylinder. On the inner surface, in black ink, was a message in Latin. He understood three out of five words, but what was plain was the description of several items of jewelry which matched with those he had seen spread out before him a few minutes before. In a separate passage, beneath the description, was the offer of a reward—not for the recovery of the gems as the jeweler had previously supposed. He read the words again, forming each one with his lips before saying it aloud.

"I, Vibius Gaius Septimus, Commandant of the Fort at Throp will pay a reward of one thousand denarii to know the whereabouts of my wife, Iavolena."

On this reading, the reward was clearly for knowledge of the woman, not for the jewels. There followed a description of the woman, a depiction which, save for the color of her hair, matched the woman as closely as the description of the jewels matched the ones she had brought. The passage finished with a mention of the seashell which, it said, she wore almost habitually.

The jeweler's watery blue eyes glittered. Here was a dilemma. Without doubt, this was the Iavolena mentioned. Just as certainly, the ornament around her neck was Druids' work, every craftsman in the north of Briton had known of the missing seashell stone for several years now.

Suppose the Roman officer was to be informed and the reward paid.

The jeweler recalled and earlier message, a word of mouth message from Medionemeton. That, too, had described the sea shell thing, the Druids wanted its return.

Well then, suppose that the Druids were informed also, perhaps they too, would be generous.

It would be dangerous.

The jeweler shook his head.

❦

EVENHOPE

"I am Optio Millius. I'm senior works overlooker."

The speaker was a large man with black hair and black eyes; his nose was broad with nostrils wide enough to admit one of his huge splayed thumbs. He was overbearing and arrogant, an attitude which his mighty biceps, bull-like neck and shoulders allowed him to indulge with impunity. He walked along the long rank of new slaves, peering at each face.

"You will each work ten hours every day, you will be given a quota of work which you have to fill during those ten hours." He smiled, a brief baring of the teeth. "Better your quota and I shall be pleased, I'll be nice. Fail and you will find out just how nasty I can be." Millius walked back again, timing his words to his paces.

He picked up a piece of timber and almost absent mindedly broke it over his knee. "And that's very, very nasty.

"I come from Tharsis where the mine shafts are so deep the rock is hot to the touch. We worked the slaves in twelve hour shifts day and night." He smiled again, for real this time, as if thinking of better times. "A slave did well to last six months at Tharsis, but now we must thank our Emperor, the glorious Hadrian, who decreed that you work for only ten hours each day. Aren't you lucky?"

Back up the line again, as though he was filled with a restless energy which demanded this constant movement.

"Let me give you this warning once.

"Do *anything* to annoy me and your lives will not be worth living." He snapped his fingers. "Nothing. The Procurator accepts that accidents will happen and that is what every one of you is, an accident waiting to happen. You understand? Good.

"You will now be taken to your work stations. Legionaries or seasoned workers will explain your tasks to you. Once that has been done, your first shift will start. How will you know it has finished?" Millius stopped in mid-stride and held his hand to his ear.

"Nobody? You will know because your lights will go out." And he guffawed at the joke and paced rapidly along the remainder of the line of men and women.

The compound reeked of brimstone. When the wind blew from the roasting pits where metallic lead was extracted from the ore, the concentration was strong enough to make the eyes water.

Marcus was made to join a file which was taken down the hillside and along a narrow valley, almost a gorge, with sides which were sheer rock faces for most of the way. It was a relief to leave the sulphurous atmosphere behind him.

There were holes in the rock faces, many with rope ladders hanging from the higher ones and notched tree trunks leading to the lower ones. From some of the holes, faces looked down at them; here and there, baskets of rock were being let down on ropes to groups of workers on the valley floor where they were emptied into carts.

The people he passed were generally emaciated, their expressions varied only in degree of dejection and hopelessness. Movements were slow and somehow, deliberate, made with exaggerated care. Most averted their gaze from the new slaves.

Eventually, Marcus was halted by a hand on his shoulder. He turned and came face to face with a boy who had also been stopped. The boy was maybe fourteen or so, flaxen haired and fair skinned. The legionary cupped his hands to his mouth and shouted. "Lethus, come down here." Again, "Lethus."

A head appeared at a hole on the lowest level. The man turned around and thrusting a foot out of the hole, felt for the first notch on the tree trunk-ladder. A moment later, he was stepping down the pole as lightly as a squirrel.

"Lethus. You're going to show these two what to do. They'll work adit five. Teach them quickly. Understand?"

Lethus, balding, hunch backed, nodded. His eyes, recessed into deep orbits, darted from the Legionary to his two charges and back again. "What about my quota, eh?"

"That's what I said, old man. Teach them quickly." And the Roman was gone after the rest of slaves.

"Come over here," said Lethus, grudgingly. "Here's where you pick up your tools."

He took them to a shallow overhang in the near vertical cliff and pointed to a variety of bronze and iron hammers, picks, wedges and pry bars laid out on rough wooden shelves. Below these were piles of wooden wedges, made from dried and seasoned timber.

"You'll need at least one of everything and I'd take several iron wedges and a bagful of wooden ones. You'll want water to make the wooden wedges swell, enough to drink and you'll want a lamp to see by."

Lethus picked up a wooden wedge and pressed it by hand into a crack in the rock. "Hammer it home and wet it thoroughly. It'll expand and break the rock. Break it up into smaller pieces, the boy will need some baskets to carry it away and tip it out of the adit."

"But what's the point? Breaking rocks, *making tunnels?*" Forced between his lips, Marcus' words were not clear, but Lethus picked up the meaning quickly enough.

"I'll show you the point in a moment. Climb up my ladder."

Marcus slowly followed the other up to the hole at the top of the ladder; every movement causing him pain from his injuries. Lethus crawled inside and led Marcus into the darkness. A few minutes later, his guide stopped and Marcus realized that it was not, in fact, dark, but lit dimly by a lamp, a piece of cloth floating on a bowl of oil.

"Lead," said Lethus pointing to a black line in the grey limestone. Where he pointed, the line was two fingers' breadth wide, further up, it tapered away and shrank to nothing at all. "Black lead we call it, but it isn't really lead until they've roasted it in the fire pits and melted the metal out of it."

Lethus raised a hammer and broke a piece free, he handed it to Marcus. For its size, the black lead was surprisingly heavy and its surface had the same dull sheen as the metal.

"It's in veins which go back into the rock. Sometimes a cubit or two, sometimes for hundreds. You follow it until it disappears. You make a hole in the rock big enough to work in and follow the lead. That's it."

"And what is adit five?"

"Outside. You'll have to back up."

Marcus crawled backwards, felt gingerly for the ladder and descended, step by pain-filled step. Lethus came after.

"There, see it? Up there. That's adit five. Norill used to work it. Now he makes talk with the Gods. Disappeared one day; went in, never came out."

"And that's all there is to it?"

"All? That's right. A basket a day of black lead. Less and you'll follow old Norill who grew too frail to make his quota. More and you're a foolish man."

"How long do we work?" asked the boy, silent until now.

"Until you're lamp runs dry. It'll burn for ten hours. When it goes out, climb back down here for your work to be checked."

Lethus turned his back and ran nimbly up his ladder. At the top, he paused and looked down. "Don't do anything to make Millius notice you. He likes killing people. He thinks it's fun." The hunched figure disappeared from sight.

Marcus went back to the tool dump and packed a range of them into two baskets and added a coil of rope. He pointed to a lamp and a brand of coiled straw. "Light the torch at the fire and follow me."

Like Lethus, the boy guessed what Marcus was trying to say through his immovable jaws. Marcus tied an end of the rope to a basket and the other around his waist, then began to climb the rope ladder. The ascent was slow and agonizing, by the time he reached the top, a matter of fifty feet or so, he was bathed in sweat and trembling in every limb.

He sat down at the entrance to adit five and hauled on the rope, bringing the basket up to him. He pulled it over the lip and untied the rope, letting it fall again to be secured to the other basket. He repeated the process and despite his new assistant's obvious fear of the height, the boy struggled to the top of the ladder before Marcus brought the rest of the tools up.

"Here we are," muttered Marcus and patted the panting boy on the head. "Our future." He moved back from the edge and made room for the boy. "What's your name?"

"Ennig." The boy looked at the dark entrance. "I'm called Ennig. I don't like it up here."

"Nor do I." Marcus' tone was consoling. "We have to get used to it though. Millius seems the sort of man who enjoys beatings, not the sort who'll listen to our fears. And if we want to be fed, we'd better get to work, I think."

The boy nodded doubtfully.

"Come on. Bring the baskets."

The opening in which they had been sitting was only half Marcus' height and somewhat less than that in width. Marcus backed further in and lit the lamp, between them; they pushed the tools along the dark tunnel.

The adit turned, first to the left and then the right, cutting out all sight of the entrance. Once contact with the outer world was lost, Marcus became conscious of the weight of rock above him, pressing down on the little passageway they were crawling through. He could hear the steady drip-drip of water, the sound of a stone falling and bouncing as a fragment of rock broke loose. The floor was gritty and damp; a trickle of water ran along one side, towards the entrance.

Claustrophobia was something which he had never felt before, even in caves, but here, with the rock squeezing in on him… *What if there were a rock fall?* Marcus realized that he could die here; crushed, asphyxiated, merely left to starve because no one would bother to dig him out.

Marcus couldn't move. His hands and arms were trembling again. He was paralyzed.

Quite clearly, he heard the boy spit. "Romans," said the young voice. "Romans. I hate them. They killed my mother and father and did horrid things to my sister. They're barbarians."

And with that, Marcus was freed. He wanted to laugh. How many times had he heard the Romans accuse the natives of Briton and Albyn of being barbaric. In reality, now he thought of it, they were just different. How many Romans—real Romans—did he know.

Four? Five? Perhaps five of his friends had actually felt the heat of the Roman sun, drunk wine in a tavern off the Forum. All the others he knew had been posted from all over the Empire. They were no more Roman than he, himself … *But I am Roman. My father's a Roman Senator. And I'm a criminal. A slave in the lead mines.*

"Some soldiers will do that sort of thing whatever side they're on," he told Ennig. Come on."

"Which way do we go then?"

"Hm?"

Marcus looked up. The tunnel widened slightly and split into two passages. He chose the left hand passage; the floor seemed to be drier. However, only a few moments later, he had to back out, the way was barred by three balks of wood which had been wedged in between the floor and roof.

"Blocked," he explained to Ennig. "Better try the other way. Have you got the water?" With just the small amount of practice, the words came a little more clearly, or perhaps, Ennig got the gist more easily.

"Here." He passed the gourd to Marcus.

Marcus held it up and let the water dribble between his lips.

"What's the matter with your face?"

"Mm? Some legionaries decided it would look better if they kicked it about a bit."

"Barbarians."

"Yes, well maybe you're right, young Ennig. Let's try the other way now, we've got to start earning our food."

They crawled along the right hand way and found that it widened a little, enough to push past two baskets stacked one on top of another close to the wall.

"Now what have we here?" Marcus reached in and brought out a handful of pebbly material. It felt peculiarly solid and surprisingly heavy. "Black lead. A gift from our predecessor I think and a lesson."

"What do you mean?"

"Lethus said if we dig more than our quota, we're fools. It seemed sound advice at the time. But if we dig more than our quota and store it for when the work gets difficult, we buy time. Let's get to the end of the tunnel."

They reached the working face and in the lamp light, Marcus found the black traces of lead in the rock.

"Here, do you see?" He showed the boy. "This is what we have to get. Now I'm going to need the light to see what I'm doing. You're going to have to fill a basket with the broken rock and push it back to the entrance in the dark. Can you manage that?"

"Of course I can manage it." Ennig was a little indignant.

"And another thing. It's not just my face, the Romans broke some ribs and I'm still badly bruised. It's going to be a while before I can dig properly. Old Norill's gift is going to have to make up our quota until I recover."

Ennig nodded. "A piece of luck, then."

"Very good luck. Now, I'm going to start. Watch your eyes."

Marcus set to work. At first, every blow he struck with the hammer wrung aches and pains from his bruises, but eventually, his body seemed to grow used to the punishment. The pain became dulled, a constant that he was able to put to the back of his mind.

He broke away the rock along the seam of galena and when he could make no more impression that way, he hammered in the wedges and wet them. The wood swelled and the limestone gave way with audible cracks. More hammer and pry bar work loosened the rock and he pushed the chips behind him for Ennig to clear away.

The galena, black lead, he pushed to one side, keeping it separate.

"What's *your* name?" asked Ennig after one of his trips to the entrance.

Marcus sat back on his heels and wiped the sweat from his face. "Uffin."

"Just Uffin?"

"Uffin Gellorix."

"Not from hereabouts then."

"No." Marcus was about to tell the boy, but thought better of it. "North," he said. "North and east, near the Wall. Let's put this black lead in a basket and see how much there is."

The basket was two thirds filled.

"We can put some in from the store; we don't have to work so hard then."

"Not a good idea, Ennig. At the moment, the rock crumbles easily enough. Tomorrow or the next day, it may be hard. That's when we use the stored up lead. Think that sounds right? After all, we're partners in this."

Marcus could see the boy's mouth open in a grin. "I think you have it right, Uffin. You know that other branch?"

"The closed off passage? Yes."

"There're birds roosting in there. A couple each would make a tasty meal."

"We'll keep it in mind if the Romans don't feed us properly. I can only take broth and wine until my jaw heals up, so we can keep your idea until later."

"Right. I'll clear this lot then. The light's going you know. Outside."

"It's going in here too, the oil's more or less gone. You clear this lot of rock and I'll pack the rest of the lead in the basket here. I think we might need a little from the store after all, not too much though."

A few minutes after Ennig had left, the lamp started to gutter and with the last of its light, Marcus filled the basket of ore from those left by his predecessor. He put the lamp on top of the basket and continued on to the entrance, meeting the boy already on his way back.

"I've tipped twenty baskets of rock out of here," he said. "Twenty baskets and we've got just one full of black lead."

"I'd guess that was pretty good," said Marcus. "How come you know so much about counting?"

"I went to school in our village and my mother grew vegetables for the garrison. She made me count, so we didn't get cheated by the Romans."

"You went to school? The same one the Roman's children went to?"

"Sure. I was the best in school at counting, better than the Romans. They just *think* they're better."

Marcus laughed at the boy's pride. He looked outside. There were people congregating, standing in line with baskets to be tallied. "We'd better get along. I'll lower our basket while you climb down."

"I hate this ladder thing."

"Believe me, I feel the same way."

"Let the basket down. I'll wait. If you go first, will you steady the thing for me?"

"I will. Gladly. This won't take a minute."

For the first time since he had been taken prisoner, Marcus felt alive again. There would be a way out of this, somehow he would find it.

⚜

ABALAVA.

Lying on her bed of bracken, Iavolena could hear the sounds of congress which was taking place on the other side of the partition wall.

Rutting pigs, she thought as the grunts and squeals grew louder. She got up and went to the window, trying to ignore the noises. The main door was almost directly below her window; two legionaries and an officer left the mansio and stood for a few minutes, talking. Iavolena recognized the voice, she leaned out a little further; yes, he was the one she had tried to sell a pendant to.

Earlier, when she heard the common room filling up with soldiers, Iavolena had gone down with two of her ornaments.

The air was already thick with the fumes of wine and small beer and the cheap perfume worn by many of the Brythonic women. None of the legionaries seemed to be interested in the jewelry; they were more preoccupied with fondling their women who seemed pleased with the attentions they were getting.

She looked for officers. There were two or three decurions there, a pair of centurions playing dice in a corner and a tribune sitting by himself, drinking steadily.

Morose expression. Probably trouble with a woman. Iavolena grinned at the thought and passed him by. She crossed to the two dice players; she leaned over the nearer man's shoulder and watched the play. He threw once, twice and won both times, scooping the pool of copper and silver coins.

"Got a nice girl, Sir?" she murmured. "She'd love this, wouldn't she?" Iavolena held a pendant out, moving it slowly so that the gems glittered in the lantern's light. "She'd love you all the more, don't you think?"

The soldier grinned and watched the sparkles. "No, Lady. I don't think I can afford that."

"Four hundred? Cheap at twice that."

"Doubtless. Who did you steal it from?" And he tried to grab it.

Iavolena, faster than he, snatched it out of his reach. "It's mine. A gift."

"Tell you what. How about we go up to one of the upstairs rooms, hm?"

He snaked an arm around her waist and pulled her closer. "If you're a bit short of money, I'll pay you, hm, twenty. How does that sound?" And he ran his hand over her breast and watched the nipple rise beneath the cloth.

Iavolena tried to back away, but couldn't break his hold.

"Look. I'll make it thirty sesterces." And he began to touch her more intimately.

Iavolena took her little pearl handled knife out of its sheath on her girdle. The officer's expression was almost comical when he realized what the length of cold metal alongside his temple was.

He removed his arm with indecent haste and making as dignified an exit as she could, Iavolena left the common room. She watched the three men leave, heading up the almost deserted street towards the distant garrison.

Perhaps I should have taken up his offer. What options am I left with, she wondered. She had very little money; she couldn't seem to sell any of her jewelry. Titus had managed to do so, what made it so difficult for her?

Suppose she returned to her husband. She could say that Titus had forced her to go with him, that he had raped her. It wouldn't be difficult to make Septimus believe her, he'd lap up the explanation and order the fellow flogged to death—he wouldn't know that Titus' was dead and there'd be no reason for her to admit to Titus' murder.

Iavolena smiled. She could return to her comfortable home again. So it was a bit dreary, it had a bath house and a full staff and...

Her daydreams ran down. Cerea was back there. She'd killed her—but she'd tell them that Titus had done it. No, it was her dagger stuck so fast in her ribs that it wouldn't come out—well, Titus could still have done it. It was his fault that she couldn't get it free, he'd shouted at her to hurry, he'd panicked her.

Oh Gods. She'd dressed Cerea in her gown, to make them think it was her, that was why she had disfigured the woman... Not even Vibius, her husband, would believe that.

There was no way back. She had to get money, get out of Briton, back to Rome, her family. Iavolena sobbed, her problems piled higher and higher every time she thought about them.

Money. Money…

The jeweler. He'd been interested in her sea shell. He'd been willing to buy it and she'd left. Why should she have done that? What had made her?

The jeweler had said he might have a buyer for it. *No*, she thought again, *he had said that he knew a buyer.* Perhaps she could insist on going to meet this buyer, sell it herself. The awful little man would want a commission, but it would get her away from this squalid little vicus where someone might recognize her and report to her husband.

She resolved to see the jeweler again the following morning and an hour later she had changed her mind. She got up, washed and left her room.

By rush light, Murrag the jeweler wrote slowly, his hand was small and neat, each character incised into the wax like an engraved line on a piece of silver. He explained that he knew where Septimus' wife was lodging and explained too, his right to the reward being offered.

The tablet would go next morning at first light. He knew several of the riders who took dispatches along the line of forts on the Wall and on the Stanegate.

Murrag considered the message he would also send north, to the Druids. That would have to be by word of mouth and therefore, must be kept simple. He had to let them know who possessed the mystic stone, that was all. He would have kept faith with the Druids and with the Gods; he could not be blamed if her husband came and carted her off back to…

"A fine evening, Jeweler," she said. "When can we leave to meet this man who desires my sea shell pendant so much?"

CHAPTER SEVEN

EVENHOPE

FOR SIX WHOLE WEEKS AND TWO DAYS, MARCUS LIVED ON BROTH and blood mixed with mare's milk. He craved food; he dreamed of food, it came to obsess his waking hours.

On his sixth visit to the physician, the man said, "Come and see me the day after tomorrow, I think your jaw is as good as it's ever going to get and your ribs have healed up *far* better than I expected."

When Marcus kept the appointment after finishing his day's work, the physician cut away the bandages.

"Hm. Not a bad job. You can spit out those chips of wood now."

Marcus did as he suggested. The wood was black and heavily indented where his teeth had bitten into it.

"Your mouth smells like a bear's den, young man. Wash it with wine, eat some fruit and start exercising your jaws. Fruit, bread but go easy on nuts and hard biscuits."

"Well, thank you. Thanks." Marcus rubbed his chin which was thick with bristles. "Do you think I could shave? We aren't allowed a knife out there and it itches where the bandages have been."

The physician nodded. "Make it fast, there's water over there, in the corner." He sorted through a box of small implements not too dissimilar from a carpenter's tools. "There's a knife. Take care; it's a lot sharper than most knives. There's a mirror too."

A moment or two later, Marcus was cutting the growth of beard away while the physician watched him closely. After shaving, he quickly took the knife from Marcus.

"Hm. A handsome lad. Pity it's wasted in a place like this." He cleaned the knife and placed it with his other tools.

Marcus moved his jaw from side to side, up and down. Everything worked as it should; even the memory of pain had gone. He examined his newly bared face in the bronze speculum. It was thinner than he remembered, gaunt almost, but then, he was thinner all over. There were one or two scars left from his beating, a pink half-moon against his pale skin just above the left eyebrow and another jagged lesion across his left cheek.

"Come on now. It's time you left." The doctor spoke sharply. "Your time belongs to Rome; it isn't for you to spend admiring yourself. Go with good fortune."

Marcus grinned briefly. "Well, thank you again though fortune has left me I'm afraid. I'd not be here otherwise."

The other held up his hand. He had often had to listen to prisoners who were convinced that justice had not been done. "Everyone here feels that they do not deserve to be—even me, if it comes to that. Speaking about it will do you no good." He put his head on one side; a quizzical expression came to his face. "No one can do anything about it; you just have to learn to live with the fact. Now off you go, there are others who need my services."

One of the buildings in the complex served as both kitchen and refectory. Here, the slaves who worked the mines and smelting pits were served by those considered unsuited to the more laborious work—mostly women and the older males.

Marcus sat with Ennig and waited for his bowl to be filled. He could not leave his chin alone, it felt unnaturally cold and the smooth skin was novel. However, when his bowl was filled with a thin soup, scraps of meat, and a large piece of unleavened bread was offered him, hunger and the smell of food made him forget his newly shaven state.

There were, he knew, second helpings for those who finished first and tonight, Marcus was certainly among the earliest to finish. Much to Ennig's amusement, he held up his bowl as others did, to attract the attention of one of the servers.

"You'll get fat," said Ennig. "You won't be able to get into the tunnel and I shall have to do all the digging, then we shall fall behind our quota and get beaten—all because you're a glutton."

"I don't care," Marcus replied. "This is the first time I've been able to open my mouth for..." The heavy bowl hit the table with a resounding *thump*; soup slopped over the edge and ran over the edge of the table. Ennig was quick enough to catch quite a lot in his own bowl.

Marcus looked up. The girl was staring at him with what he took to be a horrified expression. "What's the matter?" And he, too, stopped and looked at the girl in shocked recognition.

"Uffin? Is it you? *Really* you?"

"Asel? Callog's daughter?"

He hadn't recognized her in the first moments; indeed, she may have been here as long as he had without his noticing her. She seemed much older than when he had last seen her, more mature. She had been shy then, back at High Sil, an awkward, coltish girl between maiden and womanhood.

Asel was on the verge of weeping, her eyes bright with sudden tears. "They caught you, too?" Despair was there in her whisper.

Marcus put his hand over hers. "There'll be a way out, there always is." He saw hope replace the dejection.

"Hey. Leave the women alone, slave."

Marcus knew the voice and when he turned, it was to see Optio Villius' evil grin. He opened his mouth to speak, but the Officer's fist caught him on the temple and sent him sprawling among the rushes and food scraps.

"Slaves don't get women, they're for real men. Now stay down there where you belong. You stir from there before I've eaten and left here," he said conversationally, matter-of-factly, "and I'll kill you." He sat down in Marcus' place and banged his own dish onto the table top. "Now food, girl and don't keep me waiting."

Asel began to lift the soup bowl, in order to pour some into Villius' dish.

"Not that filthy stuff you stupid child. Bring me some meat and good bread from the kitchen and a pitcher of wine." He turned back to Marcus, still on the floor. "I think I shall probably have to kill you anyway, you've that look about you. But I'll not do it on an empty stomach."

Asel brought the food and Marcus, using common sense, stayed where he was on the floor. Villius was a huge man; he was strong and he was armed. Only a fool would have opposed him and Marcus was nobody's fool. If there came a time when he had to fight the Optio, it would be when and where he chose to.

Villius wolfed down his meal and emptied the wine jug before he spoke again to Marcus. "You've surprised me slave. I thought you would have provoked me." He kicked Marcus in the kidneys with a vicious accuracy. "Another time perhaps. We'll see."

When Villius had left, he and Ennig left the refectory to walk back to their own dormitory building.

"You know that woman?" Ennig asked, at length.

"I knew her father. Well, yes, and her, too, I suppose. From the land of the Selgovae. Where do they live, the kitchen staff?"

If Ennig found his sudden interest surprising, the lad kept it to himself. "Over there, I think." He pointed to a large hut adjoining the kitchen area. He yawned hugely. "Next to the store room."

The following morning Marcus filed out with the others for their ration of weak porridge. He watched the staff expectantly and was eventually rewarded with a glimpse of Asel although her duties seemed to keep her away from him. He dared not stand up to attract her attention because it would attract that of Villius too, so he had to content himself with watching her covertly.

He longed to ask her how she came to be here, how long she had been here, so near and unsuspected. He wondered too, why the girl had become so important to him, what had made today so different to yesterday and all those days that had gone before.

Marcus found himself taking more interest in their surroundings as the column of slaves made their way to work. There were only two legionaries accompanying them now, one at the head and one at the rear; sometime in the past weeks, the original six man guard had been reduced. The path was dark, a paler grey in the pre-dawn grayness and he noticed the frost sparkling when the torches carried by the two Romans flared in the breeze. The year had advanced without his realizing it, winter was drawing near.

Marcus found the labor becomingly progressively harder despite his injuries having healed. His inadequate diet was causing him to gradually lose weight; although his muscles were hard and his limbs tough and sinewy; there was less and less body bulk to do the work. More and more, the reservoir of galena built up by their predecessor was called upon to make up the quota.

Another day or two passed, he watched for Asel at mealtimes and ate as much as he could get to assuage his continual hunger. Perhaps the more solid food was making a difference, perhaps not; it was hard to be sure yet. He and Ennig climbed up to adit five where work had become a matter of routine. Marcus hammered, drove wedges and broke rock; he separated the lead ore from the dross. Ennig filled baskets with the waste and tipped them out of the mouth of their tunnel.

Except for the temperature outside, there was little to distinguish one day from another until a particular morning, Marcus found more water dripping from the cracks in the limestone.

Raining outside, he told himself and began to chase the drainage channel a little deeper in order to stop the water pooling around his knees. Back at the face, Marcus drove another wedge into the niche where he had cleaned the black lead from. He heard the rock crack, felt it loosen under his hand. He put in a pry-bar and levered the block out. The block was large, far bigger than usual; the surface behind it was in shadow.

Marcus raised the lamp and peered into the hole. The rock face was almost white, darkening as water began to run down it; of the seam of black lead he had been following, there was no trace.

It didn't make sense. It had been there, as thick as his thumb, he had followed it for more than fifteen feet—up, down, side to side, but always there. Now it was as if a God had leaned into the tunnel and wiped away the trace.

What would they do to him now? Villius! Villius would kill him; seal him up here in adit five to die. The rock walls pressed in from each side, the roof bore down on him. Marcus sweated and a chill spread over his body.

There was something clattering, ringing like a bell.

With a huge effort, Marcus regained his senses to find his hand shaking, the pry-bar clanging against the stony floor.

He crawled slowly towards the entrance. Two birds were silhouetted momentarily against the light from outside. They brushed past Marcus in a flurry of wings; he cringed until the sound of their flight had died away.

Ennig was sitting at the opening, far enough inside to remain hidden from observation. Turning at the sound of Marcus' approach, he put a finger to his lips—the universal signal for silence in every language of the known world. Ennig pointed out and down and made room for Marcus who slumped against the wall and gulped in great lungfuls of fresh air.

"What?" he said at last.

"Darnia's in trouble."

Marcus lay on his stomach and pushed himself close to the edge. Villius was down there standing over a prostrate man, kicking him repeatedly.

"Six years," he was declaiming at the top of his voice. "Six years you've been here and you've grown old and fat with our lenient ways. *Bad air?* How can there be bad air, no one else is complaining. None of these shafts is more than a hundred paces deep; we've never used bell pits. You don't know what bad air is except as an excuse for not filling your allotment, do you?"

Villius gave him an extra heavy kick and then stood back as the slave vomited up his last meal.

"Filthy animal." The overseer stepped back out of the way as blood followed the stomach contents. "Get him away from me, from here," shouted Villius as the man began to convulse, but it was already too late. Darnia fell still, in all probability, dead.

Marcus was ashamed to even acknowledge that he was half Roman. Rage replaced the last of the claustrophobia, his face became red with blood and he got to his hands and knees, feeling for the top of the rope ladder.

"No," said Ennig, pulling Marcus' arm back and when this had no effect, bracing his legs across the opening. "No Uffin. You don't stand a chance. You'll get killed." And after a moment's struggle, Marcus subsided in frustration.

He crawled away back into the darkness and had to duck once more as wings buffeted him around the head. He was at the point where the adit divided and could just make out the forms of several more birds flying out between the wooden uprights.

Curiosity overtook him. For the first time since they had come to this adit, he wondered why the timbers had been wedged there. To stop ingress, obviously, but why? What for?

He set his legs against the wall and heaved at the base of one of the central timbers. It came away so easily that he fell over backwards; the timber was quite rotten at the lower end. The others came away as easily. They could hardly have been put there to prevent entrance, merely to discourage it.

Marcus crawled into the opening he had made. The walls and roof were dimly visible for a few feet onward, the tunnel having much the same proportions as the part he and Ennig worked in.

He crawled on; it seemed to become darker around him. The roof disappeared into gloom and as suddenly, his outstretched hand met nothing, the floor too, was gone. He was kneeling at the edge of a void.

A cavern? Surely this might be a way of escape, the possibilities mounted as he considered them. Marcus remembered Lethus telling them about Norill who used to work adit five. "*Went in, never came back.*" But the Romans would not have left a few insecure posts to bar the way to escape, surely?

He turned back and crawled to the entrance once more.

"Ennig, pass me the brands and go and get the lamp from up near the face." The boy passed the bundles of resinous pine wood which were also soaked in oil and then squeezed past Marcus to bring the lamp.

Marcus went back to the tunnel branch which Ennig had passed without noticing the absent timber posts.

"Okay," said Marcus as Ennig returned. "We'll see what's up here." He led the way and lit a torch from the lamp. It took a while to catch from the small flame but eventually it was burning well and casting a bright glow.

"My father's spirit," Ennig whispered as he saw what was revealed.

The brand illuminated the ceiling as it rose and disappeared beyond the range of the flames; similarly, the floor fell away in a steep slope. On either hand, the walls continued, the space between them as wide as a man's outstretched arms. It was a huge fissure between two mountainous walls of ancient stone.

Marcus lit another torch and when there were two of them burning, the far side of the fissure could just be seen.

"Look." Ennig pointed down the slope where tumbled boulders had collected and covered the floor.

Where the slope, mostly clay and small rocks, met the pile of boulders, there was a heap of bones. The skull lay a little apart from the rest, on its side and grinning up at them. The skull was unmistakably human.

"Norill," said Marcus. "Old Norill who went in, but never came out. Well now we know what the posts were there for and we know there's no escape this way."

"Hm," said Ennig. "The lamp's burning its last, we'd better gather up the galena for the tally."

"The lead has run out," Marcus told him as they went back to the face and he explained how the vein had vanished. As fate would have it, Marcus had actually exceeded the daily reckoning, one of the few days when there was enough to add a little back into their hoard.

"It might be a good idea to ask some of the older workers what happens when the lead gets worked out," he suggested as they joined the column returning to the living area.

❦

SELGOVANTIA

The two men sat facing one another. Dag Liogh on a fallen log and Gavoc Mellaurig on a rock outcrop. Both had brought retainers with them, Manon and two others on Dag's side while Gavoc had come with his cousins. The five of them sat a little way off, talking among themselves and out of earshot of the two chiefs.

"They don't know the meaning of time," Gavoc was saying. "They tell us tomorrow and it means in a hand of days, a week and it means a month."

"I know. 'A signal' they told me. A sign to all the Britons and Albyns that we would chase the Romans out of our lands and what have we done? Lost many sons from both our tribes and gained a few skulls."

Gavoc shook his head. "And the rest of them grow restless." He spat into the stream which gurgled an arm's length away. "What do we do, Dag?"

Dag lifted his shoulders and let them drop. "We can send a runner to Medionemeton. Ask for guidance."

"If you think it will do any good. I think we should plan our own action. The Druids promised us good booty when we crossed the Wall and burned those forts. The only reward many of our people had was a short jump in to the next world, Dag. I think we could do it better, the two of us."

Dag smiled. "I cannot say that you are wrong, Gavoc. Let me send a message first and see what the Druids tell us. If they have nothing to say then we can do as you say."

Gavoc shook his head. "Send your message, Dag, but let us plan while he goes and returns. That way, we waste less of the time that the Druids have left us."

⚜

ABALAVA

Iavolena had been becoming progressively more frustrated over the past three weeks.

Murrag the jeweler had at first refused to take her to meet with his buyer. It was only after Iavolena had visited him three more times over the next two days that he began to see the matter differently.

Even then, he was not to be hurried. His buyer was a regular business contact from across the water, from Erin. Eventually, Iavolena realized where the land was that the jeweler was speaking of and that there was a regular trade conducted with that land.

So more time came and went and her funds dwindled. There came a time when she could no longer afford a room at the mansio out of the little money she had left. She talked Murrag into letting her stay in a dusty little store room above his shop.

It was, perhaps, fortunate that she had done so. It was only a passing remark from Murrag that warned her that Septimus had offered a reward for knowledge of her whereabouts. Now, although Iavolena had always been a fastidious woman, she dared no longer go to the public baths at the north end of the vicus and she had to prevail upon Murrag to procure food for her as well as providing living space.

She sat at the window of her room and watched the tiny world go by outside, she listened to gossip from passers-by and heard of the discovery of a man's body up at the villa near the river. *How long would it take before he was identified? Would there be people who would remember me?*

Murrag, for his part, lived in a pair of back rooms behind the shop and despite Iavolena's fears that the old man would be forever importuning her, he stayed there. They saw each other only on those occasions when she descended to give him money for food and to take her shopping from him and also when she enquired of his progress.

Finally, Murrag *did* ascend the stairs and he banged on her door.

"Oh, it's you Murrag."

"We shall be leaving in the morning. At sun-up."

Murrag had two ponies and two donkeys. The donkeys carried huge loads of goods and supplies for several days at least. He and Iavolena would ride the ponies while a boy of thirteen or so added his weight to one or other of the donkeys' loads.

Iavolena complained about the pony she had to ride. A horse would have been more fitting to her station, she said, more comfortable.

Murrag shrugged, it was the pony or a donkey. Iavolena capitulated and only an hour or so later than he had planned, Murrag's small convoy set off for Stanwyx where his regular comings and goings were well known to the Roman gate keepers.

⁂

EVENHOPE

The column of weary men and women trudged slowly past the refectory. Asel was busy at the well, she had been there for some time, in fact, already she had emptied the two huge jars back into the shaft three times and hauled them up full as slowly as she dared.

At last she saw Marcus and the boy Ennig coming and watched them draw near.

It had been a great shock when she had seen and recognized him that day, a week or more ago. After the Romans had picked her up on their retreat from the Sand Crag debacle, she had expected never to see anyone she knew again; certainly not Uffin Gellorix whose very presence had confused her and made her blush. Now he was the only glimmer of light in the darkness, the only familiar thing she could hold on to. Now that attention, as slight as it had been was her undoing.

Avoiding the notice of the bored guards at head and tail of the column, she joined the workers and walked alongside of Marcus.

"Uffin," she said and caught at his sleeve.

Marcus turned, surprised, pleased to see her.

"Uffin, it's been so good to see you, I'm so glad we met again. I don't think I shall see you again though."

Marcus frowned then he smiled again. "You mean they're releasing you?"

"No, no. Villius has told the kitchen supervisor to pick someone to replace me. He wants me for his personal slave; he's been eying me ever since you and I recognized each other." Asel bit her lip. "Everyone knows what that means."

Marcus stiffened at the news. By speaking to her it had been he who had drawn Asel to Villius' notice. Troubles did not come singly at Evenhope.

Thoughts ran through his mind, were discarded, retrieved and thrown away again. *Time*, he thought, *if only there was a little more time.* "When do you go?"

"Tonight. After the meal."

"Is there any fresh meat around, freshly killed meat?"

"There's some pheasant, a brace of hares. They're already prepared for the Tribune's table tomorrow."

"Find the lights that have been taken out and rub a loin cloth in the blood. Wear it."

"Uffin!"

"Wear it damn you, and swear it's your time of the moon. I'll think of something tomorrow, but it will give us a day or two."

"Thank you, Uffin, thanks."

"And meet me tomorrow, here. In fact," Marcus was thinking as he spoke, "get hold of as much food as you can carry. Bread, the Tribune's pheasants, anything. Cover your head with a cloth as the miners do and join us tomorrow morning. The guards are pretty lax now, nothing ever happens for them to worry about. All right?"

"I'll try."

"Don't try, just do it."

"Yes. Yes, Uffin. I'll do it."

There was a quiver in her voice, but Marcus smiled, the girl held herself erect and there was a determined look on her face. "Right."

Asel clutched his arm and stood on tiptoe to brush her lips against his cheek. Then she turned and was gone back to her water jars.

Marcus ate absently, watching Asel from the corner of one eye and Villius from the other. He saw Villius finish his meal and nod to Asel to accompany him, he did not see her again before he left.

The remainder of the night he slept fitfully, between making plans and trying to cover every contingency he could think of. He was red-eyed and weary by the morning and breakfasted poorly, Asel was not there.

The slaves trooped down the defile into the cliff-bound valley and dropped off in twos and fours. He was now so preoccupied with worry and fears for Asel that he stumbled and slipped on the loose stones underfoot.

A hundred or so paces before they reached adit five, there was a tug on his sleeve.

"Asel!"

"I followed you a while, to make sure I hadn't been noticed."

"Thank the Gods you came." He nodded to the openings in the rock face. "That is where Ennig and I work."

At the sound of his name, Ennig turned. "What?"

"Nothing. But when we stop, I want you to go and get a full basket of wooden wedges, all right?"

"Yes, but..."

"No buts. Just take your time. A full basket and two lamps."

He turned back to Asel and spoke more quietly. "When Ennig leaves, follow me as though you work with me."

A minute later, Ennig left the column and partly hidden by the gloom of the autumn morning, Marcus and Asel left and headed for the ladder to adit five.

"You are going to have to climb this rope ladder. I'll hold it firm at the bottom, but you must climb it as fast as you can. Your life, our lives depend on getting you out of sight as quickly as possible."

"Can I leave the food down here, it must weigh half as much as I do."

Marcus found a discarded basket and as she brought out bundles from beneath her cloak, he packed them in.

"Now go."

Asel scrambled up the ladder creditably fast on the lower rungs where Marcus held them taut, but more slowly as she approached the middle stretch.

"Who's that?" Ennig had returned from the stores with the wedges that Marcus had asked for.

"That's Asel."

"The girl you've been mooning over these last few days. You're mad, Uffin. You can't have a private little love nest up there, it's..."

"Don't you think I know all that?" He spoke desperately. "Now be quiet, you'll draw attention to us."

Asel was now near the top. Again, it was easier to climb closer to the pegs which anchored the ladder to the rocks, and she was soon over the lip and into the dark tunnel mouth.

"Now you."

Finally, Marcus followed them with the basket of food and at the top, found Ennig muttering furiously at Asel.

"Not now Ennig. Asel is an old friend of mine, I mean the daughter of an old friend of mine. You saw Villius kick Darnia to death yesterday, well now he wants Asel and I can't allow that."

"*You* can't allow that? What about me, Uffin? It's my life that you're playing dice with as well as yours and hers."

"That's enough Ennig. You hear me? That's all. Asel, come with me." He took the lamp and crawled into the tunnel, he took her into the branch which led to the cave. He could hear Ennig following on after.

"I'm sorry," he said to Ennig when they stopped. "I won't pretend that this has not put us all in danger. But last night I was thinking about this place. Now watch."

Marcus put the lamp down on the edge of the floor, where it fell away into the fault.

"Look at the flame. You see? It bends away from the cave, towards the entrance out there."

"So there's a breeze coming from in there."

"Which means..?"

Ennig calmed down and thought about it. "Which means there's a way out?"

"Maybe. There's certainly a way in for air, but it might be too small for us to get through."

"But it's our only hope?"

"Asel's and mine, but not yours. I'll tie you up and gag you before we go; they'll think it's just me that's escaped."

"Villius may not bother to see it like that. He just likes killing."

Miserably, Marcus nodded.

"I just didn't know what else to do."

"How much ore have we got stockpiled?"

Marcus shrugged. "More than a day's, maybe as much as two."

"Which gives us three days to work down there, finding a way out. Asel can stay here at night."

"It'd be cold, but I suppose she could."

"Unless Villius gets suspicious and thinks you're to blame for Asel's disappearance."

"He won't do that." Marcus grinned. "Not for three or four days, anyway." His face fell. "Oh, *corruption*."

"What?"

"What's the matter?" asked Asel.

"My idea with you gave us a few day's grace, I've just wasted them. They're just wasted." Marcus could hardly believe it. Madness. "He wouldn't have touched you for days, a man like that. He'd have made sure..."

"Yes, yes," replied Asel. "I know what you mean, but some men *don't* care, do they? Perhaps he would have got tired of waiting and taken me anyway."

"Well. I'm going to explore this cave place." Ennig went to the edge and began to inch his way down the treacherous slope.

"I'll get some torches."

Marcus brought the two torches he found at the tunnel entrance and tossed them down to Ennig. "I'll go and bring some more."

"No," called Ennig. "That's not what we do, someone will be suspicious if we do things that aren't ordinary. I'll go. You come down here."

They changed places, Marcus took the lamp from Ennig and began to circle the small cavern.

"What can I do?" called Asel. "I've caused all this; there must be something I can do."

"Bring the food inside, down here."

Marcus spoke absently. He had already found a place where the draught, coming through a small chink in the rock fall, was a relative hurricane.

When Ennig returned and had a brand burning brightly, Marcus carefully moved the skeleton and he also lifted a fair number of boulders aside. Asel held the torch aloft and both of them worked at clearing the obstruction. An hour and three brands later, the top of what could have been a side tunnel appeared, air blew from it, a constant breeze which kept them cool.

More was uncovered and more. A sudden fierce wind blew the brand out and then all movement of air ceased.

"What was that?"

"Perhaps this goes all the way down to Pluto's lair and he doesn't want us getting any closer."

Ennig didn't know whether Marcus was serious or not. "Pluto doesn't reign here. We Carvetians have enough Gods of our own, but I suppose it could lead to the Underworld. Perhaps Belanos the shining one will light our way if we dig a bit harder."

"Perhaps he will." Marcus smiled, forgetting that the expression was all but invisible in the dim light of the oil lamp on its outcrop pedestal. "Let's light the torch again."

They moved more rocks and more, only to eventually find the side chamber also full of rocks too.

"So much for a way down to the Underworld," said Ennig and slammed the rock he'd been holding down on to the heap of boulders they had revealed. There was a rumble and the stones began to roll. Marcus lost his footing and was swept down into the moving mass of rocks.

A minute later, the slide had finished, but Marcus was wedged between several large boulders with only his head and shoulders showing.

"Hold on, Uffin. Hold on."

"Take it carefully, Ennig." Marcus laughed. "Very carefully. My legs are free, I think I'm wedged into Belanos' ceiling."

Ennig and Asel worked hard, lifting boulders and setting them aside until Marcus was able to pull himself out of the trap. He took a torch from where Asel had wedged it against the wall and poked it down into the opening he had recently filled.

"It's free down there. Empty."

"Let's go then."

"Let's wait and discuss what we ought to do."

They retreated to the adit and sat down.

On the way up, Marcus thought he heard Ennig speak to Asel. *That's a change; at least he's talking to her*, he thought.

"How near are we to tally-time?" asked Marcus and looked towards the lamp. "Not long. We have to decide whether to make a break now or to leave it until tomorrow."

"No, we don't," Ennig objected.

"It's nearly tally-time."

"We can take out a basket of ore now and get it tallied."

"And come back tomorrow," added Marcus.

"Uffin!"

Marcus raised his hands. "Sorry, Ennig. Sorry. Have your say."

"We go back to the refectory and come back here afterwards. Nobody is going to think of us coming back here. Think of the cliffs. Climbing up those in the dark to escape?"

"Right. If they do suspect, they'll be checking the stockade."

But it was not to be that simple. Asel's absence had been noticed and Villius informed. Villius' face looked like a thunder cloud and though Marcus contrived to seem disinterested, Villius' eyes never left Marcus all the time they were in the refectory. After the meal was finished, they were shepherded back to the dormitories and locked in.

Soon after midnight, a squad of legionaries came in, waking everyone up and waving blazing torches about. Several small fires were started in the dangerously dry floor covering of rushes and were beaten out by near-panic stricken slaves. Every inch of the place was searched; every slave was lined up and identified before they were allowed to sleep again. The same thing happened again exactly two hours later with Villius himself attending the identification parade.

Marcus was ready for the third time. He and Ennig moved their sleeping position close to the door where a fire place gave just a little light and warmth. When the soldiers entered this time, Marcus waited until they were well spread out and started his own fire from a piece of kindling he had ready. He shielded the flame until it was burning strongly and then shouted, "Fire, fire. Help. Fire."

Hysteria spread faster than the flames. A couple of holes were broken through the wattle and daub walls and slaves and legionaries scrambled through.

"Now, let's be gone from here."

They made it back to the valley in half an hour, but finding adit five took longer. It was only because of Asel's vigilance that they found it in the end. The girl had heard their voices and when they had come near enough for her to identify them; she had lit the lamp as a guide.

※

Travel was slow. No matter how sure footed the animals were, dense woodland, iced-over bogs and on milder days, mud, had to be circumnavigated; long finger-shaped sea lochs had to be skirted. Murrag's weak bladder was an irritation rather than a real hindrance, but it was something for Iavolena to focus her malice on and she berated the old man unmercifully. The boy, Lyfan, shouted back at her whenever he became the subject of her tongue lashing, but Murrag remained silent. He shook his head at each new epithet and perhaps he even smiled. At night, they slept in a makeshift tent—a sheet of leather thrown over a pole or a tree branch and Murrag's snores assured him an hour's complaint while the tow-headed boy made breakfast.

It grew ever colder at a pace exceeded only by the vitriol of Iavolena's temper. She called on every God she knew to take vengeance on Murrag and Lyfan, she… but nothing happened. Days passed until she lost count and wondered where she was being taken.

⚜

NOVANTIA

Eventually the mystery was dispelled. On a fine cold morning, two hours after dawn, they crested a rise and the sea appeared, blue, with white waves rushing to the shore. Close by the seashore was a huddle of huts with a haze of wood smoke hanging above the thatched roofs.

"Ardfern," said Murrag when pressed. "It's called Ardfern. Do you see the ship at the water's edge?" He carried on suddenly loquacious. "The Captain is the one I told you of. He'll probably buy all your things as well as the sea shell."

"A rich man?"

"Assuredly. Richer than I am."

The uncomplaining beasts bore them down to the houses where the villagers stopped their errands to watch them pass by. At the quay, a man sat on a pile of netting trimming his finger nails with a knife the size of a young sword blade. Even with puddles still covered with ice, he was stripped to the waist and the smooth play of muscles beneath the sun-browned skin attracted Iavolena's eyes immediately.

"Murrag, you senile old goat. I thought you weren't going to be here this time. Thought the Romans would have flayed your tough old hide by now and hung it out to dry."

The words were meaningless to Iavolena. It was neither the rough Latin she had become used to nor the Carvetian tongue that she could more or less comprehend, he spoke in a musical tongue she had never heard before.

Murrag merely smiled in the quiet way he had developed as they journeyed north. "Captain," he said, using Carvetian. "I bring you someone who has jewels to trade with. Iavolena."

Iavolena colored a little as the Captain beamed at her. His face possessed a haughty cast to it, with a long straight nose, black impudent eyes and sandy colored beard cut into a triangular shape. A pair of moustaches flared to either side like antlers. His hair was as fair as the Carvetian, but divided and woven into two plaits.

"Lady," he said and it sounded as if he was laughing as he spoke. Murrag said a few words in the Captain's language and the other grinned again.

"Well, well. Iavolena, is it?" He spoke her name slowly, taking care with the unfamiliar syllables.

Iavolena nodded. He could not be more than twenty five years, she thought, but he has an ageless look to him, as though all the lore of the sea was inside his head. She felt just a little weak and she shivered.

"So what have you brought me?" asked the man from Erin in his own language.

In answer, Murrag signaled to the boy who pulled the wraps off the two laden donkeys. There were bundles of weapons on one of the beasts; swords of fine black iron with hilts of bronze and handles covered with supple leather. There were others with more ornate hilts and where gold wire had been used in place of leather cords and with semiprecious stones embedded in the crosspieces. Spear heads too, knives, axe heads.

The other animal was laden with small amphorae. Iavolena recognized the stamps and seals of a number of wine merchants she was familiar with. This wine was stolen, stolen from Roman supply trains.

Ferdiad, the Captain, was watching her reaction quizzically. He chuckled when she so obviously recognized the origin of the contraband.

"Only the best," he told her. "Only the best of Roman wines for Erin."

It did not matter very much, as far as Iavolena was concerned. She knew that pilfering took place, it was impossible to stamp it out; allowance was made for the expected losses.

"The Legions will cross into your lands one of these days and crucify the lot of you."

He laughed at this, long and loud. "Well, before they come, let us take food together while my men put your goods into the hold."

Murrag held up his hand. "What are you offering, Ferdiad? Those mangy beasts?" He pointed to a pack of hunting dogs tied up on the deck.

"Of course." He returned to his native tongue and ignored the insult. "So long as your trade goods are as good as you say, the dogs will be yours."

Hunting dogs such as these commanded a good price, but Murrag was careful to allow no hint of satisfaction to escape his stony expression.

"What about this woman though, what does she have?"

Murrag shrugged and spoke in the Captain's language, too. "How should I know? I am too old to judge such things, but I imagine she has whatever it is that appears to interest you."

"A trifle on the thin side, for my tastes."

"It is easy to fatten a woman up, far harder to make a fat woman into a thin one."

"What you say is true."

"All I want is the sea shell bauble that she wears at her throat."

"Hmm." Ferdiad crossed to Iavolena who was leaning against her patiently waiting pony. "Murrag tells me you have some jewelry to sell." He fingered the fossil shell on its cord around her neck. "What is so special about this? Hm?"

He turned to Murrag and shouted across to him in Erin. "Why do want rid of her, hey? What's she done?"

"She's a nuisance and she knows too much of our business."

"Why not kill her?"

And with that, Ferdiad took hold of the rough Carvetian clothes she was wearing and tore them open down the front. Her breasts tumbled free of their confines and trembled before him.

"Yes. I can see why not."

Iavolena did not try to cover herself, without pause or thought; she went for the dagger which was always to hand at her waist. The Erin Captain was quicker though. She hardly saw his arm move before his fingers gripped her wrist immovably.

"Spirited little thing, isn't she? I don't doubt she'll give some rare fun. Here." He snapped the cord about her neck and threw the shell to Murrag. "I'll just put her on board and then we'll have that meal."

Ferdiad pulled the knife from Iavolena's fingers and held both of her wrists in one hand to drag her on board the ship. Lyfan chuckled as she was led past him, but a single glance from her eyes silenced the young boy.

As he waited for Ferdiad to deal with Iavolena, Murrag examined the shell. What was its secret? Perhaps he should send the boy on with it while he returned to Luguvallium where he could leave a message for the Commandant at Throp. There was, after all, a thousand denarii riding on it. He too could be as rich as Ferdiad.

⚜

The ancient dolmen stood at his back, sheltering him from the fierce blast of the wind. It howled to either side of the standing stone, whipping the heather and the gorse until they seemed like great tides of black water racing across a rocky shore. Above, the Great River spread across the arch like mother-of-pearl dust scattered across the black sands of Ashferrix. The bright star of Vega marked the north and around it shone the familiar constellations; the hunter and broken-winged raven, there with the red star as its eye was the eagle and to one side, its legs dipping below the horizon, was the horse and the chariot.

Mandeltua let his eyes relax so that the hard points of light softened as he lost focus. The sharp edges of his sea shell bit into the flesh of his hands as his fingers tightened around it. The pain flowed up his arms and back to his heart; his heart pumped the life giving blood until every part of his being was filled with bright edged pain.

Gellorix the Champion. How went that one's journey to destiny?

Curtains of mist parted and his mind's eye gazed forth over the land. His far sight plunged down into the earth, through the soil and rocks and into deep passages.

There he was, a blazing torch held aloft and at either side was a companion. At his feet, the flames reflected from a lake of black water.

CHAPTER EIGHT

EVENHOPE

"SO WE ARE NO BETTER OFF, THEN." ENNIG GAZED AT THE BLACK water which lapped at their feet, shadows hid his expression but his tone of voice reflected the gloom he felt.

Marcus felt similarly dejected, but he still remembered the breeze which had at first blown through the hole they had cleared, a breeze that had been absent since the blast of air which had blown the light out the day before.

"Was it raining yesterday?" he asked.

"A bit," Ennig answered him.

"A lot," Asel added. "It poured with rain until the afternoon."

"And it's been dry since then?"

"More or less."

Marcus nodded. "Look," he said and held the lighted brand down close to the water's edge. "The rocks have been covered with water a lot higher up than they are now. See? The water level is dropping."

"And it may drop low enough for us to get out?"

"Perhaps. Let's get back up to the adit and see what's going on outside."

Daylight had arrived by the time they returned and most of the slaves had been rounded up after the fire and put to work as usual. There was a marked increase in the number of guards patrolling the area; in fact two of them were looking up at the entrance to adit five.

"They've noticed the ladder's gone." Ennig conjectured.

"Probably—and here comes that animal, too."

Villius was running down the hill in the wake of two more legionaries. They all came to a stop below adit five where there was a brief discussion. A moment later, the two legionaries who had accompanied him went back the way they had come.

"Will you two get the food and the torches down the rope ladder to the water's edge. I'll keep watch here."

With a grunt of acceptance, Ennig crawled back into the tunnel with Asel following him. Marcus too, followed them to the branch point and started to fill a basket with heavy boulders from the older workings. He intended these to be ammunition to ward off any attempt at entry.

Marcus pushed the basket back to the entrance and in the event, was only just ahead of the guards who were returning with a long conifer tree trunk. It must have come from the storage area where they were used for repairs to the stockade fence. The branches had been roughly trimmed, but not yet cut flush with the trunk and in this state, made a reasonable ladder.

Keeping out of sight, he watched them set the tree trunk up against the cliff face and while two men steadied it, another began to climb. When he was half way up, about twenty feet from the ground, Marcus threw his first rock. It hit the guard on the shoulder and nearly knocked him off the tree.

Seeing that they would not get unhindered access to the adit, the legionary returned to the ground and using a basket to protect himself, started up again. The other soldiers, flung javelins up at the entrance, but none of them came close enough to be a threat until Villius, mouthing curses and obscenities, picked up one of the fallen spears and threw it himself.

The Optio was a big, strong man, fuelled by hatred. Moments later, the projectile flew through the entrance and clanged off the roof, narrowly missing Marcus and startling Ennig who had just returned. Almost without thinking, Marcus picked up the javelin and threw it back at Villius. Whether he could not see it against the rock face or never thought that a slave would fight back, Marcus did not know but Villius didn't move as it flew down towards him.

He was struck in the right shoulder, close to the neck. Even so, the man remained standing and shaking his fist. Marcus did not wait to see the outcome, when Ennig told him that the supplies had been moved, he left without a second glance.

After Ennig had gone down the rope ladder, Marcus examined the rocks which surrounded the hole and moved a dozen or so with care and pulled several more out of the side of the hole. He descended the ladder with caution; he had made the rocks dangerously unstable. At the bottom, he pulled on the ropes until the ladder came free. As it did so, the rocks he had re-arranged, came tumbling through and several of them jammed the entrance they had made.

"I hope we don't have to go back that way."

Marcus looked at Ennig, but remained silent.

"The water *has* gone down, Uffin." Asel pointed to the edge. "It still is going down."

They lit a small lamp, one of several they had accumulated and extinguished the brands while they waited for the water level to fall still further. Eventually, the small flame of the oil lamp began to flicker as a flow of air developed.

Sometime later, they heard the unmistakable sounds of rocks being cleared from the blocked entrance and while the water level had fallen by a foot or so, Marcus would have preferred to give it still more time. However, after a brief discussion, they decided to try their luck in finding an escape route.

Marcus led the way holding the rekindled brand with Asel following and Ennig bringing up the rear. The oil lamp indicated that the air current came from their left and following the water's edge, they soon found it necessary to enter the cold, black water and wade knee deep, then waist and finally, chest deep.

They waded against a slow, but definite current in the water and after several minutes, the torch showed the roof descending towards the surface. Stalactites became a menace, some were quite difficult to see and one or other of the three collided with the stony columns more than once.

Soon, there was only one or two hand's breadth of air space below the roof, the torch sputtered and hissed as the water lapped about its burning point. Marcus was about to suggest that they back up a little when the sound of voices became audible. He pulled the brand underwater immediately and inky darkness descended.

"We know that the air space continues," he whispered, "because of the wind. In fact, I think it is becoming stronger. We should be able to follow the water by walking or even swimming until we find where it flows into the cave."

"Sometimes streams just sink into the ground. There isn't always a hole, you know." Ennig was determined to be pessimistic.

"There must be in this case, because of the air."

They went on slowly, feeling the way with their feet and holding their food, a lamp and spare torches above the water as far as possible. A dim glow to the rear and voices, muffled in the confined air space told them that the Roman guards had tracked them as far as the water. Whether they would follow them into the tunnel or try to find the cave entrance from the outside was an open question.

The trek through the bitterly cold water lasted, they guessed, almost three hours. The water level had continued to fall and this made it easier to negotiate the passage.

There had been neither sight nor sound of the Romans for most of the time and Marcus judged it safe to relight a torch of their own. This was a lengthy business; he used a flint to ignite the small lamp and then lit a brand from the wick. When it was burning properly, the light revealed a much larger cave with a gravelly shore and a sandy beach which they could have climbed on to—had they known it was there—much sooner.

There was now a definite movement in the air and traces of moss and an occasional fern suggested that an entrance was near. Within a half hour, though, they reached a blank wall with the stream to their left flowing from a submerged crevice.

With a cry of disappointment, Asel sat down and massaged her aching calves while Ennig and Marcus cast about for some way to continue their journey. The reassuring breeze seemed to have vanished and with it any clue to the direction they should take.

"Well, at least we can have a fire. Look here." Marcus had found a pile of driftwood at what appeared to be a high water mark. "It must have been washed in here somehow."

Much of the driftwood was damp, but here and there were some branches which had obviously been cast up when the water was higher than the recent flood. These made a cheerful blaze and dried off the wetter timber sufficiently for it to burn. Their bread and cheese, though soggy in part, helped to repair their strength and morale and as the fire died down, each of them tried to rest.

"What time of day do you think it is?" asked Marcus after a few minutes.

"Night time," replied Ennig, shortly.

"That's what I thought. Look straight up above us."

Above, contained in a narrow diamond shape, were five twinkling stars.

The gray light of early dawn revealed a shaft thirty feet deep. Its walls were damp from water seepage and tufts of grass and fern grew from every ledge and niche. The rock itself was jagged and uneven from the effects of frost and ice and had they been practiced mountain climbers, it would have presented them with an easy climb.

As it was, it took an hour to reach the top. Marcus led the way and briefly scouted the area for signs of the mine's guards before reaching down and practically lifting Ennig the last few feet.

"We're free, my friend. Escape *is* possible after all."

He lay back at the edge of the hole and reached down towards Asel who stretched up towards his fingers. A space the length of two hands separated them. No matter how they strained, they could not close the gap.

"Just a moment."

Marcus took off his tunic and twisted it into a thick coil. Asel grasped the end and he pulled her out onto the grass.

"Thought we might have to leave you there, then." He grinned.

"You know," said Ennig, quite oblivious to the last minute difficulty, "I know where we are. That hill over there is Black Pike and beyond it is Ashbend, where I was born."

Marcus looked across to where Ennig was pointing. The sky was overcast, the sun a baleful orange glow on the horizon.

"If you go there, the Romans might find you again."

"Oh, they took me from Maglona. I worked at the tannery there. I pinched a loaf of bread and some onions."

"And they took you to the mines for that?" Asel was incredulous, then remembered her own circumstances. "Still, I didn't do anything and they took me."

"Well," said Ennig. "I also took the overseer's knife to cut the onions with and they found that in my mattress."

Marcus was surprised at Ennig. In the slave camp, no one asked and no one vouch-safed the reasons for their being there, yet now the boy was unable to stop talking about it.

"Which way will you be going, back, beyond the Wall?"

"No. There's no sense in that. South, I think," Marcus replied, dissembling. "Asel has relatives down there." He saw her frown and catching hold of her hand, gave it a warning squeeze. "I'll take her there and then decide what to do."

Asel did not let go of his hand, even when Marcus relaxed his grip.

ERL-RIG

It was all but sunset when Mandeltua reached his objective, a flat topped plateau almost surrounded by mountains. A perfect ring of twenty one huge stones enclosed the plateau; just to the north of the centre of the ring was the space where a twenty second stone had stood. It too, had been flat topped, there had been grooves cut in to the surface with dark stains marking the ancient stone. It had been there for countless centuries, until the Romans came.

The Romans had dragged it away and broken it in pieces as they had with every one of the other holy circles they had found. There would be no more sacred rites at Erl-Rig until the invaders were driven out.

Mandeltua squatted on the ground and took a handful of acorns from a pouch. He placed them carefully in a rectangle on the new turf where the altar stone had been and closed his eyes.

The sun, shining between the top of a mountain and a towering mass of black cloud, stained his eyelids red and Mandeltua thought of blood. Blood spilled on alter stones, blood spilled on battle fields, blood spilled on the good rich earth of sacred groves.

He began his chant. Thanking the Gods for the land, for the streams which fed the land, the sun which warmed it and the moon that purified it. He thanked them for every live thing which ran or swam or flew or grew in the earth for without any one of these things the world would be a poorer place.

Finally, he clasped the stone which hung on a thong about his neck and thanked them for this, their great gift which, though only a half of what had been, still allowed him far sight.

Though not always when I wished for it, he added in a thought not intended for the Gods.

Mandeltua tightened his grasp on the stone and summoned the image of Uffin Gel-lorix to his mind. At first, he thought that this was to be another of those times when he strived to no avail, but then the Gods brought him what he needed.

There was Uffin with but a single companion this time. They stood on a hillside, looking down and Mandeltua shifted his sight to see through Uffin's eyes.

A roadway, not paved, but beaten hard by the passage of many feet and hooves. To the right, to the north, was a small force of Roman legionaries. They were picking up equipment and shouldering packs, their business done, ready to march on to their destination. The Roman's assignment was obvious, along one side of the road four men had been crucified on X-shaped timber crosses.

CARVETIUM

It was hard going. The virgin woodland through which they had been traveling all day had now given way to open fells; bleak areas of sandy soil and exposed rock where only the toughest of plant life managed to retain a toe hold. Tiny fist-sized hawthorn trees grew in crevices in the limestone pavement; broom and gorse filled cracks with their dark foliage; even a diminutive crab apple struggled to bare sour fruits in the shelter of a knee-high rock ledge.

Marcus and Asel failed to notice these marvels of tenacity. Marcus was dressed only in a light woolen tunic for the temperature in adit five was often suffocating even in the coldest of weather. Asel's attire was hardly better; a woolen cloak which she had originally thrown over a linen shift to hide the packages of food she had stolen from the kitchen at the mining complex.

Light snow was beginning to replace the rain which had been with them all day. It tumbled like thistledown from a low sky, the first snow of an early winter and Fall only just begun.

Marcus put an arm around the girl's shoulder and gave her a reassuring hug. He had set a punishing pace in order to keep ahead of any possible pursuit and Asel had kept up with him without complaint.

"Somewhere across there is the road to Luguvallium although we are several days south of that place. I'm quite certain of where we are, but with this weather, we're going to have to find some shelter even if it means going out of our way."

"Where are we going? You told Ennig that we were going South and by the way, I *don't* have family down here."

"No. Ennig's tongue was becoming a bit loose. I suppose it was the relief of escaping, but I didn't want to trust him with our real intentions. No, I'm heading for my mother's home, White Tarn. As I said though, we have to find some shelter and that means going down into the valley."

"If we came across a homestead, we could beg a night's sleep."

"Doubtless. And have tongues wagging from here to the Wall. Many of these people have accepted Roman rule," he explained. "Their livelihoods are bound up with the military, they sell produce to the camps and the forts, they buy Roman imports."

"No one is going to know who *we* are, though."

"The Romans will come after us, Asel. After me, anyway." He was about to say that he was too important for them to risk his knowledge falling into the wrong hands, but blamed it on Villius instead. "I may have killed Villius with that spear, I certainly injured him and the Romans will not want to let that go unpunished."

Asel turned her bright eyes on Marcus. "I hope the animal is dead, at least if he is, he won't be able to harm any of the other slaves."

"Hmm," replied Marcus and picked a way down the hillside.

The slopes were now covered with trees which were clothed in yellow and orange with a frosting of white where the snow was beginning to cling. At another time, Marcus would have enjoyed the winter beauty, but he was chilled to the marrow and he could feel Asel shivering beside him; he had eyes only for shelter, somewhere to get warm.

The path skirted a tumble of boulders and then led onward along the edge of the ice-cold swirling waters of a stream. For a moment, he wondered if the path led to a dwelling and despite his earlier warnings to Asel, wondered too about the possibility of a smoky fire and warm furs and a hot meal. He dismissed the idea as it burgeoned, though. The path was a game trail, too narrow for human use and the spoor of wild boar was plain, they were still relatively high above the valley floor and … *Wild boar!* The thought gave him pause and he stopped to look back at the pile of boulders. "Sorry," he said as Asel cannoned into him. "Those rocks."

They were of all shapes and sizes, the result of a minor rock fall at some time past and now overgrown with creeper, brambles and even a small bush or two. Marcus walked around them until he again came to the stream which lapped a third of the perimeter. He returned, not quite knowing what he was looking for, but certain that it was there to be found and almost walked past the entrance a second time without noticing it.

There was a pile of animal droppings, another a little closer to a large rock. He approached the stone and quite suddenly, what had seemed to be a crack resolved itself into a narrow passage cloaked in shadow.

Marcus had to enter it sideways. "Stay here a moment Asel, while I see what's inside," he told her from within its confines.

From the entrance, it had looked like a small cave, but inside he realized that it was a space created by the chance falling of a large flat rock on top of several others. More had piled up and around to create this little redoubt against wind and snow.

He had to get down on his hands and knees to peer in and forgetting the possibility of its being occupied, he crawled inside. Outside, it had been almost dark, for it was late evening. In here, it was Stygian and he could tell nothing except by touch and smell.

It was unoccupied, he was certain of that. There was a scent of animal, but it was old, there were rolls of hair or wool in the crevices of the floor which suggested that goats or sheep had used the place.

"Is it all right?"

Marcus' spirit nearly left his body.

"Gods, you startled me."

"I'm sorry. It's snowing more heavily now. I thought I might as well follow you. Is it all right?"

"It seems a dry enough place for the night. I…" He felt through his pockets. "I think Ennig took the flint and tinder with him which is a pity because we can't make a fire. We'll have to snuggle up close tonight and share our body heat, although I'm a bit short of that at the moment"

"Well, there's plenty of food and the stream water is clean and sweet. I've slept in worse places, I'm sure we can make do. Do you still know where we are?"

Marcus scratched his head. "I reckon us to be about two days from my mother's although we can't go directly there; the Romans will be watching the place if they aren't camped inside of it." He took hold of Asel's hand. "I only want to let her know that I'm all right. I'll try to get a message to her and then I'll take you back to your home."

Asel's nod and smile went unseen in the dark. "Whatever makes you happy makes me happy, Uffin. How about some food?"

They ate in the darkness and afterwards, Marcus wrapped what was left back into its cloth and used it for a pillow. "Let's get some sleep if it's possible."

A moment or two later, he felt Asel move alongside of him and stretch her cloak over them both. Gradually, their warmth built; that and the comfort of her presence filled Marcus with a wonderful sense of well-being. The deep abyss of exhaustion claimed them.

When he awoke, Marcus was still wrapped in Asel's cloak, but he was alone. Perhaps he had dreamed, perhaps he was back in the crowded dormitory with its smell of sweat and the ever present stink of sulphur from the roasting ore.

No. This *was* Asel's cloak; he could still smell her warmth on it.

He crawled out of their burrow, taking the cloak with him and stood up in the narrow cleft which led to the outside, taking a moment to comb his fingers through his hair. Daylight showed him several bundles of dead branches and dry grasses just inside the entrance. Asel had been busy.

He stepped over the bundles into a world gone white. During the night, snow had fallen to a depth of several hands, drifting up to waist high in some places and scarcely covering the ground in others. It had stopped now and the temperature was warmer than he remembered it from yesterday.

Marcus followed Asel's small footsteps in the snow, noticing how they led in and out of the woods where she had collected the firewood and then on towards the stream.

Asel was standing in the water when he found her, her dress was tied up around her knees and her sandals on a log on the bank. She was holding a scoop of thin twigs bound together closely and watching the water intently.

Marcus could not help but notice the roundness of her calves nor the slimness of her waist and the generous bosom. She was frozen, a sculpture rare enough to grace the villa of any well-to-do Roman. And then the magic was broken, Asel moved like a heron striking and Marcus realized how apt was the simile for a fish was scooped from the water and flew towards the bank. A flash of silver which landed, joining three others on the snow.

"What a fisherman." He applauded and realized suddenly, that he had never felt the unease with Asel which he usually experienced with women.

Asel turned and stood up straight, giving him a wide smile. She colored just a little at his obvious admiration. "Well, here is breakfast. Can you light us a fire; there seems to be plenty of flint in the stream bed."

He went to the edge of the water and gave Asel her cloak before turning over several likely looking pieces of stone. "If you have turned huntress, it seems only right that I should become cook." Marcus picked two pieces of flint. "Aha, I think this will do."

Lighting a fire with nothing to hand, nature was not easy. Marcus was more used to using a piece of iron with the flint and specially prepared wood shavings, but it could be done without such things. Some scraps of peeling birch bark straight from the tree trunk, a little dried grass.

Some minutes later, he had a small blaze going among some larger pieces of bark and fed them carefully with small twigs. Soon, he called to Asel and went to fetch her when she did not appear immediately.

Asel was returning slowly, erasing their footprints in the snow with a leaf covered branch which she propped up just inside the cleft.

"No one is going to notice our tracks now. Not easily anyway. If there's a bit more snow, it will hide our presence completely."

"I have to confess that I have always thought of you as a young..."

What was he saying? Marcus tried again. "As a youngster. But you're very talented, you're a woman."

Again, it hadn't come out the way he had wanted it to. She was indeed a woman, her sparkling blue eyes and corn colored hair kept getting in the way of rational thought. She was indeed, a very beautiful young woman.

"So," she handed him the fish, rolled up in a dock leaf, "do you think you can cook these?"

"Of course. They may seem to be a little burnt when I'm through, but that will be just imagination."

"I expect I'll get better at imagining with practice."

They both laughed and Marcus split the fish and gutted them with his fingers before setting them on a bed of hot ashes to cook.

"Where did you learn to catch fish like that?"

"Right here."

Marcus looked at her.

"I've caught them with a net before but I didn't have one so I..."

"... improvised," he finished for her. "That's very clever. You had better not show *how* clever you are too many times though, men run away from clever women."

Asel frowned. "Why should they do that? Would *you* run away, Uffin?"

"Not me, no. But other men, er..."

Marcus was on the edge of deep water again. He coughed and back paddled to shallower reaches.

"I'd guess that your father's dogs would have discouraged any legionaries from attacking your home. What happened to you? How did you get caught?"

Asel shrugged. "You're right about the dogs, I heard them barking while I was hurrying back. I'd seen some Romans in the distance and then I ran right into the three of them who'd been up to High Sil. They just grabbed me, they hit me over the head and I woke up tied to a lot of other men and women."

"They just took you back—nothing, er, nothing else."

Asel laughed though there was not a lot of humor. "I'm old enough to know what you mean Uffin. No, nothing else."

They fell silent as the fish cooked and the smell made their mouths water.

"What about you, Uffin?"

"Hm?"

"You know my father quite well, don't you? You know my family quite well. What we do, who we are. I know next to nothing about you. You don't even speak like the other Carvetian traders we know."

Marcus was a little taken aback by this last. He had always considered that his accent fitted in well with his cover work. *My speech is the same as my mother's, surely, and hers, although more Brigantean—well there*, he considered a moment, *maybe there was a difference*

"My own father was a Roman officer," he said, deciding to be honest with the girl. "He was married, he had—has a wife in Rome. He fell in love with my mother and I was born. He was here for ten years before he was posted back to Rome and he did a lot to educate me. I suppose that's the reason for my accent. Is it *very* different?"

Asel shook her head. "Not really. Just enough. I like it."

"I was raised at White Tarn, I told you that's where Mother lives, didn't I? Father had a succession of tutors for me so I learned to speak Latin and a bit of Greek as well as Brythonic." Marcus laughed, an attempt at self-deprecation. "I can write in Latin and Greek, too, and in the Brythonic runes. And, as you can see, I can cook fish to a turn—provided they're caught by a lovely young lady."

The last few words slipped out without his realizing and thus they sounded completely natural and artless. Nevertheless, Marcus blushed when he appreciated what he had said.

"So that explains why you shave your chin and cut your hair in the Roman style."

"Quite a lot of the younger men do that—shave their beards. Anyway that's all there is really." He scooped two fish out of the glowing coals and put them on a green leaf, handed them to Asel. "All there is to know."

"All! I could go on asking questions all day."

"The only questions we need to answer at the moment is when and where to go." He began to eat his own fish and spoke between bites. "I'll check... the weather as soon as... I've finished eating."

The time was early morning and the snow was melting. It dripped steadily from leaves and overhangs, but fresh snow was already falling again, enough to have completely obliterated all sign of their earlier activities.

The snowfall was not heavy, the stuff was dry and powdery as it fell and if they moved out now, it would cover any tracks they made. On the other hand, they were still tired. The circumstances at the mine had left him—if not Asel—in a weakened condition and they had poor clothes for such weather. Besides, he was filled with self-doubt; he could not really believe that they would make a lasting escape. *How could I tell her? Best to leave her at White Tarn and quietly vanish away.*

He returned. "I don't think... what are you doing?"

Asel was tearing strips of cloth from the hem of her shift.

"Bindings for our feet. They should fit inside our sandals and give a little protection; feet are always the first to feel the cold." Asel was proving to have enough spirit for both of them.

Marcus nodded. "Yes, you're right. It's too soon for winter to have really begun though, I think the snow is because we are still quite high. It will get a little warmer again. If we rest today, then I'd like us to try and leave tomorrow." He squatted down next to the remains of the fire. "I'll have to think about our journey properly. Roads are being built all over here, forts are going up. We simply can't just walk about without being noticed, we have to keep to the byways."

Asel grinned up at him. "Go inside and rest, Uffin. Everything will work out, you'll see."

"Are you coming inside, too?"

"There are things I have to do first. I'll come in a while."

A wan daylight reached inside the dark cave-like chamber, just enough light to get a sense of its size—perhaps fifteen feet deep by about eight feet broad and high enough to kneel up in.

Marcus sat with his back to the wall where they had slept and thoughts churned through his mind. Someday, the Romans were going to capture him. It might be soon or late, but the time would come. He would be crucified like those four wretches they had seen yesterday, or perhaps they would flay the skin from his living flesh. What would happen to his mother? Old Gellatorea would continue to chop wood and catch game for her and bring her vegetables—until he died, no doubt. He couldn't provide for her like a son could, though. There had to be another way, a better way. There must be, he just hadn't thought of it yet.

The day passed slowly. Asel came to sit beside him, but both of them were too restless to sit for more than a few minutes before going out to check the weather, or to pull the firewood inside or to get a drink of water or...

Night time came and dark. The snow had stopped falling and was still melting although, as the temperature had dropped with the coming of evening, it thawed more slowly. They moved the fire inside and warmed their retreat for the night.

Finally, Marcus dropped off into a restless sleep and woke some indeterminate time later to find that Asel was beside him and had again covered them both with her cloak. Then he slept deeply. And he dreamed. A dream like many others he had had over the years. Marcus lay on a bed of soft cushions and a beautiful woman came to him and disrobed in front of him.

She began to touch him with soft fingers, bending over him so that her breasts touched his skin, stroked him. The woman lay beside him and then over him. Took him inside of herself and continued to move gently back and forth, side to side. Slowly, languorously, she moved until Marcus too, moved in unison and ardor built, became more urgent, demanding.

Thus far, it had been like any of the others but now something changed. The woman moaned and clung to him, raking her nails down his chest. Marcus woke. The flickering firelight limned everything in rufus light. Asel's face was above him, inches away, her eyes tightly shut, sweat dripped from her forehead onto his.

And it crescendoed. For both of them came that ultimate moment of transportation and then relaxation. Asel lay upon him and Marcus caressed her naked skin, running his fingers along her spine, cupping her breasts, kissing her neck.

"Why do you give yourself to me, Asel. Your father would kill me if he knew."

Asel placed a finger on his lips. "He is not going to know, is he? You have made me a woman, Uffin, it might be our last chance."

"What do you mean?"

"Tomorrow, the Romans might catch us. Tomorrow, we might both be dead."

The words were true enough and were a sufficient answer to his question. They were quite chilling.

"But you are still very young."

"I'm a year older than my mother was when she birthed me and I love you Uffin. I've loved you since you first came to High Sil."

Marcus held her close and stroked her hair until she began to move again. As he became aroused a second time she smiled down at him.

"Didn't you know that I loved you?"

Marcus shook his head.

"Am I your first?" she asked.

"You know that you are, don't you?"

Any thought of leaving her with his mother and vanishing from her life evaporated.

When Marcus awoke that second morning in their hideout, he found her gone once more. Anxiously, he rose and pulled his clothing on to go outside. The blanket of snow was gone completely; the frost hardened earth had become soft again.

He went down to the stream, no Asel. He looked at the woodland, empty. Were his memories nothing but the dream that it had seemed to be at the start? Was there truly such a woman as Asel?

Marcus returned to the pile of boulders which had provided shelter and so much more and there met Asel who was returning from foraging in the opposite direction.

It *had* really happened then. He could see it in the shine and sparkle of her eyes.

Asel arms were full of nuts and roots and the white bulbs of garlic. She held the bundle up for him to see. "If we had a pot I'd make a stew, but we have no pot." She laughed.

"I thought I was to be cook and you the huntress?"

"Very well."

Marcus cleaned the roots and rubbed them with the garlic which he had mashed between two stones. He covered the roots in a thick clay and dropped them into the bottom of the fire and throwing on more wood, he set chestnuts on the hearth stones to roast.

Later, as they finished the meal, he pointed out that they had to press on. Asel nodded soberly. She seemed somehow older, wiser. Perhaps he imagined it.

⁂

DERWENTIO

Mandeltua had rested at Derwentio for the night for he had arrangements to make and messages to send. There was a small Roman presence there so the Druid had come as night was falling. He had taken a meal and seen to his business before sleeping in front of a banked fire in a hut on the outskirts of the settlement.

His hosts had provided him with food and drink and promptly gone to stay with kin in another part of the village. They wanted no knowledge of who Mandeltua saw or what he did. It was an attitude with which the Druid could find no fault and one that he actively fostered.

After the last visitor had gone Mandeltua took out his stone and gazed into the glowing depths of the fire as it flickered and flared. He looked past the flames, beyond, at the great blocks of stone which held up the monolithic roof stone.

There was movement. Slow, sensuous. A tossing of flaxen hair away from a woman's face. The movement was more intense, it quickened, climaxed, slowed, lingered, renewed.

Mandeltua nodded. Allowed the vision to dim.

"Tomorrow."

⁂

LUGUVALLIUM

Only two of the Deputy Governor's aides were present that morning and they stood behind Aemilius Karrus and witnessed the brief ceremony for the record.

Karrus stood stiffly to attention, his cropped hair was damp with perspiration, his jaw aching with tension. There was a slight but discernible tremor in his arms as the Governor presented him with the dress uniform of a military tribune and he surrendered, with some regret, the vine wood staff. The staff, the emblem of his erstwhile rank had been with him for a long time, through Pannonia, through Noricium, Rhaetia and several of the Brythonic provinces.

"I now appoint you to Tribune of the re-formed Ninth Legion, Aemilius Karrus. Take these symbols and wear them with pride."

Karrus took the helmet and breast plate and grieves and balanced the bundle on his left arm. With the hand fisted, he brought his right arm smartly across his heart.

"Sir, I accept these accoutrements and swear by Jupiter to wear them with honor."

Flavius smiled and stepped back a pace, in doing so, the formality of the occasion was broken.

"You will take command of the Veterans, Aemilius. I want you to bring them up to scratch so that they, in turn, will train the new recruits which our Lord Hadrian will be sending. I think that you will enjoy your new duties."

"Yes Sir." Aemilius Karrus rubbed a speck of dust from the gleaming surface of his new breastplate. "Yes, I shall."

"And your new salary will be twenty five thousand denarii."

It was a sum which Karrus had not yet come to terms with.

"In two or three years, you will be a rich man, Aemilius. You could take up a post in law, back in Rome. Perhaps get a Governorship somewhere."

If I live that long, thought Karrus. "Admirable, Sir, but first things first, I suppose. Where will the Ninth be garrisoned?"

"Temporary encampments at first, Aemilius, outside the forts at Vindolanda, Banna and Vircovicium. That way, the legionaries can make use of the existing kitchens and latrines and the bath houses, too. Some will go north of the Wall; I still have to discuss those arrangements later today. I want you to join me with the other officers so that we can review the plans in detail."

"May I ask one thing more, Sir? Who will be commanding the Ninth? Is the Emperor sending a general with the new recruits?"

Flavius made a silencing gesture with two fingers. He looked to where his two aides were now busy at the far side of the room.

"I am hoping," he said quietly, "that the Emperor will appoint me to that position, but the decision is still awaited. Not all good things come to he who hopes too much, eh?"

"Ah, as you say, Sir."

"Now, perhaps you would wait in the atrium until I have seen to some other appointments. You will find some pleasant refreshments on hand. Gallius..." he called to one of the aides. "Ask Praefector Milius Lestus to step in."

Karrus left and recognized the Commandant of Vindolanda as the other was ushered in. There were a number of tribunes and centurions in the atrium, all apparently waiting to confer with the Legate. Among them was at least one other he recognized: Vibius Gaius Septimus, Commandant of the marching fort at Throp.

The man seemed as nervous as ever, his hands never still, his eyes twitching and blinking. Out of courtesy, Karrus nodded to him. "Commandant." He took the seat next to him.

The Commandant surprised Karrus. Septimus turned to him and engaged him in conversation as though they had been talking for several minutes.

"My wife *is* alive you know, north of the wall in the Novantae area. Not Selgovae."

For a moment Karrus struggled to remember the situation and then recalled the reason for the Sixth's expedition into Selgovae. He shivered at the memory of their ignominious return.

"What makes you so sure, Sir?"

Septimus pulled a wax writing tablet from his tunic pocket. "Read that."

Karrus opened it and looked at the tiny characters. "The Latin is poor."

The author is not a Roman. Look." Septimus pointed to the name. "'Murrag the Jeweler,' a native craftsmen, I suppose."

"Seen two days ago. When did you get this?"

"The day before yesterday. I had heard the Deputy Governor was coming to Luguvallium so I've been waiting to see him. I want some leave so that I can go and find her."

"Recognized her seashell brooch and her description. It says here that she is in Novantae territory—ah, that's what you said."

"Yes. The writer wants the reward I posted, of course, but he won't get that until I've seen her."

Karrus did not wish to appear callous, but he could see no way around it. "Commandant. Excuse my bluntness, but you are not going to last a day out there. The Novantae are no different than any of the other barbarians. You can't hope to pass as a native, they'd be drinking out of your skull inside of a week, I promise you."

"But Iavolena. She's been seen there."

"Possibly she..." Karrus changed the words he had been about to say. "Your wife's beauty may well have saved her from death, Commandant. Certainly they don't use the skulls of women in such a fashion. But you, well you need to employ a local to act for you. One of the scouts perhaps."

Septimus nodded sadly. "I had hoped that Marcus Gellorix would do something. He seemed interested; he seemed to be a fine young man."

The name caught Karrus' attention. "Gellorix? When did you see him?"

"The day that the Sixth went north."

"And he came to see you about your wife? What did he have to say?"

"Well, he asked for a description of Iavolena. He wanted to know what she was wearing and how she got back from the party."

"And how did she?"

"She went back with a surveyor, um, Titus Severius. Gellorix suggested that I check if he arrived at his new posting."

"And—did you?"

"Not right away, I didn't have the time, but I did a day or two later, sent a rider here, Luguvallium. Disappeared it seemed. Never arrived. Posted as missing."

Karrus reached across to the table, poured a cup of wine, and thought about what Septimus had told him about Gellorix. Not the actions of a man planning to murder his senior officer, more those of someone dedicated to his job. Gellorix had been treated pretty roughly, had not been given the chance to speak in his own behalf.

He wondered if his new rank would let him look further into the matter.

"So your wife may have gone with this Severius or been taken by him?"

It was obvious that Septimus didn't care for the first interpretation.

"Seems to me that you find the man, you find your wife. Use one of the scouts."

⁂

CARVETIUM

Soft golden sunlight played across the vast expanse of water. The reflection shone in their eyes as they broke from the tree cover surrounding the great lake and came down to the shore.

Marcus cast a glance left and right. Deserted. He and Asel stopped for a moment to drink in the view.

"Wunicia," he said. "Ten miles from White Tarn and my mother's house."

He pointed across the water. "Some of my mother's relatives live at the top of the lake; they'll be able to pass a message on to her. How are you feeling?"

"I have never felt better." She flashed him a smile and Marcus knew that *he* had never felt better. "I'm thirsty." She ran down to the water line and cupping her hands, drank deeply. "You?" Asel stood up with water cupped in her two hands and Marcus drank from them. "It will be good to eat something hot again."

Marcus chuckled. Their diet over the last two days had been basic, but interesting. Asel had found all sorts of late fruits and nuts, roots and tubers and Marcus had done his best to prepare them in novel ways.

Their journey had not been unpleasant. Had Marcus not been so certain that the Romans were already in pursuit, it would have been very enjoyable. Their nights, of course, were more than enjoyable; they were memorable.

They walked along the gravel on the shore, a mile had gone by perhaps, when they noticed the figure sitting on a fallen tree and watching their approach. By the grey robes he wore, both Marcus and Asel guessed him to be a Druid. Had they needed other clues, there was the man's white hair which blew in the wind in a thousand straggles and knots and the deeply socketed eyes which seemed so used to looking into other worlds.

When ten or fifteen paces separated them, the Druid stood and came towards them. "Well met, Uffin Gellorix and you too, Asel Callog's daughter."

The two of them were dumbfounded. To be met, to be *expected*, on a lonely lake shore halfway through an unremarkable afternoon …

The man was a total stranger. Pale blue eyes, slightly shorter than himself, a huge nose though it still fit the broad face behind it. His age was difficult to guess at—more than sixty, Marcus guessed. There was a slight upturn to one end of the mouth which gave his expression a derisory quality. *Was it intended or was it a permanent quirk of the face?*

Not a handsome man, but a determined man, a man of strong character, Marcus concluded. The stranger extended both hands in a gesture of greeting.

"Puzzled? Of course you are. I am Mandeltua, a Druid. I know you well, Uffin Gellorix; I was present at your birth, I was able to give your mother, the Lady Avorocoeu, some comfort for your father was away at the time."

"Mother has never mentioned you." Marcus added ten more years to his estimate of the man's age.

Mandeltua lifted his shoulders in a shrug. "I, er," he hesitated, "I have maintained an interest in your life since that long ago day. Indeed, you are one of several of my charges."

"Why? What is so special about me?"

"The Gods themselves warned me of your place in the world. You are about to become a very important man—if you allow me to lead you on to your destiny."

Marcus did not know how to reply, but Asel had more practical ideas.

"We are very hungry. If you could lead us on to some food, we would be very grateful."

Asel's gentle mockery had no effect; her words were taken at face value. "Follow me," Mandeltua said.

Mandeltua took them on around the lakeside to Griannovix, a village somewhat closer than the huddle of farms which Marcus had being making for. Griannovix was a collection of round thatched huts which owed its existence to the good fishing to be had in the lake. The Druid swept into the hamlet as if he was lord of the place, an impression made stronger by the inhabitants; everyone they passed showed him a marked respect.

He spoke to the first man he came to, a rapid exchange of words which Marcus was unable to follow. The man, who had been chopping wood, laid down his axe and ran off at great speed. Mandeltua followed at a more leisurely pace and conducted them to one of the largest of the huts.

Inside, another man, obviously the headman of the village, bowed to them and gestured to several thick furs. Following Mandeltua's example, they squatted on the furs; three women brought them pots of soup and stew, bread and cheese and a jug of coarse wine.

Their host offered the hospitality of his home for as long as they wished. Marcus did his best to express his appreciation although Mandeltua all but ignored the fellow and shooed him out of the way as they finished eating.

"The Romans stopped looking for you two when you crossed the mountains," Mandeltua told them when everyone else was out of earshot. "They've put out descriptions of you to the various military establishments, but they are not actively pursuing you. They want you back for a public show of Roman justice, obviously—they are not going to just forget about an escaped slave who has injured an officer, but you'll be safe enough if you don't attract attention."

"I'm speaking about you Uffin, of course. Asel is not that important, she can lose herself easily enough."

"I undertook to return her to her parents' home," Marcus said. "This, I still intend to do. I intend to make her my wife."

"Oh, Fin." Asel blushed.

"Her father has already all but given his permission."

"Wonderful." His expression belied the spoken word. "Don't you think that that's a little foolish? Hmm? You're risking her neck as well as your own. You can't hope to cross the Wall with her, any couple is going to be viewed suspiciously."

"So what alternative is there? I can't go to my mother's; they're sure to keep White Tarn under surveillance. I can't go anywhere as myself." Marcus was becoming angry.

"Listen." Mandeltua chose his words carefully. "The girl should stay with your mother. On her own, she won't be recognized. I can get you north of the Wall and then return for the girl separately, later."

"All this because of my supposed destiny?"

"Just so," Mandeltua responded with equanimity. "I can't allow you to risk yourself unjustifiably, what I have suggested is the best way."

"*You* can't allow it?"

"It is the only sensible way."

"Fin. He's right."

Marcus bowed to the inevitable. The logic of the Druid's words, his forceful personality and Asel's agreement all conspired. And what Mandeltua said *was* true, he had to admit it.

"I would like to write to my mother. Can you get me something to use?"

"Of course. While you are doing that, I shall arrange for the girl's journey to White Tarn. You and I will have to leave almost immediately. Time is of the essence, we must reach our destination by Samhain."

"Samhain?" But Mandeltua had already risen and was halfway to the door.

At the lakeside, the nearest habitation was a hundred paces away. The afternoon was far gone, light was draining from the sky, a slight mist gave then the illusion of privacy.

"I didn't ask to love you." Marcus took Asel's hand. "But I do. I don't want to leave you, but it seems that there is little choice in the matter."

"It will only be little while, Fin. Days, a week or two. Give me enough time to get to High Sil, and then come to speak to my father."

Marcus smiled. "He seemed anxious enough to marry you off to me last time I saw him."

"I shan't try to change his mind—and I shall be meeting your mother."

Marcus gave her the letter he had written. "I've already told her that she will be Grandmother to our sons."

Asel took the small package of lambskin vellum. "You'll have to teach me to read; it would be a comforting thing to keep your words with me when you have to be away."

Marcus held her close, her head on his shoulder and stroked the cascade of shining yellow hair. "We've had so little time."

"But we've put it to good use." Asel squeezed his hands and kissed him. "Remember, my love, you are my man now and I, your woman, we carry each other's souls." With an effort she lightened her tone. "Now, the Druid has come with the ponies. Goodbye, my Uffin."

She turned away so that he would not see the tears that had begun to course down her cheeks.

⁂

Lyfan journeyed eastward along the estuary for the best part of a day before the waters narrowed sufficiently to put the horse in. There was a strong current running now that the tide was on the ebb, and he took the ford slowly.

A light mist beaded everything with moisture and surrounded him with an insubstantial barrier so that he moved in a world of his own.

Across the water and then east by north towards Birrans. Beyond the small settlement were the remains of the hut which had fallen in, he had come on it by accident some months before, it was covered with ivy and offered a warm, dry refuge. Come tomorrow morning, he would be within easy striking distance of Netherby.

The boy was quite at home with the Selgovae and Novantae peoples, but the settlement at Medionemeton was well beyond his previous travels. It was supposedly home to many Druids and he found himself wondering, briefly, what it was that made a man want to speak for the Gods.

He set his mind to other thoughts. Ten denarii. A small fortune which would feed his mother and his siblings for a month. Ten denarii. Old Murrag, who was more than just the old craftsman he seemed, hated to part with money. Even when they'd taken that Roman bitch and sent her off with Ferdiad, Lyfan had only gone home with six denarii. *Mind though*, he thought to himself. There was that nice little knife that had *fallen* out of a pack and it had sold for fifteen when he'd got home.

If he took the occasional such *windfall* into account, Lyfan made a decent enough living for his family; as good as before his father had been killed. And running messages and helping the old jeweler out was quite an interesting life.

Lyfan dropped from a canter to a trot, and was about to draw rein for a rest when the horse reared, almost throwing him back over its rump.

"Hey, Fleetwind. What's the matter?" And he fought for control and gentled the animal to a stop.

Three Roman soldiers stood in front. One of them pointed a javelin at his chest; a second seemed ready to threaten him with a spade. The third stepped closer and took hold of the horse's bridle.

"Nicely done, boy," he said. "Make a cavalryman out of you yet." And he chuckled. A friendly sound.

"Where do you think you're going, eh?" This was one of the other two, not so friendly.

Lyfan knew about three words in Latin, all of them obscene. "I don't know what you're saying," he replied as inoffensively as he could.

The second legionary spat. "Doesn't understand us."

"He'll understand me." This from the one who had not spoken before, he took hold of Lyfan's arm and jerked him off the horse. "Let's take him along to the Decurion; it'll give us an excuse to stop ditch digging for a while."

The legionary pulled him roughly along the line of the newly cut ditch until a wooden watch tower loomed out of the mist. Lyfan's horse whinnied as another soldier led him along behind.

"Arvius. Caught a little fish out here that doesn't understand good Latin. You want him, or shall we throw him back in the pond?"

The door at the base of the watch tower opened and an officer stood in the opening, a man with black hair and a dark skin. Lyfan stared at him; the young Briton found dark complexions and hair quite fascinating.

"Any excuse, eh, Vladius? He's just a boy."

Then he turned to Lyfan and spoke in quite passable Carvetian. "Well, where are you from and where are you going? Eh? Quickly now."

"I work for the jeweler, Murrag in Abalava. I'm delivering a package for him."

A jeweler. Wheels began to turn. "Mm. What's your name?"

"Lyfan."

And Lyfan began to tremble. The officer had narrow beady eyes and they looked at Lyfan in the way an adder might regard a frog.

"Give me the package." Decurion Arvius Sellitus imagined precious stones and metals.

"But my master..."

"The package." Sellitus held out his hand.

Lyfan gave him the sealed pouch he had been carrying. Sellitus turned away from the legionaries and using a knife to slit the leather, he tipped its contents into his palm.

He was disappointed. There was a seashell tied onto a broken cord, nothing else. Still, it was pretty. It was polished and on one side showed a spiral of crystalline segments. It might buy a night with a woman; he concealed the ornament in his tunic.

"Tell your master that the Romans confiscated your package. If he has any argument to make, tell him seek me out at Stanwyx, Decurion Arvius Sellitus." He chuckled without much mirth showing through. "We're planning on staying a while."

Sellitus turned to the three legionaries. "Let the lad go and get on with your ditches. Get it finished today, or its bread and water, understand?"

The three legionaries turned away.

"And keep those looks for when I'm out of sight or you'll all draw guard duty as well."

A few minutes later, they were picking up their spades again.

"One day I'm going to spit on Sellitus' corpse."

"Not before I shit on it, you won't."

CHAPTER NINE

LONDINIUM

CORNUA SOUNDED OUTSIDE, AND SEVERUS NODDED TO himself. Well, at least two hours later than he had expected, but that was Lucius. Senator Lucius Marcellus Vitunius. His ship had docked the day before and a runner had arrived that same evening to advise him. Now, halfway through the afternoon, and accompanied by six of the Emperor's imperial guard, he swept into the atrium and came to a dramatic halt.

"*Salve* Sextus." And he looked around at the statues of Juno and Mars and the bust of Hadrian on its pedestal. Rich hangings adorned the walls and an intricate mosaic featuring dolphins and young boys covered the floor. "You do yourself rather proud here, my boy." He gestured with a languid hand at the cedar wood furniture. "I'll just sit awhile. Get my breath back."

"Lucius, you must have walked all of two hundred paces..."

"I know, I know. Barbaric, isn't it? Now, what was I going to say? Yes. I bring you greetings of course, from our most noble Hadrian. I was going to bring you several amphorae of the new wine for your stock, this year is a great vintage, but Hadrian ordered me to make all haste. There simply wasn't time for it.

"And my throat *is* a trifle dusty, Sextus; perhaps you have a glass or two to hand. They *do* let you have wine out here, don't they?"

"Lucius, this *is* Londinium, you know, not the wilds of Albyn. Yes, we have wine. Come on into my study." To an aide, he said, "Aurelius, wine for the Senator, from my own stock." Then turning to Vitunius again, "And how's that lovely wife of yours?"

"Bessina? Fatter than ever, Sextus. Fatter than ever and all the more flesh to lick honey off, eh?" Vitunius winked and smiled outrageously. "Heh, heh."

"Well you certainly look well on the exercise, it obviously agrees with you. And here's the wine. Cassius, are the Senator's quarters ready?"

"Of course, Governor."

"Excellent. The Senator has brought dispatches from Rome which will be of interest to all the senior officers here. Arrange a meeting in the morning, will you?"

"Er, not too early, Cassius," Vitunius broke in. "Not too early."

Sextus Lulius Severus waited until his aide had gone and then leaned back on his couch. "Now Lucius, what is it that brings you here too fast to arrange a shipment of wine?"

Vitunius took a sealed roll of vellum from his robe and leaning forward, held it out to Severus. "Read that first and then you can ask me questions."

Severus studied the document at length and then looked up again. "So my young friend Flavius is becoming ambitious. I sensed that he was up to something, of course, because I knew that he was writing to the Emperor for assistance against the northern barbarians."

Vitunius shrugged and sipped at his glass. "But now, he's got Hadrian's permission to reform the Ninth."

"Well, that *is* ambition, isn't it."

"Do I need to feel threatened, Lucius?"

Vitunius pursed his lips. "Flavius has some powerful friends, Sextus, not least, the Emperor himself. Now, listen to this, Hadrian is sending three thousand recruits from Tarraconensis, Belgica and Germania; they're only auxiliaries, but they will have a legionary's basic training. The Senate will not let him send regulars, of course, that would weaken the lines elsewhere and even Hadrian must listen to the Senate."

"So perhaps I *do* need to feel threatened. I'm surprised that Hadrian has listened to Flavius and done so much. I thought the Wall was Hadrian's final answer to the Albyn threat."

"Well," the visitor from Rome lowered his voice, "it is the money in Flavius' family that keeps the Emperor where he is. Who pays for the Games, eh? And who makes donations to the temples in the Emperor's name? And who's footing the bill for the new aqueduct? Certainly Hadrian listens to Flavius. And of course he'd like to remove this threat once and for all. General Agricola reported that he had crushed the Northern tribes nearly fifty years ago when King Calgacus was destroyed and here they are again."

Vitunius moistened his lips. "I don't think you should feel threatened though. Hear me out. Our Emperor wants you to contemplate raising two alae of Numeri from friendly tribes; he would pay these out of taxes due to Rome and would consider it a personal favor."

"Hm. And how long would I have to arrange this favor?"

"It is Flavius' intention to enter Albyn in the spring."

Severus propped his chin on his hand and thought about the ramifications. "I think I see. If Flavius is successful and let us pray that he is, I share in his glory. If his scheming goes wrong then no blame can attach to me. That sounds like a fitting arrangement. So who is Hadrian sending to command the Ninth—I presume the Sixth Legion isn't involved?"

"The Sixth will maintain defenses at the Wall, as at present and Hadrian is sending no one." Vitunius winked. "It is Flavius' scheme; he sinks or swims with it."

"And the Senate can't blame Hadrian either, if it doesn't work out."

"Just so."

"Flavius can be a little impetuous if he gets a free hand."

"He has certainly been given a free hand."

"Another glass of that wine, Lucius? Now, tell me, what have you been watching at the Circus Maximus, hm?"

"I'll tell you all about that at dinner tonight, but I'm afraid that is all the time I shall have. I have to leave for Eboracum after we talk to your officers tomorrow. I have to go over these troop movements with the favored Flavius as soon as he gets there. As well as one or two other matters."

"Nothing that *I* should know about, is there?"

"Only the sentence of slavery on Senator Mansustus' son."

Severus frowned. "I *did* hear something about that." Then it came to him. "Marcus Gellorix—Marcus Uffin Gellorix, a castris, with the Sixth?"

"One and the same, my friend. Reportedly, he killed the Commandant of Vircovicium and of course, Mansustus will not believe it possible. He would be here himself, but his gout gets no better and I had to assure him that I'd give the matter my personal attention."

"And I wish you well of it, Lucius. Another glass?"

⁂

MEDIONEMETON

Medionemeton was becoming crowded. Druids had been gathering there over the past month in readiness for the festival at Samhain. Gentoricus was one of those Druids they called a Dreamer. So when he announced that Mandeltua had spoken to him during the night, he was listened to.

"Mandeltua bade me inform all of you that a message must be sent to every tribe. That the chief of every tribe should attend the New Year rites, that each one should attend on fear of banishment. Only the chiefs may enter the Holy Site, those who bring an entourage must lodge them within the forest."

Ancelitra the Younger interrupted him. "Since when has Mandeltua given us such orders when Carotach is still Chief among us? By what right does he tell us to do these things?"

"Carotach has only a short span to live," said Benolivina, an emaciated man in his middle years. "All that he is willing to discuss are the arrangements for his crossing to the Otherworld. He spends his time with his birds; he hasn't eaten for many days now and Mandeltua is the next Chief of the Druids." He spoke specifically to Gentoricus. "Did he have anything more to say? It would be wise to carry out the wishes of Mandeltua."

Seven other Druids had gathered to listen to the discussion. All of them nodded and agreed. "Let us send to Ulvinoa, the Creones have the swiftest of horses, they will take the messages."

⁂

CARVETIA

Mandeltua and Marcus passed through the gate at Stanwyx dressed as goat herds. The Druid had even mysteriously acquired six goats to add verisimilitude and made a passably good job of controlling them.

The Romans had built the Wall with no regard for tribal boundaries. While the major part of Carvetia lay south of the wall, a considerable number of families still lived and worked to the north and additionally, trade between Carvetians and the tribes of Albyn continued almost undiminished.

However, the Romans did control trade and other crossings through the wall. The inspection of wagons and donkey loads was annoying and the spacing of gateways sometimes doubled or trebled the length of journeys.

It was evident that Mandeltua knew when and at which gates security would be lax and Marcus was surprised at the ease with which the locals evaded scrutiny. He was seeing the Romans from a novel viewpoint.

The deference and respect which Mandeltua was accorded was also unexpected. As a Romano-Briton, Marcus had had little to do with the Druids and had always considered the tales he had heard as one part truth and three parts make-believe. His father, like most Romans regarded the Druids as vermin which should have been wiped out a century ago and Marcus' opinions had obviously been colored by the older man's judgment.

Avorocoeu, his mother, held an opposite view and had dealt with them from time to time. Marcus remembered quite clearly an occasion when she had traveled several miles to confer with a druid about a sick cow although the outcome was now beyond recall. There had been one or two visits from itinerant druids too who had given Avorocoeu advice on the planting and harvesting of vegetables.

For an hour, they followed the goats who seemed to know their own way, until the Wall was well out of site. At a bend in the track, a man was standing with two horses, a pair of bags was draped across the neck of each horse. Without a word, he gave the reins to Mandeltua and took charge of the goats.

The Druid mounted, Marcus followed suit and was again surprised for he thought that Druids walked everywhere. Evidently not. They rode north all of that day, sometime walking their mounts, sometimes moving up to a canter, sometimes stopping at streams to water the horses. The weather, though cold, stayed clear and even bright at times. Mandeltua did not speak throughout the day, a fact with which Marcus was perfectly content. Had it not been for Asel's absence, he would have enjoyed the journey.

Sunset approached, but the moon had been high in the western sky all of the late afternoon and continued to light their way for a further two hours before Mandeltua found it necessary to speak.

"There is a river ahead. It can be forded at a bend. We shall stay there tonight."

As Mandeltua had said, so it was. Marcus could see the moonlight reflected from its black surface within minutes and dismounted as they reached the bank. The Druid led the way along the river's edge to where a glade in the dark forest was bounded on one side by the water. Moving about and collecting twigs and branches as though it was full daylight, he kindled a fire to ward off chills and the more curious of night time's creatures.

Marcus found there to be hay in one of the bundles tied about the horses' necks and threw some down for the animals. Another proved to hold dried meat and cheese, their supper.

Later, he sat with his back against a tree and regarded the other. Mandeltua's face was outlined against the moon glow and the great hook of his nose and strong brow ridges stood out like promontories on the face of some ancient mountain. The straggling grey hair had become an almost phosphorescent white against the moon's light and his long and bushy beard hid the chin and upper torso completely.

Why had he let this complete stranger take such complete control of his movements? Did all that the Druid had said make such complete sense? Was there some power that he had, some enchantment which had taken hold of him?

Destiny? Was there a destiny which awaited him?

"What are you thinking about?" Mandeltua broke the evening's silence. "Wondering if the Romans would have truly crucified you? Perhaps you think that with your connections, you could have talked your way out of it. Mm? Perhaps they might forget the injury you did that guard and the killing of your superior."

The voice was strong and resonant. It compelled the listener to pay attention.

Marcus made a wry expression in the darkness. How could this man know so much about him? This obvious knowledge, the way that he had been waiting for Asel and himself at the lakeside. Surely there was more here than could be explained by ordinary reasoning.

"If you know so much about me then you know that I never killed the Commandant."

"Of course. But who are you to be able to convince them of that? The ones whose witness convicted you saw you there with the spear in your hands."

"But I didn't cast it, I was trying to pull it out of the wound."

"Yes, yes. *I* know that and had you been truly a Roman, you may have had a chance at convincing them of your innocence." Mandeltua shrugged, a heavy movement in the darkness. "But you are *Castris*, no one will trust you. You are a tool to be used when it pleases them and to be discarded when they see fit."

"I had a responsible position. They listened to my arguments."

Mandeltua nodded and Marcus could feel the movement in the cold air. "And they smiled to your face and talked about you when you left. Your father deserted you and your mother and he will never return. He suffers gout does he not? Too much rich food and sweet wine. No, such a journey would not be worth the effort."

"You know a lot."

"That I do. The Gods have seen fit to burden me with the gift of farseeing. They gave me a stone of power..." Mandeltua placed his hand on his chest, clutched something beneath his clothing. "Through it I see without the need to be there. It bridges the distance when I need to speak with others of my kind."

The Druid fell silent for several long minutes and the crackle of the fire was suddenly loud in the darkness.

"I even far spoke you once. When you were lying on the floor of a cell, broken and bleeding, but I think you were too far gone to hear me, or perhaps, you were not gone far enough."

The picture of that face he had seen came back. The day and a night he had been lying in that store room in agony from his injuries. It had been a dream, so he had thought, but the face he had seen then was the one which now glared at him across the fire. Marcus kept his own council on the matter.

"Why are you taking me to this place? What is the purpose? I'm an ordinary man, there are a thousand like me, just as capable."

Mandeltua sighed deeply. "He has eyes to see with, but refuses to look, ears which do not hear, a mind with a door locked and bolted. Well, the largest family is the family of fools."

Mandeltua sat up straight and pointed across at Marcus. The younger man felt the pointed finger like a pain in his chest.

"But I have a key, I shall open that understanding of yours. Never fear."

"Why? Tell me why."

"So that you *will* see the truth."

The Druid spoke no more loudly than before, but it seemed to Marcus that he shouted loud enough for his ancestors to hear.

"So you *will* recognize the invaders for what they are. *Pax Romana* and all." He spat on the ground. "What do they know of peace or want with it. Their whole empire is built on killing and subjugation and slavery. They rape the people and the land for what? Riches to please a few thousand countrymen in that anthill they call Rome."

"But the Roman rule *does* bring peace. Britons and Romans have lived in peace for generations. You don't like them, but they've brought a lot of good as well as some bad. They don't think of what they do as being evil."

"Of course not. They've grown up like that. Their soldiers are trained to think like that. Even you, after you've spent time as a slave.

"The Romans are a disease that's spreading across the world, it has to be stamped out. Can't you understand that?"

"There are other ways than yours of seeing these things."

"The Romans killed most of my kind on Mona. Our knowledge has been passed down by word of mouth for a thousand years and they almost erased that body of wisdom in a single day so that the Caesar of that time could impose *his* rules and beliefs. Even the Gods warned our forefathers and no one listened, well here *is* one who does listen." He tapped his chest. "If the Romans invade Albyn, they will learn a hard lesson."

Marcus snorted with amusement. "The Romans have no intention of invading Albyn. Why do you think we… they built the Wall? To show the border of their Empire."

Mandeltua shook his head. A gesture half seen as the fire flared in a sudden breeze.

"You'd trust them while they opened your veins, wouldn't you? If I prove to you that the Romans are wholly evil, will you help me stop them?"

"How can you prove a thing like that?"

"Oh I can prove it, if you'll let me."

"If I let you?"

"You would have to take part in the process if you wish to know. Will you do so?"

Marcus, captured by the rich voice, agreed without thought.

"Then come closer to the fire."

As Marcus edged closer, Mandeltua took a pouch from inside his robe.

"Close your eyes, Uffin. Breathe deeply of the herbs which I shall burn. The smoke will take your mind on a journey. Do not be alarmed at what you might see, you are an observer, much will be revealed to you by the shadow world."

The Druid scattered the broken leaves on the fire and a pungent smoke was generated. Marcus smelled the harshness as he breathed, but nothing else seemed to happen.

A pinprick of light shone against the darkness behind his eyelids. It grew, became a tiny circle, enlarged. *The end of a tunnel*, he thought. *I am rushing towards the end of a tunnel.*

Mandeltua was ready when Marcus slumped forward. He reached out and caught him, held him firmly against his chest, the young man's forehead pressed against the Druid's stone of power. Marcus was standing on the Wall rampart. Close beside were two legionaries—of the Ninth, judging by the insignia he could see. Deep in conversation, they ignored his presence.

"Well that's the last time I'll be mixing mortar or laying stone," said one. "Back to the Stanegate for training."

"Being moved?"

"We all are. They're reforming the Ninth. Off to Albyn in the spring."

"Into Albyn? We don't have the manpower."

"I've heard it from Optius who had it from Velitus himself. There're new recruits coming in from abroad, numeri from southern Briton."

"About time too. It's been so long that I've forgotten how to lift a sword."

Marcus' sight clouded, went dark and gradually cleared once more. He was standing behind a Roman officer. Even though he could not see the soldier's face, he recognized the man's voice: Marcellus Flavius, deputy to Governor Severus. The man who had sent him to the mines.

Looking over his shoulder, Marcus saw a group of officers.

"All of you have commanding positions in the new Ninth Legion and when the new recruits arrive, you are going to be responsible for their training. They have to be ready for the spring. Ready to enter Albyn and to remove this nuisance for good. Questions?"

"What about the Sixth, Sir. Will they be marching with us?"

"They'll stay on the Wall. We shan't need the Sixth. Our establishment will be up to ten thousand men by the spring and I think Hadrian himself will be sending at least two vexellations from the mainland, more than enough to do the job."

Marcus floated in space. It was a moment or two before he adjusted to the new perspective and recognized that what he was seeing was his mother's house.

Mandeltua pushed Marcus back a little so that his head no longer touched the stone. He re-established his position so that their two foreheads were now pressed together. Lines of concentration gathered around his eyes, facial muscles bunched, arteries bulged.

Soldiers came from the woodland and surrounded the house. Roman soldiers carrying torches. They kicked in the door and entered to come out a minute later dragging two women—Asel and Avorocoeu. Marcus shouted, but no one heard him, he swooped down but his fingers slipped through the heads and the shoulders of the legionaries he tried to seize.

Unable to do anything but watch, he watched. Watched as the house was set alight, as the two women were identified and killed out of hand.

Blackness.

Mandeltua held Marcus in a sitting position as he regained consciousness. When he was able to let the other go, the Druid was swaying and sweating profusely though the fire had died down long ago and frost glittered on the grass. He wiped his face on the sleeve of his robe.

Marcus' vision gradually focused on the dying embers of the fire. He looked up at Mandeltua, back to the fire and shivered. He was deathly cold.

Marcus huddled over the dimly glowing ashes and tried to warm himself as his mind still wrestled with the visions he had seen.

Somewhere inside him was a kernel of ice so cold it made the rest of his body feel on fire. Marcus looked at the hard white point and finally realized what it was.

Hate.

"What is it that you want me to do?"

༄

VIRCOVICIUM

Aemilius Karrus had assumed his new position as commander of the *Pillani*, the veterans; middle aged and older men who formed the core of a legion, men whose experience was so ingrained that it amounted to instinct. A hard, disciplined, dependable fighting force.

However, the Ninth had not seen active service for years, even the training had been minimal, the veterans were as badly affected as any other unit. To overcome this state of affairs, Karrus wanted a number of veterans seconded from the Sixth Legion. These men had fought several skirmishes over the years and had seen action at the ill starred Battle of Sand Crags but as well; he had chosen those he knew had a talent for imparting their knowledge to others.

The Pillani were training in small groups along the vallum outside the fort at Vircovicium. He stood for a while on the higher bank and watched them. Various maneuvers were being practiced, some of them quite dangerous despite their only being games.

Directly below him, a half century had been split into two unequal groups; the larger group formed a square with their shields locked protectively together—the *testudo* or tortoise formation, the smaller running freely with their javelins at the ready. On a shouted order, the javelins were cast up into the air to fall on the other force. At a second order, the unused shields of the larger group were flung upward to form an impenetrable shell. The spears, not the usual practice weapons without metal heads, rained down and struck the shields, sticking in or skidding and bouncing off.

There were no casualties, despite the fact that the order to take cover had not been given until the javelins were actually in the air.

"Good day, Tribune."

A centurion had approached without Karrus' noticing.

"A good day to you too, Maximus. Teaches them to keep their heads down." He nodded in the direction of the mock combat. "Sharp weapons."

The centurion grinned. "Concentrates the mind, a little."

"Many injuries?"

"The odd cut. One of them lost a finger yesterday."

"What I want, Maximus, is to borrow eight or so of the veterans. I need them to re-educate men who are good, but who have lost their fighting edge. I'd considered Arius, Fellux and Maleneus as a start, but I'm struggling to pick the rest."

"Well, you've a fine eye, Sir. I could suggest Mellus, over there," he pointed to a man, "and Crassius next to him. There's Fellonius and Tirus—they're not on duty at the moment, and Chranoc, neither is he. They've all forgotten more about fighting than I've ever learned."

"I don't think you do yourself justice, Maximus. You forget that I know your true worth." Karrus was both generous and tactful.

Maximus laughed. "Let's just say that they're the best, eh? I'm sure they'll be more than pleased to assist in your training program."

"I'm sure you're right. No guard duty for a while and a decurion's pay while they're on attachment; they're going to jump at the chance."

"A pay rise? Well then."

"Tell them to report to me for duty in three days, would you? There's no need for them to move from their nice new barracks here, the vallum's big enough for the Ninth and the Sixth to train side by side."

"How long will they be on training duty?"

"Until the spring. Say four months. They get to act like decurions and eat like optios."

Aemilius Karrus grinned, turned away and then turned back again. "No, by Jupiter, I'll let them know myself. I'll see them in the common room, in the Juno barracks. Will you arrange that for me?"

"Sir."

Half an hour later, the eight men were standing in a puzzled group as the Tribune entered.

"At ease," he told them as they straightened up. "Tribune Aemilius Karrus. Anyone here who doesn't know me?"

"Sir." Tirus, a Nubian whom Karrus remembered because of his distinctive complexion, spoke up. "We've all served with you, Sir. We know you well, and we're grateful for your bringing the Sixth back that last time."

Karrus chuckled. "I was running so fast at the time that I wasn't sure you'd kept up with me."

The sally caused laughter all round and everybody relaxed.

"When I've finished what I have to say, Centurion Maximus will fill in the details. All I want to say is this, are you willing to serve under me with the Ninth for four months?"

The reply was unanimous. "Aye." Karrus was filled with pride. He nodded. "Thank you. I'll see you in three days' time." Karrus turned and made for the door only to stop when one of the men called out.

"Tribune."

"Yes?" The man who had spoken had raised his arm, Karrus didn't recognize him and he obviously realized the fact.

"Chranoc, Sir."

"Go ahead."

"I don't wish to cause trouble, but can you tell me whether it's true that Beneficiarius Gellorix has been sent to the mines?"

Karrus stiffened a little. "Yes, that's correct. Why do you ask?"

"It's like this, Sir. I saw what happened to Commandant Pintus, Sir."

"You witnessed the attack?"

"No, Sir. Well not an attack by Gellorix, Sir. A barbarian had attacked the Commandant, Gellorix was trying to get the spear head out of his chest."

Karrus was aghast. The information vindicated the feeling that he had had all the time. The gut feeling he had never done anything about. "Would you be prepared to swear to this in front of the Deputy Governor?"

"Of course, Sir. It's what happened. If I'd known earlier that Gellorix had been sentenced for something that didn't happen, I'd have spoken out before."

Karrus nodded. "Very good, Chranoc. Leave it with me. The Deputy Governor is at Eboracum by now so there isn't much I can do until I can speak to him but I shall need you to relate your tale then."

"Thank you, Sir."

"*Thank you*, Chranoc."

As the legionary left, Karrus recalled the anger he'd felt after being harangued by Pintus' wife and how that had colored his feelings towards Gellorix and stopped him going to speak up at the man's hearing. *If it could have been called that*, he said to himself; *in retrospect, it had been more like playing politics with a good man's life*. With regret, he put the matter to the back of his mind and returned to his quarters, his head filled with training plans for the veterans.

⚜

ABALAVA

Elvin Fellaugh, second in command of the scouts working out of Vircovicium, pulled his horse to a halt a little short of Luguvallium the better to consider the instructions he had been given by Praefector Septimus. The Commandant had been quite specific, Elvin must contact the jeweler and decide if the man was telling the truth in regard to Iavolena's having been there and if so, to find out about her present whereabouts.

The first part would be fairly easy. Elvin had seen the Commandant's wife often enough to recognize her and the jeweler's description would prove the case one way or the other. Her present situation was the tricky question.

Maybe the craftsman could be persuaded to draw a map, or perhaps the place was somewhere that he, Elvin, knew of. Elvin's fingers strayed unconsciously to the hilt of his hunting knife. Either way, he would get the truth from the fellow.

Elvin carried a sizeable amount of money on his person, money which Septimus had given him to negotiate for information about Iavolena and to cover his expenses. He kicked the horse into a walk, Abalava lay an hour or two beyond Luguvallium and by that time it would be dusk.

Now, reasonable expenses meant a night or two lodging at the mansio with a good meal and enough wine to help him sleep. Elvin grinned and nodded happily to himself. Reasonable expenses would cover a decent breakfast—whatever the Romans might think about an early morning meal—and a leisurely lunch. Certainly, he would be doing less than his duty if he paid the full asking price for the information. A thousand denarii...

The fort at Luguvallium fell behind him, and Elvin rode along a low ridge which paralleled the shore of the estuary. The air was clear and the sun a red patch on the western horizon; a haze of smoke marked Abalava's position—evening cooking fires. Elvin rode just a little faster.

Really, there was no need to think in terms of just a day or two. He did not have to report back until he had a definite conclusion. Just because he considered the business to be a wild goose chase was no reason to be less than thorough. Two or three days, several, in fact…

The mansio, when he reached the vicus, was busy. A party of officers had just arrived and were speaking Latin very slowly and loudly in the hope that the local Carvetians would understand them. Elvin sniggered and walked his horse past the inn and along the single, rutted street.

There was the jeweler. Looking through the open doorway where a lantern cast a glow, Elvin could see a dark shape hunched over a workbench which glittered with metal and what he guessed were semi-precious gems.

Elvin left his horse in the alley which cut down the side of the tradesman's shop and walked back. He had read the letter which had been sent to the Praefector; he knew that the man had claimed to have recognized the jewelry that Iavolena had been wearing. Soon, he would determine the truth.

Murrag was perched on a stool behind his workbench. He was alternately hammering thin strips of metal and bending them between two posts set into an iron base. The jeweler, as yet unaware of his visitor, took up one of the strips and riveted the two ends together at the center, when he laid it down, Elvin realized that it was an oval brooch in the form of a knot, a fastening for a cloak.

"Good day to you," he said and Murrag jumped with surprise. The jeweler leaned back so that his eyes were outside the lamplight and scrutinized the other; his lank yellow hair and narrow beard, the watery blue eyes and thin lips. It was evident that he did not like what he saw. "It's a fine evening outside."

Elvin, for his part, thought the other looked like a toad, hunched up in his black cloak with a cynical not-quite-smile spread across his face. Elvin's pleasantry was ignored. "Buying or selling?"

Elvin shrugged. "Buying, if you have what I want."

"Now what would that be?"

"I'm looking for a lady's pendant; it's shaped like a sea shell." Elvin watched the jeweler carefully as he said the words, but beyond a slow blink of the widely space eyes, there was no response.

"A lot of ladies like that sort of thing. You don't come by them too often though. I could probably make you one from jet with a bit of brass trim, silver or gold, even, if you've the right sort of money."

Elvin stood back a pace and leaned against the door jamb. He crossed his arms. "I'd prefer the real thing. What I have in mind only looks like a sea shell. In reality it's quite heavy, they can be found in the right sort of rocks if you know where to look."

The jeweler leaned forward so that the lantern reflected from his eyes, turning them to a pale yellow.

"My pocket's ample enough to buy one," the Scout said.

"You're not from round here, are you?"

Elvin smiled at the non-sequitur. "No. From the east coast. But I've as much Brythonic blood in my veins as you have in yours. Perhaps you have a mistrust of your eastern cousins?"

Murrag shrugged and sat back again. "Your coin is as good as anyone else's, cousin. What I would like to know is why you should come to me asking about such a pendant."

Elvin told the first lie that occurred to him. "I was just down at the inn and talking to someone about it, they told me that a woman had been in there trying to sell just what I was looking for. Furthermore, this woman had been seen riding out of the village with you. I thought you might have bought it from her." Elvin was stabbing in the dark and from the look on Murrag's face; he had just scored a hit.

"Some people have overlong memories and nothing better to prattle about." The corners of Murrag's mouth were turned down. "Still, what if this person was right and I did have this thing? What would you be willing to pay me?"

Elvin had the fellow weighed up now. Profit, money; greed was the master here. He understood the jeweler perfectly, as well as he did himself.

"I don't think that you purchased the pendant, did you? If you had, we'd be talking about a price, not about offers." Elvin looked up at the ceiling, lost in gloom. "Why don't you just tell me where the lady went? Then I can ask her myself."

"I don't know which lady you mean." Murrag rearranged some of the trinkets on his workbench. "And I'd be careful if I was you. There are some powerful Romans who are interested in this bauble you're talking about."

"Powerful Romans..." Elvin debated as to whether to identify his principal when there was the sound of hooves pounding down the street and coming to a careless stop outside.

A young man ran into the shop, a boy.

"Master." The boy was breathless. "Some Romans stopped me and..." Belatedly, he became aware of Elvin's presence but his tongue wouldn't stop in time... "took... the... pendant."

"Quiet boy." Murrag threw a finger up in front of his mouth. "I have a customer in."

Elvin came out of the shadows by the door and smiled. He put a restraining hand on the boy's arm and simultaneously, plunged his dagger into the workbench where it quivered, glinting in the light from the lantern. "What was that? A pendant, you said. A seashell pendant?"

Miserably, Lyfan nodded, knowing that Murrag was going to be very angry, but knowing, too, that he had little choice but to tell the truth.

Elvin let go of the boy and pulling another stool out from the wall, he sat down opposite Murrag. The jeweler hastily swept some of the bits and pieces away from Elvin's side of the bench as he put his elbows on the board and propped his chin on his hands.

"So, cousin. You did have the pendant that we've been discussing." He turned back to Lyfan who was standing uncertainly in the doorway. "Don't go away boy, I want to talk with you some more. There'll be some money in it for you."

Without waiting for a reply, he turned back to the jeweler and flicked the dagger's handle so that it shivered in the lantern light. He pulled it free and felt the edge with his thumb.

"Now cousin, unless you wish to grin from ear to ear," Elvin pressed the back of the blade against his own throat, "you'll tell me all about your dealings with this lady and what has happened to her."

"She wanted to get away from Briton," said Murrag who was blessed with neither bravery nor a strong bladder. "I'm a poor man, when I couldn't afford to buy the pendant from her; she gave it to me as payment for a passage on a ship to Erin."

Elvin looked over his shoulder at Lyfan. "Is this the truth?"

"She went aboard the ship all right," affirmed the boy.

"And you saw the ship? You'd recognize it again?"

"Probably."

"What about the master? Did you see her captain?"

Lyfan nodded again. "I'd certainly know him again."

Back to Murrag. He put the point of his knife under the old man's chin, pressed so that the old and wrinkled flesh dimpled. "The truth now, who was the ship's master and when will he be back? I take it that he was a trader?"

Murrag started to nod, but felt the point of the knife bite more deeply.

"Yes, yes, a trader." Murrag was almost weeping with fear and felt the warmth flood down inside his trousers as he lost control of his bladder. "Ferdiad, Ferdiad from Dun Croach. He'll be back in seven weeks, regular as clockwork he is. Same place."

"And if that's not the truth, I'll swear I'll be back and cut you up into little bits and I'll feed you to the fishes piece by piece. That *is* the truth, old man."

"Oh it's the truth." Murrag misunderstood Elvin's last words "I swear by Lugh that I tell you the truth."

"I'm sure you do," Elvin said quietly. I can *smell* it. You'd better go and get cleaned up." And he stood up, sliding his dagger back into its sheath.

"What's your name, boy?" Elvin crossed to the door.

"Lyfan, Sir."

"Come with me, Lyfan. You can sup with me at the inn tonight and you can tell me where this ship will berth and what sort of a ship it is and all about it. Eh?"

Lyfan nodded and taking a last look into the gloom inside the shop, followed on behind Elvin Fellaugh.

Murrag hated them both, but most of all, he hated Lyfan for seeing him brought this low by that arrogant pig from the east.

CHAPTER TEN

EBORACUM

SENATOR VITUNIUS, SPECIAL ENVOY FROM THE EMPEROR HADRIAN arrived at Eboracum five days after leaving Londinium. He was pleased to see Marcellus Sextus Flavius there, ready to conduct him into the warm interior of the *pallatium*. They had made good time, the mansios along the Ermine Street had been comfortable and well chosen, the horses had been changed at regular intervals, all had been well managed. Everything but the weather, however, which had been bad and worse by turns. Vitunius was tired. He was a large, not to say corpulent, man and while he had boundless energy for intrigue, for bureaucratic scheming and even a well developed understanding of military tactics, he detested physical exercise unless it was of the carnal variety.

The Senator dismounted and stepped carefully, his legs a little rubbery.

The two men embraced.

"My dear Marcellus," opened the envoy. "Fancy, we share a name. I feel that I know so much about you that we must share ancestry too. Your mother sends her love, of course and pines for your return. The Emperor sends his best wishes both for now and for your future plans."

"Senator, if I call you Marcellus, it will be like addressing myself."

"And I shan't know to which of us you're talking."

Flavius, the Deputy Governor, laughed. "Well, I could not wish for a more dignified namesake. How went the journey?"

Vitunius smiled inwardly. *How like myself in my late twenties.* He thought, *Gracious, charming and oh so ambitious.* "The biggest problem, until we came to the shores of Briton, was dust and since then it has been mud. How do you live in this country-wide quagmire?" Vitunius felt that all journeys—even good ones—were to be deplored. Travel broadened nothing but the backside, he would say, he remembered only the worst things about journeys.

"There are some good points to the country, Senator. Allow me to show you one—a long hot bath after arduous travel."

Vitunius looked up, rolled his eyes. "Am I come to Elysium?"

"Afterwards," continued Flavius, "we can talk while we dine."

"Already the gracious host, Marcellus. You read my mind except in one respect. A glass of wine before either would not come amiss and of course, there is my honor guard to accommodate."

"All in hand, Senator." Flavius snapped his fingers. "Wine. A very smooth desert from my family's vineyards. A barracks is ready for your guard."

Afterwards, when they were propped up on thick cushions, dressed in loose togas, Flavius asked, "So why the personal message delivered by so eminent a person as yourself?"

"One thing our Emperor wished me to tell you was that your reinforcements are on the way. No more than ten days behind me, Flavius."

"Well thank you for that. I must admit that I already know that. I have friends at home who keep me posted."

A braggart and not very polite to point it out, though, thought Vitunius. "I see that not even the Senate can keep its secrets safe."

"Well not when the issue is as large as transforming a legion of masons and road builders into soldiers again." He smiled and Vitunius admired the disarming effect that Flavius could wield.

"And of course, you will also know who is to command the Ninth?"

Flavius' expression changed from pleasant to serious. "Not so, Senator. Oh no. There would be very few people who are party to that knowledge."

"Three, actually. Hadrian, myself and Governor Severus. I have the official authorization with our Emperor's signature in my strong box. Allow me to congratulate you Marcellus; you are the youngest Legate ever to command a full legion at war. The Emperor feels that not only do you have great administrative acumen, but will instinctively make the right decisions. I'll make this observation Flavius, you're just one victory away from making General. Enjoy that victory and return to Rome to receive your just rewards."

It took several long seconds for Vitunius' message to sink in. Flavius' face portrayed surprise, incredulity, elation, and finally pleasure tempered with apprehension.

"Jupiter." Flavius was almost tongue tied. "Well I asked for it, I hoped for it, but I don't think I really believed it would come to it. Let's drink to it. Victory. Victory over Albyn." He raised his goblet.

"Victory over Albyn," echoed Vitunius.

They finished the wine, Flavius called for more and a few minutes later, a young local girl brought in a tall earthenware jug.

The Senator glanced at the girl, the long blonde hair plaited and braided and reaching below her waist, the bright cornflower eyes. "I see that this country has good points beside its hot baths, Flavius."

Flavius laughed. "An excellent example, Senator. Um," he wondered if Vitunius had been hinting, "perhaps you're interested..."

Vitunius held up a hand. "Not enough flesh on her, my friend. I like them... better endowed. And anyway, what if my dear Bessina... hm? If word got back, well I'd be... no, it wouldn't be worth the consequences."

"Well, if you ever feel that, um, anything can be arranged."

"Thank you, Flavius. But no, I'm astonishingly faithful to my wife, you know. Incredibly so."

Flavius heaved a sigh. He wasn't sure if he had complimented the Senator, or cast a slur on the man's honor.

"I must confess, Sir, that I'm still in shock from your news. It might take several days to get over it. How long would you care to stay with us?"

"It all depends, Flavius. I have some other business to attend to."

"Other business. Anything that I can assist you with?"

"I have something to look into for a friend of mine. Senator Mansustus, you know him, perhaps."

Flavius shook his head. "Know *of* him, of course."

"Hm. Well, his son was enslaved, sent to the mines. Marcus is the name. Marcus Gellorix, I believe."

Flavius was instantly alert. "Yes, Senator. I believe it is. Marcus Uffin Gellorix. I sentenced him to the mines sooner than having him crucified out of respect for Senator Mansustus."

"Enslavement or crucifixion. Both bitter medicines to swallow when it's your own son."

"But the one is not as permanent as the other."

"True enough. Mansustus heads a powerful lobby, a very powerful lobby in the Senate. Powerful enough to harm even your charmed future. Were you on solid ground when you passed the sentence?"

For the first time since he had given the sentence, Flavius considered the matter. He recalled the Scout, badly beaten—which was not surprising given the crime. Unwilling to speak, as he remembered, not a word of defense. There had been the testimony of three legionaries; how he had thrust the spear into... what was his name? Commandant... The name escaped him for the moment, but the circumstances of the case were quite clear.

"I *was* on solid ground Senator. The testimony was clear, no defense was made. However, if *you* feel that the punishment was too severe, I'm sure that he could be released into your custody. Take him back to Rome for the Senate itself to put him to the question, perhaps. Perhaps the Emperor could be persuaded to pardon the man."

Vitunius admired Flavius' adroit handling of the matter.

"I'd like to speak to the young man concerned before I make a decision."

"Quite so, Senator. I can set the arrangements in hand immediately. Help yourself to some more wine; it will only take a moment."

Flavius left the room and had his aide summoned to his office. When the man arrived, Flavius smiled briefly. "The former Beneficiarius Marcus Gellorix. Send an authorization to the mines at Evenhope and have him released and brought here as quickly as possible."

Flavius turned to go then stopped as the man made no move.

"Well, something the matter? What are you waiting for?"

The aide was a man of advancing years; he tended to stutter at moments of stress. "B-but S-sir, Gellorix. H-have you n-not read your m-messages?"

"Messages. Not since this morning."

"Gellorix escaped from Evenhope, Sir. Some days ago. The whole of the Wall knows about it, all of the guards have been warned to watch out for him. The Scouts have been told to report any sightings at once."

When Flavius returned to the Senator, he was composed and had looked at the problem from all sides. In this case, only the truth would suffice, the truth of Gellorix's escape, that was; not the fact that the dispatch had been waiting, unread.

"There is a complication, Senator. It seems that Marcus Gellorix has left the mine and his whereabouts are, at present, unknown to us. We do know that he is unharmed and we are doing everything we can to find him."

"*Left* the mine? What do you mean *left*?" Senator Vitunius was too old a statesman to miss the discomfort in the other's features.

"Well. It seems that, for the time being, he has escaped."

MEDIONEMETON

From the brow of the hill, Uffin marveled at their destination which was a clearing in the oak forest below them, a forest which itself was hemmed in by cliffs and impassably steep screes. The clearing was large, a hundred paces at its widest and dominated by three huge stones which pointed at the sky like three giant fingers. To the side of these was what appeared to be a well and beyond was an area covered by uncountable burial mounds. Medionemeton, the most fabled of the *Temenes*, the sacred precincts, perhaps more revered than Mona had been before the Romans ravaged the Holy Island.

Uffin, who was becoming used to thinking of himself by his Brigantean name, could see how difficult it would be to find. They had come by secret ways over the mountains, by mist shrouded passes and finally, by a narrow and winding cleft which was the only way down the sheer rock walls. The passes could each be defended by a handful of men while that last fissure could be held by a single guard, no army could ever come at the community in force. The place was a natural fortress, palisaded by the gods.

Mandeltua stood at Uffin's side. "I am home." He gestured, taking in the open area and the surrounding forest in one movement of his arm. "I hope that you will come to feel the same way. It is a pleasant place to live, a gentle way of life, a shedding of burdens."

Uffin shook his head. Mandeltua's words were quite at odds with what he had, so far, gleaned of the Druid's intentions which seemed entirely warlike.

"A little further down here is a stream, you can hear a waterfall if you listen carefully. We can bathe our feet there and drink of the pure mountain water before we descend the rest of the way."

They walked a little further and there was the stream, a rush of ice-cold water frothing over stones worn as smooth as a woman's body.

"In one day's time it is the eve of Samhain. We are in good time for the celebrations. The gods have indeed smiled upon our travels; such a timely arrival can only be a good sign."

At the side of the stream was a tiny shrine, three upright stones which mirrored those in the glade below with a handful of brown acorns between them.

"Go ahead," said Mandeltua. "Wash the dust from yourself while I perform my duties."

Uffin stripped off his sandals and trousers and waded into the water. He gasped at the numbing coldness even as it cooled and refreshed his feet. He bent over to wash his face and not for the first time, was suddenly conscious of the heavy beard he had grown. Finally, he drank deeply before wading to the bank and donning his clothes.

Mandeltua was kneeling at the shrine, the sun full on his face making a halo of the wild hair. The Druid was chanting, but in a language quite unknown to Uffin. He waited several minutes before the other fell silent and opened his eyes.

"Mandeltua."

"Yes, Uffin."

"Do the Gods really hear you and aid you?"

"They hear me. Sometimes they help me."

"Religion is something which I have not studied. I am quite ignorant in these matters. Tell me then, how do the Gods help you? Do you call on them today and expect help tomorrow? Or the day after, perhaps? Or in a week's time?"

Mandeltua gave him a look of mild reproach. "Uffin, you have a lot to learn. Our Gods have no notion of time as you or I know it, one event after another. In *Annwn*, today and tomorrow are the same, or yesterday for that matter. When I wish to speak to them, I must free my spirit from its bodily shackles and send it forth into their presence."

Mandeltua bathed his feet and splashed a little water onto his face, combed his beard with his fingers.

"If the Gods happen to see me, if they are not too preoccupied with more weighty matters—things which mortals would find incomprehensible—they will offer advice."

"Do they ever come to our realm?" asked Uffin as they resumed their progress.

"They leave *Annwn* only rarely these days; when they do come, they manifest themselves as wind or as water, birds, animals. They come briefly, to take a swift glance at our world. Do you understand?"

Uffin thought over what he had been told. "Not really," he said at last.

"Well, I can sympathize with you. I have traveled the one true path all of my life and still do not fully understand."

The Druid bent over to take water in his cupped hands and as he did so, an ornament tied about his neck slipped free: Mandeltua's stone of power. He stood up and it slid back behind his clothes once more. Uffin experienced a sense of familiarity at sight of it, a nagging thought that he knew more about the amulet than he had reason to.

"Let us hasten, Uffin. Great events are about to unfold, events which you are a part of." Mandeltua's enigmatic words broke into his thoughts and dispelled his concern.

As they neared the holy site of Medionemeton, Uffin saw that houses had been built among the trees, small round houses capable of housing no more than six people or so. The style was quite unlike that of the neighboring Selgovae or Votadinae where each house could sleep anywhere between twenty and a hundred. Then the reason came to him. Larger buildings would mean that trees had to be cut: to a Druid, this would be sacrilege under most circumstances. More practically, the trees provided a perfect cover against the sight of any scout stumbling on the location by chance.

Some of the roundhouses were occupied and men lounged outside, leaning against the walls, sitting with their backs against trees, whetting axe or sword blades, spear heads, polishing metal ornaments, greasing leather harness. There were many different tribes represented, Uffin saw. All of them sporting different hairstyles and facial whiskers, some with tattoos, some without, yet there was a common theme. Each one of the men he saw was a chief or at least, a nobleman of his tribe. Their clothes told him this, richly embroidered with circles and swirls and the representation of knots. The weaponry confirmed the impression, beautifully wrought sword blades with intertwining designs or runes incised along the length, gold and silver torques and armbands, all of them old and much used and carefully maintained. All of them handed from chieftain father to heir apparent son or won in contest by a challenger.

What they had gathered here for was something that Uffin could not guess except to suppose it was connected with Mandeltua's comment concerning *great events.*

Several men who could only be Druids came to meet Mandeltua and looked at Uffin with mild curiosity. Staring back, Uffin realized that a mature age was not, as he had supposed, a prime requirement of the Druidic vocation. The ages of this group of robed and whiskered Druids varied from relative youth to patriarchal.

Mandeltua spoke rapidly and at length to his colleagues in a voice too low for Uffin to make out more than a word or two. However, after being the object of several perplexed glances, Mandeltua drew Uffin forward.

"I bring you Uffin Gellorix," he said loudly and with some force. "Cocidius himself came to me in a dream and foretold that this man would unite the tribes. I place him in your charge. Feed him, clothe him in fitting raiment and let him rest until dark. Tonight will be momentous, I promise you."

So they did as they were bid. Some with antagonism: *what are these momentous events?* Some with acceptance: *Did Cocidius bless you with his presence?* Others with neither questions nor interest.

By evening, he was well fed and clothed in fine woolen garments, his beard had been trimmed and he was rested. At sunset, they roused him and escorted him from the oak grove to the three gigantic fingers of stone.

A strong wind was blowing and with it came rain. Colors seemed to drain away leaving the site etched in so many shades of grey; voices became tiny, childlike against the background of rushing air and the creaking of great, wind-tossed oaks. The wind searched the land, fingering cloaks, groping through the trees, flinging dead leaves into the air like a cloud of ragged bats.

The visitors—the tribal chieftains and their closest supporters, stood in a packed circle with a clear area at its center. Druids ringed the area, while Mandeltua stood at the uncannily still center of the violent wind storm.

Mandeltua stood as straight as the three menhirs (a large upright standing stone), by some trick or echo from the mighty stones, his voice reached every one of those who listened.

"You have been summoned here," he told them, "to a meeting of chieftains, the like of which has never before been seen. A meeting watched over by the Gods." And it might easily have been so, for Mandeltua continued to defy the forces of nature as he went on, his voice even falling slightly. "Here present are members of all the free tribes in Albyn, from the islands of the far north to those living in the shadow of the Wall. Many of you have fought long and bitter feuds, one against another and you have come here to neutral ground to hear of your one and only chance to sweep the invaders back into the sea that brought them here. They have built one wall across our land, leave them be and they will build another and another to hem us in like sheep into folds."

Mandeltua paused. He turned in all directions, his eyes were alight, his hair stood out like a dandelion clock. He pointed to all quarters.

"There is one way only.

"Those of you from the north and from the far west may doubt what I tell you, but ask your brothers of the Selgovae and the Votadinii and of the Novantae, for theirs is the land divided by the Wall. Ask them too about the battle of the Grampians and the three generations of their dead.

"There is a way, one only."

Mandeltua licked his lips.

"These invaders of our land come from so far away, you could not walk there in ten hands of days. They speak so many tongues that one tribe may not speak to another, may not eat with another, may not live with another. And they come to Albyn as they came to Briton. With but one purpose."

Again he paused and the roar of the wind came back momentarily.

"They come to kill and subjugate and to turn us, the last free men, into slaves. Surely there must be a way to beat these vermin, these men who have given up their souls, from our shores.

"Yes.

"There is such a way."

Mandeltua was a master musician and the instrument he played was his oratory. He lifted his voice and his audience tasted aspiration, he lowered it and they knew despair. He spoke slowly, they held their breath, fast and they panted like a dog in a chase. Every man there stood in two places; on the hard, windswept dirt and in the palm of Mandeltua's hand.

"Brothers. My brothers. Be you from the Epinii, the Carnovi, the Caerrini or from the Creones or Smertae or the Taezali. All of you. Listen to the way."

Mandeltua beckoned and druids pushed Uffin forward. He shuffled, as mesmerized by Mandeltua's voice as the others.

"Here is one chosen by Cocidius himself."

"Ah!" said his audience at mention of the God's name. "The horned one" and signs were made to protect them from the God's anger.

"A man who's grandsire was King of the Brigantes, a man who has been trained by those same invaders of our land and who has more reasons to hate them than most of us. A man destined to lead us to victory and to fulfill the prophecy that stone will be their downfall."

Reaching behind him, Mandeltua grasped the sleeve of Uffin's garment and pulled him into the charmed circle which surrounded the Druid.

"Uffin Gellorix!"

And Uffin felt the hairs of his head begin to stir. His scalp prickled, it felt as though a thousand tiny sparks crawled over his skin and swarmed up into his head. He stood there, looking at the assemblage not knowing what was expected of him, but waiting for some event which seemed to be rushing from the future to take hold of him.

The wind died, a dead calm pervaded Medionemeton. A bright glow seemed to come from the stones and then even from Mandeltua and from Uffin themselves. The light intensified, streaming upward from Uffin's head like long white flames which writhed and burned without consuming.

Blue and white, silver, blinding colors flashing around him so that it was impossible to tell what was real, what imaginary. For long seconds, Uffin felt as though he had been lifted up from the ground; he was on a level with the tops of the standing stones and he was outlined in brilliance.

Then the lights dimmed and he was lowered, his feet once more solidly on the ground and the rain fell hard enough to hurt, long straight darts from the heavens.

"Belenos the Shining One has conferred his blessing on he whom he has chosen." Such was the faith in Mandeltua's shouted words that even Uffin believed him.

He took hold of Uffin's arm and turned him so that the Druid's eyes burned into his own. "You *are* the Chosen One, Uffin," he said earnestly. "Do not doubt it for an instant. Say something to your followers; they *will* follow you now, wherever you lead them."

Uffin stood there with scarcely a thought in his head. To be told this out of the blue, to be expected to address these powerful men. He felt absolutely inadequate, his limbs trembled, his muscles felt like water. *Why him? Surely there were a thousand men more suited to the job than himself.* He peered through the sheets of falling rain to where the Chieftains could be dimly seen. Words welled up in his throat without thought and the trembling passed from his body although it remained in his voice.

"If the Gods have chosen me to lead you, will you follow?" His tone was almost uncertain but strengthened as he went on.

"Aye!" The reply was thunderous.

"Then let every one of us celebrate this together. No matter what tribe we come from, we must leave here as brothers."

Afterwards the chiefs came forward to where Uffin stood beside the well and cast into its depths, their votive offerings: a sword, a spear, a piece of jewelry. Mandeltua stood behind Uffin and when all had passed by, he made prayers to usher in the new year, a year in which a new movement was given birth, a new beginning.

That night, Uffin dreamed that he was in a dark wood surrounded by a high stone wall when suddenly the path was illuminated by a bright shaft of light. A tall figure came towards him but although it had the outline of a man, there was something wrong, something unreal which he could not place for a moment. Then Uffin saw that the head was the head of a stag with spreading antlers; the mouth opened and the creature's breath steamed in the still, cold air. The voice was sweet and melodious.

"Destroy them with stone."

⚜

Uffin awoke instantly as though the words had been physical blows which left his senses reeling. He was bathed in a cold sweat, his limbs were shaking and he had a raging thirst. He got up from the pallet and drank from an earthenware jug of water. Emptying the remainder over his head, Uffin rubbed his face, massaged his eyes.

While the water still ran from his hair and shirt, he pulled on his outer garments and pushed through the curtain which covered the doorway of the hut.

It was early dawn with watery sunlight gleaming between the sere leaves of the oaks. He realized that he had hardly slept. The festivities of Samhain Eve had continued for many hours, it must only have been an hour before when he had sought his bed.

He did not desire company and climbed the wooded hillside behind the huts until he was high enough to see Medionemeton below and the whole spread of the basin shaped hollow which held the Druid's stronghold in its palm.

Here and there were small herds of long horned cattle grazing in the infrequent glades of the forest. A river, child of the many streams which tumbled down the slopes, wound its way towards the center. It terminated in a small pool which soaked into the ground, without doubt, finding its way to the outside by means of subterranean cracks and caverns. Food and drink: A self-sufficient community hidden here and unknown to the Romans, guiding the resistance against the Romans' encroachment into Albyn.

The events of the past few days had gone much too fast for him to take them in at the time. Like a leaf in a gale, they had swept him along with no time to think, no time to pause and wonder if what he saw was the truth.

Now, secluded, Uffin took time to think about these experiences, about Mandeltua and his strange access to knowledge, the weird acceptance of himself as some sort of strategist for the tribes of Albyn.

Uffin, always a realist, placed his faith in hard facts and his own observations and there was no denying that the events which he remembered had actually taken place.

However, there was another and more difficult thing to accept. Part of being a realist was his reluctance to place a blind faith in the unseen gods and goddesses which his fellow legionaries had looked to for support. It was the same with dice and games of chance, there was no such thing as luck he maintained and would not wager on anything where the odds were less than favorable. Now he had witnessed things which could only be ascribed to supernatural forces, even—perhaps—been visited by a God.

Everything was conspiring to urge him in one direction, both the supernatural and the mundane. Did he wish to comply? Was there a choice?

He was being given a monumental task: to lead an unknown number of uneducated men of various tribes against the might of Rome. The Albyn tribesmen were highly individualistic, craving personal glory: concepts of tactics and group maneuvers were unknown and quite foreign to their way of thinking. No man trusted another not to steal his chance of renown.

A gaggle of individuals against the most highly organized and disciplined professional soldiers in the world. And...

A new thought occurred to him.

The Ninth? Being re-formed? It could only be for invasion, there was no other reason. Did that mean that there would be one legion or two? The Ninth and the Sixth?

Uffin did not know enough. He did not have enough answers. At the moment he did not even have enough questions. He stayed on the mountainside for a long time in his attempt to come to terms with the task he seemed to have little chance of refusing.

Suddenly Asel's face swam before his mind's eye and he could think no longer. Tears streamed down his cheeks and a great spasm of sobs racked his body. So young, such a waste of a life, such a brutal, ending. Never a chance to be mistress in her own home, nor a mother, nor...his wife.

Finally, he retraced his steps and he had been missed, there was no doubt about that when he saw one of the druids running to meet him.

"Uffin. The Chiefs are waiting for you and are becoming impatient. They want to know what to do."

Uffin sighed and nodded. "Lead on then. Let's see what we can tell them."

As they approached the gathered chieftains, he counted them. Seventeen. Uffin had not realized that there were so many. Seventeen. More tribes than he had realized, more than half of them must be unknown to him but then, he had traded only with those closest to the Wall.

"So, Brigantean," one of them shouted, "are you going to teach *us* how to fight? A man from a tribe that kisses the arsess of these invaders?"

Uffin ignored the comment, did not acknowledge that he had heard it. Under other circumstances, he would have bristled with rage, made a challenge but for the moment, at least, a sense of calm had descended upon him. He felt a steely purpose within him, a rush of power through his body that swept aside the childish insult, trivialized it, withered it away to nothing.

He drew closer.

"Let us see *you* fight then." Seeing that the first insult had missed its mark, another tried to be more direct. "If you're going to lead us, show us what skills you have, how brave you are."

This was easier. Too near to ignore it and it could be turned to advantage, a demonstration was easier than a speech. Uffin shrugged. *This was of no consequence*, it said for him. "If that's what you want? Hm?" He had little interest, his tone of voice told them. "I'll not deny you your entertainment. Find a volunteer," Uffin walked on a few more paces, "one who won't mind a few bruises."

In front of Uffin was a tall thin man with his hair plaited into two braids which hung down in front of his ears while the rest was spiky, thick with grease.

"Can I borrow your sword?"

The man lifted an eyebrow and with a sardonic smile drew his blade, passed it over. It was a massively broad weapon, the length of an arm and half as long again, it curved slightly towards the end. He said nothing as he offered it to Uffin.

"Thank you." Uffin took the sword and walked over to a hut which was still being constructed. Several bundles of saplings were piled at the side, intended for working into the roof structure. He picked one out and choosing a spot where the diameter was right, cut it with the borrowed sword. He measured off a forearm's length and cut again.

He returned the sword to its owner who received it back with a puzzled expression. Then he turned to one of the others who carried a tall oblong shield, a little unusual among the Albyns; this too, he borrowed.

By this time, several druids had joined them and were looking askance at the odd preparations.

"Do you have any blood?" he asked.

"Blood? What sort of blood?"

"Any sort. Animal blood would be best, we don't have to harm anyone then."

"There'll be blood behind the kitchens. We've butchered enough cattle for tonight's feast."

"Then bring me some, a cupful. Now," turning back to the Chief who had required proof of Uffin's skill, "who's to be the volunteer?"

"Any of us would fight, but not against a stick. Where's the honor in that?"

Uffin gave him a thin lipped smile. "If I'm to lead you, I can't go around killing. I've enough enemies among the Romans without building feuds with your tribesmen."

He stood back and addressed them as a whole.

"I've been trained by the Romans. I want to show you the difference between your sort of fighting and theirs. Is there a volunteer?"

No one answered so after a moment, Uffin picked the biggest man among them. A man a finger's length taller than himself and broader by the width of a hand. Muscle bulged along the man's arms.

"You?"

He shook his head. "Salmane, Chief of the Lugi. If I draw my sword, it is to kill."

"Then kill me. Try to kill me."

"Take that silly stick and spank him with it, Salmane," someone called, which only served to embarrass Salmane, who blushed and knew he was blushing.

"So be it, then," he said. "If no one else will do it, I will."

Uffin looked across at the druids where one of them held a leather bucket filled with entrails.

"Chickens."

"No matter. It's as good as any." Uffin dipped the end of his stick in the mess and drew it out wet with blood. "Stay here, I might need a little more, yet."

Uffin grinned at Salmane. "Come on Salmane. Have at me, man."

The Lugi Chief shed his cloak and hoisting his great sword aloft, came on with a rush. At about thirty summers, Salmane was a fine looking man, a physique to rival any of the sculptures to be found in Roman houses and temples. He wore a short skirt which reached to just below his knee and his chest carried a thick matting of ginger hair.

The sword slashed sideways, singing through the air with a high keening sound. Had Uffin remained where he was or been slower in moving, his head would have leaped from his shoulders, blood spouting from arteries in his neck.

But Uffin dropped to one knee and the blade shrieked past above his head. Simultaneously, he reached forward, the stick caught Salmane in the chest, stopping the man's forward rush with a jolt. A red mark was left on his skin; later, it would bear an ugly bruise.

Salmane roared as if his body rather than his pride had been wounded. Almost without a break in the swing, he brought that mighty blade round in a backhand slash which Uffin parried with the shield and, at the same time, thrusting the stick into his opponent's thigh.

The Chieftain raised his sword high in the air and brought it down in an almost vertical chop which would split Uffin from crown to groin. Had he been there.

Uffin stepped aside as Salmane became committed to the blow. The momentum of the heavy weapon could not be killed, the blade hit the ground in a shower of sparks as Uffin's stick punched into the other's ribs, just under the heart.

The shock stopped Salmane breathing and he stepped back. Uffin leaned all the way forward and jabbed at Salmane's ankle and then twisted the stick between his feet. Salmane fell as heavily as one of the oak trees he resembled.

Before Salmane could even begin to struggle to his feet, Uffin had his stick thrusting into the hollow of Salmane's throat, Uffin's foot was on his sword arm.

The contest was over. It had lasted four minutes, long enough to run a Roman mile.

Before he took the stick from Salmane's throat, he turned to the ring of silent onlookers. "Chief Salmane is a brave man like all of you. He's brave in a different way too; he is brave enough to risk fighting a man with a stick."

Uffin stepped back. "It will take more than bravery to defeat the Romans. King Calgacus had twice as many men as he faced when the Roman Agricola met him in the Grampian mountains, but they lost the battle."

He bent over and assisted the still-breathless Salmane to his feet. He grinned, used a conspiratorial tone of voice. "It isn't bravery that kills Romans, it's technique and it's discipline. Now this," he held up the stick with its bloody tip, "is the same length as a Roman sword. It's light and it is pointed and it's made to thrust with. Not slashing and stabbing."

Uffin pointed out the blood stain on Salmane's ribs, now surrounded by a purple halo. "If I had used a sword, Salmane's breath would be whistling through his chest. So it wouldn't have killed him but he wouldn't be fighting too well. Here," he pointed to the other chest wound, "it would have found his heart. Here, on Salmane's leg, his life blood would have drained away and here on the ankle, his foot would have been useless."

He punched Salmane on the shoulder. "I did not intend insult, my friend. But I had to show them these things."

"Where is the honor in fighting like this? Who will sing of our deeds?"

Uffin rounded on the speaker immediately.

"The Romans do not fight for honor, they fight to kill and for the land you stand on. They fight like this because it is the quickest and the easiest way. None of them seek to be first or to be the finest. They fight side by side; if one man falls, another steps into his place—no gaps are left in their ranks because gaps allow ingress."

Uffin sought for an example. "Does a boar learn to fight? Does it need to think before it gouges?"

He lowered his voice once more. "The Romans train every day so that they fight like a boar, without having to think about it. Does the snake have to hate you before it strikes? The Romans don't hate, they don't work themselves into a rage. They're natural killers. They're good at it."

Before Salmane or any of the others could reply, Uffin offered his hand to the defeated Chieftain. "Friend?"

Salmane paused a single moment, a long one, then he seized the proffered hand and held it in a crushing grip.

"I have a tribe who will follow me to the death if I ask it. My tribe is yours whenever you wish it. I doubt that my men will change the swords they have inherited from their fathers, but they will fight for you." He rubbed at the bruises on his ribs and grinned. "I am very pleased that you chose to use a stick, Uffin and not a Roman sword."

One by one the great Chiefs of the Albyn tribes came forward and clasped Uffin's hand. Two of them impressed him greatly for they seemed to trust one another and seemed too, to be quite happy to join in a joint venture. One was Chief of the Selgovae and the other, a huge man covered in blue tattoos, was Chief of the Callatae, the man who's authoritative voice he had last heard at the ritual execution he had witnessed before the attack on Fort Throp. They invited him to visit them at their homes.

Mandeltua had taken no part in these proceedings; he had not been seen since the ostentatious events of the previous night. However, he was present at the feast and made a point of coming to speak to him. "You have done well," he said. "You have gained the trust of the Chiefs." Evidently, the duel and his words had been reported. "You have started things moving, you must not let the momentum die down. After the feast, we will talk and you must outline your plans."

My plans! Uffin nodded and filled his trencher with meat.

⁂

THROP

Elvin marched into Praefector Septimus' office and saluted as smartly as any uniformed legionary.

"By the right arm of Mars," Muttered a startled Septimus. "Two days gone and back already."

Elvin made a mental note to stay away longer next time. Most of his time had been spent in Luguvallium buying food and wine with Septimus' money. And girls, the sound of coins jingling in a pouch was a powerful aphrodisiac.

"I have discovered certain facts, Sir. I thought I should let you know as soon as possible. It may take more money to er, to redeem your wife."

"You've found her?" The relief in Vibius' voice was manifest. Elvin knew that he had to be careful with his replies.

"Not exactly, Sir. I know that she's alive and I know where she's been taken."

"Taken?"

"The jeweler who sent you the message only knew this. He had seen her in passing and recognized her and being a jeweler, he recognized what she was wearing. I found someone else who knew what had happened to her. The Lady Iavolena has been taken to Erin, against her will, of course."

"Erin. There are more barbarians there than in Albyn. Not even the Emperor wants to go there."

"Not yet,"

"How can we get her back?"

Elvin scratched his cheek and replied in a thoughtful voice, "I know the name of the Captain of the ship she was taken on. I know roughly when he will be back and where. He may be open to business suggestions, if there's money to be made, most of them from that place seem happy to buy and sell."

"When will he be back? And where? I'll take my cavalry..."

"Oh no, Sir." Elvin was aghast. "With respect, Sir. This man is as wily as a fox. He isn't going to come ashore if he even suspects a Roman presence and your cavalry isn't going to swim after him back to Erin."

Vibius' flushed face paled. He sat back with resignation. "So what do you suggest?"

Elvin grinned to himself. This could become a very profitable venture, better even than the trade he did as a Roman scout when much of his income came from selling goods provided by the Romans.

"He's returning in six or eight weeks. I'd suggest that I go to the docking site and, incidentally, that's in Albyn, north of the Wall. I'd meet with the man and talk business with him, report back to you. Your decision to pay the ransom, or not..."

"There's no other way?"

"We could have a ship ready, follow him and try to steal her back. Risky though. You said yourself how many barbarians there are on the other side of the water."

Septimus Vibius thought the matter over. *There really didn't seem any other way.* "Very well. We'll do it your way, but six weeks seems like a lifetime."

"Keep busy, Sir. The time will pass more quickly."

LUGUVALLIUM

Decurion Arvius Sellitus finished his twenty eight day tour of duty as overseer on the Wall. The job was not that onerous even in Novantae country, but watching men put one stone on top of another and living in a leather tent with nothing but bread and the odd hare to eat was boring.

He wanted a good meal, a large drink and a woman, and not necessarily in that order.

Several men—both officers and infantry—had got back to Luguvallium before him and were already gambling on a dice game when he reached the mansio. Their voices and laughter could be heard out in the street and there was no need to wonder if they had been at the ale and wine yet.

The crowd in the main room was mostly men, too early for many girls to be in as yet so Sellitus ordered a jug of wine and found a bench where he could watch the game in progress.

After settling his bills for kit and a new knife, there were twenty day's wages jingling heavily in his pouch. He had a mind to invest a few coins in bets.

Only two men were playing. They were using a squared board where they had to move stone counters from the outside to the center on each throw of the dice. The object was to avoid those squares which had been blacked out, failure meant the loss of the counter, those who were out of the present game sat and watched. The players were well into the end game and progressing slowly with much whispering to the dice and invoking the aid of favored deities.

Sellitus poured some more wine and watched and waited as it ground to its end.

The game finished and two of the previous players, having no more money or grown bored, left the table. Sellitus and another, an infantryman, joined in, taking the vacant seats.

At his turn, Sellitus threw well and advanced swiftly. He increased his bet and promptly threw a four on his next turn, a four instead of the five he needed placed him on a black square. His reaction was quick; he knocked the board with his elbow, pretending an accident. Sellitus was almost fast enough, the legionary who had sat down with him was the only one to see what had happened and it was he who took offence, accusing Sellitus of cheating.

The wine on an empty stomach had turned things hazy and Sellitus was quite aware that his fighting in such a state might end badly; nevertheless, he loosened the sword in its scabbard and rubbed his bristly chin.

"I may have been hasty," he admitted. "I'll pay my debts as though I'd lost fair and square. How's that?"

The other looked at him, stony faced. Sellitus brought out the bauble he had confiscated days earlier.

"I'm short of money." He lied. "But this is worth a small fortune. See, it has a golden ring set into it."

"Money," said his accuser. "I don't want a worthless snail shell. You owe me a hundred sesterces."

"I don't have it. It's this, or it's cold iron." And he put his sword on the table.

"Leave it be, Claudius. Make him pay later, we'll witness the debt."

"He's got money. I saw his pouch; it's bulging."

"You telling them I'm a liar?" Sellitus grew suddenly angry; he caught at the scarf around the other's throat and twisted it tight. "Nobody calls me a liar." Their faces were inches apart.

"Liar," said the infantryman. "Liar and cheat."

Unseen by Sellitus, the infantryman had drawn his sword and he pushed it into Sellitus' fist, where he held the chain, drawing blood from a cut on the thumb.

The fight which followed was short. No more than ten or eleven blows were traded before an officer pushed through the watching crowd. "Stop it," he shouted and had to shout again to drill through the fog of drink. "Stop it, the pair of you."

But the infantryman was already crumpled on the floor bleeding from the neck and even more copiously from a chest wound.

"Bind his wounds and take him to the hospital," said the centurion to two onlookers at random. "Him," He pointed at Sellitus who was smirking at his own prowess, "secure him. Take him back to barracks. He's from Stanwyx; tell the guard room to send him there on my authority, he'll await trial for this. I'll confirm the order when I return."

***

MEDIONEMETON

Mandeltua lay between the great calling stones and shed his spirit to roam freely over the world. As on other occasions he saw vast numbers of spirits entering and leaving the Underworld through the various vents and cavern entrances which connected with the subterranean realm. The spirits—blue, blue-grey, wispy in appearance—seemed to drift without purpose. To Mandeltua these were the spirits of the dead who were returning to the Underworld and those going out to unite with new born babies.

Choosing an entrance, he willed his spirit to float towards it and then to drift down into it. The rocky walls passed him by, layer upon layer of stone until it opened out into a vast space where he searched for landmarks by which to guide himself.

This was the abode of Arawn, King of the Underworld; Arawn at whose right hand stood Cocidius who had shown Mandeltua the fate of Uffin Gellorix and given him the prophecy.

Mandeltua's spirit moved slowly, searching. Memories of that past visitation came to him as he traveled the cold dominions of the Dead.

Cocidius had come to him in his sleep, wearing the guise of a raven rather than the more usual form of the great stag. Cocidius had shown him the farmhouse at White Tarn and the woman who would soon give birth. Mandeltua watched as the days sped by; one, two, he counted and twenty and thirty.

"This is the man who will unite the tribes of Albyn," Cocidius said as the woman went into labor. A night and a day passed and he saw himself enter the house as the child's head pushed free. "Watch over him, Mandeltua. He will live as the Romans live and as the Brigantes live. He will learn from both worlds."

Cocidius had faded away, and the Druid had gone to White Tarn in time for the birth and had indeed watched as the boy grew from babe to early manhood. And now, as in every year that had passed, Mandeltua entered the Underworld at the time of Samhain in search of further guidance.

Now that the prophecy was on the cusp, Mandeltua hoped that guidance would indeed be forthcoming. Too often were the Gods intent on their own business and spared no time for the affairs of the world.

And there in the misty distance was the mountain where dwelt Arawn and Cocidius and who knew how many more gods and lesser spirits. And as he approached, for distance here was a thing of the mind rather than the measure, another spirit floated near. For all its airy appearance and near translucence, it was familiar to him, a face he knew better than his own for he had conversed with its corporeal body on numerous occasions.

Here was Carotach the Arch Druid bent on some task similar to his own.

Carotach's mouth opened and words sounded in Mandeltua's mind. "Why waste so much time in trying to speak with the Gods, Mandeltua? Ever the impatient one though I have counseled you these forty years that the Gods will speak when they wish to, not when you desire it."

"Times change Old One. The Romans have killed all but a handful of us and like the Gods themselves, you seem to be unaware that the Druids and the great heritage of our wisdom are at risk. Perilous risk."

Carotach seemed almost to shrug. "Perhaps that is what they want, Mandeltua. The Romans themselves are praying to Cocidius now and soon they will adopt the rest."

Carotach's spirit drew near. "Mandeltua, are you certain that your guidance comes from the Gods or only from the dreams brought on by fasting? The line between one and the other may grow very indistinct."

Mandeltua became angry, as far as that was possible without the glands and organs of his body. "Carotach, you have always been a fool. Your spirit eyes are as milky white as your earthly ones and as good at seeing. Why are you here now if not to forestall my plans, eh? Cocidius has always been my guide, why should he not guide me now?"

Cracked laughter sounded in Mandeltua's mind and Carotach's filmy body shook with laughter. "You think I came here to stop you? You who I rescued at Mona, you whom I taught everything I knew. How many times have we discussed the spirit world since then? And still you don't see what is in front of *your* eyes. Mandeltua the new Arch Druid. Look at me and look at yourself and tell me what you see."

Mandeltua turned his spirit eyes from Carotach's blue-grey form to his own—a likeness sculptured in sparkling silver white.

Mandeltua looked again at Carotach. Carotach's semblance was a smoky blue and the old Druid's meaning became clear. Carotach was dead. This was his last journey.

CHAPTER ELEVEN

VIRCOVICIUM

FLAVIUS MOVED HIS HEADQUARTERS TO VINDOLANDA, CLOSE enough to the build-up of troops, but far enough away so that his staff would not feel that he was breathing down their necks.

He had traveled with two tribunes and six centurions all of whom had been serving with the Twenty Second Legion in Germania Inferior. There was also a praefector from Cohort II Breucorum Equitae, a cavalry officer from Mauritania who was taking over as Commandant at Vircovicium.

There had been a hard frost over the past two nights and the ground had hardly thawed throughout the day. The officers from Germania took the temperature in their stride, but Silvanius Platonius, the Tribune, had been used to warmer climes and was obviously having difficulty. On the second day he gave in, wearing trousers to hide his permanently blue knees and to Hades with what his fellow travelers thought of him.

The Deputy Governor was quite pleased that the man was the same age as himself as well as somewhat greyer in the hair. The praefector seemed rather in awe of Flavius' rank, a fact which fed his ego a little.

As they traveled along the Stanegate, Flavius considered his plans, eventually deciding to continue on to Vircovicium and point out the facilities which had been built and which were still under construction.

As they neared the fort, Flavius indicated them.

"As a cavalryman, you'll be interested in that." He pointed to a large circular stockade.

"Horse training? That's good."

"Exactly, and above there, see? Graded slopes for putting them through their paces while further along there, posts for lance practice."

"All for Vircovicium?"

"Not just yet. I told you about the Ninth, didn't I? That's for the Ninth Hispana, but it will remain here afterwards. Yours to use as you see fit."

"It's very impressive, Sir."

Flavius lifted his voice a little, so that the rest could hear him. "And down there, along the Vallum we have men undergoing basic training; the Wall conceals most of what we're doing from direct observation. We have maneuvers, war games, hand to hand and formation fighting. And our soldiers don't have to walk too far to get anywhere." He laughed.

"Except for their regular route marches. Eh? Sixteen miles, three times a month with full packs and weaponry."

He looked at the contingent of officers. "Featherbedding them. You gentlemen will all be billeted in nearby forts, of course. I don't know where, but you'll get instructions at your preliminary meeting up there at Vircovicium."

He spoke to the new Commandant of the fort again. "You'll be looking after the Sixth, of course, but with all the extra men for the Ninth, every spare bunk is being pressed into temporary service. It needs quite a bit of co-operation with both Legions living and training alongside of each other.

"Rest assured Sir, there won't be any problems."

"I'm pleased to hear it. I'm coming up to the Fort with you, I want to discuss one or two matters. I'm rather anxious that the Scouts are put to proper use again. Your predecessor was a little reluctant to deploy native scouts. What are your thoughts?"

"I'd consider it essential to use men born to the territory. Intelligence, I believe, is the most important part of any invasion plan."

Flavius smiled. Was the man saying what he thought or what he thought Flavius wanted him to say? Well. He was either clever or accomplished in appearing clever.

Vircovicium was the most imposing sight for many miles, from this—the south side of the Wall, the whole fort could be seen as if drawn by an architect. Its northern rampart was the actual Wall which ran along the crest of the ridge. The southern gate, some one hundred feet lower than the northern, gave onto a wide natural valley which here separated the Wall and the Stanegate road.

With such a vantage, the guards on duty at the fort had known of their approach well before their arrival, and little time was lost in formalities at the entrance, where staff were already waiting for them. Flavius was, himself, surprised at the number of new buildings which had been erected during his absence. There was none of the green grass areas that he remembered within the fort area and the vicus outside had also grown considerably. One or two shops had been extended at the rear and work had started on an extra story to the butchery.

Suddenly, he remembered the shrines he had sanctioned after the Sixth had returned from Albyn. There they were, up on the western side and nearing completion by the look of it. Progress could not be stayed, Commandant or no Commandant.

They dismounted and as the animals were led away, he nodded to the headquarters building. "An hour, gentlemen, to wash up and change. Then I would like you to attend me in the main briefing room. Issue a general order, will you?" This to one of the aides who had met them at the gate, then he turned to the new Commandant. "Silvanius?"

"Sir?"

"If it's no imposition, perhaps I could wash myself at your villa; then we can have that discussion I mentioned. Particularly about the deployment of the Scouts."

"Of course, Sir."

Sixty centurions, eight tribunes and two cavalry praefectors were gathered in the long, elegant room of the headquarters building. Standards were arranged at one end and a group of small altars bore offerings to several of the Gods. A brazier at either end of the room had taken some of the chill out of the air and the body heat from seventy men soon warmed the place up to a comfortable level.

The men were of the Ninth Legion; those having become used to overseeing building work standing alongside others who had been drafted from overseas and who had had recent fighting experience. They could not yet be called a fighting force and most of them knew it; the knowledge lent an air of unreality to the proceedings.

Flavius entered, coming into the room from a door partway along its length and making his way through the assembled officers. On the dais, he chose not to take the central chair, but to perch a buttock on the end of a table.

"Men." He smiled at them and was rewarded by a few smiles and grins in return. "Officers of the Ninth. Your Legion has a long and honored history. General Agricola took the Ninth into Albyn before most of us were born. The Ninth fought with great distinction against Calgacus in the Grampian campaign. The Ninth suffered some losses at the time, but defeated the last barbarian king in this island so decisively that there have only been petty uprisings since then."

Flavius stood up and walked to the center where he faced them again, his arms folded.

"The Emperor himself gave you your next task. You have built much of this great Wall; many of you have sweated and labored on it yourselves. Six long years. Well, that's all behind you now. Like the Wall, we are rebuilding the Ninth itself, rebuilding it so that we can do what we joined Rome's army to do—fight.

"Any comment?"

The atmosphere, which had been quiet and somber in mood to begin with, had gradually changed during the short speech. The initial smiles, tentative, uncertain, had become grins; cheers burst forth.

"Mars has blessed this day," shouted someone in the rear and a collective roar of agreement erupted. Flavius held up his hands for silence.

"Thank you. Now listen. Our present establishment is six thousand three hundred, a thousand more than usual thanks to the generosity of our Emperor. I have also had a message from Governor Severus to tell me that, along with his good wishes, he is raising two alae of native cavalry to add to our strength. And finally," Severus again had to signal for silence, "finally, out of my own coffers I shall pay to recruit a further three thousand native cavalry to serve as scouts in the vanguard of our advance."

Again, there was spontaneous cheering and Flavius had no option but to wait it out. When it had died down, he continued.

"I'm a great reader of history. I've studied all the reports and the evaluations of Agricola's campaigns in Albyn. The General did great and remarkable things, but he didn't finish the job; he left behind people who were enemies of the Empire. Whatever his reasons were, he can only discuss those with the Gods now. It is we who have to eradicate the problem, the Ninth. If we attain this goal then I shall personally decorate every officer in the Legion.

"Soldiers of the Ninth, will you follow me?"

There was no hesitation. The loud concerted "Aye' was followed by yet more cheers and shouts of accord.

Flavius grinned broadly and left before the noise died away.

Aemilius Karrus left the meeting deep in thought. He had shouted as loudly as any, the charismatic Flavius could charm bravado from the stones themselves. For Karrus and one or two others though, the elation had died with the applause.

Karrus too, knew history. Perhaps not in the detail that the Deputy Governor knew it nor from the favored chroniclers of Roman history, but he knew that in the Grampian battle, Agricola had had twice as many troops as the present Ninth massed. There had been two legions and five thousand auxiliaries as well as numeri and every single man had been needed to put down the barbarians.

Why, he wondered, *should the present day Albyn be any different?* The question was to remain unanswered. He reached the entrance to his old Sixth Legion barracks and almost collided with a stranger bundled up in so many clothes that he looked a caricature of a fat man. The fabrics were rich, the leather fine and embossed with gold leaf. *High rank*, he realized. *A senator perhaps?*

"Aha! Tribune. I'm looking for an Aemilius Karrus. Also a Tribune, I was told that he might be found here."

"Sir." Karrus saluted, forearm across his chest. Dumbfounded.

"Relax, man. I'm here quite informally. Tribune Karrus?"

"I am he, Sir. How can I help you? Come inside." Karrus was quite flustered.

"Thank you. A Tribune, sleeping in a legionary barracks?"

"It's just temporary, Sir. I was promoted some time ago to another Legion, the Ninth. While I'm here, I thought I'd use my old quarters. Um, you were looking for me, Sir?"

"Indeed, Tribune. Allow me to introduce myself. Marcellus Vitunius. Senator, in fact. I'm here—among other things—to look into the matter of Marcus Gellorix."

Karrus almost winced as the name came up. No sooner did he think of the man and decide to do something than duty reared its head and pushed Gellorix to the back of his mind again.

"I believe you knew him. In fact, I believe you were there at the Battle of Sand Crags, where Gellorix committed the act for which he was sentenced to the mines."

Karrus nodded. His mind's eye back with the Sixth, ankle deep in mud and blood.

"Senator." From Rome, he realized and guessed as to why he had come, on whose behalf. "Senator, are you here to find evidence of Gellorix's innocence or, at least, to ameliorate his guilt?"

"I merely wish to make certain of the facts, Tribune. His father is a friend of mine and unable to make the journey himself."

Karrus nodded, not really hearing what the other had said. "I may have some new evidence; it certainly points towards a miscarriage of justice." At least, he was able to do something positive about what seemed, increasingly, to be an error.

"Well, that *is* good news, Tribune. Excellent news."

"I've been waiting to discuss it with the Deputy Governor, but this is the first time our paths have crossed since I heard the testimony myself. I feel that he should hear this as well."

"Then let us go and see him, Tribune Karrus."

"Well, he's only just got here. There was a meeting and I expect..."

"I'm sure that Marcellus Flavius' door will be open to me."

And woe betide him if it wasn't, Aemilius thought, and woe betide himself if this evidence could not be corroborated, the thought continued on.

The two men crossed once more to the headquarters building where they were shown into Flavius' presence without delay. Senator Vitunius shed two cloaks and remained as fat as ever.

At the Senator's urging, Aemilius Karrus repeated what the eye witness had told him.

Flavius, not a man to be ruffled, nevertheless took several seconds to reply.

"Bring this Chranoc to see me at, um, noon. In the meantime, have him sign a written statement avowing what he saw." Flavius turned to the Senator. "As I said before, Senator, we are trying to find Gellorix—without success so far. However, in the meantime, I will issue orders that the Beneficiarius will be reinstated in the Legion's register; all his back pay will be available to him on his return. Senator, perhaps you would convey to Senator Mansustus, the urgency with which we are trying to repair this mistake and convey, too, our apologies—my apologies—for the anxiety which this has caused him."

Vitunius nodded, his expression carefully bland. "I'll do that, certainly. I have some other business to see to, but I'm certain that Aelius, that is, Senator Mansustus will be in touch with you just as soon as I report back to him."

"I'm sure he will, Senator. By then, I am certain that we shall have good news for him."

There were further formal pleasantries before Vitunius took his leave and as Karrus followed him to the door, Flavius spoke up.

"A moment, Tribune, A few words."

Jupiter's fist, said Karrus to himself. *Here it comes. Why did I have to open my mouth?*

"I know you're a busy man, Tribune, you have the veterans to retrain and so on, but I have decided to make the scouts answerable to you and not to the new Commandant of Vircovicium."

Karrus looked surprised. "A number of reasons, Aemilius. First, the Scouts are going to be used by the Ninth and so they need to be commanded by an officer of the Ninth and not the Sixth. Secondly, I know what it has cost you to stand up for Gellorix."

Karrus was pleasantly surprised, he had expected a reprimand. "I've known him since he joined the Scouts, Sir, but quite apart from that, I'd do the same for any man under my command"

"Be that as it may, Aemilius, in truth, the matter has embarrassed me. I know that that's not your affair but it *has* shown me that you respect the Scouts and I'm sure that it is a respect that will be returned. I think you will pay more attention to their information than the former Commandant of Vircovicium did."

"Well, thank you Sir. I certainly will listen to them."

Flavius made a dismissive gesture. "I've already ordered them to cover a more westerly route than General Agricola used. I want to subjugate these tribes once and for all, but not to suffocate them. I shan't deliberately seek aggression although I'll not be hesitant in using force against force if we are subjected to it. Many of the Brythonic tribes welcomed the *Pax Romana*, I'm sure that as with the Britons, so it will be with the Albyns."

"The Scouts will tell us what the mood of the tribesmen is."

"Exactly, Aemilius. There will be those who wish to fight, of course. The scouts will also find out which ones they are and mark their maps accordingly. But you, Aemilius, I want you nearby to give me good advice. Your counsel will not be ignored."

Karrus bowed slightly. "Be assured, Sir, I will always give my best."

⁂

MEDIONEMETON

Uffin and Mandeltua sat at a rough board table outside the hut which the Druid called home. Although the frost had gone during the day, there was still enough chill in the air to make Uffin wear his cloak. Grey clouds scudded overhead, presaging rain.

"So that was the first step," observed Mandeltua. One hand fiddled with a small bone carving, the other held the circular amulet suspended on a thong about his neck. "Successful, I think. Quite successful."

"They certainly seem to have taken to the idea," Uffin agreed. I think that was due to the Gods' timely display of lightning. Without that, they would have been much harder to convince."

Mandeltua leaned back. He made no reply although he smiled knowingly. "So then, what plans do you have?"

"Plans? You want plans already?"

"Come now. You have a score of chieftains pledging their fighting men to the cause. How do you plan to use them? How are you going to train them to kill Romans?"

"Train them? It would be a complete waste of time. Useless."

Mandeltua's mouth opened, closed. His shocked expression conveyed everything.

"Split me into fifty men and with every tribesman willing, I still could not do it. Not even in five or six months, if Rome gives us that long. No I must think of something better than that."

Uffin chewed his lower lip and thought for several minutes. "I need to be back, closer to the Wall. I need to know what's happening and I need to know while it is still going on, not several days afterwards as it would be if I stay here."

Mandeltua was still mulling over Uffin's first reaction. "But if all the tribes of Briton could not prevail against the Romans with their traditional tactics, how can the Albyns do better unless they are trained in Roman ways?"

"The Britons and the Albyns will never fight in the way the Romans do. It takes months of basic training drilled into new recruits by veterans who have used the methods all of their lives. I know how they fight, how they think. That's why you picked me, isn't it? I'm not a fool, Mandeltua."

The Druid did not respond. His eyes looked into the middle distance, his expression betrayed nothing. "They choose where they stand and do battle. If the Romans have to fight without selecting their fighting ground, the outcome is no longer certain." Uffin's words had been coming slower and slower as he thought about what he was saying.

"That is the single Roman strategy that we can use, pick our own place to fight. It will probably be Severus who leads any expedition into Albyn. He's a very able General, won a great many battles. He will use his scouts to make certain he isn't forced into fighting on marshland or in some narrow valley..." Again, Uffin's thought had outpaced his words. "I'll have to find a place which suits us rather than the Romans and tempt them into attacking us there. Hmm. Tempt them to follow us..."

"So you propose a single battle, a large one?"

"Oh no. We'll find a site so far from the Wall that their supply lines are too long to be of any use. There'll be no reinforcements then, they'll never get there in time. And on the march, we'll snap at the Roman columns like a dog at the heels of a beggar. Agricola chose his last battleground near enough to the east coast for ships to supply him, we'll make that impossible."

"There, you see. You have plans already."

"It's called thinking on the move, Mandeltua, and it still needs a lot more thinking and planning than you realize. I have to go south so that I can find out what's going on. I'll organize scouts from the Selgovae and the Callatae who can pass through the Wall just as the Romans send theirs north.

"Of course. You'll know how their scouts operate."

"Yes, and unless they've disbanded them and recruited new ones, I also know the individuals. There's no real reason they'd have done that, though. They shouldn't know that I'm working against them and not for them, so I know what routes they'll take, who they'll see."

"And you can have them killed as they show up?"

"No, that will only warn them, I'll let them carry on. I'll tell the chiefs what I want them to know, a little truth and a lot of lies."

"Ah." Mandeltua began to realize that there were different levels to warfare. Unsuspected levels. The comprehension cheered him, the complexity appealed to him. "This is excellent news, Uffin Gellorix. Excellent. You will need an assistant, someone to act as a runner for I need to be kept fully informed of your progress."

"You do not trust a traitor."

"I trust you Uffin Gellorix. I have made… I have shown you the true nature of those you worked for. Surely you have no choice but to fight them now."

Uffin closed his eyes as the wave of pain swept across his mind. "No. No choice. Send who you will, Mandeltua, but make it soon. I intend to leave as quickly as I can."

"The boy will leave with you. His name is Finnul, an acolyte. A boy with a memory like a sponge, you will find him as useful as I do."

Uffin nodded, hardly listening to the Druid. "I shall go to see Gavoc of the Selgovae and Dag Liogh of the Callatae. I think they could help me a great deal, perhaps they will ride south with me, we can talk as we go."

⁂

BRIOGIX

The two young chieftains did indeed ride with Uffin and the acolyte, Finnul, went with them. Uffin's earlier appraisal of the two men proved to be correct. One, the Callatae, was tall and serious with a breadth of judgment unusual in the chief of a small tribe—or any tribe that Uffin knew of for that matter. The other was shorter, broader and filled with a natural humor.

Dag Liogh he now learned had been present on the raid at Fort Throp, although he burned with curiosity as to how the assault had been achieved, he dared not ask. Trust was a long time in the earning and to risk a question which might be misconstrued would have been foolish.

It was Gavoc of the Selgovae who offered a place which Uffin might use as a base. Briogix was not far from the Wall and space would be made in his own broch, or there was a small round house kept for visitors that he could use. Uffin thanked him, but begged leave to reserve his judgment. His undercover work for the Romans was, so far, unknown; he played the innocent and asked where Dag's tribe dwelt.

"Aha. A good three hours' ride to the east of Briogix. In a vast woodland, along secret pathways."

Uffin grinned. From his scouting activities, he knew that there were mysterious defenses though he had never been near the settlement. "Is it nearer the Wall?" he asked.

"It is," Dag replied.

"And darker and more dismal than our Briogix," added Gavoc with a chuckle.

"That may be," Dag answered, "but we don't have Romans visiting us, any who enter our woodlands fail to find their way out again."

"No trade?" asked Uffin, knowing full well he had traded with the Callatae in hand weapons and metal tools.

"We have a house just within the trees. A watch is kept and if our friends come there, we meet them." Dag shook his head and said no more while the horses walked a dozen paces, the mud of the thawed ground sucking at their hooves. "We Callatae have more reason than most to distrust these Roman invaders."

"And why is that?"

Dag's mood had grown somber, Gavoc's too, in sympathy.

"We were all that escaped Mona when the Romans slaughtered the Druids there. When they ran out of Druids to kill they turned on the rest, killing men, women and children in their bloodlust. A few escaped, a few Druids too, in *curracks* which they took up the coast to the lands of the Epinii who allowed them to come ashore because of the Holy men with them."

Uffin knew of the wicker and hide boats, frail things in which to ferry whole families along the western coast with its tidal races and rocks. As much as he hated the Romans though, he could not believe they had killed in bloodlust; the idea was quite foreign to Roman commanders. More likely, they had used the opportunity to set an example in order to prevent the uprising spreading.

"Your ancestors stayed with the Epinii?"

Dag shook his head. "My tribe became nomads. We encamped each Fall, moved each Spring. It was not until our chief found friendship with Alluston of the Selgovae that we settled. Alluston was, I think, brother to Gavoc's grandsire?"

Gavoc was listening and responded to the query in Dag Liogh's tone.

"Aye. He ceded a valley to the Callatae and enough hunting land to support them."

"And the two tribes live together?" Again, Uffin knew scraps of this history, but found the full story fascinating.

Dag shook his head. "Our tribe grew, as happens. Perhaps we poached too much from the Selgovae because the next generation saw many squabbles between us and until Gavoc and I reached an understanding, we were uneasy neighbors."

It was Uffin's turn to fall silent. Romans, it seemed, sowed hatred wherever they went. There was too little understanding of the peoples they subjugated.

He could understand the Romans' loathing of the Druids; he was not happy with his own relationship with the priestly order. Their schemes were too political, their goals reeked of subversion and guerrilla skirmishes, the Romans could not abide that sort of thing; too costly, too drawn out. And the Druids nurtured the hatred which the Romans planted, nourished it, cultivated it. One more tool to be used by Mandeltua.

"I'd like to visit there one day. Perhaps..."

"Down girl, settle down will you." It was Finnul. His mare had been startled by a fall of wet snow from a branch overhead. Uffin left the question unfinished.

They arrived at Briogix on the following day. The two Chieftains were welcomed by a populace warned of their coming by sentries and along with Dag and Gavoc, Uffin was welcomed as their friend. Preparations for food and drink were well in hand when they arrived and soon they were sitting in front of Gavoc's house, their hands full of juicy meat.

"So, Uffin, my friend. Where do you wish to stay? Hm? My house or the guesting house over there?"

Uffin held up his greasy hands and explained that he wanted to be as close to the Wall as he could. Gavoc's face fell a little and he sighed and nodded. "You need to question as many of the travelers as you can?"

"Yes," replied Uffin, "but I could do with some help here." Briogix was close to the main route to the north and west, and a steady flow of travelers passed through on their way south, beyond the wall.

"These men will have stopped here and will be known to your people," Uffin explained to him. "You might ask a few of those you consider reliable to take special note of what the Romans are doing."

"Of course. And any who spy for the Romans, we..." Gavoc mimed an exaggerated disemboweling.

"No such thing," said Uffin. "Send them back with tales of how frightened everyone is. How much you wish to be friends of the Romans."

Gavoc spat in the dirt. "This is a hard thing you ask of us, my friend. A hard thing."

"What are your plans then? To keep on attacking the Wall?"

Gavoc snorted. "I want to. The young men will do so whether I order it or not, but too many Selgovae end up dead or as slaves whether we attack it or no."

"I don't understand."

"Whenever a spear is cast at the Romans, they come here and take slaves. It is easy to find us, easy to blame us."

"The only Callatae who are slaves are those caught along the Wall," said Dag. "With our tattoos, they know who to blame, but they don't know where to find us and punish us."

"Perhaps the Callatae can teach the Selgovae how to paint themselves," suggested Uffin. "After they have played games with the Romans, they can wash the paint off."

Gavoc tugged at his beard. "You will have to teach us how to shave too, so we can paint our faces," he said it with a grin and Dag grinned back. "The Romans will think your women are bearing full grown men, Dag Liogh. There will be so many Callatae." The grins became chuckles, the chuckles turned to laughter.

"It is like telling lies to the Roman spies," said Dag. "A different sort of fighting. Is this not so, Uffin?"

Uffin shrugged. "I suppose so. I'd not thought of it in that way before. Anyway, if you do raid along the Wall, I have a request."

"Speak it."

"I want a prisoner. Preferably a young soldier." Uffin drew a figure in the dirt. "He'll be wearing this on his tunic." It was the symbol of the Ninth Legion.

"And he must come from the Wall?"

"Well, yes. Why do you ask like that?"

"There are plenty of them wearing that over by Birrens. They're building one of their holdings there."

"At Birrens?"

Dag nodded.

"Then let's try, it will be easier. If not, we can get one off the Wall later."

"You wish to put him to the question?" asked Gavoc, grinning with relish. "The torture? If you're not staying here, where shall we bring him?"

Uffin ignored the first of Gavoc's questions. "Bring him to Liogh land if Dag will let me stay there and if you will keep the young Druid here for me."

"Of course, Uffin. You are welcome at any time. You don't trust the lad?" Dag nodded at Finnul who was watching some of the younger boys and girls of the tribe practicing with small spears.

"I just don't want everything I do reported back to Mandeltua."

Gavoc shrugged. "Whatever you wish, Uffin. Let him stay here and we shall bring you a fine specimen of the Roman ditch diggers tomorrow. The fools are cutting trenches and building wooden walls as though the whole of Albyn had bade them welcome. We've left them alone because the land is Novantae, but the Novantae will not mind our poaching a Roman..."

CALLA

Later that afternoon, filled with roasted duck and enough ale to make his head swim, Uffin followed Dag Liogh along a game trail. Eventually, they came out onto moorland where the shrubs were brown from the recent frosts and the horses had walked fetlock deep in mud where the ground was soft.

The two passed along streambeds and at last, forded a small river before stopping in the fringes of a dark forest.

Dag held up a woolen scarf. "With all due respect, my friend, I have to blindfold you now. No one, no matter how much trust we have in them, comes this way with uncovered eyes unless they are Callatae." He tied the scarf over Uffin's eyes. "Perhaps when we have grown to know one another better, I shall make you Callatae, but until then..." Dag adjusted the cloth. "Take a hold of my harness and do as I bid you."

Uffin accepted the blindfold willingly and rode alongside Dag for perhaps half an hour or more. At one point he had to lean on his mount's neck to avoid an overhang; at another, Dag led the animal along a narrow ledge where Uffin felt rock to one side and listened to the blankness of empty space on the other.

"There now," said Dag at last. "You may use your own eyes again."

Uffin pulled the blindfold away and looked about him. He had expected to be in front of a house at the least; more probably on the edge of a settlement like that at Medionemeton. Instead there was nothing. An occasional bush and tall columns of rock sculptured into fantastic shapes by rain and wind were the only things visible..

"Where are we?"

"Tell me what you see."

Uffin looked again, again expecting to see other than what was there. "Nothing," he said. "Trees and brambles, thick bushes. Rocks."

"Just so. Which way would you go?"

There were at least a dozen routes from the small clearing they had arrived at and Uffin did not even know which direction they had come from. He searched the ground for clues. It was bare rock, no sign of hoof prints, no horse droppings. There were clumps of fern although none where they might be trampled, neither were there broken twigs on the bushes nor any other sign of passage.

He shrugged and grinned at Dag. "I don't know, try at random?"

"A bad choice. Look up."

Uffin looked up at the tops of the columns of twisted rock; most were crowned with grass and small bushes. Several of the bushes moved aside and men with small compact recurved bows in their hands looked down at him.

"Even a small army making it this far—and it would have to be small, you don't know what you have passed on the way here—a small army would be divided and dead in minutes."

Dag urged his horse on and the beast, used to what lay ahead, walked between two of the rocks. Uffin followed on into a maze of pillars and passages, all of them open to daylight twenty feet above their heads. A maze, a labyrinth which filled a small gorge some sixty, seventy feet wide. Perhaps a hundred feet long, it had been an underground stream until, at some time, the roof had come crashing down and left the old water courses open to the air. At its end was more woodland and a clearing within which were three large round houses.

Dag was grinning widely. Not the grin or joke of someone discomfited, but the huge grin of pleasure a man has when he comes home. "Welcome to my house, Uffin, and to the houses of my brothers. We Lioghs of the Callatae know how to honor a new friend, I will show you what Callatae hospitality means."

As they had ridden into the clearing, there had been four children on the steps of one house. Young children, four or five summers; they had disappeared as Dag spoke and as he fell silent so the adults appeared. Seventeen, he counted as they came towards them and surrounded them. Seventeen men and women and half grown adults.

It was curiously silent. As Dag grinned, so did they; the grins grew wider and finally changed to outright laughter and whooping cheers.

"Come inside Uffin," Dag shouted. "Bring him in here." He directed those who had their arms around his shoulders.

"Now here," he continued when they were inside, "are my younger sisters, Melga and Vena. They are not married so they live with me until then. Mind you, I think that Vena will always be here, she's a man hater, aren't you, my dear one?"

Vena was diminutive and while curvaceous, her young breasts and rounded hips might go unnoticed at first because of her small size. She had long fair hair tied in a bun and a crooked nose that could only have come from a fight at some time or another. Her eyes were blue and her chin firm, both smaller editions of her brother's.

Despite the unfortunate nose, Uffin thought she was attractive although, as always in the presence of a woman, he felt uncomfortable. The serious expression he put down to Dag's comments. "I'm pleased to meet you," he said and bowed slightly.

"If that's what you think, you should listen to what my brother says more carefully."

Uffin's eyebrows shot upward, his discomfort increased. "Wasn't he joking?"

"Certainly, he wasn't. I've yet to meet a man who was better at anything than a woman and I doubt I'd change my mind if I did."

"You see, Uffin. I tell you no lies. Here is Melga though, what Vena has lost, Melga has twice over. The greatest cook north of the Romans' Wall."

Melga was obviously cast from the same mold as Vena, but being a year or two younger, she still had a little of her puppy fat about her. There were dimples in her cheeks and a roundness to her figure which was already promising a ripeness that would get her noticed.

Uffin found her company easier to accept. "Hello, young lady."

Melga cast him a swift glance and then turned her gaze back to the floor as she walked back to the fire at the center of the room.

She reminded Uffin of the time he had been at Asel's home before coming to know her at the mine. He wanted to reach out and touch her, but instead he spoke to Dag, his voice rough with emotion.

"It seems that I haven't succeeded in impressing either of your sisters."

"Just wait. If she brings you a bowl of stew, you'll know she likes you," and as Melga dipped a ladle and filled a bowl, "there now. What did I say?"

He turned to his sisters. "You'd better get used to my friend, Uffin, girls. He's staying here for a while, going to hatch plots to kill Romans," said Dag.

Even Vena looked up at that.

"Oh yes. Hates them worse than we do. That so, Uffin."

Uffin nodded, his throat too tight to speak for a moment. "Yes," he said and coughed. "They killed the two women most dear to me." He spat at the fire. "I think that if I couldn't kill them, I might've killed myself."

Uffin took the bowl of meat stew and found a seat to one side where Dag joined him a moment or two later, after he had had a quiet word with Vena. The two men talked as darkness fell outside; Uffin talked about the mine and Asel and his attack on Villius. He made no mention of course, of his scouting duties, emphasizing his trading activities instead.

"So why do the Druids rely upon you to lead us against the Invaders, Uffin? How does a trader come to know so much about the Roman tactics, eh?"

How indeed. Uffin was non-plussed for several long moments. "Would you believe that I am the chosen of the Gods?" he asked to give himself a little time.

"There are many who would, Uffin."

"Let me tell you this then. The blood of Brigantean kings runs in my veins, my mother would be a princess if the Romans had not come."

Dag leaned back, not a little impressed.

"The blood of Rome also runs in these same veins for my father was a Roman officer."

"Ah!" Uffin supposed that Dag assumed his mother to have been raped. He let the surmise lie.

"I was trained in the Roman army until I knew their ways."

"And you revolted and they sent you to the mines."

"I was sent to the mines for killing an officer." *Half-truths and half-lies.* Uffin did not care for such things yet what choice did he have? Mandeltua had told the chieftains that he knew the Roman ways; the reasons had to be credible. He went on to outline his plans for spying beyond the gates in the Wall and for questioning travelers coming through. Melga brought them more stew while Dag considered the proposals with care.

"I have almost ten hands of family here in our village and many times that number elsewhere. I can think of no more than three times three who could take to this new sort of warfare. The Romans fight like this?"

"The Romans do. The Druids do."

"Ah. The Druids."

꧁꧂

The less than sturdy palisade of timber had little protective value for the legionaries who were refurbishing the Wall between Netherby and Birrens. It provided some psychological courage to the Romans mainly because the Novantae had never bothered to put the defenses to the test. The small band of Selgovae waited in the bushes beyond where they had been cleared, a bow-shot's distance from the building activity. There would be fog that evening, their old men had said and as foretold, the fog came down and hid the timber wall from view.

Then, ten men of the Selgovae, ten mounted men simply stood upon the backs of their horses and rode along the palisade. A single leap and they were at the top, balanced on the rough hewn stumps, as silent as the ghosts that drift to the Otherworld.

The guards, few, for there was little worth the stealing, were taken by surprise. Their token resistance was soon overcome and the workers, asleep in their leather tents slumbered on unaware.

What the Selgovae stole was one of the guards. They stripped the dead of swords and pila and found a stockpile of more; these were made into bundles and taken when they left… although the guard was the object of the raid, there was no reason why it should not be a profitable foray, too.

⁂

Mandeltua turned on the hard pallet and groaned as the pictures moved before his inner eye. How many times had the dream visited his sleep?

The Romans' advance had been implacable. More than a thousand druids had been put to death and every grove of oaks they could find had been set alight. Now they rooted out the tribe's people, standing them in long lines and guarding them until a centurion or a tribune arrived.

The soldiers were almost silent. A word of command here, another there, but the overwhelming impression was of a silent and ruthless machine. The officer would arrive, give the word and the legionaries would work their way along the line of waiting people, killing, killing.

Or, in some cases, not. Inexplicably, whole villages would be left alive, or a family from a village would be made to watch as the impassive genocide was carried out. Here, all the men were slaughtered. There, every woman over the age of twelve or so. Another place, every child would be killed.

Reasonless killing. Killing with no purpose to it.

Mandeltua did not bear that name then. He had been six; his mother had called him Brin. Brin had seen the sword end his mother's life, she had not had time to scream, just a sigh as the breath left her body.

Brin had hidden in the well, his eyes just above its parapet. When the soldiers had gone and he had climbed back out again, he had tried to wake his mother, wiping away the blood that trickled from the gaping wound in her ribs.

That was when the Druid had found him and pulled him away, taken him down to the north shore, away from the Romans.

Mandeltua stirred. He was chilled by his own sweat. "Gods," he muttered, "how much longer?" The Druid was not really awake though and the moment of lucidity fled.

He drifted once more through the vast blue and grey spaces of the Underworld until he was close to the misty foothills of the mighty mountain, the abode of his Gods. His spirit lifted and climbed the slopes effortlessly to the peak which seethed with movement. Blue grey forms stepped in an endless and intricate dance about a group of figures in earnest conversation. They sat upon the blue grass, Cocidius' head was bent to listen to the words of Arawn and his hand rested on the arm of Belenus. Sionan sat a little apart smiling to herself, her beautiful face lighting all about her like a warm spring morning.

"Cocidius," said Mandeltua. "Cocidius." The Being either failed to hear or ignored him. "Cocidius," he called, louder. No response.

Lugh bent down to speak with the others. So tall, so huge was the old God that Mandeltua had not noticed him until he moved.

"Cocidius," he shouted. "What must I do to make you hear me?" Still his patron God gave no sign of hearing him although a raven, symbol of death and battle, raised its head and fixed Mandeltua with a single gleaming eye.

"Cocidius. Must I call a curse on you before you deign to notice your disciple?"

It grew instantly quiet. All sorts of noises: muttered conversations, the soughing of a spectral wind, the rustle of grasses, chirpings of birds, insects; all stilled; sounds so common that the ear hears none of them until they are gone. Now Cocidius *did* hear, the great antlers on his head swept up and back as he raised his face and looked directly at Mandeltua.

He paused. "Ah. Mandeltua," he said finally, his voice so soft and quiet, scarcely raised enough to carry. "You must believe that your visit here has great importance to interrupt the Gods in their deliberations. Hm?"

"Just so," whispered Mandeltua, appalled at the still, small voice which seemed to reverberate through his skull.

"Then tell me."

Mandeltua's brain was frozen, no thoughts stirred, not a word came to him.

"TELL ME!"

Now he could speak, his mind raced, the words coming fast. "The Romans. It is time to wreak our vengeance on them for what they did at Mona. Time to drive them from our shores..."

"Yes, yes. I remember. And your protégé, Uffin..."

"Yours, my Lord, your..."

"Oh Mandeltua, interrupting me now." Cocidius chuckled and then he laughed and his laughter echoed back and forth across the Underworld. "Well, I suppose so. What to do?" Cocidius nodded to himself thoughtfully. "There is a place," he said, "Uffin will know it, I will send a sign. Still, it needs some preparation. Wait."

Mandeltua waited; he felt that the God's mild amusement was more frightening than his just displeasure might have been. There was the sound of a storm in the distance and far off, away at the edge of the unimaginable horizon of this weird place, he saw lightning and heard thunder.

There was rain, torrents of rain and rivers, lakes and oceans of rain pouring across primeval land, cascading down ancient mountains, wearing them away and washing away the ground. There had been people there, a village; a herd of deer gave them blood and milk and meat. The village was washed away, its long houses uprooted and smashed, the big logs like dried straws, the deer were swept along over a sudden precipice, the inhabitants drowned.

All this was as clear to Mandeltua as if his eyes floated, disembodied, only feet above the inundation. Mandeltua watched the waters flow for a million years and when the deluge was over, when the water was gone and the land was scoured clean to bedrock, there was not a single sign of twenty seven hundred and eighty four villagers. The same number of men, women and children had been killed by the Romans on Mona, when Mandeltua had been a boy.

A single golden eagle turned and spiraled in the updraft from the bare expanse of rock.

The vision faded and Mandeltua awoke shivering and as tired as when he had retired. He rose and washed himself suddenly reminded of his grim dream by the sound of the cold water falling from his fingers.

⁂

CALLA

Uffin woke and cast about him like a man drugged. A dream had left the taste of bile in his throat and a clammy sweat over his body. He threw off the sleeping furs and stood up, trying to remember where he was.

He was still dressed in the robes given him at Medionemeton; they were dirty and smelled badly of his own sweat.

Dag was still sleeping, snoring loudly and it was his face, as much as anything which brought Uffin back to reality.

There was a pool outside, he remembered, fed by a small stream. At least he could clean himself a little.

It was a damp and misty morning. Last evening's fog had persisted and floated in a shoulder high layer that shrouded the clearing held the three round houses. The pool, partly natural, but enlarged, was twenty feet wide and deep enough to swim in.

Uffin shed his garments and dived cleanly into the icy water. He was halfway to the other side when the cold hit him and he trod water for a moment before swimming back to where he could stand on the bottom. Here, he rubbed at his chilled body trying to keep warm as well as cleansing himself.

"My Lord Uffin, is that you out there?"

It was a voice he did not recognize. "Yes," he said. "Is there a curse on this pool that it may not be used to bathe in?"

"Not that I know of, Lord." The voice sounded relieved as well as a little amused. "There are visitors coming Lord, from the Selgovae. They are bringing a prisoner for you. Chief Liogh has also been informed; he commanded that you be told."

"For me?' And then he remembered. "Are they coming here? Blindfolded?"

"Yes, my Lord."

Uffin found his new title rather pleasing. "Unless Chief Liogh has other plans, do not take the blindfold from the prisoner. I'll be there directly."

Uffin waded to the side of the pool and put on his clothing then made his way back to Dag Liogh's house. There, four men sat on their horses; a fifth horse had a body tied across its back. The four horsemen, he supposed, were Selgovae, but adorned quite grotesquely. The hair of the nearest was stiff with clay and grease, standing up in red and brown and white spikes; his body was covered in the most bizarre tattoos, severed heads and polished skulls hung from his belt and the horse's harness.

With a start Uffin looked more closely at the figure and with difficulty, confirmed his fist impression. This was Havoc Maloria, with a grin so vast that Uffin wondered if the top of his head might not fall off.

Dag stood on the steps and laughed at the sight. He was about to greet Uffin, but Uffin put his finger to his lips and motioned the Chief to one side.

Out of earshot of the prisoner, Uffin spoke to Dag. "Is there an empty shed we can put him in?"

"Um, yes. What do you have in mind and why the secrecy?"

"Get him into the hut, leave him bound and gagged. The secrecy is because I don't want him to hear my name."

"What will it matter? He's never going to leave here with his life."

"A new kind of warfare, remember? Sly, like the fox. Listen and you will understand. Put him in the hut and leave him bound and gagged."

Once the legionary had been taken away, Uffin turned to Havoc. "Well done, Chief of the Selgovae," he said for the benefit of his retainers. "I like the painting. No losses?"

Havoc preened a little, he threw out his chest. "No losses. They never expected us, we struck while the fog was thick and they never saw us coming."

Dag returned after supervising the incarceration of the Roman.

"Have you any Roman clothing?' asked Uffin. "A bit of armor?"

"We must have," Dag replied. "Verin?"

The man addressed frowned. "I'll see what can be found."

While this was being done, Dag and the visiting Chieftain, Havoc, went inside with Uffin for breakfast and Uffin explained what he was going to do.

Later, after the Roman had been alone in the hut for an hour or so, Uffin dressed himself in the military clothing that had been found. As they approached the hut, the Callatae began shouting; the hut was opened and Uffin was thrust roughly inside. The door was slammed and bolted behind him.

Valorous Senecus, a legionary with the Ninth Legion, lay in the dark on the hard dirt floor. His limbs were tied tightly with animal sinew, his mouth was filled with a piece of dirty cloth, he was bruised and hurting all over. Additionally, he could smell himself; at some time since he had been captured, he had urinated in his loincloth.

The Roman was glad that he was alive but the pleasure was mixed with a large measure of terror. It was obvious that his life had been spared so that he could be tortured or sacrificed by the barbarians. He had heard of captives being beheaded, of their blood being drained into kettles and used in weird rites.

The Gods grant my death be a quick one, he prayed.

There was a great deal of shouting going on outside. The door opened with a crash and before he had time to anticipate his death, another body was thrown into the hut and the door relocked.

"Mmf?" It was all he could force past the gag.

There was no answer although he could hear heavy breathing.

"Mmum," Valerius tried again and was rewarded by a groan.

"What?" asked the new arrival, in Latin.

"Hmm."

"I guess they must have gagged you. Just a minute, my hands are tied behind my back, but I may be able to do something."

There was the sound of movement and Valerius felt the other groping around him.

"I may be able to pull your gag out."

The hands fumbled about and eventually found his face; a moment later, they had tugged the wad of cloth from his mouth. The blindfold came away next and Valerius saw that he was in a hut lit dimly by light seeping through chinks in the walls and roof. The newcomer was also a legionary, tied and blindfolded.

"Can you get this cloth off my eyes?"

Valerius twisted about until he could reach the newcomer's blindfold and tug it free.

At length the two men lay on the floor looking at each other.

"Mansus Ferrus," said Uffin. "From the Sixth."

"Valerius Senecus of the Ninth Legion," the other replied.

"How long have you been here?"

"Two or three hours. I got caught during the night, on guard duty and they brought me here over the back of a horse."

"Much the same as me. There were three of us on duty, the other two were killed, but they brought me here. How well are you tied, do you think you can get free? What do they want with the likes of you and me, anyway? It's officers that have all the information."

"They won't try to torture us for information, will they?"

"Can't see any other reason for keeping us alive, but it's stupid, what do we know about the invasion?"

"Nothing except it's going to be too late to be any use to us."

"What do you mean?"

"Well, it's going to be months before the Ninth's ready. My squad was about ready to start training. Only just been sent there, too. We'd been building that new watchtower at Banna until a day ago. If the savages had come the day before, they'd have caught someone else."

"Months, you say? As long as that? I didn't realize it would take all that time."

Valerius spat some filth from his mouth. "Well, there's thousands more coming from all over. That's what takes the time."

Uffin continued making conversation. He found out that auxiliaries were coming from abroad, that rumors of raising a Brythonic force were circulating and that invasion was expected as soon as the weather improved in the spring.

"Jupiter, I'm cold. Messed myself, too, when I was on the back of that horse. Could do with a nice warm bath."

"I don't know about a warm bath," Uffin replied, "but we can give you a bit of food." He shouted to Dag outside.

"Well, that went quite well," he said, changing from Latin as Dag pulled the door open. "A rough idea of when and how many. We can improve on that another time."

"Shall I kill him now, or is there any other use you have for him?"

"Do whatever you want, Dag. It's a pity. He has no real hate for us, fighting is his work; it's what he does to eat."

Dag Liogh bit his lip. "You feel sorry for this misbegotten dog? I cannot understand you, Lord Uffin."

"I feel sorry for a bird caught in a cage, Dag, but I'd still kill it and eat it if I was hungry. Don't worry, Dag, you and I see this in different ways; it won't stop me accomplishing what I've set out to do."

Dag shook his head and bolted the door.

"You must use this sort of ruse to gather information, my friend. I have to leave and choose our battle site."

CHAPTER TWELVE

VIRCOVICIUM

LONG BEFORE THE SUN, AEMILIUS ROSE AND WASHED, READY FOR another day of making decisions and giving orders. Since being promoted to Tribune, he had rarely had more than a moment's spare time to sit back. Somehow, there was little personal time left, and that seemed to be spent sleeping. He needed to reflect on his career, to try and choose his direction rather than being carried along like a stick in a mountain stream.

Today was mapped out for him already. Address the scouts, deal with that vindictive decurion who had half killed a gregarious and oversee the veterans' training. Aemilius checked a mental list as he donned his uniform. That was before noon. Afterwards, he had to check that Chranoc had made that deposition and signed it. And what else? Something to do with his belongings… Aemilius sighed, it would come back to him.

Unlike Flavius who had stayed away from the build-up of troops by moving in at Vindolanda, Aemilius lived with his veterans, ate with them and slept with them whenever other duties allowed. It formed the sort of bond which he considered to be important. *But it would have been nice to get away from it all, take a ride across the moors for a few hours, through the forests, but… no time.*

He had been allotted a room in the headquarters building at Vircovicium, larger than his quarters as a senior centurion although the furniture was a bit sparse. Aemilius hadn't really wanted to move, but rank had its penalties as well as its privileges; he had to be seen to assume the benefits as well as the responsibilities.

Ah! Aemilius remembered the other item on his agenda. *Move my stuff to the new quarters, of course.*

Aemilius, like the vast majority of soldiers in the Roman army, took only a drink of water for breakfast. He swung his cloak about his shoulders and stepped out into the pre-dawn darkness for a brisk walk across to the headquarters building. As well as dark and cold, the morning was foggy; he pulled the cloak a little closer against the chill.

Inside the meeting room a clerk was already sitting at a table busy with his styli and tablets. The clerk looked up briefly and nodded. Aemilius returned the gesture although protocol demanded that the clerk stand and salute when someone of tribune rank entered.

As Aemilius looked through his notes, two legionaries knocked and entered, saluting correctly as they did so. "Scouts are here, Sir," said one.

"Very good. Have them come in."

Between twenty and thirty men came in. All of them were dressed in local costume, a mixture of homespun, leather and furs with a sprinkling of brighter checks and stripes. These men looked the part because they *were* the part; every one native to Briton and working for the Romans purely for the money. Aemilius knew that they were mercenaries and trusted them accordingly. He looked them over carefully.

"I'm Tribune Karrus. The Deputy Governor has appointed me to be your overseer so you follow my orders from now on and you report to me and to me only. Is that understood?"

There was a rumble of low-voiced assents followed by a query from a lean saturnine individual with lank greasy hair.

"I'm currently on detachment to Praefector Vibius of Fort Throp. I expect to be away on his business for two months."

Aemilius Karrus raised an eyebrow. He knew the man, had in fact, received reports from him in the past, but he could not recall the fellow's name. "And you are. .?"

"Elvin Fellaugh. Sir. Senior scout since Gellorix left."

Aemilius didn't like the man. His attitude lacked respect, another officer would have had him punished for dumb insolence, but he was good at his job.

"Return to Praefector Septimus after this meeting and present my respects. Inform him that Deputy Governor Flavius has ordered that all scouts are to be instantly available for missions. That is *all* scouts, not all scouts but one, Fellaugh. Is that clear?" His final words were sharp, an admonishment.

Fellaugh nodded, obviously put out, but he stood a little straighter, appeared to show a little more respect. *A glimpse of the iron hand within the soft glove, a lesson for all.* "Now gentlemen. I want an outline from each of you so that I know which tribal areas you work in and what you were last doing. Give your name before you start so that the clerk can note it down. Since you are the senior, we'll start with you, Fellaugh."

There followed the better part of an hour's discussion and Aemilius guessed that the scribe's hand must be aching by the end of it.

"Good. Thank you. Now, to future work. The Legion, the Ninth Legion, that is, needs to know which of the tribes to the north of the Wall are friendly to us. Not just on trade and domestic matters, but which ones are likely to genuinely accept the *Pax Romana*. We need to know this so that we can estimate the numbers of Albyn fighting men who would bear arms against us if we decided to extend the peace to the whole of Albyn. That is your first task.

"There is also a secondary issue, but one that I think you will all be interested in. Beneficiarius Gellorix has been cleared of the crime he was accused of and sentenced for. His name has been replaced on the Legion's roster. Unfortunately, no one knows where he is."

The meeting turned into uproar. Everyone, even the clerk laughed at Aemilius' joke.

"Now this is quite serious. If you see him, tell him that all charges have been dropped. Tell him, too, that he has ample back pay to spend."

Again, there was laughter. The formal part of the meeting had ended on a good note; the tribune was satisfied that, as a first encounter, it could not have gone better.

"Any questions?"

"Trading goods, Sir. What do we have to work with?" The question came from the back.

"Two horses and you'll be issued with double packs of goods since you're going to be away a bit longer than usual. There's time to visit your families or friends before you leave and on that note… check with the clerk here. We don't want you all going north at the same time or all of you through Vircovicium. There will be orders for each of you: which gate to use, what time, what area we need you to concentrate on."

Aemilius looked around. "That's it my friends. Get to it."

Elvin Fellaugh was fuming, although he kept the fact well concealed. The chance to earn more money than he'd ever dreamed of before was falling through his fingers like sand. Was there a way around it? *Perhaps my arrangement with Septimus could be combined with this unwanted business that Karrus had handed them.*

Aemilius didn't notice the look of venom which Fellaugh cast in his direction on leaving. His mind had already turned to the next item on his program, he looked round at the clerk.

"What do we have on this Sellitus matter?"

The clerk had been at his job a long time. His thoughts switched smoothly in midstream as he handed a scrap of vellum to the last Scout.

"Decurion Arvius Sellitus, Sir. Optio Samec who was present at the mansio at the time and the arresting officer, Centurion Gladdus; both here and waiting on your pleasure, Sir."

"And the man that Sellitus attacked?"

"Still in hospital, fractured skull, Legionary Didius Lupus. He may not leave there alive."

"Right." Aemilius Karrus sighed. "Thanks. Would you bring in the Centurion first?"

The Centurion was a grizzled officer older even than Aemilius' forty six years. Deep scars cut through the seamed cheeks and forehead, the scars of a seasoned campaigner not afraid to stand in harm's way.

Aemilius indicated a chair. "Water?"

Gladdus accepted both the seat and the refreshment. "Thank you."

"So what can you tell me about this Sellitus?"

The man's voice had the soft creakiness of a well worn chair. "Was a good man," he said. "A good man to have at your side in a battle, but he's been supervising building for six years. This…," Gladdus edited the obscenity before it emerged, "has ruined too many good fighting men. He's changed; he's quick to take offence, any excuse to take a drink."

"So there's every reason to believe he committed the offence and you've nothing to say in his behalf?"

"Oh, there's little doubt that he did what, um, Samec, witnessed. If the Legion had been re-formed six months earlier, it might have saved him, he's a born fighter."

Aemilius nodded. "And is the re-forming going to suit you?"

Gladdus nodded too and smiled, a smile made crooked where one of his scars met the edge of his mouth. "Never fancied taking a pension, not while I can still swing a sword. I'd sooner die fighting than rotting in some Brythonic village."

The sentiment reminded Aemilius of his own thoughts on the subject. "Yes. I'd thought of retiring. Not too long ago, either. It's odd, what life has in store for you, isn't it?" Aemilius turned to the clerk again. "We'd better see the Decurion now."

The moment that Sellitus entered flanked by a pair of *legionaries*, Aemilius knew what Gladdus had been talking about. The size and color of the man's nose could only have come out of a wine bottle, but he still held himself well, despite the first signs of a pot belly. There was plenty of muscle left, plenty of fight.

The witness, Optio Samec, followed them and stood back against the wall.

Sellitus came to a halt in front of the Tribune's desk. Aemilius read the charge without looking up at the man.

"You have been brought here to answer to the charge of causing a public affray and of seriously injuring a fellow legionary."

Karrus looked up.

"What do you have to say in answer?"

Sellitus stood stiffly to attention, giving no sign of remorse or of regret. "We were gambling, Sir. Small stakes and the man from the Sixth wouldn't accept what I offered as payment. Said I'd probably stolen it and he insulted my mother." He shrugged slightly. "I disagreed with him"

"You disagreed with him?"

"We, er, fought, Sir. It just happened. It was him or me and I was proved the better man."

How often had he heard such stories in his twenty eight years with the Army? The man was probably lying, adding bits of the truth where it fitted and doubtless; there was blame on both sides. "What was it you offered him?"

"A stone pendant, Sir. A gift for a woman, sort of sea shell. I'd lost a hundred sesterces, the thing seemed worth at least twice that."

"And where is it, this pendant?"

"Centurion Gladdus has it, Sir."

"Centurion?"

Gladdus stood up and handed Aemilius a package. The Tribune unwrapped it and stared at the contents. *A man's life, possibly, for this.* He put it down on the table where its black involutions glittered in the light from the window.

"Optio, do you agree with what the prisoner has said?"

"I didn't hear the argument itself with the injured man. I saw the fight break out and I saw other men pulling them apart. But for that intervention, I think that the prisoner would have probably killed his opponent."

"And no one actually heard what was said in the argument?"

"Only the injured man, Sir," interjected Centurion Gladdus. "And with respect, his version is unlikely to be the same as the prisoner's."

"Quite."

"Sir," said Samec.

"Carry on, Optio."

"Well Sir, both men drew swords at the same time, Sir."

"Thank you. Anything else?"

Samec shook his head.

"Then, leave us please."

Samec saluted and marched out of the room; Aemilius looked up coldly at Sellitus.

"At this moment your victim is still alive. For the purpose of deciding on punishment, I have to assume that he will continue to live."

Aemilius massaged his temple while he thought.

"You will lose your rank. You will have no wine ration for three months. When you leave here, you will report immediately to the Centurion in charge of training the *hastati.*. This pendant will be sold along with your other personal possessions, things that will no longer be required by an ordinary legionary. The proceeds will be paid into the account of Legionary Didius Lupus, the man you put in hospital."

Sellitus breathed in sharply.

"Yes, Legionary Sellitus, you have something to say?"

"No sir." Sellitus may have wished to say any number of things, but he was a soldier; a soldier took his punishment silently.

"Then you may leave us."

When the Centurion, too, had gone, Aemilius leaned back and eased his uniform across the chest. He picked up the pendant. *Quite attractive*, he thought, *a hundred sesterces.* He rubbed his fingers across the surface; it was quite smooth, a tiny tingle seemed to run along his fingers. It seemed in some weird way, to *desire* him to touch it, hold it.

At the clerk's table he counted out five hundred sesterces from his pouch and put them down. "Post Sellitus' goods for sale, show that the trinket was sold for five hundred." Aemilius placed the pendant's cord around his neck and slotted it down inside his tunic.

⁂

CALLA

At last a morning had dawned without the usual shroud of fog and the Callatae settlement enjoyed a watery sunlight. The previous day, Uffin had set several matters in motion and felt able to leave.

Somewhere there existed a battle site where the Romans' fighting strategies would be useless. At the moment, he could not visualize such a place. *I would recognize it when I saw it or perhaps,* Uffin smiled at his flight of fancy, *perhaps the Gods would lead me there.*

As he rose to see to horse and provisions, Dag Liogh approached.

"You'd better change out of those things before you leave."

Uffin raised his arms and looked at himself. He had lodged with Dag Liogh for two days and had, unconsciously donned the Roman shirt and kilt he'd used to deceive the prisoner. The clothing felt so familiar that he had forgotten that he was wearing it, but at least there had been no slipping back into his old persona.

"You'll be dead before you leave these woodlands."

"You're right. My own clothes needed washing; I'm not sure what I did with them."

"They've been cleaned. Keep them to change into, I bring you these instead."

"These?" Uffin fingered the garments which Dag had brought. "This is chieftain's garb. In fact, the most beautiful that I have seen."

"Last night, I dreamed of my father in the Otherworld way across the ocean. He smiled at me and told me to trust you; he told me you would lead our tribes to great honor."

Which is not the same thing as a great victory, Uffin thought, but kept to himself.

Dag unfolded the tunic and held it out at full length. Uffin shook his head. "I can't accept this, Dag my friend, it is far too fine for me."

The Callatae chief turned the garment so that he could see it himself, the entwined serpents embroidered in gold and silver thread, the green stones sewn into the fabric to represent eyes, the line of intertwined knots along the lower hem.

"Yes," he sighed, "it is very beautiful. My mother sewed it for him; it took her two years to make it. I want you to have it, Uffin; my father wants you to have it. You see, my brother, you are now a chief among chiefs; if you do not dress the part, how will anyone know?"

Uffin looked at the other. There was the suggestion of a twinkle in his eye, even so there was also a note of gravity in his words and he knew that Dag was perfectly serious.

"Then, yes, thank you. I accept these things."

"Of course you do." Gavoc had approached unseen and in time to hear the last part of the exchange. "And when you are next at Briogix, I have something that will complement Dag's gift. Dag and I have talked of this while you slept the night away."

Uffin realized that there was no alternative. To refuse the generosity of these two young Chieftains would be an insult to them. "I thank you, too, Gavoc. I suppose that I must call there before going north, anyway; Mandeltua's ear will have to go with me."

"Mandeltua's..? Aha. Young Finnul."

"Yes. Now, let me change and Dag can find a blindfold for me."

"No blindfold, Uffin. With these clothes, you are as much a Callatae as I and a Callatae needs no blindfold. May Bele shine upon your journey."

⁂

BRIOGIX

At Briogix, Finnul watched as Gavoc brought three items from his house.

"My father's war shield," he said, leaning the great shield against the steps. "My father's sword and his torque. Now you are Selgovae, too."

The shield was rectangular with rounded corners and built from laminated wood. Three iron bosses with garnet centers crossed it diagonally, bronze plates reinforced the face and silver inlays outlined designs beaten into the bronze. The sword of the old Mellaurig was bright and strong with runes carved along the blade and a handle wrapped with gold wire and leather. Both were beautiful as well as functional, but the most beautiful was the torque. It was made of gold wire twisted into a gleaming rope as thick as Uffin's thumb; at each end a golden stag's head—twin works of genius—bound the metal fibers together.

"These are beautiful, Gavoc. Truly beautiful. How can I thank you?"

"Unite the tribes of Albyn, teach them to fight Romans, lead them against the invaders and drive them into the sea."

Uffin swallowed.

"Try," said Gavoc with a grin. "If any man can succeed then it's you, Uffin Gellorix, for there is an aura about you that no clothes or weapons can hide. You are the chosen of the Gods, Uffin. These gifts are fitting."

"With a tongue as silvered as yours, Gavoc Mellaurig, you should be talking to the tribes of Albyn."

Gavoc shook his head. "I think not, Uffin. You are the one who has the backing of the Druids and they are our voice to the Gods. Even Chiefs listen to you now, you saw that at Medionemeton."

Gavoc embraced him, spoke in his ear. "Do what you have to and call me when it is time to take arms. I and my Selgovae warriors will be at your side."

Uffin and Finnul reined in and pulled their horses to the side as the trader approached them on his way to Briogix. The trail was narrow and the two pack horses were heavily laden, the trader raised his hand in thanks as they squeezed past.

A few minutes later a Selgovae sentry stepped into the path and stopped him. "Oh, it's you Donach. What have you got?"

"Usual sort of thing, Arden. Tell me, who was that I just passed?"

"Dark fellow, rich clothing?"

"That's the one, had a boy with him."

"That was Uffin Gellorix, Donach, the most powerful man in Albyn. Step carefully next time you meet him."

"The most powerful? How do you mean, chief of a great tribe?"

"Chosen by the Druids themselves. Chosen to be chief of *all* the tribes, my friend."

"Is he now?"

"Indeed, he is."

⁂

MEDIONEMETON

Further north the sky was blue and cloudless; the sun was stronger and warmer. It was a fitting dawn to herald the ceremony of Ascendancy. No breath of wind, no birds, no sounds. Stillness, silence. Only the sound of bare feet on dew damp turf accompanied Mandeltua's procession to the Arch of the Gods. He strode purposefully ahead of the thirty or so druids and priestesses and their apprentices along the avenue still strewn with the Fall's golden oak leaves to where Endorr the Elder awaited them.

Mandeltua looked to neither right nor left. At the arch, he stopped and let the loose robe fall to the ground. Naked now, except for the stone of power which sparkled at his chest; tall and thin with the knobby joints of old age, he approached the portal. Here, he walked slowly, entering the symbolic gateway of rebirth and stepping through into Druidic lore.

Unconsciously, Mandeltua's hand crept upward to clutch the stone as his followers, still fully clothed, walked around the stones to form a circle on the far side. Mandeltua stepped out of the shadows of the archway into the circle, a brief expression of gratification crossing his face.

Endorr stepped into the circle, too, and raised his arms to the sky. He spoke the prayers to honor the aged Carotach who now sat with the Gods; he thanked the elements for the omens of sunlight and dew. He threw earth at the new Arch Druid, he breathed air in his face, he tossed newly kindled tinder and sprinkled water.

"Mandeltua, pledge your life energy to the faith of the Druids. Lead us along the true paths of knowledge and by example show us how to live a devout and humble life."

Mandeltua bowed to those present and intoned his reply. "I do pledge my life energy and I will lead you along the true paths of knowledge. My life will be an example of devotion and humility. I pledge this on my oath. Let the earth open up and take me, let the air leave my lungs, let me be consumed in hot flames, let the rivers overflow and drown me if I should break this oath."

"Having pledged by earth and air, by fire and water, I pronounce that you, Mandeltua, are our new Arch Druid." Then to the others, "Give us your omens."

"I saw the sun and moon in the same ascendancy," said one of the Druids. "It foretells a great battle."

"Three magpies flying in a circle, a fourth dead upon the ground. It will be a hard winter and a long one."

"I watched a leaf rising where there was no wind. An early spring."

Each of the lesser druids made some declaration or other and when they had finished, Endorr came to Mandeltua with a white robe of new linen over his arm. He held it out open and Mandeltua stepped into it, closing the robe and hiding the stone of power from sight.

"With the robe of purity I welcome the Arch Druid Mandeltua. Let the spirit of Carotach and the spirits of those who have gone before him, reside in your body and offer guidance in all your deliberations."

Mandeltua remembered his astral visit to the Halls of the Gods and his meeting with the newly dead Carotach. *Do I wish for Carotach's guidance?*

Whether it was the fact of Mandeltua's three days' fast or relief at the end of the ceremony, he didn't know, but Mandeltua suddenly felt as light as a wisp of swan's down; he felt that he could climb invisible steps into the air.

Mandeltua threw open his arms and smiled at everyone, turning to everyone in the circle.

"Let the feast begin."

<hr/>

DAMNONIA

Although the day was fine and bright, it was cold enough to snow and a high layer of hazy cloud lent weight to the possibility which imbued Uffin with a growing sense of urgency.

For the past week, he had been traveling northward through desolate lands uninhabited by other than birds and animals. High heather covered moors, grey blue hills formed the backdrop while rocky water scoured gulley's with rushing streams and flat waterlogged lings thwarted his progress and frustrated his need to make haste.

Perhaps there was no need for speed, he thought. *After all, I still have no idea what I'm looking for.* It was only the firm conviction that he would recognize it when he saw it which made him continue. Now, even that confidence was becoming eroded and his mind began to wander as the day grew less bright and the sky less blue.

For several minutes, he let the horse guide itself, following the black cloaked figure of Finnul on the pony ahead of him. Finnul's head swiveled left and right, a glance at a finch, another at the twisted fingers of a leafless alder bush. He gaped at a high waterfall cascading from a hanging valley so high that the water blew away as spume before reaching ground level.

The boy, it seemed, had never left Medionemeton before, had never been beyond the closed home of the Druids where there was never time for an acolyte to just stand and stare.

Everything was a wonder and a joy, everything seen for the first time, everything amazing. Only the morning before, Uffin had caught him staring with rapt attention at a spider's web jeweled with beads of moisture.

Uffin's mind turned back to memories of his father. As with Finnul now, so it had been with the young Uffin. Mansustus, the grand senator from Rome, tall and wide shouldered, gleaming helmet and scarlet cloak. The pictures were in the bright primaries and had the heroic proportions envisioned by a child.

But the figure was distant now, a person who had loomed large in his childhood, but whom he had not seen for twelve years. *Too high in the nobility, too busy in government, to visit Mother and her bastard son.*

Uffin discovered with surprise that the warm affection he had felt for the man had faded. The man who had educated him, trained him, provided for him, those were childhood memories, faded memories.

In those far off days when Mansustus had been stationed on the borders, Uffin had been too young to comprehend the casual cruelty of the Romans. Unbidden, he suddenly recalled the image of a centurion who had been unhorsed and had then thrashed a Carvetian boy within a finger's breadth of his life for laughing. That sort of unthinking cruelty came from the arrogance of the conqueror. Like the three women he had once seen dragged into an alley by a gang of drunken legionaries and raped; they were the conquered, with no rights to justice or dignity.

They were not all like that, of course. There were the decent ones, the officers who accepted the Britons as human beings rather than animals. Karrus for example, Karrus had saved him from being injured by a stampeding horse. *Too bad he hadn't been there when they'd blamed him for Pintus' murder. Karrus wouldn't have let it go at that.* Briefly, Uffin wondered why Aemilius had not been at the court martial. *No one there had known me well enough to speak for me.*

Uffin felt a pang of guilt, for until recently, he had been as much a Roman as any legionary, he had seen the offhand atrocities and done nothing, ignored them. He had repressed the memories like…

Uffin felt his throat swell and stiffen with emotion… like the more recent memories he had done his best to hide, the casual killing of his mother and of Asel who had only just begun to live.

Was it revenge which drove him now? He wondered and considered the question a long time. The answer, when it came was not convincing. His mind told him *justice*, his heart said otherwise.

He looked up and saw that Finnul, now quite a way ahead because of his slow pace, had reigned in and was staring fixedly at something. *Now what?* wondered Uffin. *What new little miracle had he found now?*

Uffin rode forward and as the sound of the horse's hooves on the turf reached the boy, Finnul turned. "There are men up there, Lord Uffin. Up among those rocks that look like broken pots."

"You're certain?"

"Certain. I think..."

Uffin stayed the boy's words with an upheld palm. "Stay here until I have gone ahead and then follow twenty, thirty paces behind. Let me do the talking and if necessary, the fighting." Uffin reached behind and undid the leather thong which held the sword at his back, concealed beneath his cloak; he pulled the blade from its scabbard, letting it fall to the side so that he could carry it at the ready. The handle fitted his hand as though they had grown up together and the shield, hanging from his saddle was ready to take up in an instant.

As he was readying himself, Uffin's eyes were searching the rocks that Finnul had indicated. Several were large enough to hide a man, but they were spaced well apart; if more than one man lay in wait, they were too far apart to jump out and take him in concert. *How many are there?* he wondered. *Can I handle them all? Perhaps ride at speed, take them by surprise...*

In the event, Uffin stood his ground and shouted.

"If you are enemies, come out here and prepare to die." He brandished the sword. "If friends, there is no need to hide, I intend you no harm."

Uffin sat there relaxed, ready for whatever might eventuate; five heartbeats, no more. This was what he had been trained for, second nature.

Three men leaped from the concealing rocks and jumped and skidded down the short incline. The largest and the scruffiest was clad in a filthy brown tunic and leggings, a single lock of yellow-white hair hung amongst the tangle of dirty brown.

"Listen to him, lads," said the leader of the brigands. "Prepare to die, says he and we're the best three fighters in the Lunnif Hills."

Closer, Uffin saw the fellow had thick bushy eyebrows which met in the middle and grew long moustaches which fell below his chin. Rings of jet did little to restrain the bushy hair as he stood there, chuckling with his two henchmen, smaller and more tattered versions of himself.

"What is it you want?" asked Uffin, his voice a little gruff with tension.

"Not much." The other laughed. "Your horses, your clothes, anything else you may be carrying like that fine shield hanging at your side." He put his foot on a rock and leaned forward, his forearm across his knee. "Maybe I'll even take your lives, or maybe I won't."

Uffin smiled a thin lipped smile and felt goose bumps rise all over his body. He gripped the sword a little more tightly. "What tribe are you? All the tribes have pledged to the High Druids that they will offer no hindrance to us. Surely you know that I am the Lord Uffin."

Uffin's pronouncement was met with silence, a silence that was broken by one of the brigands sniggering.

"Tribe? Why, we are a tribe of three, Lord Uffin. This is our land you are crossing." He swept his sword around. "We demand the proper taxes."

Uffin heard a sound off to his right and knew at once that it was no wild animal that made the noise. *More than the three of them, then.* In a single silky movement, Uffin tightened his feet under the horse's belly and urged it forward, the sword came up ready to parry or wound.

The three would-be robbers were taken off guard; the sword rose, swung, fell and rose again to chop downward. The nearer of the thieves lost an arm. The second, his life by way of a huge slash across his throat. The third also forfeited his life; the final chop had opened him from neck to sternum.

Uffin turned his horse on a shield's span and he took it up the slope to the side of the rocks, where the fourth robber had been waiting. Instead of a fourth, however, there were four of them who broke cover and fled in four different directions as fast as their frightened legs would take them.

Uffin let them go. There was no sense in trying to ride any of them down; they knew the land and he doubted that they would be back. Uffin dismounted and walked his horse back.

Of the three that Uffin had attacked, one was still alive. He held his left hand to the stump of his right arm, attempting to staunch the flow of bright red blood. He was a dead man; *he* knew it, Uffin knew it. Without warning, Uffin plunged the great blade into the brigand's chest, cutting short the last few pain-filled minutes of his life.

Young Finnul had not moved from where his mount had faltered to a stop. He sat there, as white as a spirit and clutching the reins in nerveless fingers.

Uffin walked back to him, elated at the ease of his victory, slightly sick at the efficiency with which he had killed.

"No need to worry about those others," he said to the young man. "Disappeared like chaff in the wind, gone back to whatever hole they crawled out of."

Finnul roused and shook himself. "Are they dead?"

Uffin turned to look at the three bodies. "We would have been," he said obliquely, "if we had shown any sign of fear. They respected neither man nor god, now the Gods will be pointing out the error of their ways. Come along now." He took hold of the pony's bridle and walked it nearer his own horse. "Look away if the sight offends you, but I promise you this, young Finnul, you'll see far worse before you're through with life. Of that, I'm sure."

Uffin remounted and patted his horse's neck. Finnul now rode alongside him having studiously avoided looking at the corpses. A few minutes later he spoke.

"Shouldn't they be buried?"

"As soon as we're out of sight, the corpse takers will come. We don't need to do a thing."

"Corpse takers?"

"Crows. It will take them a while, but if we come back this way, all you'll see is a few scattered bones. They deserve no more."

They rode on again in silence and again, Finnul broke it.

"You saved my life, Lord Uffin. One against three. Truly, you are the chosen one of the Gods and now, Mandeltua is not the only one to know. Those... those robbers that got away will spread the word."

Uffin looked sideways at the young druid. Privately, he had called him *Mandeltua's ear*. Now, perhaps for the first time, he saw him as something separate from Mandeltua, a person in his own right. The fellow was extraordinarily neat, considering they had been in the wild for almost a week. His fair hair shone, his face was clean shaven, the black cloak, the tunic and leggings looked as though they had been washed that morning.

Finnul turned and caught Uffin looking at him. Embarrassed, he turned back to face ahead, the cheeks and the long straight nose blushing pink. Uffin chuckled, here was one who could be a warrior, but for his calling.

"So why was Mandeltua the only one to know it?"

Finnul gaze remained ahead. "I uh, I speak out of turn, my Lord."

"By the Gods, Finnul, you don't speak out enough. For a week you've watched and listened and kept your own counsel. I'd begun to think it was some long dead spirit riding with me. Now answer me."

Finnul colored slightly and chewed his lip. "Mandeltua wears the Stone of P-p-power," he stuttered and was silent for several seconds, collecting his thoughts. "For a time, for some generations, it was lost. Fanolina cast it aside at Mona when the Gods refused to hear his pleas for help and now Mandeltua wears it. It gives him the power of far sight, he knows all."

Uffin was intrigued by the story though not taken in by what might well be a clever piece of propaganda on Mandeltua's part. Nevertheless, he remembered the night he had been shown the soldiers on the Wall and the death of his loved ones. Something had conveyed those scenes to him.

"I have experienced this far sight you mention," he told Finnul. "Mandeltua himself showed me, but I don't see how this would make him aware of my being chosen, as you put it."

Finnul shrugged. "Mandeltua knows these things; it is said that he eavesdrops on the Gods through the trumpet of that sea shell. He walks his own path. I know this and I have heard others say it, too, but he has knowledge that no one else has."

Again, Uffin was reminded of his first meeting with the older Druid, on the lake shore not far from the high waterfall.

"I think the others are frightened of him. They whisper in his presence and talk behind his back, but they never question what he bids them do."

Talk of Gods always left Uffin feeling uncertain. He had never more than half believed in them for they were never seen by ordinary men, never spoke to ordinary men. Were it not for the things which had happened at Medionemeton, he would have found it hard even to consider the possibility of their existence.

"That stone, you said it was the Stone of Power?"

Finnul nodded. "Yes."

"Hm." Uffin remembered the stone he had seen slip from beneath Mandeltua's cloak at the waterside and now he recalled where he had seen its like before.

"A sea shell, did you say?"

"That's right."

There had been a carving of just such a thing on the bust of Septimus' wife. He remembered seeing it at Fort Throp, remembered saying how distinctive it was. "How long is it since Mandeltua first wore this stone?"

Finnul raised his eyebrows. "Years. Since before I came to Medionemeton, anyway."

"Well. Interesting." Uffin had suddenly had a feeling that there was a connection, but it was a rather absurd fancy. *Obviously, the two ornaments could not be the same object.*

That night, they camped on the banks of a wide stream which ran into a long, long lake running north east as far as the eye could see. Hills had grown around them into mountains and now hid much of the night sky from view.

⚜

THROP

Praefector Vibius Septimus was overseeing cavalry training in the new stockade outside of Fort Throp, one of several new, purpose-built structures along the middle west section of Wall. There was the sound of hoof beats behind him, a trot slowing to a walk and finally stopping.

"Sir."

Septimus turned. The scout, Elvin Fellaugh, sat his horse a few feet away. The scout saluted.

"Tribune Karrus sends his complements, Sir. I have to tell you that on orders of the Deputy Governor Flavius, I am being deployed north of the Wall."

Septimus' face expressed several emotions. Shock, despondency, resignation, even for a moment, a touch of relief. *Perhaps it was best that he would never know.* But, unbidden, his mind moved on. "And what happens to my Iavolina? Is she to be left to the barbarians?"

"I really don't know, Sir. I shall try to keep on her trail while I am about the Emperor's business, but I have this much to tell you. She was taken by a man called Ferdiad, a bit of a sea trader by all accounts and perhaps a bit of a pirate, too. He returns to trade cargoes every couple of months or so, due back in six weeks although I don't know where."

Septimus gave him a withering look. "I thought you knew where. That's what you said."

Elvin trod carefully, indeed he had said so. "Within twenty miles, I know, but the coastline is rugged, hundreds of coves where the meeting could take place, take an army to watch them all."

"So?"

"So it will cost. There are two people who know. Neither one will talk. One because his life depends upon secrecy, the other because his livelihood depends on it. A thousand denarii will compensate him for the loss of earnings."

Septimus appeared to accept the other's lies without comment. "How soon will you find out?" If Elvin had listened, he might have heard a trace of bitterness in Septimus' voice.

"Within the day, Sir. After that, I must ride north."

"Very well then. I shall be finished here in an hour. Meet me outside my villa, I shall have to have the aquilifer unlock the treasury, but listen to me, scout," Septimus grasped the reins of the other's horse and pulled it closer, "if I do not have this information before the sun goes down, no place in the world will be safe for you. Do you understand?"

"I most certainly do, Sir." Elvin was quite shocked at the sudden change in the once mild Commandant. "Be assured, Sir."

As Elvin rode towards Throp's eastern gate, his thoughts veered between puzzlement at the Romans' sudden belligerence and consideration of how to spend his fortune.

There was that farm at Velswater…

CHAPTER THIRTEEN

VINDOLANDA

DEPUTY GOVERNOR FLAVIUS AWOKE TO A WHITENED LANDSCAPE. Unlike the legions, he did not rise before daylight, and as he looked out of his window, he could see legionaries and officers trudging along, ankle deep in the snow. Flavius swore and hit the windowsill with his fist. It would further delay the training which was already beginning to fall behind schedule.

The new troops had arrived some ten days before after weeks of forced marches. Flavius recalled his dismay on seeing them for the first time; they were not regulars as he had expected, but lightly clothed auxiliaries with minimum arms and even less experience.

At the time, he had suppressed his reactions, hoping that first impressions would be wrong. Now, he allowed himself to wonder why Hadrian had sent such forces. Politics of course, in Rome even a born soldier like Hadrian had to play the political game. The Emperor was covering his back; he would be under pressure from the Senate to keep all the Legions which were strung out along the borders up to strength. So, in acceding to Flavius' request for more men, Hadrian had sent him forces needing rather more than a refresher course.

The mercenaries had come from Rhaetia and Pannonia where they had been maintaining an uneasy peace with the Marcomanni and the Quadi, barbarians all, little more advanced than these here in Albyn.

He had had to strip the store rooms of blankets and winter clothing to protect the newcomers from the cold. Now, with the coming of the snow, they would have to issue better rations or suffer losses from poor nutrition.

Flavius also knew that many of the auxiliaries would be better off employing their traditional fighting skills; these would be placed in the van when the Legion finally left. However, those who were to be integrated into the Ninth, bringing it up to full strength, would have to learn to fight Roman style and think Roman style. It was these men which Flavius was most concerned about; their training could not be skimped. Their reactions simply had to be the same as those of the rest of the Ninth, tactics and fighting methods acquired over the Legion's lifetime—hundreds of campaigns, tens of countries all now parts of the Empire.

He sighed deeply and called for his slave. In one way he wished it were Spring already; in another, that he had much more time to spend. At the moment he was in a *lose or lose* situation, a problem which was not going to disappear as a result of wishes.

The body slave came in followed by Flavius' aide. He sighed again, looking up at the ceiling. As well as coordinating this mammoth training exercise, the logistics, the fortune it was costing, there was the usual day to day problems of running the northern provinces.

Flavius felt a headache coming on. Not that he could escape by pleading illness.

"Well?" he asked.

"Two native scouts, Governor. Sent on by Tribune Karrus."

Flavius nodded. "After I've dressed and had a drink."

The two scouts entered the Deputy Governor's office; they came to attention and saluted. Flavius nodded to them and indicated that they should stand at ease.

"Well, what is it? I'm sure it's important or the Tribune would not have sent you to me."

"Yes sir," said one, obviously chosen as spokesperson. Probably on the spin of a coin, Flavius suppressed a grin.

"You may know that we've been scouting the country north of the Wall. So, I was at Briogix a week ago, where the Callatae chief is. I saw Beneficiarius Gellorix there. Dressed in finery more suited to an Albyn chief than to a tribesman or a trader."

Flavius sat back. That mongrel scout was going to haunt him for the rest of his days.

"And? Something more?"

"The Callatae are calling him the *Chosen One*. The *One* to unite all of the Albyn tribes. I would have told him about his re-instatement, but I wasn't any too sure at the time that he was Gellorix and I could hardly chase after him."

"Hmm." Flavius was mystified, but took the report at face value. "Have you anything to add?" he asked, turning to the second scout.

"I've heard the same story. A hundred miles or more from Briogix, I come from Votadenii territory. *Chosen of the Gods* is what they call him there and aside from their Chief, no one's even seen him. Lord Uffin, they say, Lord Uffin who will unite the tribes."

"And what happens if he *does* unite the tribes? Unite them for what? What do you think will happen?"

The two scouts looked at each other and the first one continued again. "We think he could put more than thirty thousand warriors into the field, against you."

"Thirty… How long would it take him?" Flavius was starting to show the first signs of the anger building inside of him.

The scout shrugged. "A year? A year, Sir, or maybe a little longer for it's a huge territory to cover."

"Any way to prevent it? Any weak links in the chain?"

"Two ways, maybe."

"Well get on with it, man." Flavius allowed a little more annoyance into his voice.

"Do something that's going to cause the tribes to fight among themselves; they do it all the time usually, but that sort of thing has more or less stopped. Or, um."

"I do not have all day to listen to you *umming* and *urring*. Or what?"

"Or kill him. Kill Gellorix."

The last idea had already crossed Flavius' mind. Quick, expedient, no mess. Only a very irate Senator away in Rome. He thought about it. When he finally spoke, his voice was strained.

"There will be an order made for his apprehension and questioning. I shall issue the order this morning. However, *this* will not be on any official order list, but you can pass the word, it will not be secret. I shall personally pay the sum of five thousand denarii to the man who kills Gellorix."

Flavius took a handful of gold coins from his pouch and laid them on the table. He divided them in to two small piles.

"That is for being the first with this news and for realizing its importance. Go and see your families and then get off. You know what you have to do."

Flavius called his aide. The letter to Senator Mansustus would have to be composed with care.

⁂

CREONIA

As it snowed along the Wall, so it dawned fine and cold in the lands of the Creones.

Uffin and Finnul rode side by side along a wide valley enclosed by harsh mountains. Some of them seemed to consist of nothing but towering slopes of scree while others were firm enough for a few hardy pine trees to have colonized the lower slopes.

Uffin had now been traveling for two weeks with no clearer view of what he wanted than when he had set out. He had looked and tried to visualize plans for maneuvering a host of wild barbarians into something which would stop the Romans and here was another example of the same thing. Nothing fired his imagination; nothing called out to what he knew was lurking in the back of his brain.

"Look," said Finnul as excited as ever over a new sight. "What is it?"

Uffin smiled. "Lovely isn't it, majestic. It's a golden eagle. You see how white its underside is? If the clouds were a little heavier, you might not have seen it against them."

The bird had been hovering, laying on the wind and watching for prey. As they rode up the length of the valley, the bird seemed to float just ahead of them, then, with effortless grace, it circled and soared away to the north, leaving them behind.

"Isn't the eagle the Romans' symbol?" asked Finnul.

"Well, yes, it is. So, you do know something about the world outside Medionemeton."

"Oh, indeed. We know a lot about the Romans."

But Uffin had no great faith in symbolism. They continued up the valley. It opened up into a wider space further on. A fast shallow river crossed its width, sweeping out of a narrow gorge and tumbling into a boulder strewn chasm on the far side. Half a mile further on, the circular plain narrowed again into a deep V-shaped valley before once more opening into a huge space locked in by mountains; no way out, a dead end. Above them the eagle was back, circling and hovering, balancing against gravity and wind.

"Oh!" Finnul said no more, merely pointed, open mouthed.

Like a stone, the eagle stooped, falling from a thousand feet in the air. At the last moment, the talons extended, the wings spread to half break its fall. Beneath it, in its shadow, there was a flash of white; a long sinuous form was suddenly grasped in the talons.

Ermine, a stoat, but still alive and active. Only one of the eagle's claws had taken hold and it flapped into the air with the animal writhing frantically. The small head darted, small razor sharp teeth fastened in to the eagle's belly. The bird's ascent faltered, the wings beating erratically. Long seconds passed as it tried to gain height.

"Taken on more than it could manage," said Uffin quietly.

Even at fifty feet, they could see the blood soaking the pale plumage, the sudden pumping spurt as the stoat severed an artery. Both bird and animal plummeted to the ground, locked together in battle.

Uffin found that he had been holding his breath; he released it and looked around. "Nowhere else to go, Finnul. Shall we camp here tonight or head back again and find somewhere else?"

"Here," said Finnul. "It will be dusk before we've finished pitching the tent anyway. At least we'll have time to cook before the light goes."

"Whatever you say, lad. Whatever..." Uffin's attention had suddenly been taken by another movement. A wolf, he thought, looking down on them from a ledge and behind the animal, a series of darker markings on the flanks of several cliff faces. "I'm not trying to give you all the work, Finnul, but I've just noticed something. It's only because of the position of the sun that I saw them. Will you handle the tent and the fire while I go for a closer look?"

Finnul had worked for nothing except his meals and a sleeping space above the kitchens since he had been taken in by the druids. He had been a drudge until Mandeltua had noticed him and since then he had been a student—as well as a drudge. He had no life of his own.

"Lord Uffin, I don't remember the last time I left Medionemeton, I don't remember when I last had time to think. Go wherever you will, I will not be the one to argue."

Uffin smiled. "Thank you lad, thank you, my friend."

Uffin left his mount to graze while he climbed the tiny ridges that generations of goats had made. The going became steeper and harder and he had to use hands as well as feet to climb up to the area he had first noticed as a discoloration in the rock face.

The darker colors were due, as Uffin had suspected, to the shadowed entrances to caves. The particular strata he had reached seemed to be honeycombed with caverns.

He climbed over the edge into the nearest entrance and stood up. If the wolf had been here, there was no sign of it now, no sign of a lair or of droppings. The roof was a foot or two higher than his head and smoothed by centuries of silt-laden water. Here and there in floor and ceiling and in the walls were bowl shaped depressions where stones had been swirled around and around, grinding away at the soft sandstone.

Uffin walked through the echoing spaces lit by shafts of red sunset light from the openings. Suddenly, there was an explosive flapping of wings and Uffin's heart pounded wildly until his reflexes caught up with his brain and spotted the birds flying off into the dusk. The cavern system could hold an army, he guessed.

There was a constant seepage of damp in some places, the dripping of water loud in the silence but most of what he could see was dry. He stood at one of the cavern entrances and looked out across the almost circular plain. Uffin was familiar with the way in which water could wear away at the land, he had seen rivers alter their courses in the space of a few years and knew how huge areas of land could be washed away in the space of a handful of winters.

He pictured the floor of the huge basin below him raised by a hundred feet and a wild river—perhaps that which they had crossed a few hours previously—rushing along the flanks of the confining mountains. Uffin kicked at the sandstone and watched the soft rock flake away, water made these caverns—it seemed obvious to him. Perhaps the caves extended right the way through the mountains, right through to the other side. The next morning Uffin volunteered to strike camp and pack their gear onto the animals.

"Mandeltua told me you had a memory like a sponge," he said. "I want you to take a look around. Climb a tree or scramble up the cliff over there and memorize this place."

⊰❦⊱

CALLA

Elvin Fellaugh turned over on to his back and stared up through the trees. A chill wind whipped the upper branches into violent motion and drove clouds wildly across the gray sky. This was the woodland which he knew to hide the small settlement where the Chief of the Callatae lived. Elvin had followed several of the tribesmen deeper into the woods, employing all his skills and wood craft to ensure that his pursuit was not noticed. Each time he had lost his quarry, each time the man had melted away into the forest and each time, there had been no trail to follow.

Except once.

Two days before, he had followed an older man, confident that this one would not elude him. There had been a tall rock, he remembered and the sound of smaller rocks falling. There had been a resounding blow to the back of his head and... nothing. He had woken up on the edge of the forest with his bow broken in two, his small stock of knives and metal arrow heads looted and a bloody lump on the back of his head with the size and feel of a hedgehog. Elvin rubbed it tenderly; memory had made him conscious of the ache once more.

It had been a warning. Elvin had not tried again. He had decided that the wisest course was to lie here, at the top of a small bluff and watch for his quarry on the busy pathway below him.

He had heard that Gellorix and the Callatae chieftain were firm friends and sooner or later, he felt certain, he would have the chance to kill the one-time scout. For the tenth time that day, he checked his sword, the several spears and the new bow he had acquired. One good strike and away on the horse he had tethered nearby. It was a three hour ride to the Wall, two, if he pushed the horse. The Deputy Governor's reward would be his.

Elvin had no doubts as to his ability or his will to kill; he and violent death were old companions. The only imponderable was time. How long could he remain here? There was plenty of water, but his food supplies were dwindling and it could only be a matter of time before discovery.

Decisions. Buy food or hunt it and risk missing Gellorix. Well, he remembered trying to calculate how many pigs he could buy for the five thousand denarii on offer, how many cattle to put on the farm which he had already partly paid for courtesy of Praefector Septimus. Elvin's stomach rumbled, a haunch of pork would do very well at this moment.

He could wait a little longer though, put off the decision a little while.

The snort of a horse brought an abrupt end to his reverie and he rolled back onto his stomach and watched for the hundredth time to see who passed below. He chuckled, all the waiting had been worthwhile after all, there was Gellorix, accompanied by two Callatae and a youth.

They rode single file. An arrow then, an arrow would be the best chance and he knocked an arrow to the string, brought it to bear on the party, aimed, released as something heavy struck his shoulder. So concentrated was his attention on the flight of the arrow that only belatedly, after he had seen it strike the mark, did he register the blow.

He turned in time to receive the sword hilt on his temple instead of on the wound he had already acquired. He saw no more for several hours.

Uffin felt the arrow rip through the flesh of his right arm, pinning it to his chest. The arrow head had gone right through, scraping a rib and emerging at the back, warm blood seeped down his side. Urged on by his companions, Uffin rode like the wind along the secret pathways to Dag Liogh's dun.

As he waited for Dag to be made aware of his arrival, Uffin stripped off the splendid tunic more concerned, he was amused to discover, that he should not spoil the garment which had been Dag's father's.

Dag chuckled too, when Uffin mentioned this to him. "The tunic can be repaired easily enough; your blood will wash away. What will not wash away is my failure to protect you on my land."

"The failure is none of yours," Uffin protested. "I should have been more observant."

"No. Come inside and let my sisters bathe these wounds, or you might not live to wear the tunic again, however well they mend it."

The arrow head had gouged through the inner layer of his right biceps and torn a groove along the edge of the trapezius. Neither wound was life threatening so long as rot did not set in.

"You see," Dag continued as the girls cleaned the torn flesh, "I have known about the fellow for some time. We have kept a loose watch on him in the hope he would lead us back to whoever was employing him. If I had realized that you were returning, I'd have had him picked up and put him to the question."

"Don't blame yourself, my friend."

"I do. I do."

"Is the fellow dead?"

"No, no. We have him outside. You can decide what to do with him."

"Let me get dressed then, Dag and bring me something to drink, would you? Something to eat to, if that can be managed. For Finnul, too. Then we can see to this, Roman?"

Dag pursed his lips. "No, my friend," he said quietly. "A Brigantean, like yourself."

Later, they went outside and Uffin was met by the sight of his assailant bound, gagged and hanging by the feet from a convenient branch.

"Still unconscious, you see."

Uffin bent over in order to see the upside down man's face more clearly. He nodded. "Perhaps you would have him blindfolded and then throw a bucket of water at him."

His requests were carried out with enthusiasm and as the man was doused with cold water he spluttered back to wakefulness, Uffin had been right. He thought that he had recognized Elvin Fellaugh, once his second in command at Vircovicium.

The gag in Elvin's mouth was beginning to swell with the water and he was in danger of choking. Uffin pulled it free and used the sharp point of his dagger to trace a pattern on the exposed throat.

"You have your desire granted, my friend," said Dag as a trickle of blood ran along Elvin's chin and down into his hair. "You have tried for a week to reach my house. Now you are here."

"Why did you wish to visit the Chief of the Callatae?" asked Uffin; deliberately roughening his voice and thickening his accent. "And why kill our honored guest?"

Dag heard the words and looked sharply at Uffin and then watched him more thoughtfully.

"Answer quickly before we cut your throat and be done with it. Who sent you and why did you do this?"

Elvin was, or had been, a good scout and as was often the way with bullies, Elvin made an even better coward. No further persuasion was necessary.

"The Romans," he gasped. "They wanted him dead."

"Murdered. Why?"

"They heard that he was trying to bring all the tribes together. They fear the numbers he could have brought against them. I'm just a scout, I have to follow orders."

Uffin reached out and took Elvin's chin in his hand and squeezed. "Who told the Romans all this?"

"Another scout who was at Briogix. He saw him there, heard about him. Dunnoch, he was called Dunnoch."

Uffin knew the man and cursed himself for not being more circumspect.

"And what about the Romans? Do they really intend to invade Albyn?"

"Oh yes. Yes, it's true."

Elvin's face was becoming red as the pressure of blood mounted.

"How many men do they have, hm? What sort of forces do they have and when do they plan to come?"

Elvin groaned and answered as best he could. With careful goading and questioning, Uffin extracted more information. He learned the strength of the invasion force, the type of auxiliaries they were bringing in and that a springtime invasion was definite. Even the planned route came out unintended, a bonus that he would not have had, but for the assassination attempt.

Uffin motioned Dag away. "We should place him in a pit somewhere and let him escape. He'll tell the Romans that I'm dead, they won't worry about me anymore, and they won't send any more like him." Uffin jerked a thumb over his shoulder and winced at the unexpected pain from his injury.

Dag, his face set in serious lines, shook his head. "This cannot be. He was brought in here without a blindfold. My men never expected him to live; now he cannot be permitted to do so."

Uffin nodded.

"If he escapes to tell them, the Romans will wipe us out."

Uffin put a hand on the other's shoulder. "Yes, I understand, Dag. I just want to know one thing."

He crossed and pulled the blindfold away from Elvin's eyes. "Hello Elvin. Surprised to see me? Tell me Elvin, how much were they paying you to kill me?"

It took a moment for Elvin to realize who he was looking at. "Marcus, I thought..."

"I was dead? No, no. How much?"

"Nothing Marcus. Nothing. We were ordered."

Uffin brought his dagger into play again, nicking the other's cheek so that blood dribbled into Elvin's eye. "Don't lie, Elvin. You forget that I know you and I know how the Romans' work. There was a price on my head; you wouldn't have sat there waiting for me if there wasn't. How much? Hm?"

Still, the scout said nothing.

"I can ride down to the Wall and find out from our friends there; you'll have to hang upside down until I get back, of course."

"Five thousand denarii," came the reluctant reply.

"As much as that? What did I ever do to you Elvin, that you'd take blood money to kill one of your own kind?"

"I keep telling you Marcus, it was orders, no alternative."

Uffin heaved a deep breath. "I hope you're at ease with your Gods, Elvin. You'll need to be before these Callatae get through with you."

"Marcus. You're not going to let them kill me?" Uffin thought that he could see tears in the man's eyes. "I could be useful to you, Marcus. I could act as your scout amongst the Romans. I hate them as much as you do; they order us around and treat us like dogs." A veneer of cunning crossed Elvin's face. "I could kill Flavius for you."

"Flavius? What good would that do?"

"He commands the Ninth now. It's his plan to subdue the whole of Albyn."

Flavius. Why Flavius? It should have been Severus. He was the most experience commander in Briton. Why would Hadrian favor the Deputy over the Governor?

Dag leaned forward and spoke in Uffin's ear. "You know you're going to have to kill him soon, Uffin."

Uffin turned and frowned.

"You cannot afford to lose face, my friend. He tried to kill you, you have to be the one to dispatch him otherwise it will be seen as weakness. Your loyalties are going to be questioned."

True, thought Uffin. He had never killed in cold blood before, but he could see that he was going to have to. It was not an easy thing though, he had to steel himself. And then he thought of Asel and his mother and the killing rage rose in him. With a face like thunder he plunged the dagger into the scout's throat. Such was the force of the thrust that the blade severed the spinal column.

Unrealized, Uffin had collected quite a crowd. He jumped with surprise as they burst into shouts and cheers.

"Now they will follow you anywhere. Now you have my heart as well as my arm."

⁂

MEDIONEMETON

Two days later, Uffin and Finnul were back at Medionemeton where Mandeltua greeted them. He used the right words and phrases, but it was obvious from his manner that progress was all that he was interested in. *Did the Druid want justice or revenge?* wondered Uffin.

They were offered a meal, but Mandeltua persisted with his questions even while they were eating and Uffin had to divide his attention between eating and speaking.

"Yes, Arch Druid… I have found a site… yes, far enough inland to prevent supplies coming from Roman ships… too far for reinforcements."

Uffin took a great bite of goat's meat and listened to the next question.

"There should be no difficulty in getting all the tribes to merge there."

"Where is it?"

"In the lands of the Creones where the mountains are very high."

"Hm." Mandeltua scratched his chin and ran fingers through his beard. "Finnul, draw me a map."

Now Uffin realized why Mandeltua had sent the young man. Finnul went away and came back a minute or two later with dried sheets of white birch bark; he pulled some charcoal from the fire and began to sketch. Before his eyes, Uffin watched the route they had taken marked out. Along its length were mountains and rivers, moor land and swamp with identifying marks like curiously shaped rocks or exceptional trees, waterfalls. And finally, on a separate sheet, Finnul drew a plan of the circular plain-like valley and the approaches.

Uffin was amazed, almost speechless. He had told the boy to memories the area. The instruction had been quite superfluous, Finnul had soaked everything up like—as Mandeltua had remarked—like a sponge.

Mandeltua nodded his white head. "So, why have you chosen this place? A place with no way out of it? Is it a form of madness with you? Do you enjoy being penned in like sheep?" He scratched his head. "And why so far north? Will the Romans go that far?"

"The Romans intend to go all the way unless we stop them, Mandeltua. And who says that we are going to be penned like sheep? Hm. The further we are from the Wall, the longer the Romans will take to reach us. Time Mandeltua, time is what we need. There is much to do between then and now and I haven't told you yet about the eagle."

"Eagle? What eagle?"

"The golden eagle that the Gods sent as an omen. The one that led us to the place."

"Of what relevance is… an eagle, you said?" Mandeltua remembered a dream he had had when an eagle had flown across a land of bare rock.

"The eagle," explained Uffin, "is a symbol for the Romans; they carry it everywhere atop their standards. It's the official badge of Rome, the *Aquila* which is carried into battle by the standard bearer. Now do you see the significance?"

The Druid held his head and rubbed his fingers against the temples. "I'm sorry. What was it you said?"

Uffin repeated himself.

Mandeltua closed his eyes and bowed his head, nodding. "Of course, yes. Yes, I do and you're right. It must have been sent by the Gods to show us where." He closed his eyes, bowed his head.

"There is more."

"So? Tell me."

Uffin related the incident.

"And the eagle was killed?"

"That we could not see, nor the fate of the animal. Anyway I leave for the site tomorrow; I want Finnul to go with me."

"Very well." Mandeltua sighed.

"I want a meeting with the Caledones arranged, and with the Creones, their two Chiefs. I want five thousand men with axes and mattocks and spades and supplies organized to feed them all.

"As quickly as possible."

"And doubtless, the Gods sent you signs to say how this will be done?"

VIRCOVICIUM

For once, Aemilius Karrus found himself with no duty more onerous than checking the daily training exercises. His walk along the vallum was casual, his pace measured. There were one or two others with no pressing duties, too; he passed by two in discussion, an Actuarius and an Optio. Karrus could hardly avoid overhearing their words; the Optio said everything at full volume.

"Looks as though it was painful," said the Actuarius.

The other fingered a livid scar at the junction of neck and shoulder and Aemilius noted the man's musculature, a strong man, he stood out even in a legion of very fit men.

"Don't remember. I was so angry at the time that I just pulled the spear out and threw it away. Accursed slave at the mines. Gellorix by name. Threw the spear at me from above, didn't see it. One of these days I'll come up against him and I'll wrap these two hands," he held out a pair of oversized hands, "around his neck and squeeze, separate his head from his body."

"You mean he got away with it? A slave, how was that?"

"Found a way to escape. Through some caves he'd broken into at the back of the mine shaft. I'll find him..."

Aemilius coughed to let them know of his presence. The two men turned and came to attention in the presence of the senior officer.

"Optio," opened Karrus. "I don't think I know you."

"No, Sir. Optio Villius, Sir. Transferred from the post of mine supervisor. At Evenhope."

"Ah, yes. Deputy Governor Flavius has ordered a general recall of all experienced officers. You're in short supply, Optio. And you've had experience in battle?"

"In Dacia, against the Sarmatians, Sir."

"Good enough. I er, overheard you talking about a man named Gellorix."

"That's right, Sir. A slave, an escaped slave."

"Yes. I'd heard that. Innocent though."

"*Innocent*, Sir?"

"That's right. Miscarriage of justice. You allowed him to escape and you'd like to wring his neck? That so?"

Villius frowned, his arm muscles flexed. "Well yes. Didn't know he was innocent at the time."

"No, no. Of course not." Aemilius struck a conciliatory note. "Still, you might get your wish fulfilled yet."

"How's that, Sir?"

Aemilius Karrus smiled wryly. "You want to wring his neck and the Roman army now wants him dead. You are going with the Legion to invade Albyn and Gellorix, for reasons best known to himself, has joined the barbarians in Albyn."

"Well, I don't know what to say."

"Don't say a thing, Optio Villius. Get on with the exercises, all ranks up to and including Centurions are expected to take part. All right?"

That same evening, there was a party at Vircovicium, in the headquarters building. Its purpose escaped Aemilius, but he was still expected to attend. As the evening wore on, a number of officers, their reserve softened by wine, surrounded him.

Magnus Maximus, a long serving Centurion with the Sixth who had helped Aemilius select officers for training duty, posed the question that was on all their lips.

"You knew this Gellorix, didn't you, Aemilius?"

Aemilius smiled and inclined his head.

"Knew him well, Magnus. Worked with him; he was a friend, truth be told. A good man, dedicated to the Legion, reports were always accurate. What more can I say?"

"So why do you think he changed sides, then? Been a lot of talk about his being wrongly accused of murdering the last Commandant here, at Vircovicium. Reaction seems a bit extreme for wrongful accusation."

"That's true, too." Karrus considered his words carefully. "Our Deputy Governor sentenced him to life in the mines at Evenhope. He based his sentence on the evidence presented to him, flawed evidence as it turned out. Now Gellorix escaped from the mines; he's been at large since then, doesn't know he's been reinstated. In his circumstances, what might you have done? Thrown your hands in the air and declared it to be the will of the Gods?" Hm?"

"Well. I suppose not."

"I'll put a wager on that and be certain to collect."

"So he's some sort of leader over there, now, is he?" asked someone.

"Some kind."

Maximus asked another question. "If he does succeed in uniting all those tribes, what kind of enemy is he going to make?"

"Formidable, Maximus. Wager on that, too. He knows how we fight, what our strategies are going to be in any given situation. Formidable."

"Agricola destroyed the best that they had," said another voice from the group.

"After a five year campaign," Aemilius replied.

⁂

MEDIONEMETON

It was dark, the fire had burned low and most of the Druids had retired.

"I've been learning my lore for thirty years, my teacher was Alfare. He taught me that compassion was the greatest quality a druid must strive for."

The speaker cleared his throat. "I find our Arch Druid singularly lacking in compassion. It worries me. I find myself asking questions I'd rather not ask. Is there really a one true path to follow, or must we all find our own way through the darkness?"

"As usual, Liaghm, you speak too much and say too little. What are you really asking?"

"I am asking this. Are we individuals following the teachings of our mentors or a flock of sheep being herded by an egoist?"

"I think sheep being led by a wolf might be nearer the truth."

"We should not have elected this man. He bends the truth, he utters false wisdom."

"This is fishing in a lake when the fish have gone. We have no rules by which an Arch Druid can be removed. No laws."

When Melandae duly reported the discussion to Mandeltua the following morning, the Arch Druid smiled.

"Children lost in a fog. They refuse to face the one certainty in this life. The Romans will destroy us all and with us, all the knowledge that we possess. Compassion? What use is compassion to dead men? Most of them have never seen unnatural death; the *vates* perform the sacrifices and the divinations. They think of death as nothing more than a transition 'twixt waking and sleeping.'"

Mandeltua suddenly sat up in his bed. His face was a mask of hatred. "My whole family was murdered by the Romans and my whole life has been devoted to bringing about their downfall, driving them from our shores.

"The day is coming. I can feel it and when it does, these children will worship me for it.

"Now leave me, Melandae. I must gather my strength. Open your ears as always, but do not come again until I call for you."

CHAPTER FOURTEEN

NOVANTIA

A LONE FIGURE LAY IN THE BRACKEN STUDYING THE SCENE below. A ship rode the swells at anchor just a few yards off the rocky coast. He guessed that it was a Roman trader, or had been, but it might just as easily have been Byzantine or Phoenician for the observer was no expert on shipping.

A small boat, propelled by a paddle and looking like nothing so much as half a pomegranate at this distance, was slowly crossing to the larger vessel.

An oarsman from the trader wielded the paddle while a more familiar figure sat, gripping the sides with both hands.

Septimus had come to know the man being ferried rather well. He was Murrag the jeweler from near Luguvallium and had been Septimus' guide over the past week.

Septimus had undergone a minor transformation since Iavolena had disappeared. From despondent and tearful, his attitude had gradually hardened; his manner had become more forthright.

Still, however weak his character had been, the Praefector had never been a fool and when Elvin had asked for the one thousand denarii to pay for information, Septimus had made other, parallel enquiries, setting on a scout to watch the scout. The money was of no importance to him and he gladly paid another five hundred to Murrag when his second scout followed Elvin Fellaugh and brought Murrag's name back to Septimus.

Murrag had confirmed the meeting place with the Erin man, Ferdiad and on sight of Septimus' gleaming sword, had readily agreed to take the Praefector along with him.

As Commandant of a minor marching fort, Vibius Septimus had become somewhat soft of muscle and flabby in the torso. The week long hike had toughened him a little, had shed some weight and he felt surprisingly good. It was with an almost-eagerness that he watched the captain from Erin, evident by his swagger, step out onto the deck.

Murrag was not sure where Septimus had secreted himself and played carefully by calling out in the language of the Sons of Erin.

"Ferdiad, it's me, Murrag. I have an uninvited guest, a dog of a Roman who misses his wife."

Within the cabin, Ferdiad, who had been busy making the beast with two backs with the wife in question, paused in his labors. Iavolena grew petulant. "What do those stupid men of yours want now?"

"None of mine, my playmate. This is the worthy Murrag who sold you to me."

"Sold?"

"The price, as I remember was the seashell you had at your throat."

Iavolena's hand went to her neck. "Am I worth the price?"

"That we shall have to see about later." And Ferdiad withdrew and began to pull on his leathern trousers. He was secure in the knowledge that Iavolena would wait, perhaps not contentedly, but with anticipation for her passion for lovemaking seemed to know no bounds. He slapped her rump.

"Murrag tells me that your husband has come to fetch you back." Then, to Murrag: "I am coming, my friend."

Iavolena kneeled up and put her arms around her lover, pressing her breasts against his hairy chest. "Kill him, Ferdiad. Just stop him bothering me."

Ferdiad plucked her arms away and stood, looking down at her thoughtfully. She was worth keeping around him, she knew how to pleasure him and what was more, she added to the pleasure by enjoying their antics as much as he. But to kill a Roman officer. He shook his head.

"No."

"Why, you're craven. I'll..."

Quite casually, Ferdiad backhanded her across the mouth. "You. .?" he said. "Mm? You'll what?" He pushed away and Iavolena wiped her bloodied lips with the back of her hand.

"Killing a Roman officer would bring the might of your husband's army down upon us; we don't know who he has told about his journey, or how many men he has with him. No." Ferdiad thought a little further. "No, that way is folly. Now what was it you told me about your traveling companion, you killed her, didn't you? Because she might be mistaken for you?"

Slowly Iavolena nodded. This man of Erin was the first she had met who would take her more than once a day, every day. Never before had she known such vigor, he was a find she did not intend to lose.

"Yes, she had a similar build to me. I dressed her in my robe."

"And what was her name?"

"Cerea."

"Cerea." Ferdiad practiced the pronunciation a few times. "And where did you put her body?"

"Behind a water cistern. I expect they've found it now."

"If that's so, why is your husband here looking for you?"

Iavolena shook her head, feeling a little frightened now.

"Stay in here. It may be that I can deal with this." Ferdiad pulled on his shirt and stepped outside.

"Well, well, Murrag. Last time you were late, this time you're early. And what's all this about a man looking for his wife?"

They sat, Ferdiad on a heap of sacks, Murrag on a coil of rope, while the jeweler explained the circumstances and Ferdiad nodded, putting the finishing touches to his story and making certain his sword was loose in its scabbard.

"So. How many legionaries does he have with him?"

"Legionaries? Why none. He and I came alone."

"Well, I fail to see the problem. Come. We'll go ashore and see what happens."

Back on dry land, they walked slowly up to the low roofed houses and sat down on a bench set by a lime washed wall. Ferdiad reached out a hand and knocked on the door. When it opened he smiled at the woman who peered from within. "Perhaps you have some ale you'd care to sell two thirsty travelers?" And he held out a dull copper coin.

From his vantage, Septimus watched them return to the village and take their seats before backing down from the small hill and retrieving his waiting horse. The horse, hired from Murrag, was somewhat short in the legs. *Lacks the sort of response I get from military mounts*, he thought, *but it will have to do*. He gripped the animal with his knees as they went down the steep slope. He turned on to the dirt road which led into the village and walked the horse to where the two men were sitting.

"A fine morning to you, Roman," opened Ferdiad in heavily accented although perfectly understandable Latin. "Come and join us; there's enough ale to stretch to three."

I'm shaking, Septimus realized and decided that it was anger rather than fear which caused it. *Iavolena's abductor, I could split him from crown to gut from here.*

"I haven't come here for pleasantries," Septimus said at last, gasping a little with the effort of control. "You've taken my wife, how much do you want to bring her back from..." Septimus gestured out to sea. "From your land."

Ferdiad stood up casually and moved a pace or two, taking him to the left, away from the Roman's sword arm. "I don't have your wife," he said, keeping his voice even and friendly. "So..."

"I don't suppose you have, but you can buy her back from whoever you sold her to, can't you?"

"I was going to say, so I cannot accept money for her return. Things are not as you suppose. Sit down here, take a cup of ale and let me tell what I know."

Septimus was certain that the swaggering seaman was patronizing him. The anger which had been building over weeks burst through his control, he drew his sword. He made a backhand sweep which should have taken Ferdiad's head from his shoulders.

Ferdiad had no intention of letting such a thing happen. It seemed to Septimus that a sword appeared in the trader's hand instantaneously and his blow was blocked so effectively that the shock ran back up his forearm. The hired horse, unused to singing metal and unruly riders, reared and unseated Septimus who slid over its rump and landed on his own, heavily winded.

When the mists of the mishap cleared, it was to find a large knee on his chest and the point of a very bright blade just touching his throat.

"I've no wish to kill you, Roman, so just listen to me. The woman I took in trade from Murrag here was called Cerea and she now resides in a brothel across the sea from here. Before I sold her I had the full story from her, your wife was killed by a Roman named, er, Severius and he dumped her body at a fort. Where are you from?"

"The Roman fort at Throp."

"That's the one. Behind a water tank."

"But I had her traced. Her jewelry, her favorite pendant..." Septimus could not grasp what he was being told. Iavolena was really dead, that pendant... Unaccountably, for no reason he could fathom, Septimus felt just a little better. *I suppose the thing was actually mine, since I purchased it, but somehow...*

"The two women were of an age, there was a similarity?"

"I suppose," Septimus allowed.

"Cerea took your wife's jewelry and fled with the man, this Severius."

Well, for a quick lie, the story had had the ring of truth to it; he thought and eased the pressure on the Roman's throat.

Septimus coughed and climbed to his feet. *That incompetent Elvin Fellaugh,* was his immediate thought. "I'll look into it." He nodded and caught hold of his skittish horse. "I'll check." The Praefector climbed on to the horse and turned it round; he took one last look at the two others and shook the reins.

At least that shell pendant's gone. I don't think I ever liked it. The pendant really had nothing to do with Iavolena's fate, but somehow the irrelevant thought kept intruding.

Ferdiad drank off the last of the ale and watched the winter sun's light reflected from the white wave crests on the incoming tide. "I hope the trade goods are better than last time, Murrag. Most of those swords were chipped and the axes couldn't hold an edge."

"They were the finest you could wish for," replied the jeweler who also traded in many things.

"The tide's turned, let's get them aboard before it's really on the ebb."

"I hope the meal's ready," Ferdiad shouted when he had returned to his ship. "Do you know that your husband took a swing at me?"

Iavolena dropped to her knees and hugged him about the thighs. "Your meal is just as you like it, my lord." She looked up and then dropped her eyes again. "And so am I."

Ferdiad chuckled and reached down to tug gently on her long locks; she stood up. He turned her around and gave her bottom a pat. "Be off. If the meal's to my liking, I'll join you in my bunk."

Ferdiad used his sleeve to clean a smudge of dirt off the bulkhead. *I think I like this Roman woman the best of all. After my little Roman ship, anyway.*

CREONIA

It was bitterly cold. The wind which howled out of the north shook the pines along the mountain sides like a bunch of straw in a man's hand. Despite the conditions, as Uffin rode up the valley from the lower clearing, he saw men lining the route ahead. And not just a few, but hundreds, perhaps even thousands; it was difficult to tell with the wind whipping tears from the eyes.

Five deep, he saw as he and Finnul rode through. Harsh faced men who would neither ask for quarter nor give it, unspeaking, unsmiling, stoic against the gale.

Briefly, Uffin wondered if these were the allies he had expected. Were they perhaps, some huge band of robbers of the kind he and Finnul had encountered before? They were dressed similarly in skins and in tattered woolens with here and there a faded check.

If indeed they are such men, Uffin found himself praying to the half-believed in gods, then help me, for there's no use in my taking out my sword.

They forded the swift and shallow river and came to the second of the two clearings and close to one side a windbreak had been erected and rude wooden tables and benches assembled. A man was sitting there, he rose as Uffin approached and Uffin gave a sigh almost audible above the wind's cacophony.

Uffin vaguely remembered meeting this man at Medionemeton. It was the fellow's dignity which struck the chord and proved beyond doubt that the forces he and Finnul had ridden past were not the vagabonds he had envisioned. He brought his horse to a stop and swung stiffly down from the saddle. He held out his hand and they gripped each other's forearm; the one, thick with corded muscle and massive bones, his own, thinner and hard with sinew and long tight muscles.

"Corvoniti, Chief of the Creones. These are my men, Lord Uffin, what will you have them do?"

They still held each other's arm in greeting and Uffin smiled into the other's eyes, taking the chance to assess the Chief. A decade or more older than himself, he guessed and a finger's length shorter. His head was crowned by a shock of red hair, his face by a mass of red whiskers which hid all but the nose which thrust through and the eyes which laughed out at him. Uffin felt an instant liking. *This was a man that loved life,* he thought, *and probably lived it to the full, a man who was looked on with great affection by his tribe.*

"How many have you brought me, Chief Corvoniti?" he asked. "I see they've built you a nice windbreak and all the comforts of home, anything I might ask will be of small consequence after this."

Corvoniti smiled, his eyes crinkled up and his chest shook as he chuckled. "We have waited for you for two days, my Lord. It gave them something to do. Tell me, is it true that you wish to fight Romans here?"

Uffin nodded.

"On Creone territory?"

Again, he nodded.

"CREONES," roared the Chief above the wind. "COR-VON-ITI, COR-VON-ITI" chanted his warriors at the tops of their voices loud enough for even the echoes to be heard above the noise of the wind.

"This is a great honor. We thought that there was some mistake in what we heard for it is many days from the lands of the Wall." He laughed again. "How many tales do you give us to tell our children, Lord Uffin, how many songs for our bards to sing around the winter fires?"

"You know," said Uffin, "it's strange, but you are the first person who has *not* asked me 'why.'"

"What does it matter? You have chosen the place, *this* is what matters. You asked how many I have brought. *This* many." Corvoniti poured a heap of pebbles from a small bag on to the table. "One stone for a handful of men."

Uffin did not count the stones, but guessed at around six hundred or so warriors; he made a mental note to get Finnul to do a head count later on.

"Thank you," he said. "My companion has drawings of what needs to be done. Do you wish to discuss them now, or when the Chief of the Caledones arrives?"

Corvoniti's good humor died and he turned a bleak look upon Uffin.

"Is there a problem with the arrangement?" Uffin showed concern.

"No problems. I give you my word—as long as Alventicus gives his also. No problems."

"Alventicus." This must be the Caledones' chief.

"Chief of the Caledones," confirmed Corvoniti. "Our tribes have warred against one another since the time of my Grandsire's father."

Uffin winced. Here was the reality. *Two neighboring tribes who had feuded over four generations.* The fact that they were neighbors had suggested that they would be reasonably friendly to each other. *The Selgovae and Callatae are quite amicable, but these two...* He shook his head at the perversity of human relationships.

By the mid-afternoon, Uffin had the Creones working in the almost circular plain at the far end of the blind valley. Most of the force was felling and stripping trees although a hundred or so were digging post holes in as straight a line as any Roman road.

It was his intention to put up a stout palisade across the center of the area which would effectively halve its size. There were two main objects to the exercise, to hide the true size of his fighting force from the Romans and reduce the amount of room within which the Romans could maneuver. He also intended to build it like a Roman fortification, with watch towers and crenellations—a whim, something to wrong-foot the Romans when they saw it.

Mid-afternoon became late afternoon with dusk an hour away, poles had been erected along fifty percent of the fence line. Corvoniti was always at Uffin's right shoulder, never more than a pace away; he asked no questions, but watched everything, his bellow always at the ready to relay an order. Uffin overheard him talking to one of his lieutenants.

"Why?"

"Mm, why what?"

"Build a stinking Roman fence, we're Creones, not spineless Romans who have to hide behind fences."

"This is what the Lord Uffin wants. The Gods have spoken to him and made plain what is to be done. If they say that a Roman fence must be built then a Roman fence will be built."

Uffin grinned to himself. The time would come when he would have to try explaining his reasons, but not yet, not before the Caledones' Chief arrived and he could make do with a single lecture to both.

"Chief, Lord Uffin!" The call had all the urgency of a surprise attack being reported. They turned with worried expressions and heard the rumble of wheels over rocky ground. "Supplies," the lookout added.

Corvoniti beamed, his eyes disappearing behind tufts of hair. "Now we can make a feast, Lord Uffin. Tomorrow, we'll send hunting parties out into the forest but tonight— all we need is here."

The carts were pulled by oxen and driven by women who lost no time at all in bawling at the men to light fires and make hearths so that the dozens of cooking pots might be heated. The women themselves prepared unleavened dough and baked flat bread cakes as soon as the stones were hot enough.

In reality, it took something like an hour, but it seemed scant minutes to Uffin before they were sitting down eating belly filling soup rich in chunky meats and as much bread as he wanted. There was ale in abundance and even fruit which had been brought from the storehouse where it had been set aside for winter.

"Chief, Lord Uffin!" Reaction to the second such cry was slower and less anxious than before. "Warriors, guard yourselves."

A hundred conversations fell silent and an instant later, a thousand spears and swords, axes, cooking knives and even shovels and iron spoons were grasped and held aloft. The Creones turned to face the valley from which the unmistakable jingle of harness and arms could be heard.

A weird cry emanated from the darkness, a warbling ululation which set the teeth on edge and the hairs at the back of the neck rising.

"Gods! That's a Caledone war-cry," came a frightened exclamation.

"Hold," shouted Corvoniti. "The Caledones come as *brothers*." The Chieftain laid heavy emphasis on the last word, warning everyone that he had given his bond.

Riding into the firelight came a huge group of men whom Uffin knew could only be Caledones for there were a dozen subtle differences between the newcomers and the men he had been working with all day. Dress differed, bearing, many wore helmets, a few had scraps of armor strapped onto chest or fighting arm. All, every one, brandished a weapon.

They halted and the front rank stood straight and solid, their eyes reflecting the fire-light's flickers a hundred times or more. Comments, low and unintelligible, passed among the Creones who stood facing the Caledones.

Uffin recognized the signs and walked quickly forward. Action, action would defuse the situation, he hoped.

In the center of the Caledone's front rank, there rode a stern faced man with hair laced liberally with grey, an ugly scar crossed his right eye and nose, but it was the man's hands upon which Uffin's eyes fastened. Huge, banded across the back with thick tendons. *Easily, twice the size of mine*, he decided.

"Welcome, Chief Alventicus." He walked straight up to him and spoke loudly enough for all to hear, from the cooking fires behind him to the far side of whatever force stretched away into the darkness in front. "Chief Corvoniti has been telling me that between them, the Caledones and the Creones could move a mountain if it was necessary. Now that you have come, I see that he spoke no more than the truth."

Alventicus cleared his throat and unbent enough to lean down from the saddle and grip Uffin's right arm.

"So you're this Lord Uffin. You seem different to when I saw you at Medionemeton. Perhaps you've grown."

A joke? A censure? Uffin chose to laugh. "If your two tribes can work together, Chief Alventicus, it bodes well for Albyn. It pleasures me to see two such willing bands of men. In truth, if the Romans came here at this very minute, they'd think twice before starting any trouble."

There was a veiled message in his words which did not escape the Caledones' Chief. He raised his right arm above his head, a young oak rising in the firelight. He, too, spoke loud enough so that no one might fail to hear him.

"I have given my pledge to the Druids on fear of excommunication. I have pledged that my tribe will aid the Lord Uffin. Still, we came here prepared for war because the air between Creone and Caledone is bitter with anger."

An angry muttering rose from the Creones, but Alventicus put a hand forward, palm upraised.

"There will be no bloodshed if none raise their hand against us. If the Creones accept us as brothers, we, too, will accept them. Our vates have filled our memories with tales of the valor of King Calgacus in the battle of the Grampian Mountains. We Caledones stood against the Romans then, we will stand against them today. While there is breath in my body, they shall take no more slaves."

Alventicus had made his point, had shown strength and magnanimity. His pride had been served. Uffin relaxed, felt the tension drain away, muscles ease their knotting.

"Then join us brothers," he told them. "Dine with us and drink your fill, rest your aches and pains, for I know only too well how far you have had to ride. What say the Creones? Welcome our brothers to the fight, for Rome is foe to all of us."

There was a mixed response, from lukewarm to enthusiastic. Uffin heard no dissent, for which he was grateful and as Chief Corvoniti's stentorian roar took to the air, the reception grew degrees warmer.

"Escape routes?" queried Alventicus later. "I'd kill the first man to run away."

"Lord Uffin has curious ideas, brother Alventicus. Some of them take time to understand. Perhaps there are even a few that we shall never comprehend, but I ask you to listen to him, humor him a little if need be."

Uffin did not know whether to be pleased or annoyed at Corvoniti's intervention as they discussed plans after the enormous breakfast eaten by the two Chiefs.

"So. We search the caves for an escape route, to the other side of the mountains. These here?" Uffin had shown them the caves at first hand, as soon as the light had grown strong enough and Alventicus now picked out the depiction of the cavern system on Finnul's finely drawn maps. Alventicus had grasped the idea of the maps much more readily than had the Creone Chief.

"Right," agreed Uffin. "And remember, I mentioned piles of loose rock on timber staging so that we can tip them onto the army as it comes through. We shall need steps and pathways cutting into the steep mountain sides over here, so that we can build similar platforms on both sides."

"You know," Corvoniti had been looking around Uffin's site long before Uffin had arrived for the meeting, "some of that rock is so rotten, we could wedge timbers into the cracks and lever out blocks the size of a broch when the time comes."

"Fine. Whatever we can. Now here, where the valley joins the first plain, I want a tunnel constructed. Across from one side to the other."

"Aha. We make holes and poke spears up the Roman backsides as they march along," Corvoniti guffawed.

Uffin grinned politely, but Alventicus ignored the sally.

Uffin continued. "If we dig two shafts within the trees on each side," he pointed to both spots, "as deep as two men are high and three man-heights wide, we can then dig across underground until they join. Every foot of the tunnel needs to be propped with timber and two timber rafts built over the shafts themselves. They will act as bridges which we can pull up or drop from one side only."

He looked from one chief to the other. "Can we do it?"

Corvoniti spoke first. "Of course, my men have mined the ground for iron; their fathers and their fathers before them have mined for iron, for years beyond counting."

Alventicus shrugged. "My men, too, can dig. What is a little earth moving, after all, when you compare it with a life time of slavery?"

"Well put," said Uffin with a mirthless chuckle. "I was a slave in the Romans' lead mines until I escaped."

Now it was the turn of the two Albyns to look from each other to Uffin. "Escape?" said Alventicus.

"Lead mines?" said Corvoniti.

Briefly, Uffin gave them a few of the facts, but quickly returned to the project while it occupied the forefront of his mind. "Suppose the Caledones start from the north side and the Creones from the south, hm? I'll make sure there's enough wine brought in so that every man on the side that digs the fastest can get as drunk as he likes."

"Ha!" said Corvoniti, his huge voice turning every head. "I've a mind to dig the whole thing myself."

"No need for that. The Druids have promised to bring enough wine to celebrate Samhain all over again."

Corvoniti frowned. "Why Uffin?"

"To keep up morale."

"No, no. The tunnel."

"Just get it started, my friend. I will reveal all of my plans very shortly. Finnul is building a model of this site, I can explain then. I had better go and see about that section of palisade where the bog is."

"Before you go, Uffin." Alventicus pulled Uffin to the side. "That trick you pulled at Medionemeton, think you could teach me that?"

"Well, gladly. It's a training exercise where I come from. I'll be pleased to show you and anyone else who wants to learn—after the day's work is done, yes?"

VIRCOVICIUM

"So, Tribune Karrus." Flavius leaned back and picked at his teeth with a split goose quill. "How goes it with the veterans?"

Aemilius settled himself down in the cushioned chair and looked across the table at the Deputy Governor. "Better than I had expected, Governor. At present, they're off on a full field exercise with other infantry cohorts. My centurions tell me that they are running around like ten year olds."

"And they'll be ready—when?" Flavius raised his eyebrows.

"My men are ready now, Sir. I don't think you'll have to worry about the veterans, the new men have settled in well, they're working well. You won't have to worry."

"Ah. I'm pleased to hear it. Would that it were so with some of the others. I have tribunes telling me another month, another five weeks. And the auxiliaries, they can do what is required, but not yet fast enough to be satisfactory."

"There must still be a month before the weather changes and we've not had a lot of snow since November."

"True, but the ground still needs to dry out sufficiently to take the weight of the wagons. The Legion marches at the speed of the slowest ox, we need firm ground underfoot."

"That is in the hands of the Gods, Sir, but I *do* have some other news for you."

Flavius inclined his head. "Good news, hopefully."

"Some of it is certainly good. The scouts have been returning on and off over the last month. They've contacted several tribes who seem willing to become a part of the *Pax Romana*."

"And they are?"

"The Novatae, the Selgovae, Votadinii and Damnonii, oh, and the Venicones. That's so far. There are still some scouts to report back, Fellaugh amongst them. He's not been heard from for a month, at least."

Flavius then surprised Aemilius with his obvious depth of knowledge. "So that leaves us with the Caledones, Vacomagii, Taezlii, Creones." He was ticking them off on his fingers. "Let me see. The Epinii, the Decantae and the Carnonocae not to mention some we have yet to hear about. So at least seven tribes have not yet agreed. Is that not so?"

"Quite correct, Governor, but the five tribes who have agreed represent half of Albyn. Provided we can trust them to keep their word, we have eliminated half the forces that would be bearing arms against us."

"Well, yes. What you say is true. Now that must be the good news. What of the bad?"

"I didn't say it was bad. It's just news. I've a report in that Gellorix is dead, killed in hand to hand combat with one of our own scouts."

"Won't the scout confirm it?"

"The report is second hand. The scout in question is Elvin Fellaugh, the one that hasn't been heard from for some time."

"Hm. How much credence do you give this report?"

Aemilius smiled. "If I were Gellorix, I'd want you to believe me dead. The Callatae are a close mouthed bunch at the best of times, no one seems to know where they sprang from. They certainly weren't on the register in Agricola's time."

"That's true." Flavius propped his chin on his hand. "And something else, have you noticed that the tribes you mentioned are all those closest to the Wall? If one had a suspicious nature, one might suspect that if we *must* fight then our, er, new friends don't intend it to be around here."

In point of fact, Aemilius had noticed it, but had thought that if Flavius were to observe it then he would prefer to let the Deputy Governor take the credit. "I'm sure that there is something in what you say."

Flavius nodded, more to himself than to Aemilius. "Have you ever read Tacitus, Tribune?"

Aemilius shook his head. "A professional soldier like me doesn't find much time for reading, Sir."

"No. It's a great pity, Aemilius." The Tribune's mouth tightened a little at the informal address. "He was an extraordinarily shrewd observer. Let me quote you a few words. He was reporting Agricola's address to his troops on his last campaign. 'These Albyns' said

Agricola, 'are those same men whom last year you swept from the field of battle with no more than a shout after they had fallen on a single legion in a stealthy night attack. These are the men who excel at running away from the enemy. That is the only reason that they have survived so long.'"

Flavius had closed his eyes. He opened them and grinned at Aemilius. "You see, like you and your colleagues, Agricola's officers had their doubts too."

"I'd not question your orders, Sir."

"Very diplomatically put." The Deputy Governor continued his recital true to the spirit of Tacitus' writing if not to the words.

"All the bravest animals burst out at you when you pass through the forests, but the timid and slothful are driven off by the sound of your column on the march. Even so, all the fiercest of the Albyns have long since confronted us and fallen before us. All that are left are the craven, but now that we have found them, they have no choice but to stand and face us. We have overtaken them in their flight and their extremity and their terror has rooted them to the ground where they stand. Here, you are fated to take part in a great and a glorious victory."

There was passion in every word that Flavius uttered. His eyes had closed again and it was plain that his imagination stood before the same legionaries that Agricola had spoken to. Aemilius was a great believer in reincarnation. *Was Flavius no less than Agricola reborn?* he wondered.

"Very moving words, Sir. Very moving." He meant it.

"Just so, Aemilius," Flavius almost whispered. "The Grampian campaign. Can you see how everything is the same now? They're running away from us again. I mean, they cannot fail to have heard of our expedition by now, and they're on the move. I feel it in my stomach, Aemilius, the Albyns are running, but sooner or later they have to stand or else they must swim across the northern ocean.

"Agricola made one mistake, Aemilius." Flavius held his index finger up. "Just one. He stopped after winning the Battle of the Grampians. He had them, but he let his fish off the hook."

Flavius stood and pushed his chair back, stretching and bending his back. "I'll not let the hook slip."

❧

MEDIONEMETON

The red embers of the fire shed a dim light across Mandeltua's stringy body. He lay on the floor of his dun, chanting under his breath those conjurations which compelled the spirits to carry his messages, willing them to carry his thoughts to Uffin.

He had starved his body for days so that his spirit could better touch those less corporeal than himself. Unfelt by his brain, his limbs thrashed across the rush strewn floor and his eyes stared sightlessly into the darkness of his home. The muscles of his sparse frame spasmed and every joint locked rigid as the power of the sending coursed through his nerves. The stone clutched in his right hand bit into the flesh and seemed to glow.

❦

CREONIA

Uffin sat bolt upright in his tent as the figure of Cocidius, the horned One, approached him from the darkness of a huge cavern. The stag like muzzle opened and un-human words came forth, words which nevertheless, Uffin could understand.

"The prophesy will be kept," said the God. "The invaders rush towards their fate and will be destroyed by stone. The Gods who watch over you are not those who deserted their people in elder times."

The figure faded until only the vast and splendid blackness remained, a space far bigger than could ever be contained in the small tent that Uffin occupied. He sat there gazing into that Other region until the grey light of dawn dispelled it.

Slowly, Uffin put words to his feelings. There must be more to his being here than merely human machination.

VIRCOVICIUM

Aemilius was sweating, a cold sweat which ran down his body in beads and soaked his bedding. He saw Cocidius come, heard the words that the God uttered and though he could not understand the distorted language that the stag's mouth uttered, he was filled with an ominous dread, a foreboding of great evil.

Gods, I'm frightened. More frightened than at any battle. Aemilius was man enough to admit it. He had never worshipped the Britons' God, but he determined to visit the shrine at Virsa and sacrifice a healthy white cock.

The pain in his hand registered. His fingers were locked about the stone shell, its hard edges biting deep into the flesh. It felt red hot and he dropped it on the floor. Aemilius pulled on a tunic and went to walk in the cold and frosty night air.

❦

VINDOLANDA

The Deputy Governor and three of his officers stood on the gate tower looking down on the seething mass of cavalry. He waited patiently until the milling had settled down and some order had been created, then he spoke with pauses for the Centurion at his side to translate his Latin into the Brythonic words.

"Welcome to Vindolanda, all of you." Although he appeared not to raise his voice, it carried, heard by every one of the assembled riders. "You serve with the Legion, Ninth Hispana, a glorious Legion, one with a great history of achievement. You will form a part of the largest invasion force now assembled on this island and in honor of this great event,

I name you Brytonnica Flavius. You will be detailed to your respective *alae* by your officers after this assembly.

"Whilst you are with the Ninth, you will be well paid and well fed and in expectation of a glorious victory, every man of you will receive generous bonus money. You men are the wings of my army, like birds, free spirited. I expect great things of you for I know of your bravery and fearlessness.

"I know that I shall not be disappointed."

As Flavius left the tower, he signaled Aemilius Karrus to accompany him. The Tribune followed him down to the Deputy Governor's office.

Flavius went to stand by the open window which looked out across a steep, almost miniature, valley where a stream sang and burbled its way down the steep slope.

"Aemilius, I understand that you speak this outlandish Brythonic like a native."

Aemilius coughed. "I, er, not exactly, Governor though I've been here eight years and it rubs off on a man. Actually, since the Sand Crag incident, I've made an effort to learn more of the tongue."

"Spending more time with your woman? Mm?"

Many long serving men had a woman, or even a family in the local *vicus*. Often, if not usually, the arrangement would be made official by marriage when the man retired. Despite its being so common and Aemilius wise in the ways of the world, he blushed. Flavius saw the color rising. "It's all right. I know life is lonely up here, I meant no intrusion and I have a good reason for asking... about the language."

"Let's just say that I have a reasonable understanding of it, Sir."

"Of course. The point of all this," he took a deep breath and Aemilius had a sense of fate looming over him, "I've been watching your progress. You are a resourceful and competent man, Aemilius. That's why I appointed you Tribune and you've impressed me further with your dedication and abilities."

"Well, thank you..."

Flavius held his hand up to stop whatever else Aemilius might have been going to say.

"You're ahead of schedule, are you ready for a new challenge?"

There was no way out, what could he answer but "yes"?

"Excellent. I want you to take responsibility for those men outside. Five thousand of them." Flavius' eyes were alight; his eagerness was almost contagious.

Aemilius however, was immune to the enthusiasm of political officers. Five thousand cavalry?

"I'm an infantryman, Sir."

Flavius didn't hear or chose not to. "They have their own leaders, naturally and I want you to work your way into their confidence. Keep them aware of the long arm of Rome and how punishment and reward are dealt from the same hand. Many a rebellion has been nipped in the bud by having a good man on the spot."

"You think they might rebel?" Barbarian cavalry, it was the last thing he wanted, he had hoped that that seashell bauble might bring him a bit of luck, but it seemed that it was not very powerful.

"No I don't. It has been known for such men to change sides if the tide of battle turns against them, but er, not with you there."

"I've only ever worked with infantry."

Flavius' good humor became a trifle strained. "Every man who is destined for the top has to have worked with cavalry; it's a mark of nobility. You can do this, Aemilius, you're born to command. You brought home the Sixth; do you think I'd forget that? Now?"

"Yes sir. I'll do my best."

"Good. I'm glad that's settled, I'll rest easier knowing you're in charge there. However, on the march, I shall want you by me. I shall want your advice on deployment and a dozen other matters. This," Flavius thumped a fist into the opposing palm, "this campaign is going to catapult us into the very top of the Roman command."

"I'm certain it will do wonders for us, Sir."

"Haven't heard any more about Gellorix, have you?"

DUN CROACH

At the back of the bay, landlocked and hidden by high coves, a settlement of five duns was concealed among the oaks and ash trees.

A sizeable stream ran between two of the buildings and a dam created a pool deep enough for some good sized fish to fatten contentedly. In season, salmon would leap the barrier and rest awhile before continuing up to their spawning grounds—if the men from the Dun did not catch them first.

When he was not away across the seas, the largest of the three duns was home to Ferdiad the Trader. Until recently, it had also been home to several women who had taken the Trader's fancy. All but two had gone now, banished to one or other of the smaller places where Ferdiad's crewmen and one or two hunters and farmers lived. Those who stayed were mothers to Ferdiad's son and two daughters; their role, now purely domestic.

When the new woman had come, the Roman woman with the hair like spun gold and the contemptuous look in her eyes, Ferdiad had dug his heels in and point blank refused to deny their parentage and Iavolena had had the sense to submit to the arrangement.

Still, Iavolena was more or less content with the compromise. She was undisputed mistress of the small holding and over the winter months, had made the big dun as comfortable as any Roman villa.

That is, except for bathing arrangements. These, she was determined to have, come the Spring. In the summer, the floor would be excavated for a *hypocaust* to be laid and a decent cellar made for the wine that Ferdiad had had filched from the Roman supply trains.

By then, she planned, smiling happily, to be well into her first pregnancy. Her child was going to be the one that mattered; it would be born in the late Autumn and the following year …

Ferdiad grinned and let her have her own way. Here, at Dun Croach, he was a self-made noble. His retainers were happy with their chief, their *Ferdiad the Pirate*, for life was interesting and exciting by turns and a comfortable one, too.

Like his new woman, Ferdiad had ideas about the future, too. Happily, they more or less coincided with those of Iavolena. A family of half Roman children, an invitation—secret at first—to Iavolena's parents followed by shrewd commerce with Roman traders and the traders who traded with the Romans.

Once, many months before, when the drink had softened Ferdiad a little more than usual, he had confided his ideas to Murrag the Jeweler.

"Who signs agreements with the Romans must sit at a long table." And he had closed his eyes and nodded his toad-shaped head.

Ferdiad thought about the comment for a long time before he realized what Murrag was saying. *Keep them at arm's length*, was what the enigmatic little Carvetian had meant.

The possibilities for the future had not occurred to him straight away of course, nor had Iavolena's domestic aspirations met with his full approval. But, little by little, Ferdiad had seen the opportunities, Iavolena—or rather, her family—was just the sort of insurance he had been looking for.

⁂

THROP

As he returned to Throp, Septimus' mood changed and changed again. There was the relief of finally knowing what had happened to his lovely wife; there was distaste for the unsavory facts which would have to be heard if the surveyor, Severius was ever brought to justice and as he approached the fort, the search for Iavolena's body loomed larger and larger in his mind. The concluding ordeal, a dreaded finale.

As he made his way through the gate, Septimus told himself that he did not wish to know the truth, just let it go—he descended from the chariot which had brought him from Luguvallium and entered the villa. Five minutes later, he had changed his mind, Septimus called an aide and gave orders to search behind all the water cisterns.

There were three of them. One near the north gate which was used for flushing the pavement drains, a second near the eastern gate which provided drinking water, the villas included and a third in the south western corner where it acted as a reservoir for the supply to the latrines. They were all lead lined and built within a foot or so of a wall of the timber palisade, rubbish collected in the narrow space, it was rarely cleaned out.

Using hooks secured to pila, it took no more than an hour to pull out a year's accumulation of debris. There was the skeleton of a piglet behind one, a helmet and a battered breastplate behind another and five swords behind the last besides dirt and animal feces. The arms and armor had probably been put there by the raiders of last Fall, for collection.

But there were no human remains.

Septimus became angry. Angry at himself for being duped, at the slimy little jeweler for leading him on a wild goose chase and at Ferdiad and Elvin Fellaugh... Wait though. The Surveyor had stayed at the mansio, he had enquired and learned of his leaving for Luguvallium.

"Centurion..." Septimus gave the appropriate orders and returned to his villa to wait. Not for long, he heard the slow steps half an hour later, he knew what to expect, could almost have said the words that the officer uttered.

"You had better see this for yourself, Sir."

Septimus looked at the decaying body, it rested on its back with the head turned away. It was difficult to look at, the action of pulling it out from between the wall of the mansio and the large cistern had damaged the corpse, the smell was indescribable.

Tears filled his eyes, real tears, sorrow for the death of a lovely young woman with twice his vitality. There were the two silver combs in her hair, she'd been just twenty one when he had given them to her, a birthday present. A brooch still held together the edges of her dress, a brooch which her father had sent last year.

Septimus made to move around so that he could see Iavolena's face but the Centurion put out a restraining hand.

"I wouldn't, Sir. It would be better if you didn't."

Septimus pulled away. He wanted to, had to...

Decay and the inevitable maggots had left very little to recognize and the empty eye sockets seemed to stare into his very soul.

He stood there for an indeterminate time, not really seeing the horror before him but imagining the face he had known, in repose, asleep. At length, he turned and walked mechanically back to the fort and the quarters which echoed emptily about him.

Tired, he realized that he had neither washed nor changed his clothing since he had arrived back. Again, Septimus had to concentrate to make his mind work. He called for hot water and discarded the soiled clothes. He sat in the warm water, remembering happier times when Iavolena had found him attractive. He had delighted in her, shown her off like a beautiful doll at the various parties. He had indulged himself, clothing her in the finest fabrics and adorning her with jewels and silver and gold... *That seashell, the one from the rock... never liked it. I wonder what she saw in it that I didn't.*

It seemed the best thing to do, the right thing. He placed the point of his knife against the veins in his left wrist and pushed, then he did the same to the other one.

He sat there, calmly watching the water turn pink.

CHAPTER FIFTEEN

CREONIA

HIGH IN THE MOUNTAINS OF THE CREONE TERRITORIES, AT A place that had come to be known as the Valley of the Plains, a constant trickle of arriving tribes people had gradually swollen the numbers. Upward of five thousand men and women worked at a pace limited only by the weather and the local abundance of game. Considering the generations of hostility between the Caledones and the Creones, there were few disputes and Uffin's orders were followed with little or no questioning.

In the higher of the two plains, the mountain-locked grassland, the Roman style palisade was completed. It cut the roughly circular area into two halves and towered twenty five feet into the air with watch towers every two hundred feet apart. Behind the palisade, a multitude of ladders gave access to the walkway which ran the whole length of the barricade. A semi-permanent camp had been established on the far side of the palisade thus, anyone approaching along the valley would find no clues as to the strength of the workforce. More people—mainly the Creones, Corvoniti's force, were camped within the stratum of caves.

These people, who had a great experience of mining, hauled logs and rough planks up the two and three hundred foot cliffs. No way through the cave systems to the other side of the mountains had been found, but it was discovered that the caves extended some hundreds of feet along both sides of the valley. Accordingly, racks had been built and piled high with boulders gathered from within the caves or broken free from the mountain sides above. Wherever the rocks seemed loose and unstable, huge timber pry-bars had been inserted and used to lever the gigantic slabs of stone away from the main mass, poised to fall on command.

The flanks of any invasion force making its way along this part of the valley were going to have to contend with a continual bombardment of rocks and stones. A natural ledge had been eroded into the cliff walls on a level with the caves and these hid the booby traps from sight. Above this level, the mountains continued upward with a more gradual slope for a further three hundred feet or more to the snowline which towered up into the clouds.

Uffin was disappointed that there was no back way out through the caves, it meant that if the worst came to the worst, the Albyn forces would be trapped, unable to escape whatever the Romans might have in store for them.

It was a minor matter to the Creones and the Caledones; they were not interested in escape plans. Around the camp fires there was talk of the Otherworld across the sea, the land of plenty that all would go to after the last battle, but defeat was not a serious consideration. So long as one died with honor, there was no defeat and no hero was ever turned away from the next world, death was not an end to the great adventure.

It was more than a half hour's walk along the valley to the next plain and Finnul had been put in charge here, his capacity for cunning coming to the fore. Uffin saw holes being dug—deadfalls with a dozen sharpened stakes at the bottom and covered over with flimsy branches and concealed by a layer of dirt and thin turves. He had young fir trees brought in from the higher slopes and replanted to mark safe passage among the traps.

Further along, consternation reigned. The two gangs of men—Caledones and Creones, had been constructing the tunnel which Uffin had asked for. They were now standing, arguing and but for Uffin's fortuitous arrival, would have gone on arguing for some time.

This particular project had been dogged by small and annoying delays due almost always to the silly contest which Uffin had set in motion. "Calm down," he cried. "Now, what's the problem?' Everybody started to speak at once. "One man at a time."

"Come into the shaft, Lord," interposed someone into the ensuing silence. "You will see."

Uffin nodded and climbed down the ladder. He had assumed that the ground here would have been a continuation of the sandstone which comprised the mountains above them. In fact, it was nothing more solid than compressed sand and mud with a liberal fill of rock rubble and water worn gravel, the bed of the river which had once worn away the caves and flooded this valley. The sides of both shafts were continually crumbling, the foot of the ladder down which Uffin had climbed was buried in the latest fall.

He stood on top of the fall and looked at each side of the rectangular shaft. The first five or six feet were stable, the shallow roots of the fir trees formed a mesh which reinforced the alluvium; below that, there was a continual trickle of sandy soil. While Uffin had been assessing the situation, two or three others had climbed down and tried to press their own solutions upon him. He shook his head and gestured for silence.

"Cut trees that are long enough to shore up the sides when it is fully dug..."

"But we shall never get it dug, the sides..."

"Listen. Do as I say. Cut the tree trunks in half, sharpen one end and hammer them into the floor around the sides." Uffin used his hands to show how the flat sides of the split trunks should face the walls. "Dig the floor out and hammer the trunks down further. Do it in sections—no more than knee height at a time."

"We still have to dig across the valley."

Uffin nodded impatiently. "The crossing is only fifty paces. Cut a deep groove where the top of the tunnel will be and place a horizontal timber. Cut two upright grooves and hammer in supports for the overhead." Again, he mimed the actions with his hands. "Dig the tunnel out—no more than a hand span at a time—and place a new roof support and uprights as close together as possible."

The Caledones nodded dubiously.

"It'll take longer, but it doesn't matter, the whole tunnel will be lined with timber."

They regarded Uffin with new respect. He had come along and solved their problems without a second thought. "Yes," they said. "Yes, Lord."

"Fine. Get to it. I had better go and see your cousins on the other side."

One of the Creones spat upon the ground. "They have not yet dug deep enough to find out the problems."

"Well, we'll see."

As the Creones had said, on the far side, the Caledones had not dug as deep a shaft. However, they had made some attempt at shoring up the sides with boards woven from flexible fir tree branches, a solution used back in the mines of their homeland.

Uffin suggested his own method as diplomatically as possible and after some discussion, it was agreed to use the split tree trunks. He then went on to describe the difficulties he foresaw in the digging of the tunnel and his solution to these. Again, the merits were recognized.

A single voice was raised. "Lord."

"Yes, lad," said Uffin although the speaker might have been old enough to have fathered him.

"This wood is difficult to cut. It blunts the axes faster than hard oak trees do."

"Hm. Let me see one of your axes, will you." An axe was handed to him. A fine tool cast from bronze and honed to a keen edge.

"Iron, too. We have to whet the edge after every tree is cut down."

Uffin looked at the edge which appeared to be sharp. "This is one that needs re-sharpening?"

The man nodded. "One tree. Now it must be sharpened again."

The blade was coated with a brown gummy substance, sticky to the touch. Uffin knew what the problem was immediately. "Don't you work with this sort of wood?"

"Oak and ash. Beech, sycamore. This fire wood makes good quick fires, not good for much else, even the fires don't last."

"Resin. You see." Uffin pointed out the layer. "It interferes with the blade cutting into the wood. These particular pines must be highly resinous. Is there a fire nearby?"

They went through the trees to where a small fire was heating a pot of stew. Uffin held the axe in the flames for a few moments, the resin softened and ran and then burst into brief flame. He brushed away the soot and tested the edge.

"There." He handed the axe back to its owner. "Clean them like that as often as you need to." Uffin was about to walk further down the pass when he saw a band of warriors approaching. There were several carts pulled by horses and a dozen or so riders. Even at a distance, he recognized Druids and as they closed, saw Selgovae tribesman. These, he recognized from differences in cloth patterns and colors, differences which were becoming more obvious to him as time passed.

One of the messengers, obviously recognizing him, rode closer and reigned in. "Lord Uffin."

Uffin nodded.

"I bring news from Chief Mellaurig."

Uffin thanked him. "Have you rested?"

"My thanks, Lord. I have eaten and rested; these," he nodded at the Druids and their attendants, "do not ride as hard as may be. The news, Lord."

"There is no great hurry, my friend; it has been a long time on its way. What is your name?"

"Reven, Lord. Reven, son of Cadog."

"Dismount, then Reven Cadogson. We will walk over here, a little way away from the others."

"Oh, they know what I have to tell you, Lord. We have talked about it often enough."

"Then tell me, but out of earshot. They will always wonder what else you had to tell me and why it was so secret that you did not discuss that with them."

Reven grinned, enjoying Uffin's cunning. "The news, Lord, is this. Five days ago—five?" Reven counted on his fingers, held them up. "Five. The Romans welcomed thousands of mounted Britons to their camps along the Wall. They are being paid to fight against us."

Uffin nodded. *The power of Roman coin,* he thought. "And they are prepared to march north with the Romans?"

"My Chief believes so. He bids me tell you that when they leave the shelter of the Wall, the Selgovae and the Callatae will welcome them too, with a party which will last a long time."

Uffin nodded and frowned. *Two weeks,* he thought. *Perhaps a little more before preparations are complete.* "Well. This is certainly news. Is there more?"

"Only that we captured a trader." Reven jerked his thumb at the group he had been riding with. "We have brought him with us, in that cart. Chief Mellaurig sent him as a present to the Druids and they have brought him with us. As well, all the weapons captured at the Sand Crags are here, in the carts."

"That is welcome," said Uffin. "And more than welcome, it is very generous of Gavoc to send us such booty." Plunder from a battle was regarded as almost magical by the tribesmen and to give this up to the common cause showed just what breadth of vision the Chief of the Selgovae possessed. Gavoc would know, as did Uffin, that the average tribesman carried little more than a spear and the extra weapons would make a tremendous difference to their fighting efficiency.

"Thank you, Reven. The news is interesting. You must guest with us tonight before you return. I may have messages for you to take back with you."

Uffin went back to the main group and to the cart which carried the captured trader. The man's ankles were bound together, but otherwise he was free. The fellow had been badly beaten and would not have been able to get far on his own. In fact, the beating had been bad enough to seriously disfigure the man—even if he had been a Scout from the Roman forces, Uffin would not have recognized him.

He looked up at one of the druids with raised eyebrows. An unspoken question.

"The Arch Druid Mandeltua has sent us to give knowledge and guidance to our people. He remains at the Holy Place where he communes with the Gods."

Uffin could only nod; for once he was lost for words. Here was he, planning a battle campaign and the man responsible for elevating him to this position desired only to confer with the Gods.

What was he doing here? He had no real knowledge of such things, no experience of leadership beyond the Scouts. Events had carried him along without a chance to stop and think. *Just let it be over,* he prayed.

For long weeks now, he had thought of nothing but preparing the battle ground so that there would be half a chance of breaking the Roman's ambitions. Now he knew that there would be other Britons fighting against them. Men who had once been just like these Albyns that he was trying to help. Men, he recalled suddenly, just like he had been—paid by and working for the Romans.

Uffin whirled around and began shouting orders, voice harsh with emotion. How many men and women had to die before the Romans and the Druids would be content? Where in Hades was the sense in it all? In anything?

Corvoniti, Alventicus, Finnul and Uffin sat wrapped in their furs around an open fire.

The weather had been kind to them. Snowfalls had been lighter than the average for these northern climes and while there was still a great deal on the higher mountain slopes, there had been none on the plains now for more than a month. It could still come, Uffin realized although now that the season of spring had come, any covering would be light.

He watched the flames dance and become a golden blur as his eyes lost focus.

Snow. The first snow of winter, when he and Asel had sought refuge in the rock fall so long ago. He remembered how, both of them virgin, had both become adult, learning love and the pleasures and pain of caring for someone else. And the terrible loss, the end of what should have gone on and on.

Tears hurt his eyes. The Romans would pay.

"I think it time to send out the messengers," he said. Having asked for the meeting, he spoke the first words. "It is time to call the tribes to war. I'd like to assure you that all who hear will come, but there will be many reasons why this will not be so. Albyn is a huge territory, the distances are too great for some tribes to make it here in time and leaving families and homes and crops for the Romans to ravage will be an impossible request for some."

Uffin saw the converging of warriors in the flames, the gathering of an imaginary army. "I can understand the problems and the difficulties and I can sympathize, but even those who answer the call are unknown to me. Shall I have ten thousand warriors to fight with or twenty? Twenty or perhaps, thirty thousand? Will they be mounted or on foot, will they throw spears or wield swords." Uffin turned to right and left, the faces of Alventicus and Corvoniti stared straight ahead, bright silhouettes against the darkness of the night. Finnul sat nearly opposite him, the flames leaping between them.

"We, none of us, know what strength, in men and warriors, we can put into the field when the Romans come. This is the reason we are here, to even the odds between the Roman multitude and whatever army we can send against them. Until now, you have humored me; you have carried out my wishes as if they came from the Gods. I owe you an explanation."

The two Chiefs smiled, but kept their own council, waiting for Uffin to continue.

"But your wishes *do* come from the Gods," Finnul said into the silence and the fire crackled and sent a shower of sparks high in to the air. "You are the chosen; you express to us the wishes of Cocidius. That is why those wishes are carried out."

It was Uffin's turn to smile. *What a comfort such certainty must be.* "Finnul," he said, "bring out your drawings while I light these brands."

Uffin rose and took a piece of burning wood from the fire and lit four torches already set upright in the ground. By their light, Uffin and the two Chieftains could see the maps which Finnul had prepared and which had been used for weeks to plan the constructions.

The maps were drawn on four beech wood boards which fitted together to give a full plan of the Valley of the Plains.

Uffin pointed out various features to make certain everyone was looking at the drawings from the same point of view. "Here is the upper pass to the main plain, where we are now. This line," he took up a small stick to act as a pointer, "is the palisade we have built. It is my plan to have five thousand of the bravest men with me here behind the palisade."

"Then that will be me and mine," put in Alventicus with finality.

"And mine," added Corvoniti, not accepting so blunt a statement.

"Without doubt, there is nothing to choose between the two of you." Uffin poured a little oil before the waters could become troubled. "Listen to what else I say." Again he pointed out the palisade and the area behind it. "Those of us here will die, if the Romans win this battle. There is no escape and they will kill us all, every one."

"It will be an honor to die with my Lord Uffin," interjected Alventicus stolidly. "We shall journey to the Otherworld together and the bards will sing such songs about us as will make all others jealous of our honor."

Uffin shared the views of neither Alventicus nor of Corvoniti who both nodded vigorously in agreement. Uffin regarded most killing as a waste which could have been avoided with better understanding, however, he conceded that such understanding was an ideal and that killing often could not be averted.

Our main strength will be positioned here and drive forth from the gates of our palisade. They will remain hidden until then, the Romans must not know how big or small our force is. Now here, outside the pass," he indicated an area of dense woodland, "will be a thousand on horseback and they will join with our friends the Selgovae and the Callatae, who will have been harrying the Romans from the rear since they started marching."

Uffin stopped and poured himself a cup of watered wine.

"Now the Romans will follow a small force of our men who will lead them through the first pass. If they react as I expect them to, they will stop and send a scouting party to discover our deployment and our strength. What they will see is a large palisade behind which the craven Albyns are hiding. There is nowhere these Albyns can escape to and there is a large area where they can encamp and lay siege against us barbarians as long as they wish."

"I do not like this talk of running away and hiding. It is a dishonorable thing to do," put in Alventicus.

Uffin made no reply. He carried on regardless.

"Flavius will order his forces to enter the valley, but no further than the first plain where he can camp temporarily and make sure that none of us escape while he plans his assault."

"Lord Uffin, do the Gods tell you all of this?" Alventicus would not look at him, pretending a great interest in some detail that Finnul had drawn onto his map.

"This is what our messenger will tell Flavius to do."

Alventicus looked up frowning. *What did Uffin mean?*

"You recall the trader that the Druids brought with the intention of sacrificing for the sake of the omens?"

Alventicus nodded. "Almost dead. There was little honor in killing him."

"I asked that he be spared and allowed to escape."

Again, Alventicus looked up. Corvoniti seemed less disturbed by the idea.

"Finnul, under my direction has allowed him to overhear various conversations. That we are a few thousand disaffected barbarians, that morale is low, that I talked you into building a Roman fortress with no thought to provisions and water. We fight amongst ourselves, we are lazy and most tribes will have nothing to do with us."

Alventicus considered what he had been told. "Lies and misinformation."

"Lies and misinformation. The trader, who is a Roman scout sent to spy on us, thinks he has a lot of useful intelligence to share with his paymasters."

Alventicus nodded. "And how will he escape?"

"He will be taken to the end of the valley with several others, all supposedly to be sacrificed by the Druids. One by one, his companions will be taken to be killed. There will be screams and laughter. The trader will discover that his bonds are not tied properly and will lose no time in running away as fast as his legs will carry him."

"Back to the Wall."

"If he is clever enough, he might steal a horse to speed him on his way."

All of them refilled their beakers and the two Chieftains had a brief discussion between themselves. "What are our forces doing all this time?" asked Alventicus, at last.

"Before they start unloading their carts, we shall attack from the palisade. We shall ride out—a smallish force—and make contact with their front ranks."

Corvoniti grinned for the first time since the discussion had started. "And we shall start to reap a harvest of heads."

"No." Uffin put steel into his voice and Corvoniti recoiled almost as if he had been slapped. "This is a feint. It *must* not be anything else for everything depends upon it. After a few minutes, we shall retreat up the valley and come back here, behind the palisade. I want the Romans to think that we are frightened."

"By the Horns of Cocidius," muttered Corvoniti, "I myself will kill any man I see running away."

Alventicus nodded. "And I also. No Creone will be branded a coward on his own land."

Uffin sighed. He knew that it must come to this. Try as he might; hope as he might, he knew in his heart that even the semblance of cowardice was a burden too great for most Albyns to bear.

"They will not be running away, Corvoniti. They will not be cowards, they will be fighting to orders. We must lure the Romans into coming all the way up the second pass so that when the mounted men—they will be in the van—have all come through and the Legion itself is in the pass, we bring the rocks tumbling down on them from above the cliffs. While that is happening, the Selgovae and the Callatae with our reinforcements will charge in from the rear while they are still in disorder from the barrage of rocks. Now, we open the gates once more and our full force rides out to confront the cavalry."

"This is all very complicated. Complicated fighting never works."

"Nor does–" Uffin almost said *your* but changed it in time, "nor does *our* sort of fighting work against the Romans. The only way to win this battle is to fight it the Roman way—by planning everything first."

"Go on."

"This way, the Romans will be fighting on three fronts. We shall push them towards the pit-traps we have dug and gradually push them into an area too small for them to fight in effectively."

Alventicus was nodding slowly, Uffin noticed, a little smile playing across his face. The smile became a grin, a chuckle and then a full bodied laugh. Corvoniti joined in as did Uffin and Finnul. Uffin believed that he had them convinced, all he had to do now was to make it all work. The messengers to the tribes would leave the following morning. The specially prepared messenger, to Flavius, would leave tomorrow at dusk.

⁂

VINDOLANDA

It really was a fine spring morning and had been for some time when servants roused Flavius from sleep. The rest of the Legion had risen before dawn and had been busy at their various duties for two hours as he took his morning bath. Later, as his servants helped him on with his armor he promised himself that he would add a second inscription to the altar which had already been raised to the Gods, this one would thank them for this chance at glory.

One campaign, the subjugation of Albyn and his career would be assured. A generalship? It would be the least honor that could be bestowed and with his connections... *Daydreams, of course, but it was not impossible that Hadrian would groom me as his successor.*

⁂

VIRCOVICIUM

Outside the newer fort at Vircovicium, the troops were gathering. All final preparations had been made and now they awaited their new leader to take them on to battle. Centurions used their vine wood shafts to slap at slow movers; they shouted and bullied and fussed until everything was to their liking.

During the past week, a new altar stone had been erected at a high point above the vallum, its inscription listed Aurelius Flavius' name and those of his officers right down to decurion and recorded today's date, the day they were to march into Albyn and finally settle the problem of the barbarian hostilities. It was here that Flavius rode to with his retinue and here that he received the tremendous ovation from the legionaries.

Flavius held up his hands for silence and he dismounted. Priests came forward dragging a white ox, the aquilifer brought forward the Ninth Legion's eagle standard and others bore a large iron dish upon which a brazier of coals burned: the holy fire from the temple of Jupiter.

At Flavius' bidding, the priests cut the ox's throat and caught the blood in a great iron kettle. When its death throes were over, they opened its carcass and examined the internal organs. Only when they had nodded to signal that all was as it should be, did Flavius finally speak.

"The Gods are truly with us today," he said loudly, though there was a proportion that could not hear him. "The omens speak for themselves and the Eagle of the Ninth is our genius, we are blessed."

With this, he took a flask of oil and perfume and poured it over the brazier causing the flames to leap high into the air. The troops cheered again and again.

Once more, Flavius called for silence. He knew to the moment when to engineer a cheer and when to silence it.

"We go today to find that hole where the rats of Albyn have hidden themselves. Those rats which have nipped at our soldiers on the Wall. Although our search may take a long time and lead us over mountains and rivers, we shall find them. In the days ahead when you wonder if we shall ever find them you must remember what I say now. If we find empty holes it is because the sound of our coming has flushed them out and they have run to hide elsewhere. But there will come a time when a rat will turn and fight. It is then that we will exterminate them and this whole island will have peace, the Peace of Rome."

Again, the Legion cheered Flavius, and this time he did not foreshorten the adulation, letting it die by degrees in its own time.

"Of course, you know and I know that things will not be so simple. Some of us will die for Rome's greater glory. General Agricola walked these same paths three generations ago, remember what he said. 'Be prepared to die with honor, it is better than living in disgrace and all paths of glory lead to salvation. There will be no disgrace in perishing at the very edge of the natural world.'"

Again Flavius paused, letting the import of his words sink in and for those who could hear to pass back what he said to others who could not.

"On this campaign," he continued with a new subject, "we shall travel light. No siege weapons to slow us down, no oxen. Only mules which move as fast as we can march. Each day, we march forty miles and we have supply ships on the way to provide us with rations when we need them.

"I promise all of you a victory before the next winter. So all of you, are you ready for war?" he shouted at the top his voice.

"Yes," came the reply.

"Are you ready for war?" he asked again.

"Yes, yes."

And a third time. "Are you ready for war?"

"YES." The answer from twelve thousand throats was truly deafening.

"YES, WE ARE READY FOR WAR."

"THEN LET US MAKE WAR."

Once the Legion was properly under weigh and the Wall out of sight, Aemilius Karrus dropped back from his position at the head of the cavalry to walk alongside of Aurelius Flavius' horse drawn carriage.

One of the four guards recognized him and let the Deputy Governor know of his presence. Flavius invited Aemilius to join him. Aemilius slid off his mount; he handed the reins to the guard and clambered up into the heavy covered cart which Flavius had dubbed his *carriage*.

The cart was protected by layers of beaten bronze and furnished with large cushions and furs; Flavius intended to sleep there each night. There was a jar of wine, another of water, but what surprised Aemilius were the maps. They were fastened to the walls and

Flavius was studying them intently, making notes on a wax tablet and marking off items on a list written on vellum.

Karrus noted that all of them showed different areas of Albyn and wondered where they had come from. He forbore to ask and said instead, "Tribune Karrus, Sir. Reporting as requested."

"Good. Pleased to see you, Aemilius. How are the cavalry doing?"

How do I answer that? he asked himself. Flavius had delegated responsibility for six thousand auxiliaries and one week to get to know them. Aemilius scratched his chest where the sea shell pendant itched against his skin. I have met each of the leaders and eaten with them, learned about where they have come from and watched as they showed off their riding skills, listened to their boasts.

Basically, he considered them to be no different from the Albyns that they were being paid to fight. How, he wondered, did Rome succeed in paying one tribe to fight another? When the historians wrote about this campaign would they tell of the bravery of the Ninth Legion, or would they say how Hadrian had bought success with the gold donated by Flavius' family.

Of the Britons, he knew nothing of any practical use. "Fine, Sir. They seem very keen to fight. I think it must be in the blood."

"Good. Good. We are going to need them, I assure you. I want an ala at the front at all times and where there is space enough, one to each side of us. Three at our rear."

"Three, Sir?" A rearguard of a single ala was usual.

"Two in reserve, as it were."

"May I ask the reason, Sir?"

"Of course." Flavius smiled mischievously. "You see, I don't believe that Gellorix *is* dead. I won't believe it until I see his head on a stick. Gellorix knows our usual deployment so I ask myself what would I do if I were him?"

"And what is that?"

"Why, I'd send bands of warriors to harry my flanks and then my rear. Normally, if a column is attacked along its length, the rearguard cavalry is brought up to protect it. That so?"

"True. So you can do this and still leave your rear protected."

"Exactly so. Gellorix won't know that though, will he?"

Flavius was no fool. It was a point which Aemilius Karrus had noted time after time. Young, impetuous even, but no fool.

Dag Liogh was thinking almost exactly the same an hour later as he lay in the newly greening heather at the top of a rise and watched the approaching army. He had heard the progress long before he had seen them and now, as the vast extent of the forces being fielded by Flavius dawned on him, he realized how difficult it was going to be to slow the Legion down.

There were no lumbering wagons, no siege engines, no wheeled vehicles at all except the one at the center which moved as speedily as the rest of the forces. The legionaries marched briskly, fresh and alert.

Weeks before, he and Gavoc Mellaurig had planned their attacks, had decided the best places for ambush, but Flavius had changed his route or had never let his intended route be known.

Dag shook his head in frustration, all for nothing. He backed away from the ridge; he would have to discuss this with Gavoc in person before making any more decisions. Out of sight of the Romans, he gathered the small band of men together and set off.

Their last plan of action had been to disperse their forces along the sides of a deep burn which they had assumed their enemy would be fording and to trap them in the gully as they crossed.

Gavoc and his men were already in place and as angry at the lost opportunity as Dag had been.

"So where to now?" asked Gavoc.

Dag shook his head. "I don't know. They seem to be keeping to open country as much as possible, we cannot attack them there, their mounted forces number more than both our tribes."

"Where do they all come from, Dag?"

Dag spat on the ground and turned to his brother. "Those that I have seen are from the southern parts of Briton, Manon. Dogs. Dogs working for money. There are others too, others that I don't recognize. What does it matter where they come from? I only know that wherever we attack them, it must be some place with an escape route else it will be the end of us, Lioghs."

Gavoc's face had been made to grin and laugh, worry sat incongruously on his features. "There is one place, if they continue in the direction you said they were going."

"And where is that?"

"I doubt you know of it. It's well north of the Selgovae territory, it means we must trespass on other's lands, but we must try to slow this column down or we fail our Lord Uffin."

"Then tell me about it."

"It's called Annag Valley.

"There's a narrow gorge with little water in it at this time of year, that would be our escape route; six men on the heights above the gorge could stop an army following us."

"How long? How long before they reach the place?"

"Tomorrow afternoon. Sometime in the afternoon. And we can be there in four hours."

"Manon. Fetch our men; we'll ride with the Selgovae."

The warriors of the two tribes arrived in the steep sided valley at dawn having ridden through the night by the light of a quarter moon behind scudding clouds. They hobbled the horses and lay down to sleep under bushes or overhangs—anywhere that was not soaked with dew.

Two hours later, Gavoc awoke to find his fellow chieftain already painting himself with the now familiar patterns of sun and moon. He watched in silence for some minutes as Dag applied the dyes with his fingers and in the more inaccessible places, with a stick.

"How did you come by these skills?" Gavoc asked eventually. "In my tribe and all the others that I know of, the custom has died with our great grandsires."

Dag paused a moment before replying, to finish a sweeping line across his shoulders. "I learned it from my father and doubtless, he from his. The custom had been put aside on Mona, even as you have done here but my grandsire who was chief when the Callatae fled Mona, swore that we would ever wear the blue in battle while the Romans hold our lands in thrall."

For once, Gavoc's face was a study in seriousness as he watched Dag finish his designs. "Perhaps you would paint something on me?" he asked at last, almost apologetically. "Something appropriate."

Dag stood up and grinned. "Appropriate. Let me see." He walked around Gavoc and stood before him again. "Appropriate. How about the horns of Cocidius? Hmm? Growing from the trunk of a mighty oak tree?"

"Why that?" asked Gavoc, still serious, still diffident.

"Because… you are as strong as an oak, as wild as a stag and, hmm, because you wish to be a god." Gavoc's hand began to tighten into a fist and he half rose from his kneeling position. "And that's the way I like you and I'd not have you any different."

Gavoc responded to the joke and grinned as broadly as Dag. He nodded. "An oak tree with the horns of Cocidius. Yes, I think I'd like that." He nodded again and abruptly changed the subject. "Do you like the Lord Uffin? Do you think he is the man to defeat the Romans?"

"Lord Uffin? He has many strengths and that's true enough. Not the least being that devious streak of his." Dag thought about the question as he sketched the outline of a tree on Gavoc's torso. "He's taught me more about my own lacks than I'd admit to anyone but you, my friend and he's taught me that there is more than one way of seeing things."

Dag painted in a pair of antlers and stood back to judge the effect.

"Yes, Gavoc. I like him. More than that, I trust him. Do you have doubts?"

"No. No, I like him too." Gavoc shook his head slowly. "He doesn't say a lot, but what he does say makes a lot of sense when you think about it. He has an aura of strength about him which makes him seem invincible."

Dag laughed and clapped Gavoc on the shoulder. "I hope you're right, my friend. Now, I think that will loosen the bowels of our enemies, it will be dry in a moment or two then we had better find the best place for our ambush."

The ensuing battle lasted four hours and slowed the Romans by exactly that much. Gavoc's escape route worked successfully enough, but the losses during the fighting were as unexpected as they were heavy.

"I have lost nine hands of warriors," said Gavoc as they counted the men remaining.

"And I, two hands," said Dag, a great sadness in his voice. "One of them was my brother, Manon." He paused for a long time and added, "But then, I had fewer to start with."

"I grieve with you, my friend. Manon was *my* friend as much as your brother, We cannot go on like this. Every day we fight them, we shall grow less until we wither away because they have the numbers to outlast us."

"And armor, too. It's a wearisome thing to score hits and see your enemy fight on."

"Then we must think of some other way."

Mandeltua lay on the floor where he had lain these past seven days. His body was pitifully thin and his skin looked like yellowed parchment. Only water had passed his lips during that time, he had steadfastly refused to eat. His belief in his Gods was so complete that he preferred to die rather than give in to mere desires of the flesh.

He had been with his Gods. Camulos had sat at his right hand while Cocidius had been to his left. They had talked about the coming battle. They had acknowledged that they had sent the omens of eagle and ermine to show Uffin Gellorix where it must take place, they had discussed tactics which Mandeltua would later, relay to Uffin.

He had seen the running battle between the Selgovae and Callatae on the one hand and the Romans on the other. This, too, must be passed on to Uffin. And now that the time was at hand, Mandeltua could not force his spirit from his body. Mandeltua's sight grew dark and dim; the stone of power bit into his flesh and seared it with white heat. *Without me, the battle will be lost*, he thought as oblivion swept over him.

⚜

Too late. It was too late to stop the one death, but now the incipient massacre had to be prevented. Gods, if only he had never thought of that foolish wager. Uffin was standing inside the nearly completed tunnel beneath the pass, by the fitful light of a single torch; he was gazing sadly at the body of a man who need not have died.

"Why?"

Alventicus and Corvoniti stood on either side of him, sharing his concern. Alventicus, brusque by nature, answered shortly. "The Creones say they have dug more of the tunnel than the Caledones."

A Caledone spoke up. "Everyone can see that this is a lie." He pointed down to the body and looked at his chief. "The Creone drew a knife and Verone did what any Caledone would have done, he drew his own knife and killed the Creone first."

So simplistic. Uffin felt sick. *The logic of killing a man for... for what? A line drawn in the dirt?* And the consequences might yet be more devastating than could be imagined.

"It is an excellent tunnel, built by exceptional warriors. I intended to reward all equally because the difference between what one tribe has done and what another has done is trifling. But I cannot condone the killing of a man whatever tribe he comes from and whoever drew a knife first."

He looked from one Chieftain to the other.

"I must give the decision for what has to be done to Chief Alventicus and to Chief Corvoniti. Let them deal out justice."

Alventicus was a big man, but agile. Almost before Uffin had finished speaking, the Chief had drawn his own knife, had turned, plunged the blade into the chest of the man called Verone. Alventicus looked from one to the other of his tribesmen; each pair of eyes glittered for a moment in the leaping light of the torch and then looked down.

"I gave my word," he said and spoke quietly, menace laced every word. "I gave my word and Verone broke it. I said we would keep the peace between Creone and Caledone. Those who broke that peace and made my word into a lie are both dead; let that be an end to it."

Alventicus marched to the shaft and climbed the ladder. No one there doubted that as Alventicus had commanded, the matter was ended.

That evening, messengers arrived from the Selgovae. They told Uffin of the lightning fast advance of the whole Ninth Legion, and of the failure of the delaying tactics. Uffin gasped at the news, he felt his heart begin to race. The Romans might well be here before his own force of Albyns could assemble.

⁂

Aemilius Karrus was, for once, feeling happy with his cavalry command. They had fought two engagements with the barbarians and had suffered few casualties while inflicting quite heavy damage on the enemy. The Brythonic mercenaries had proved their mettle and were themselves, pleased with their success.

Karrus had, of course, led from the front and the cavalry had responded to his authority. After the second of the attacks, they had started to chant his name.

"KAR-RUS. KAR-RUS..."

Aemilius wore a grin as wide as his helmet. For the first time, he began to believe that the Ninth could do all that Flavius wanted and be back, as he had said, in time for the next winter.

He became aware of the pendant under his breast plate. Perhaps it was, after all, bringing good luck.

The Scout was picked up later the same day and taken before Karrus and Flavius. The Tribune recognized him and his story was told.

"I don't know, Aemilius." Flavius frowned as the Scout finished his tale. "I told you that Gellorix was alive, didn't I? But the rest, I don't know whether to believe it or not."

"These Albyns are not a subtle folk, you know. They don't know how to lie."

"If he's half as wily as that old fox Mansustus, Aemilius, then he *is* Roman and he'll lie like a whole Legion of troopers."

CHAPTER SIXTEEN

DAMNONIA

AT FIRST, THE MOUND HAD BEEN A LOW HEAP OF WORN WATER washed stones from a nearby stream, grey, burnished, skull-like. But as more arrived, so the mound grew, changed: jagged, broken pieces of sandstone, glittering knobs of quartz, lumpy balls of lava deposited by some ancient glacier, far from their origin.

The warriors arrived in dribs and drabs from across the land of Albyn. A few were on horseback, but most came on foot. Some carried weapons: old spears, a sword; there were a few—a very few—came with new forged spear heads or gleaming swords with keen edges and dressed in bright colors and warm furs and cloaks. Most though, were poorly shod and worse armed.

But the pile of stones grew.

A tatterdemalion army. No two looked alike, were dressed or armed alike. Their clothing ran the gamut from checks and stripes to dun colors and homespun untreated woolens. Weaponry ranged from sticks with fire hardened points to swords with notched edges and old boar hunting spears.

Uffin could have shed tears as they came. He had expected armies, thousands of men armed to the teeth and ready to fight. And what had they sent? Hundreds of men and women: some of them seemingly no more than children, others almost too old to wield a stick. Virtually every one of them was worn out and hungry.

This was Uffin's force, the troops with which he had to oppose the Roman legion which was already on its way. Was their some magic he could utilize to fashion this collection of lost souls into a living breathing fighting machine which could withstand the seasoned veterans of a hundred campaigns?

Uffin shook his head and sought the solitude of his tent. All the preparations, he thought. The Palisade copied from the Roman style rampart, the carefully planned rock falls, the mantraps. The bards would sing of history's greatest blunder. In celebrating the bravery of the hundreds of warriors bound to die here, they would be recording the foolish dreams of one insignificant man who had dared to swear vengeance on Rome.

He closed his eyes and suspended all thought. It was the only way he could relieve the black despair he felt, a despair where death was to be preferred to life.

Mandeltua. Here was the author of all misfortune. Mandeltua had convinced him that the Gods had chosen him. *It had been so simple,* he told himself, *a word or two and his own conceit had done the rest* ... Deliberately he drove the thought away. *Not the Druid, but his own arrogance had been the cause.* His thoughts died away and Uffin stared into oblivion for many hours until he finally roused when Finnul came for him.

"Lord Uffin, supper is made and messengers are here."

"Lord?" Uffin's laughter was ragged. "Lord of what? Eh? Lord of a few hundred tired old men and women too tired and hungry to crawl away when the Romans come."

"I think that you should come to supper, Lord Uffin," Finnul said, taken aback. "There are more than a few hundred, Lord. They have been arriving all day, the volunteers. Chief Salmane has come with his warriors. He's brought supplies and extra weapons too."

"Salmane." Uffin frowned. Salmane, he remembered the man, he had fought him with sticks at Medionemeton, a big man. Bigger even than Alventicus. Uffin cursed himself. He would have to shake off this mood, even with the certain knowledge of defeat, he could not afford to present this face to the world.

"All right, Finnul. I'm coming, tell them I'm coming."

Dusk was falling as Uffin left his tent and looking up at the heavens, pulled his jerkin open. *Must be a change in the weather, seems to be two cloaks warmer than at midday.* There was, too, a new hill on the plain behind the Palisade, where the warriors had been dropping their counting stones, a hill where before, there had been a mound. A broad based hill where there had been little more than an overgrown cairn.

And round the cooking fires, more people than he had ever expected to see. Where were the halt and the lame he had watched coming in that morning? Where were the oldsters and the children? As he approached, the people got to their feet and began to move towards him. Salmane was there, his huge stature drawing the eye.

"Hail, Lord Uffin." Salmane saluted him. "As I promised you, seventeen hundred men and three hundred women of the Lugi to fight at your side. A few more too, we picked up perhaps three hundred more as we came through the mountain villages."

Uffin smiled, his dark mood of premature defeat gone in the space of a breath. "Welcome Chief Salmane, welcome to all of you," Uffin clasped the other's forearm and raised his voice, "whatever your tribe, all of you are welcome." Salmane drew the smaller Uffin close and threw both his great arms around him in a bear hug which all but crushed Uffin's ribs.

"I have never been more pleased to see anyone," said Uffin when he had been released. "I had feared that too few would heed the call."

Salmane stood back and roared with laughter. "Never have I been late for a party, Lord. If there are, indeed, latecomers, they will have to find their own Romans to kill for we shall leave none for the tardy."

Uffin turned to where Finnul stood. "Make a head-count, Finnul. Not the Creones and the Caledones, I know their strength."

Finnul grinned. "Already done, Lord Uffin. I counted them as they came. Three thousand and two hundred have come today."

"Three thousand." Uffin added in those he knew about. "Eight thousand in total and less than a half of them mounted." Uffin pursed his lips. *Still nowhere near enough, even*

with those Callatae and Selgovae who would be following the Romans—but getting better.
To Salmane, he said, "I have to see what news the messengers bring then we must dine
together."

"It will be an honor, Lord Uffin."

"Now, Finnul. The messengers?"

"Here, my Lord."

There were two of them, one from Dag Liogh and one from Chief Callum of the
Smertae whom he spoke to first.

"What news do you bring me?"

"Chief Callum is three days distant with two thousand warriors. He begs you wait
until he arrives before starting to kill the Romans."

Uffin grinned. "This I promise. Return to Chief Callum tomorrow and tell him so."
He turned to the Callatae. "And what does Dag Liogh have to tell me?" The man still wore
his blue as though he had only just come from battle. He limped a little; a linen bandage
was wrapped around the man's right calf.

"Chief Liogh said to me 'tell the Lord Uffin exactly what I tell you.' He said to tell
you that the Romans are moving fast. They have neither carts nor war machines to slow
them down. From the Wall, they reached Briogix in less than one day."

Uffin raised his eyebrows. *Thirty five miles a day, or more.* "And what else?"

"We have attacked them twice, but half of their number is on horse and they alone
outnumber us three to one. They carry long spears and stick us like pigs, we and the Selgovae have lost many hands of warriors. Chief Liogh says they will be here in two days,
but he and Chief Gavoc of the Selgovae will stay close to the Roman tail."

"Two days." Uffin frowned. Two days and he had just told the other messenger that
he would hold off beginning the battle for three days, as though he had power to make the
slightest decision in the matter. "Two days," he muttered. "Two days and I need a week."
Perhaps we can pray for bad weather, it'll hold up the Romans more than the Albyns. To
the messenger, Uffin nodded his thanks. "Eat your fill and rest. Tomorrow you may stay
or return as you wish."

The messenger smiled back. "My thanks, Lord. I'll return to my Chief, he has lost too
many men to spare me. His brother, too, has gone to sit with the Gods."

Uffin joined the Chieftains at supper and after they had eaten, he explained the situation to them. "Unless there is some miracle, the Romans will find us in two days," he
finished. "Their mounted strength is twice our own and their foot soldiers about the same
as ours though they must be more experienced. The delaying tactics we had worked out
have not been successful." He stared into the flames and lapsed into silence for a minute
or so. "Whichever Gods you petition," he said thoughtfully, "start praying now."

Corvoniti spoke first in much the same tones as he combed his fingers through his
moustaches. "If praying is what you really need then tell the Druids. That is what they
are here for. If it is fighting that you want, then that is what *we* are here for. Tonight or
tomorrow my own carts will be here and they will be filled with whatever weapons we

have mustered from among my villages. There will also be a hundred chariots with enough throwing spears to darken the skies twice over."

"Throwing spears? How long are *throwing* spears?"

Corvoniti stood up and held his arm out, palm downwards. "As long as you are high, Lord."

"Throwing spears. Bring me the messenger from the Callatae."

When the fellow had been called, Uffin questioned him further. "These horsemen who use long spears against you and the Selgovae, where do they hail from?"

The messenger shook his head. "We don't know for certain, Dag Liogh believes the southern kingdoms of Briton."

"Britons." The mercenaries, he had all but forgotten the information he'd had earlier. "If the Britons can learn new ways then so can we. Tell your Chief that I say this. Tell them to think of ways of making their own spears longer, so that they can reach the Britons who ride against them. If the Britons can use lances, so must we... Finnul."

Finnul was at his side on the instant. "Finnul. What is the best way of making a spear shaft longer?"

The boy thought for a moment. "I've seen the way they make fishing poles to fish from the middle of rivers."

"Then for me, discuss the problem with this warrior of the Callatae, so that he can talk to his Chieftain about it, then you can talk to our warriors, too."

As the night closed in, Uffin left the others and walked out to the growing pile of stones. One for each warrior. When the battle was over, so the custom went, each of the survivors would take away a single stone so that those remaining would number the fallen. Looking above the pile, his eyes found the dark scars of the cave mouths. Up there, unseen, the prepared rock falls and the unstable rocks which had been levered away from the cliffs were ready to be nudged onto the Roman Legion below.

Uffin left the ground behind the palisade and walked along below the waiting avalanches to the first plain where mantraps had been dug and camouflaged and then on to the first valley where he had had the tunnel built. The tunnel had been completed and was more or less filled with dead bracken, dried and soaked in oil. Doors had been fashioned and even now were being fitted and lowered into place over the shafts at each end. As Uffin watched, they spread pine needles and more bracken over each one to conceal the shafts. A fire had been lit at the southern end, close to the rift where the river flowed alongside, those men no longer working were cooking meat.

"You have done well," Uffin said in a voice loud enough to carry and every man jumped with surprise at his sudden presence. "I know that none of you knows the reason I have for asking you to build this tunnel. Soon, you will see the use I want to make of it. For now though, rest. The day after tomorrow, we may well be fighting for our..." Uffin was about to say *lives* but it smacked too much of cowardice. "... For Albyn." He continued with scarcely a break and his words had them cheering as though he had brought them the best news of their lives.

Perhaps he had, for they were clapping each other on the shoulders and cheering him.

At least, he thought, *Caledones and Creones are treating each other like brothers.* If they were successful in discouraging the Romans from annexing Albyn, perhaps such unity would spread to all of the tribes north of the Wall.

⁂

DAMNONIA

Two days from the Valley of the Plains, Flavius was as near indecision as he had ever been. The column was running short of food, those so-called tribes with whom they had expected to trade for victuals had been not so much unwilling as missing. Flavius' scouts had counted hundreds of empty duns over the past several days; the villages had been emptied of provisions and occupied only by packs of barking dogs.

The Ninth Legion traditionally ate fish, but they were now too far from any coast to be supplied from Roman ships. While traditions could be forgotten on campaign, marching men still needed a great deal of food to sustain them. If they had now to stop and forage, the pace could not be maintained.

Frustrated, Flavius punched the cushions in his carriage. The previous day, they had captured and tortured a woman. She had stoically suffered burns and only when she had seen her toe cut off had she screamed out the name. The Valley of the Plains.

Once started, she blurted it all out. The Valley of the Plains in Creone territory, close by the great lochs which separated Caledone from Creone. Flavius had consulted his maps. The place was almost central, it might almost have been chosen with the purpose of keeping the Ninth out of range of his supply fleets.

He shook his head. There was no real alternative if he was going to follow the Albyn barbarians to their hiding place; they had to live off the land. Having at last made the unwelcome decision, Flavius lost no time in giving the necessary orders. The Ninth was halted and a marching camp set up; simultaneously, the Brythonic cavalry was sent out to hunt... it was the speediest alternative. If they could not come back with sufficient provisions then the only other course of action was to turn east and rendezvous with the supply ships.

Flavius felt that the second option was wrong. Too much time would be lost, too much distance would separate him from the fugitive hordes. He was irrationally afraid that the Albyns would build impregnable defenses or even disappear into the boundless north, slipping away like mist on a summer morning.

Just let him catch them unprepared and he would crush them like walnuts under a hammer. He could be back in Eboracum by the summer, let alone winter. The winter would see him back in Rome receiving accolades from Hadrian himself. But food. Without food, the Ninth was twelve thousand grumbling stomachs, a liability.

In the event, the Britons found gold. An outrider heard the lowing of an ox in need of milking, following the sound, he found the place where the deserting Albyns had penned twelve beasts. Now that they knew what to look for, other scouts climbed hills and spotted further herds.

By nightfall, they had rounded up enough meat on the hoof to keep the Ninth moving for a fortnight. Every soldier ate well that night and packed enough to keep him marching for three days, a small contingent would be detailed to drive the remaining beasts on behind the advancing column.

Flavius personally made offerings to Jupiter and Mars at the Legion's portable altars. It was a fact, the Gods were truly smiling upon him.

⁂

Behind Uffin, the pile of stones stood half a man high and spread in a rough hemisphere some twenty five or thirty feet in diameter. Eight thousand warriors were numbered here, their live counterparts gathered inside the Palisade to listen to Lord Uffin.

The sun shone warm and bright, heralding a glorious spring. A light breeze tossed his dark hair and cloak as he stood on the rampart and waited for silence. He ran fingers through his short beard and looked from face to face below him with no idea as to what to say to these expectant men and women.

Uffin coughed to clear his throat; he raised both arms and began.

"My friends..." he paused. What should he say? "I have just heard that the Romans draw near. Within a few short hours we shall be joined in battle. They are confident of our defeat. *Over confident.* They come to claim the whole of Albyn but Albyn will *claim them.* Even now they are marching to their doom. *Albyn will never be theirs.*"

He looked over the rows of intent faces; men and women, young and old. *How many would there be left at the same time tomorrow?* It was not a thought he wished to pursue.

"We have come together to make certain of this. King Calgacus, king of the Caledones, said that his were the last free men before the Romans won that battle in the Grampians, but both he and they were wrong. *We* are the last free men and *this* is the last battle.

"Your bravery is without question, every one of us would sooner die than be taken into slavery, but I want you remember this." Uffin paused again, he was breathing heavily not from exertion, but from an excess of emotion that he had not known was in him. He started again, tears falling from his eyes.

"Remember this," he whispered. "*Remember,*" he shouted. "We fight today not for our own honor, not for the honor of Albyn, but for all our children and their children yet to be born. If *we* fail, then it is *they* who will be taken into slavery." Uffin's voice broke and he was unable to say what he wanted for some moments. "If we fail," he said, forcing the words from a throat grown tight and aching, "if we fail, then *we* fail those generations yet unborn."

Uffin wiped his face with the hem of his sleeve and held up his arms, palms outward to his silent audience. "The future of Albyn lies in *our* hands, now let us drive these cold, arrogant Romans out of our lands, let us teach them the lesson that Albyn is and always will be, too expensive for them to take.

"ARE WE READY TO DO THIS?"

"READY!" came the reply. "AYE, WE ARE READY."

"Gellorix." shouted someone. "*Gel-or-rix.*"

"GEL-OR-RIX… GEL-OR-RIX…"

And the words echoed across the plain and back from the ring of cliffs which hemmed them in. Flocks of birds rose from the grassland and wolves looked down upon the gathering before slinking off to their holes.

And as the acclamation died away and the reverberations dwindled, the figure of a druid made its way along the rampart towards Uffin. Behind, four more of them dragged a reluctant man in his wake.

"Lord Uffin," said the first, Endorr; in Mandeltua's absence, the most senior Druid. "A spy. We caught him this morning; he'd joined with one of the bands of volunteers who arrived yesterday. I would speak to our warriors."

Uffin looked at the man, still recognizable despite the obvious signs of torture. He had been born into the Votadinii tribe. "I think you have been too clever this time, Dunnoch. Far too clever," he said in Latin, then, to Endorr, "Certainly, go ahead."

Dunnoch, the scout was held up for the Albyns to see. As far as he was able, Dunnoch stood straight and stiff, knowing what his end was to be.

"I have always preached peace," began Endorr. "I have believed all my life that all men can be brothers. Those of you who know me, know this too. But Mandeltua has traveled a different road. He has warned us that the Romans would never be content to stop once they owned Briton. Well, now his words are proven true and I find myself stepping in Mandeltua's footsteps.

"Mandeltua sought guidance from the Gods, now we must do the same. You see here a spy. Not one of the Romans or their mercenaries who at least have the excuse of coming from foreign lands, but like yourselves, he is an Albyn, a traitor."

There were many shouted suggestions for dealing with him and watching Dunnoch, Uffin saw him shiver once or twice.

Almost as if he had heard nothing, the Druid signaled for silence and continued. "His capture will let the Gods speak to us." He nodded to one other who had followed the druids, a *vate*, a man skilled in interpreting the signs and omens which were the Gods' preferred means of communication.

The soothsayer reached around in front of the captured scout and drew his silver knife blade across the man's throat. A fountain of life-blood gushed from the wound, staining the timber Palisade a dire crimson. Uffin had looked away at the last instant, thankful only that the scout's end had come too quickly for him to even cry out.

The *vate* waited until the spray of blood ended and then slit the man's torso from sternum to groin, letting the entrails spill out across the walkway. He spent long minutes in examination, noting the way the organs lay and looking for abnormalities. He looked up at length and nodded.

"The Gods have spoken to us," shouted Endorr. "The Gods have promised us that their hand in our victory will be plain enough for every Roman to see. Albyn is safe," he screamed, "Albyn will not be invaded and conquered for a thousand years. No one who casts greedy eyes on our fair hills will succeed where these Romans have failed."

Uffin smiled to himself and shook his head. *If only the Gods* would *take a hand in the battle.*

Down at ground level, he clasped forearms with the three Chieftains, Corvoniti, Alventicus and Salmane. "How long do we have?"

"My scout reported them two hours away and half that is now gone." Corvoniti grinned. "And none too soon."

Uffin, who still wished for three days rather than the hour he had, grimaced.

"You look unhappy, Lord Uffin." Alventicus was always puzzled with Uffin's reservations and treated the worries he voiced almost as jokes.

"I'd be looking forward to it a great deal more if our numbers had been greater."

Alventicus patted his shoulder as though he were commiserating with a child. "Today, Lord, is as good a day as any to die on. My head, my heart and my arm are ready to kill Romans. You heard what Endorr said, the Gods themselves have promised to play their part in our battle. If I die, then my ghost shall stand on yonder hill top and watch as the Romans are destroyed."

As Alventicus spoke, great rain drops splashed around them. Uffin sighed; if this was a sign, then the Gods were against, not for them. His strategy hinged on clear signals and careful timing, how could there be such a thing when curtains of rain hid one side of the plain from the other?

⚜

Mounted Britons had been riding up to two hours ahead of the legion all day and discovered the valley well in advance of the main body. In fact, there was hardly any avoiding it, the trail—though unused for several weeks and returning to nature—led nowhere else.

The horsemen made no attempt at concealment, even if the terrain had been open enough to spread out; the size of the cavalry unit made it impossible to hide, consequently they simply rode ahead employing reasonable precautions against ambush.

They passed through the valley to the first plain where the shallow river wound across it to cascade over its southern edge.

There was, as yet, simply nothing to report. This was the trail which had been reported earlier, there was no doubt about it, signs of men and animals having passed this way were abundant, but appeared quite old, the trail was already growing back into the wild—thanks to the pains with which Finnul had disguised the Albyns' presence.

They forded the river and marched more slowly along the second valley until the Palisade came into view. The sight of the Roman type fortification gave them pause; why had they not heard of this, they wondered and wondered too, if scouts coming this far had been captured by whoever was behind the enigmatic rampart.

There was a hurried conference before they turned about and rode back across the plain and through the first valley.

The trees along the north side of the first plain concealed Salmane and fifteen hundred mounted warriors with four thousand more on foot. It said a great deal about Salmane's qualities that he was able—by example—to restrain his forces from breaking out and simply eradicating the Britons. Instead, they waited quietly, knowing that the main force was still to come. Each of the mounted warriors had a spear which had been made an arm's length longer, each foot soldier carried two throwing spears, a sword and a shield. Many wore conical leather or metal helmets and a few had chain mail cuirasses which had been captured in earlier engagements.

From the Palisade, Uffin had seen the arrival of the mounted outriders, had watched as, non-plussed by his imitation rampart, they had conferred and ridden back the way they had come. Behind the barrier were fifteen hundred mounted men and over two hundred two man wicker chariots, not the five thousand which he had hoped for. There were no foot soldiers; when the battle reached this point, there was no place for them in his plans.

Uffin had made no move to conceal himself or the lookouts, but he was undecided when the Britons had come and gone, as to what they had seen. *What would they report to Flavius?* he wondered.

"Soon," he said to Alventicus who was standing closest to him. The wind was rising and rain swept across the plain, obliterating everything for minutes at a time; there was no use in trying to make himself heard above the elements. "Pass the word on, they will be here soon."

There was a persistent tattoo of rain on the roof of his covered carriage which made it impossible to hear anything for the moment. When it had passed, Flavius nodded at Aemilius who was sitting astride a shaggy brown horse alongside the entrance.

"Again. What did you say?"

"We have found them, Sir, no more than a half hour's march away."

"*Right.*" Flavius punched a triumphant fist into his palm. He had been so frightened that the Albyns would simply melt away when they realized the size of force that they were about to engage.

"The scouts report that they've built a huge fort at the center of the plain. The second one that's on your charts, Sir. Very tall walls and everyone inside it. Not a sign of anyone anywhere else."

"I knew that Gellorix was still alive—he's built that. Trying to teach Roman ways to barbarians, but..." Flavius frowned. "We've had reports of twenty to thirty five thousand men, Aemilius. They can't all be inside a fort."

"Hardly seems possible, Sir. What orders do you have?"

"Let us see for ourselves, Tribune, then we can decide what to do."

Dag Liogh and Gavoc Mellaurig with better than three thousand mounted Callatae and Selgovae warriors trailed the Legion. During the past days they had maintained an hour or so's distance from the rearguard although now, they had closed it to less than half of that. A succession of riders reported back continuously, keeping the two Chiefs informed of events.

Dag reached out an arm. "It starts soon," he said. "May we fight bravely and if need be, die bravely. I could wish for no better companion at my side."

"Nor I." Gavoc caught hold of the other's arm as they brought their horses closer. "Today we will fight side by side not on opposite sides of the valley as we were at the Sand Crags." Gavoc nodded ahead. "Should we move in closer?"

"I think not, any closer and their rearguard will see us."

"If this rain gets worse, they'll not see us if we ride amongst them."

Dag's clothing was already a cold weight on his back and he wondered whether to cast it away now. It was the custom of the Callatae to ride naked into battle so that the spirits of the fallen might hasten to their place in the Otherworld, but he decided to wait until the moment of battle came. With the rain, the darker clothing hid them effectively from chance sightings, he grinned at Gavoc and checked his sword, something he had done countless times over the last few hours.

⁂

The first valley was broad enough to accommodate the whole width of the Legion. they entered without breaking stride, mounted troops to front, sides and rear, enclosing the infantry. Flavius stood at the front of his carriage as it swayed over the rough ground, his scarlet cloak marked him out as a noble. Before him and behind came rank after rank of legionaries, picked groups of men surrounded and protected the *signifers* bearing the battle standards and the *aquilifer* with the golden eagle.

Over twelve thousand men from many nations marched under the badge of Rome; from start to finish, they stretched out for half a mile.

Trumpets sounded and like the scouting party before them, the Legion came to a halt as Flavius' carriage came to the far edge of the first plain. He called for his horse, but Aemilius, riding alongside, gave a barely discernible shake of his head. Closer to his Commander, he spoke in a low voice.

"This valley is steeper and narrower, Sir. It's an ideal place to cast stones from above and therefore doubly dangerous for our supreme commander."

Flavius looked at the towering cliff on their left hand side and at the scree covered slope to the right and let himself be persuaded to seek the bronze plated protection of his carriage. From where he stood, high on his wagon, Flavius suddenly realized that it was possible to see all the way up the valley even to the Palisade beyond, a distance of a mile or so.

"Tribune. That construction is more than just a fort. Come up here and look at it. Even from here you can see it's a tremendous thing."

Stepping up to the platform at the front of Flavius' carriage, Aemilius Karrus saw what his superior saw and agreed with him.

Despite his impetuosity and his desire to get to grips with the Albyns' rag-tag army, Flavius knew when caution was necessary. "I think we should, perhaps, camp here and send out the scouts again for a proper survey."

"And roast their feet for the sloppy work they already did," added Karrus again agreeing with Flavius.

It was at this point that several events occurred. Men emerged from beneath the pine-needle covered traps above the tunnel shafts, lifting the stout wooden doors and wedging them between tree trunks. Almost at once smoke began to billow from the shafts as flames caught hold in the tinder dry bracken below the pine staging. Air rushed in through a ventilation tunnel cut through to the edge of the waterfall and fire roared along the tunnel's confines.

Salmane and his main force emerged from the trees to charge, screaming and roaring as they came. Caught between the fire now erupting from the collapsing tunnel and the barbarians pouring down on them from their left, the Legion edged towards their right, to the south side of the plain. Just as they found the man traps set there by Finnul, the main gates opened in the Palisade. Huge and wide, the portal allowed the chariots and Albyn cavalry to emerge ten abreast; Uffin, Alventicus and Corvoniti led the charge down the incline at the thoroughly unprepared Romans.

Aemilius, seeing Salmane's horde thundering in on the flank, wheeled his horse about and shouted orders to his cavalry leaders to take the weight of the charge. Flavius, concentrating on the warriors attacking from the Palisade, turned to say something to the Tribune only to find him gone and already defending them against Salmane's charge. The Governor bellowed his own commands, ordering his regular cavalry forward to meet the attack from the valley. After some minutes, Flavius began to realize that the meticulous timing of the Albyn offensive was more apparent than real.

Salmane's charge had been made too soon, before any signal had reached him and long before Uffin could engage the Roman cavalry effectively. The lines of vicious man-traps had taken a few Roman legionaries and, panicked, a few more had plunged to their deaths where the river surged over the edge of the cliffs but this was barely a handful of Flavius' forces. The fire which had been set behind them, presumably to cut off retreat, would burn out soon and the ditch could be bridged under cover of Roman shields.

Flavius heaved a sigh, the situation was not as bad as it had seemed, he decided. However, in this, he was both right and wrong. Although the charge had been a long one, Uffin's charioteers still slammed into the Roman lines without slowing. Riders were thrown from their horses and trampled by the Albyn cavalry coming in the wake of the chariots, infantry were cut down by the second man in each chariot.

The smoke from the burning trench began to subside and blow away, but only to reveal the Selgovae and Callatae warriors milling furiously on the far side. Dag and Gavoc might well be angered at their exclusion from the battle, but if there were to be a later, Uffin had no intention of ever confessing that he had planned it thus—that they were his *cork in a bottle*.

Uffin's cavalry followed the chariots through and wielding their long spears, skewered both horses and men until the lances were broken or wrenched from their hands. Several of the light wicker chariots overturned where their handlers had pulled corners too tightly, but the riders leaped from the tumbling baskets and plunged furiously into the fray.

However, despite the sudden onslaught and the Roman's lack of prudence, casualties remained light on both sides. The victory, though firmly on the Albyns' side was a moral rather than a military success.

As the Roman forces pulled themselves together and began to regroup, Uffin ordered retreat and with poor grace, his orders were obeyed. Again, the retreat back to the Palisade went according to plan and now came the start of Uffin's final stratagem.

Flavius looked about him as order was restored.

Karrus and his cavalry were holding off Salmane's warriors with little trouble and the traitor Gellorix and his barbarian friends were herding the Albyns back to their fortification.

Flavius narrowed his eyes, once behind that, it might take weeks to starve them out or they might even have some escape route over the mountains planned. The *bête noire* of Flavius' imagination: a hugely augmented legion, far into the Albyn interior and no enemy to conquer.

Now, then, while they are on the run.

He gave the orders. Aemilius Karrus was still holding off Salmane's warriors, there was little danger, Flavius decided, from that quarter. He gave the orders and the Ninth regrouped and gave chase to the Albyns.

Uffin climbed to the walkway behind the Palisade and watched as the greater part of his forces streamed through the gateway and the last few hundred turned to block the progress of the Roman horsemen.

Salmane had moved too soon, had he broken cover when Flavius had been making camp, more—much more—could have been achieved. Now, if the Chief of the Lugi would only wait until the Legion was bunched at the head of the valley, where the rock falls would do the most damage there was still a chance that they would succeed. Just let that covered wagon with Aurelius Flavius come within range of one of the rock emplacements, just let them cut off the Legion's head as had happened at Sand Crag and …

The rain was still coming in heavy showers rather than the downpour they had expected. At the moment, he could see most of the way along the valley, almost three quarters of a mile. Some of the Roman cavalry was already clear, out onto the plain and maneuvering uncertainly. The Infantry was double timing along behind them.

Three minutes. Two, one, now…

Uffin nodded to the signalman who raised both burning brands high. In answer, ropes were taken up tight, pulled, poles strained against huge boulders, water poured on to great wedges of dry timber.

Retaining posts creaked, shifted. Boulders rocked. Timber swelled.

The cliffs were a mass of flaws, every slight strain, every little stress added cracks to those already there. There were sudden bangs, creaks and groans as the rock stirred. Caves collapsed, strata slumped, stones fell. At first only those which had already been loosened fell, but these struck the weakened cliff faces and triggered fresh falls of virgin rock.

Just as they entered the valley, darker because of the tall trees to either side, a legionary paused to listen. The centurion marching just ahead of him caught the change in movement and wheeling about; hit the man hard with his vine wood staff. The legionary staggered for two steps and started to regain his position but the noises persisted and as he slowed again, so did many others.

Legionaries marching along the valley saw the showers of pebbles coming down. The width of the ranks had been halved so that heavy rocks flung from above could not reach them in the narrower valley but even so, smaller missiles were making painful impact.

"Shields," shouted Villius. It was a call echoed up and down the line.

Automatically, without thought, they lifted their oblong shields and locked them together to deflect the falls. But the pebbles were followed by larger stuff, small boulders, rocks the size of a horse; weights and quantities that reached further and further across the valley floor. Shields were just not proof against such a barrage.

The *testudo*—the interlocked shields held like an overhead tortoise shell—began to cave in where large weights crashed down on to it. Men stumbled and moved out of line. Following ranks bunched up against those in front. A huge lump of rock hit the edge of Villius' shield, breaking the corner and numbing his arm. The Optio looked wildly about him, stones and dirt, boulders, great slivers of sandstone were falling all around, men were being crushed to death before his eyes, screams punctuated the thud of falling stone. Villius saw a man fall with his shoulder and right arm torn away.

He was not going to survive this. He was going to die, he was going to be crushed, squashed like a beetle underfoot. Villius did not consciously search for refuge, it was just there. Just in front of him as he broke rank and stumbled away. The Governor's carriage. He heard a centurion bawl at the men, trying to keep them moving because more would survive that way than by standing still.

Not Villius. It took no more than a second or so. A leap, a quick crawl and into the darkness. Safe.

Uffin watched the falls from a mere half mile away. He saw the platforms give way and tumble their loads of rock onto the Legion below, saw the huge boulders fall down the cliff faces, bouncing and crashing into the valley. He watched the great ribbons of rock flake away from the mountain side.

No matter how bad it seemed from here, thousands of legionaries would escape and he and the Albyn warriors would have to confront them. The final conflict was postponed, not revoked.

Curiously, the prospect exhilarated him. He found himself impatient to be out there, facing them. Sweat ran down his face, his heart hammered away within his chest and he gripped the great sword that Gavoc Mellaurig had bequeathed him in both hands. Now Uffin was a Briton, his heritage rising in him like the lava in a once dormant volcano, gone was the cool and calculating Roman, he could hardly control himself, could hardly wait for the proper time.

At first, Uffin thought that it was thunder and looked up at the skies which had boiled with black clouds for much of the day, but these were now clearing. The sky was a polished steel blue, dry and clear. It was not thunder though, the sound became a huge hollow grinding noise, a gut-wrenching sound that came up through the soles of his feet and shook every bone in his body. It came from the very bowels of the earth below him.

A movement caught his eye and he turned again to watch the rock falls. Not just rocks and stones, but bushes, trees, men with flailing limbs and finally, the entire cliff face began to crumble and slip. It seemed to slip sideways as the base was pulverized by its own weight and the sheer mass of falling stone made the ground heave.

The rock, rotten and honeycombed, had finally succumbed to the barrage of boulders.

The noise rose to a crescendo, Uffin and those around him clapped hands to their ears in a vain attempt to shut it out. It had an evil quality to it, something that might herald the end of the World.

Marcellus Flavius grinned as he heard the rocks striking the bronze armor of his carriage, secure in the knowledge that it would take more than a few stones to breach his defenses. The horses which drew the conveyance stopped and he realized that he might have to wait out the barrage.

No matter. Victory was too close to worry about such a minor delay. He pictured himself riding into Rome at the head of a column of picked troops. The noise of stones on the carriage roof became applause as hundreds and thousands of Roman citizens welcomed him back.

General Flavius. He tried the sound on his tongue much as Julius Caesar might once have done and grinned afresh.

Flavius never saw the stone which ripped through the bronze plating and killed him, never heard his own scream as the breath was crushed from his body. He died as he had lived, in a rush to reach his destination.

Villius heard the rocks smashing into the bronze sheets above him and clasped the helmet tightly onto his head. The whole carriage bounced as something struck the roof and came all the way through. Quite distinctly, he heard the snap of bone breaking and the scream of pain as Flavius died. A second missile struck the wagon and an axle broke, and then came a continuous barrage, impossible to hear individual impacts. The bed of the wagon was gradually pressed lower and lower, pinning Villius to the ground. Try as he might, his huge muscles cracking, sinews tearing free from the bones, he could not move it.

When at last, his skull split, it was almost a relief as the pain receded and the World went away.

The avalanche of stone continued almost unabated for a quarter of an hour and then diminished. Little by little, the rocks became stones and pebbles and dust and finally died away to an occasional trickle of debris dislodged by the wind."

The entire valley, as far as Uffin could see was filled to a depth level with his vantage point. Buried forever beneath countless millions of tons of rock was the Ninth Legion. The horsemen who so lately had confronted one another on the plain stood in shock, some horrified, some disbelieving. Albyns on the far side of the Palisade clambered up to peer from the walkway at what had happened.

The silence after the cataclysm was as appalling as the noise had been, a silence that stretched on and on. The World, every living thing in the world, wild animal, bird or human being, held its breath.

After many minutes, there came a whisper from one of the Romans, a whisper clearly heard by all. "Today, our Gods have deserted us."

Endorr the Druid nodded and spoke to Uffin. "The Roman is correct. Now, you have seen *our* Gods truly take a hand in the affairs of men. Let those who disbelieve look on their work and weep."

On the far side of the rock fall, the Albyns who had set light to the trench slid the trap doors back across the shafts once more and signaled to the Callatae and the Selgovae. Dag Liogh and Gavoc Mellaurig led their men over the trap doors which now covered the shafts. They could see, further along, where Salmane was harrying the Brythonic mercenaries and some way beyond them the new barricade of fallen rock.

Forming ranks across the width of the pass, each warrior knee to knee with the next, they rode at a trot towards the milling men and beasts ahead. Their pace increased, swords were raised; "CALLATAE" screamed Dag Liogh's forces, "For MANON", shouted Dag himself. "SELGOVAE" roared Gavoc's band as they thundered along the valley.

The fresh warriors carved their way through the fighting men, cutting and slashing. A third of the remaining Brythonic mercenaries were dispatched in that first rush which so demoralized them that they attempted to disengage and retreat, something so out of character that Salmane suspected some devious strategy and stopped his own men from following. Dag and Gavoc followed suit and watched as the Britons huddled among the rocks and debris of the landslip.

"It's snowing," said someone, looking up.

"The sky is clear," said another, a woman's voice this time.

"Still, it is snowing."

"Back," shouted Dag Liogh. "Back. Get away."

In a panic, both the mercenary forces and the Albyns raced back down the valley. Around them the sudden snow became a blizzard, hampering movement and confusing the sense of direction.

Softened by the recent rise in temperature and the rains, the snow fields of the upper mountain levels had been disturbed by the landslip. Now, it too, began to move. Slowly at first and inexorably. Faster it slipped and as it reached steeper inclines, faster still. The accumulated winter snow slid down, burying the grave of the Ninth Legion in a shroud of pure white.

Aemilius Karrus stood next to his fallen horse, grasping the lance which had transfixed it, for support. Better than six thousand men snuffed out while he stood by and watched. It was more than his brain could cope with. His arms seemed numb, lifeless, the short two foot sword simply too heavy to wield any more. He reversed it and handed it wearily to a Lugi warrior who, equally shocked, was sitting his horse nearby. Instead of striking at the Roman, the Albyn took the sword and walked his horse away.

It was not the same with all of them, Callatae and Selgovae had come lately to the conflict and were in a hurry to make up for lost opportunities. However, they soon found that there is no honor to be gained in fighting an enemy who simply stands and waits for his head to be taken, the killing stopped almost as soon as it had begun. Instead, they backed the Brythonic mercenaries up against the steep cliff and bound every one of them hand and foot.

The situation in the upper plain was almost the reverse. The Roman cavalry could see that they were outnumbered and that there was nowhere to go. They laid down their arms and awaited their fate.

More than a hundred miles distant, Mandeltua sat bolt upright on his thin mattress. He looked straight into the eyes of one of the serving women who had taken turns in kneeling by his bedside for a week.

"The prophesy is fulfilled," he said, his voice weak and hoarse. "Bring me food and drink and tell those druids that are still here to prepare a ceremony of thanksgiving to our Gods."

AFTERMATH

THE HILL OF STONES WAS GONE. TWO HUNDRED, PERHAPS, TWO hundred and fifty; these were all that were left to mark the Albyn dead.

So many Romans dead, the end of the Ninth Legion.

So few Albyns.

Uffin was still in two minds when the Druids spoke of the Gods. Had he *really* witnessed divine intervention?

"Karrus?" said Uffin as he passed the bowed figure. "Is that really you, Aemilius Karrus?"

There were over fourteen hundred of the Britons who had served as Flavius' vanguard and a handful of Roman officers left alive. Uffin was looking at each of the officers and trying to decide what to do with them.

"Aemilius?"

The Tribune looked up. "Well, Lord Uffin. We meet again under altered circumstances." There was the ghost of a smile on the Tribune's lips.

Uffin shook his head, not in disbelief—after the past few hours he could believe in almost anything. "I have a problem. What do I do with you? I can talk my friends into releasing the Britons, but you Romans are a different matter. What would you do if you wore my sandals?"

"I'd let me go, of course." It was forced bravado, Uffin could see the defeat in the other's eyes. Uffin *could* probably let them go. After the extermination of a whole Legion, the Albyns would almost certainly grant any request. "I can even pay my ransom, look."

Aemilius reached into the neck of his tunic and pulled out an ornament that suddenly took Uffin back six months in time.

"The pendant." He breathed, reaching out and taking it.

"Thought it would bring me luck," Aemilius said. "Perhaps it did, I'm still alive."

The words were lost on Uffin. As he clenched his fingers around the shell there came a feeling of revulsion, evil. He snatched at the ancient fossil, breaking the cord around Aemilius' neck and drawing his arm far back to cast it into the river where it cascaded over the brink.

Something stayed his hand for an instant, between one heart beat and the next Uffin's eyes looked into other places, far places.

Cocidius came and took him by the hand. The God spoke, his voice was soft and melodious, cultured, perfectly understandable. He revealed how the Druid's machinations had led him every step of the way, how Uffin had been driven by Mandeltua's will.

The God gestured and showed him the vision he had had.

He had watched Mother and lover being taken from his home and foully murdered by the Romans.

The old vision faded, but more followed.

There was his mother standing at the door of her house. There were flowers there, winter heather and jasmine in full bloom, so that it must be spring. Now. The present.

There came a vision of Asel sitting on a log outside her home at High Sil. Asel with rounded belly and blooming cheeks.

Asel pregnant with his child!

Uffin opened his eyes to find his arm still drawn back, the pendant still clutched in his tingling fingers.

- THE END -

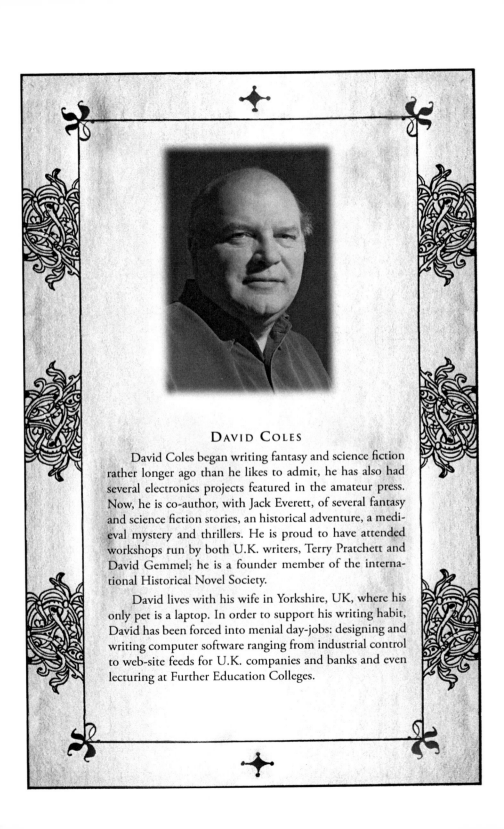

DAVID COLES

David Coles began writing fantasy and science fiction rather longer ago than he likes to admit, he has also had several electronics projects featured in the amateur press. Now, he is co-author, with Jack Everett, of several fantasy and science fiction stories, an historical adventure, a medieval mystery and thrillers. He is proud to have attended workshops run by both U.K. writers, Terry Pratchett and David Gemmel; he is a founder member of the international Historical Novel Society.

David lives with his wife in Yorkshire, UK, where his only pet is a laptop. In order to support his writing habit, David has been forced into menial day-jobs: designing and writing computer software ranging from industrial control to web-site feeds for U.K. companies and banks and even lecturing at Further Education Colleges.

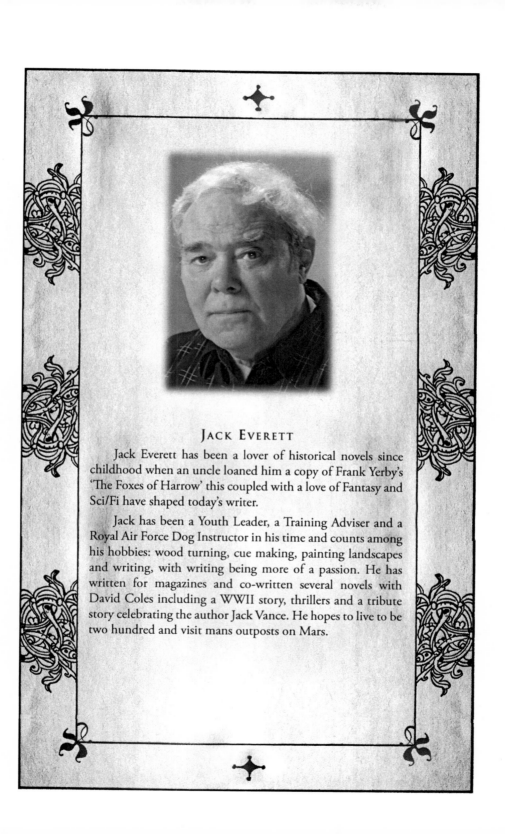

JACK EVERETT

Jack Everett has been a lover of historical novels since childhood when an uncle loaned him a copy of Frank Yerby's 'The Foxes of Harrow' this coupled with a love of Fantasy and Sci/Fi have shaped today's writer.

Jack has been a Youth Leader, a Training Adviser and a Royal Air Force Dog Instructor in his time and counts among his hobbies: wood turning, cue making, painting landscapes and writing, with writing being more of a passion. He has written for magazines and co-written several novels with David Coles including a WWII story, thrillers and a tribute story celebrating the author Jack Vance. He hopes to live to be two hundred and visit mans outposts on Mars.

Challenge of the Red Unicorn
Jack Scoltock

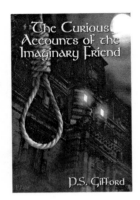

The Curious Accounts of the Imaginary Friend
P.S. Gifford

P.S. Gifford

DRY RAIN
B.J. Kibble

Earrings of Ixtumea
Kim Baccellia

Figgy-Dowdy
Frank Minogue

The First Vampire
Alicia Benson

The Further Accounts of the Imaginary Friend
P.S. Gifford

Hannah
Sharon Poppen

ALSO IN PRINT FROM VIRTUAL TALES

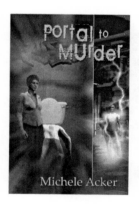

Lightning Source UK Ltd.
Milton Keynes UK
22 November 2009

146585UK00001B/6/P